I0824357

The Other Side of Silence

By Jamie Klinger-Krebs

This story is a work of fiction. All characters and events are the product of the author's imagination. Any resemblance to any person, living or dead, is coincidental.

The Other Side of Silence © 2017 by Jamie Klinger-Krebs
All rights reserved. This book or any portion thereof may not be reproduced or used in any manner whatsoever without the express written permission of the author. except for the use of brief quotations in a book review.

First Printing, 2012

Cover design by Jamie Klinger-Krebs
Edited by Signe Jorgenson • signejorgenson.com

For more information about the author, visit jklingerkrebs.com

ISBN-13: 978-0615725772 (J Klinger-Krebs)

For my daughter, Charley, and my great-grandmother, Agnes.

Prologue

October 11, 1975

Grace twisted the gold ring on her left hand as she sat silently on the porch. It was a cool, early autumn evening and the scent of newly fallen leaves left a musty smell in the air. She rocked slowly and looked down at the ring as she spun it around and around. It was the only object in the world that she still felt connected to; everything else had slipped away and seemed to hold less meaning. She had made many mistakes—this she knew—yet she had held little regret until these past few years, when Alfred's anger had grown deeper. She never meant to trap him in a life he didn't want, but how could she have known?

She heard children playing in the distance as she rocked, and she rested her head on the back of the chair before closing her eyes. The rocking calmed her and she wondered what made the laughing children so happy. She smiled slightly, imagining the children running up and down the street, chasing one another and laughing when they couldn't be caught. She reveled in the thought of feeling that free and alive—she could barely remember what it was like to be truly alive. When the children came closer to the yard, she lifted her head to see them pass. They didn't notice her watching as they raced by, unaware of anything but the street ahead.

Grace didn't turn when she heard the screen door slam behind her but continued to twist the ring on her finger. She wasn't afraid.

The sky had grown darker and the streetlights began to dim, casting an eerie yellow glow on the blacktop. A slight breeze whirled a patch of dry leaves on the street, and she leaned back again. The children were gone and their laughter barely reached her now. Heavy footsteps came closer as they crossed the porch, but she didn't turn. She only twisted the ring faster.

When she felt the cold, hard metal barrel against her head, she closed her eyes tight and heard a fast *click.* She wasn't surprised when the sharp, hot wind rushed across her face. She felt herself float above the street and saw the children again. But they were too far away and hadn't heard the shot. Alfred was below, shaking as he stood over her lifeless body with a gun in one hand and a bottle in the other. His thin, sickly frame was trembling and hot, angry tears streamed down his leathered face. No one would understand what had brought him to this.

Chapter 1

February 2, 2006, 4:47 p.m.

Ellie didn't remember the impact. But the sounds echoed inside her head.

The snow had been blinding as it hit the windshield like tiny, glistening daggers. She was exhausted. Her hands were cramped from steadying the steering wheel against the heavy, blustering wind that pushed against the car. A quick shot of pain flashed through her abdomen and she winced. As the windshield wipers slapped back and forth, she became hypnotized by their motion. Back and forth, back and forth, they slid across the windshield until the slide of rubber on glass was all she could hear. Even the radio blaring an unfamiliar song became background noise to the wipers' deafening slap. As the pain in her stomach subsided, even the cold blast of air from the partially open window couldn't keep her eyes from closing. Beyond her headlights, the sky was thick and black, but the snow seemed endlessly bright as she slowly blinked, fighting off the arms of sleep that tried to pull her closer. It was a losing battle.

As the car suddenly began to slide, her eyes snapped open and her hands froze on the wheel. She didn't know what she had struck, but she heard the windshield's slithering crack as her body jolted forward. Everything slowed as she slipped out of the moment. She expected the sudden onset of pain, but it never came. She just felt weightless as she ominously drifted into a slow darkness.

She wasn't sure how she had gotten there or how long she had been lying on the ground, but Ellie soon began to feel something cold and wet beneath her, and she was wretchedly thirsty. She licked her lips, which were salty and dry. Before she managed to open her eyes, she felt light, soft snowflakes gently landing on her face. At first it stung as the twinge of the cool flakes hit her skin, but it was soothing as she became lucid.

The brightness of the newly fallen snow hurt her eyes as she blinked and strained to sit up. She expected to see her car somewhere nearby, immersed in a tangled mess, but it wasn't there. In fact, there were no road, no emergency vehicles, and no people rushing to her aid. Instead she found herself lying in the middle of a vacant, snow-covered field.

For a moment, she thought she had been thrown from the car, or maybe she had walked there in a state of shock. But there were no footprints in the freshly fallen snow, and the sky, which had been pitch black before, was now bright and sunny. She looked down at her arms and grabbed at her legs to make sure she had feeling in her extremities. She felt her face for blood and looked at the ground for evidence in the snow to indicate whether she was injured. There was nothing. She was fine. Even the pain in her stomach had subsided.

She sprang up from the ground. The light snow had stopped, and although it was cold here, she didn't feel cold. The snow stung her fingers when she touched it, but she remained warm as it melted in her hands.

“Am I dead?” She said the words aloud, not knowing what to do next.

There was no answer.

As she stood in silence, Ellie tried to comprehend what had transpired. Moments ago, she had been driving home from work in a snowstorm. Now she was in this strange, unfamiliar place.

As she stood motionless, a light wind sent a dusting of snow swirling about her feet and she became dizzy. She had never seen this place before and she could see nothing in the distance that gave her any indication of where to go for help. There were no houses, no roads—just snowy plains and gatherings of trees for as far as the eye could see. Bewildered, she put one foot in front of the other and headed for a grove of trees in the distance. She didn’t know where she was going or why she was going there; she just knew that she needed to move forward. She told herself the answers would come if she just started walking. If they didn’t, maybe she would snap out of this strange dream and wake up at home, safe in her bed, next to Joe.

Chapter 2

February 2, 2006, 4:10 p.m.

Joe sat on the edge of the couch and stared at his feet. His head was heavy and it ached from drinking too much the night before.

Ellie had left that morning in a rage, ranting and threatening him like she always did when he didn't respond to her questions. His lack of response fueled her anger, but even though she couldn't see it, he was sorry for what he had done.

To her, it was the same old story. He had starting drinking early in the day and left home before she returned from work. He knew she would give him that look if she saw him—it was a look he hated. He was never sure if it was disappointment or utter disgust. Either way, he couldn't take the glare of her dark eyes judging him.

He knew she would try to call him once she left work and reached their dark, empty home. But he ignored it. The laughter around him in the crowded bar helped pull his thoughts away from where he knew he should be. Right then he didn't want to be at home; he wanted to be away—not forever, just for now. He wanted to feel free and irresponsible, though he knew he would pay for it later.

But his moment of freedom was over. After his brief escape from reality, he knew he had to come back and face what he had done.

The house was silent when he opened the door, though he knew there was no way she was sleeping. He could feel her anger hanging heavily in the air.

He crept in quietly and let himself drop clumsily on the couch. There was no movement from the upstairs bedroom, and he closed his eyes as the room began to spin.

Seconds later, or so it seemed, Ellie's voice tore at him, but he didn't allow himself to comprehend the words. Her voice trembled, but she was angry and he knew his best defense was to say nothing at all.

Soon she gave up, like he knew she would, and in a frustrated fluster, she gathered her things and walked out of the house. He jumped as the door slammed behind her.

Joe grabbed the blanket off the back of the couch and pulled it over his head. He didn't know why he had done this to her again. He had known she would be upset, and in all honesty, he hadn't even enjoyed his time away.

When he awoke hours later, he searched his mind for a way to show her how sorry he was, but he knew she wasn't interested in apologies. She wanted a change in him, but he was determined to keep that part of himself away from her grasp.

When it began to get dark outside, he glanced at the clock and sighed. It was past the time she normally came home.

She's really angry, he thought as he struggled to get up and prepare to leave for his second-shift job.

He pulled on his shoes and stepped into the darkness, believing it would be better to give her some time to calm down and forgive him—again.

Chapter 3

February 2, 2006, 5:15 p.m.

The snow crunched beneath her feet as Ellie made her way toward an unknown destination. She wanted to cry, but something inside her prevented the tears from reaching her eyes. She just kept walking.

Though the last thing she remembered before waking in this place was a thick, dark sky, the sun now shone brightly as she trudged through the snow. The clear afternoon sky was warm and her breath became heavy as she began to sweat.

She spun around to judge the distance she had come, but all she could see was her own footprints in the snow. She headed toward a grove of trees that never seemed to get closer, yet she continued to slowly walk. As the snow deepened, she began to breathe more heavily.

Finally, she stopped walking. Lowering her head and bringing her hands to her face to wipe the perspiration that flowed freely on her forehead, Ellie sighed in frustration and tried to clear her head.

Why is this happening to me? She thought, wanting to cry, but still no tears came.

When she opened her eyes, Ellie was startled to see that the grove of trees was suddenly right before her. Again she spun around, only to find that her footprints in the snow had vanished.

"This has to be a dream," she said, hoping to wake herself like she had done many times when her dreams took on strange twists. She had always been able to wake herself from bad dreams, but this one seemed to hold onto her tightly.

The trees gently swayed in a light wind that pushed past her, and she was drawn to walk forward again. There was solace in these trees, though she didn't know why.

As she passed each tree, she began to feel a sense of welcome. The branches extended toward her, like hands, and they seemed to beckon her forward, as if to lead her somewhere. The trees were in full bloom, which struck her as odd considering it was the dead of winter. The dark green of their leaves made her think of spring, and for a brief moment, the thought gave her a warm feeling even in this cold place. She began to feel a bit calmer.

As she reached the other side of the grove, a hawk cried above her. Looking up, she saw the bird soar against the wind, swirling as it dove toward Earth, then catching itself and looping back toward the sky. She wished she could be that free and fly above this place.

Beyond the grove, Ellie could make out rising smoke that came from the other side of the slight hill that now rose before her.

"My car!" She shouted as she ran in the direction of the dark, billowing cloud.

Gasping in the cool air, she raced through the snow and trudged up the hill. When she reached the top, she was surprised to find herself peering into a slight valley. Her hopes were dashed when she didn't see her car at all—just a lone cabin that poked out of the snow. Smoke flowed from the chimney up toward the sky and then disappeared into the atmosphere.

Her breath was labored and her steps were heavy as she walked toward the cabin. Maybe the people there would have a phone and could at least tell her where she was.

As she approached the cabin, she made out a figure moving on the porch. She hesitated but, realizing she had no other options, kept walking. When Ellie was close enough, she focused on a woman with a broomstick who swept the light snow that had blown onto the stoop. The woman's back was to Ellie. As Ellie approached, she thought the woman could sense her presence, though she said nothing.

The woman's tiny hands had a tight grip on the broom as she slowly moved across the porch. Her grayish hair was long but tidy and neatly wrapped into a bun on the back of her head. She wore a faded blue housedress that covered her feet and a red plaid apron, but no jacket even though the snow kept a chill in the air.

"Excuse me," Ellie said as the woman spun around, startled by the sound of another voice. "I'm sorry," she continued. "I didn't mean to scare you, but…"

"Oh no, dear, that's quite alright. I just wasn't expecting you quite yet." Her voice was friendly and warm, but her response was surprising.

"You've been expecting me?" Ellie said, taken aback.

"Why, yes, but I didn't know when you would be coming."

The woman smiled and reached out a hand to welcome Ellie onto the porch, but Ellie hesitated. She didn't know this woman, who peered at her as if she were a long-lost friend. Ellie's stomach began to churn and she froze in her tracks.

"Don't be afraid, Ellie. It's alright," the woman said, sensing the younger woman's hesitation.

"Did…did you hear about the accident?" Ellie replied. She searched her mind for some indication of who this woman might be, but she could find nothing. "How do you know my name?"

"I've always known your name," the woman said with a slight laugh. "And yes, I know of the accident. Please, come inside."

"I'm sorry," Ellie said, still afraid to move forward. "Do I know you?"

"Why yes, dear," the woman said with sparkling eyes. "But we've never met in person. Please come inside and I will tell you all about it."

As she slowly stepped forward, Ellie's head began to spin and she suddenly felt dizzy. Who was this strange woman? How did she know her name?

"Oh dear. You don't look well. Perhaps you should sit a moment," the old woman said as she helped Ellie to sit on the top step.

Ellie looked into the woman's gentle, dark eyes. Her face was somewhat wrinkled and worn, but her eyes were soft and almost familiar, though she still had no idea who this stranger was.

"If we've never met, then how do you know my name?"

"My name is Grace." Ellie looked away, knowing she had heard the name before, but her mind couldn't access the information.

"Am I dead?" Ellie said, almost afraid to know the answer.

"That's a question only you can answer," Grace said as she stood and moved toward the door. "Come inside and let me tell you a story."

Ellie slowly moved toward the door, and the old woman's hand touched Ellie's arm as she welcomed the younger woman inside.

Within the walls of Grace's home, Ellie felt strangely at ease. The cabin was tiny, only two rooms and stairs that led to a darkened second floor. As she shook off the coolness of the outside air, Ellie walked closer to the fire that roared in a large stone fireplace. Grace watched her visitor closely as a warm smile stretched across her face, and then she turned to place a black, dented teapot on an old wrought iron stove in the corner. The stove almost looked like some kind of strange, fire-breathing animal with claw feet that held it firmly to the floor. Between the animal-like stove and the fireplace's roaring flames, the room should have felt extremely warm, but to Ellie's surprise, it was just right. In fact, it almost felt chilled.

On the mantle above the fireplace, there were black-and-white photos of what looked like Grace when she was younger. She was with an older gentleman who wore a fedora hat that almost seemed out of place against his crisp, new-looking dungarees and what was probably a dark-blue button-up shirt, though she couldn't be sure of the color. He was dressed neatly, but Ellie knew he must have been a laborer of some sort.

In another photo, Grace stood beside a tall, magnificent-looking horse. Then there was one of her and a handsome younger gentleman wearing overalls. Though his eyes looked soft and kind, Ellie noticed something odd about his stare. It seemed blank, as if he were thinking about something else at the moment the flashbulb snapped.

The last photo was of a young girl in a floral-patterned chiffon dress. She sat on the front stoop of a charming little house with a wrap-around porch. She was smiling as if it were the first time she had ever worn that dress. Her hands rested proudly on her knees, as if to show off the dress even more. Her eyes, too, looked oddly familiar.

"Sit, Ellie, sit," Grace said motioning toward a chair near the fireplace. The fire was warm and comforting, and the old woman watched as Ellie continued looking around the room, searching for anything familiar.

"I bet you're a bit confused and wonder why you're here," she said as she motioned toward the chair again.

"Yes. I feel like I'm dreaming," Ellie replied, still taking in her surroundings.

"I'm afraid it's more like fate, dear," Grace said as she rose from her chair and moved toward the teapot, which now whistled on the stove.

"Fate? I don't understand. I was just in a car accident," Ellie said, watching the expressionless old woman pour the tea into two white porcelain cups. One of the cups had a crack down the side. The old woman didn't respond as she set the un-cracked cup on the table beside Ellie and then sat in the chair across from her. She looked at the fire for a long time, saying nothing.

"Grace?" Ellie's voice was a half-whisper, and it snapped the old woman back to the present.

"I'm sorry, dear. I was just thinking of someone. My husband, Alfred."

Ellie looked up from her tea and saw a look of sorrow on the old woman's face. She thought of her own husband and wondered where he was right at that moment. Did he know she was gone? Did he care?

"He murdered me," Grace said as her eyes drifted back to the fire.

Ellie was speechless. She simply stared at the old woman and felt fear rising in her throat.

"I was a maid once," the old woman continued, never looking away from the fire as she spoke. "I came home from work one evening and found my whole world was turned upside down. And then Alfred ended it all."

"If he murdered you, does that mean we're both dead?" Ellie's heart was pounding so loudly now that she wondered if the old woman could hear it.

"It was my fault," the woman replied, not acknowledging the question. "Ellie, sometimes infatuation can be an awful thing and can lead you to the darkest places. You may not get there right away, and you may even have some good years in between, but when you turn someone's course of fate…well, that's a sin that you can't repent."

Ellie was bewildered, and she watched the old woman closely as she spoke. She was suddenly aware of how dark Grace's eyes were; they seemed deep and hollow, like there was so much pain behind them that any color they used to possess had been wiped away long ago.

"Alfred was a sweet man," Grace said, then paused for a moment, as if she were afraid to finish her thought. "Until everything changed."

Ellie didn't quite understand what she meant, but Grace looked down at the floor, again lost in a memory, before she spoke again. Ellie stayed silent.

Chapter 4

February 2, 2006, 8:26 p.m.

The factory sounds caused a deafening pounding in his head as Joe dialed the phone. It rang once, twice, three times, but there was no answer. It was odd for Ellie not to answer at this late hour.

He sighed as he hung up. He knew she was deliberately trying to torture him, to make him pay for the night before. But she didn't understand how twisted he was about the conversation they'd had just a few nights ago. It had driven him away from her again, afraid and unsure.

He forced himself to put his mind back into his work, though he couldn't help but continuously glance at the clock. He wanted to call again, but he knew she wouldn't answer even if she were there. As much as he tried to fight it, her voice kept replaying in his head.

"Joe, do you think we'll ever have a baby?"

It was a simple question that had come out innocently enough. But, before he even allowed himself to comprehend the words, he fired off a sharp response: "You know how I feel about that."

"No, I really don't," she said, scanning his face and reading the anger. "I know you said you weren't interested in having a baby, but…"

"And I'm still not," he retorted, growing uncomfortable and shuffling in his chair.

She sighed, stood up from the couch, and walked into the next room.

"Why is this conversation perpetually off limits?" She mumbled.

"Because I've never lied to you, I've never given you any indication that I wanted a family, and you said you were okay with that."

He said nothing as drawers slammed in the kitchen. He shook his head, growing more irritated with every slam from the other room. He had never lied, and he had never given her false hope about having a baby. But lately she had started to continuously question him about it. He had told her this would happen before they were married. He'd said that she would try to change him as soon as they were married, that she would want a baby. But she had told him she wouldn't.

"I told you this would happen," he snapped when he walked into the kitchen. She passed him by, not meeting his glance, and went back to the couch, flopping down heavily.

"People change…except for you," she said. She heard the clink of ice hitting his glass. As the liquor cabinet door creaked, she cringed and shook her head. "Here we go," she said.

Joe walked back into the living room. He set his glass down, plainly in her view, and returned to his chair. He knew this would bother her.

"Why can't we talk about it without you having a drink?" she asked.

He said nothing; as far as he was concerned, the conversation was over.

She wasn't satisfied. "I didn't say we *should* have a baby, Joe, I just want to understand why we can't discuss it like two normal married people."

He raised his voice. "Because you know how I feel, so drop it!"

Ellie stood and walked toward the stairs. Joe waited for her to turn around and fight, but she didn't. He knew there was only one reason why she would react that way. She was trying to fight tears. Tears made him angrier, though he didn't know why. He hated when she cried during arguments. It made him meaner than he intended to be. So, on the verge of opening the floodgates, she went upstairs and closed their bedroom door. He imagined her breaking down into a pillow so he couldn't hear. Though he felt guilty, he didn't dare try to comfort her. Downstairs in his chair, he took a long, slow sip of his drink as he tried to choke back the seriousness of what had transpired.

As the conversation replayed in his head, Joe slipped back to the reality of his pounding head and the monotony of his work. He wanted to apologize to Ellie, to tell her why her question bothered him so much, but it wasn't a simple thing for him to explain. It wasn't that he didn't love her, because he loved her more than he could love anything. But, the thought of having a baby chilled him to the bone. He'd had a son once, and he had chosen to leave his son behind. It was something he was sure his wife couldn't understand, though deep down he knew it was unfair of him to keep her in the dark about his past. Telling her now would change things between them, he was certain of this, but not telling her would make her bitter and want a child even more.

Frustrated with his own thoughts, he stopped his work and walked to the phone. He just wanted to hear the sound of her voice, to talk about everyday things, and calm the fear inside of him.

The phone rang once, twice, three times. Still there was no answer.

Chapter 5

February 2, 2006, 6:30 p.m.

"The first time I saw Alfred, I was seventeen," Grace said with glimmering eyes as she reveled in the memory. "My father hired him to work on the farm and it was so hot that day. My friends and I were going to the lake. Oh, he was so handsome standing there in his overalls."

Ellie smiled and leaned back in her chair as Grace talked. For the moment, she forgot about her own plight.

"My friends and I talked about going to the lake that day. We were all walking out of the house as Alfred and my father came up from the barn, and we locked eyes instantly," she said. "My father noticed this right away, but he never said anything. He trusted Alfred…at first."

The sound of Grace's voice relaxed Ellie as she imagined what Alfred might have looked like. She glanced up at the photos on the mantle.

"Yes, that's Alfred and me," Grace said, motioning to the photograph that Ellie had already spotted. It was the photo of the young man with the distant look in his eyes. Alfred was indeed handsome. He was tall and lean, and his dark, wavy hair made his eyes look brighter even in a black-and-white image.

"The other photo is of my father and me." She motioned toward the photo of the man in dungarees and a dark-colored work shirt. "And the other is of my mother's horse, Belle."

As Grace spoke, a black-and-white tabby cat came out of her hiding place and settled on the arm of the old woman's chair. "Ah, Mayda, there you are," she smiled. "This is Ellie," she said motioning to her visitor. "She's come to visit us."

Ellie smiled as Mayda purred and Grace gently stroked her fur. Ellie said, "How long have you lived here?"

Grace looked at Mayda and then back at the fire.

"Since that day."

"But what is this place?"

Grace avoided the question as if she hadn't heard it.

"Ellie, do you still have the ring?"

Ellie was unsure of what she meant. "Ring?"

"Yes dear, your mother's ring."

Unable to speak, Ellie stared at the woman. Grace half-smiled as she lifted the younger woman's right hand to take a better look at the tiny gold object. Ellie's mother had given her the ring when she was seventeen. She said it had belonged to Ellie's grandmother, and her grandmother's mother before that.

"Are…are you my great-grandmother? Was this yours?" She realized that after all the years of wearing the ring, she still didn't know much about it or where it had come from. Though it had shown signs of wear, the gold-leafed ring was still beautiful and unbelievably strong. It had never bent in all these years, not even a little.

"Yes I am, and yes it was," she said. Ellie removed the ring and placed it in the old woman's palm. Grace looked at it with a cold, blank stare. Ellie couldn't take her eyes off of the woman now. As she watched, she became even more conscious of her surroundings. Ellie looked around the room and out the window at the snow. *What is happening?*

"Do you know why this ring is so special?" Grace asked.

"N-n-no," Ellie stuttered, her head swirling with confusion.

"It was my mother's wedding ring," she said as she ran her fingers across the leafing. "My mother died when I was a young girl and she gave me this ring before her passing. It has a lot of history, this ring."

Ellie watched the old woman study the object like she was looking at an old friend, but she never slid it onto her finger.

"Would you like to keep it?" Ellie finally asked, beginning to feel guilty that it had obviously been so special to Grace yet had little history for her.

"No, dear, you keep it," she said as her eyes began to mist over. She reached out, grabbed Ellie's right hand, and quickly slid the ring down her finger. Grace's hands were cold to the touch, and she quickly wiped the wetness from her eyes.

"Can you tell me about it?" Ellie asked, wanting to know why it seemed to evoke so much emotion from this woman and how it had managed to continue down the family line, eventually resting on her own finger.

She also wanted to know about Alfred and why he had committed murder, but she wasn't bold enough to ask those questions, not yet. There was already too much she didn't understand about her current situation and this odd, cold place. As much as she turned the circumstances over in her mind, she couldn't come to terms with the fact that she was sitting in front of a woman who had lived a lifetime before she was even born. As Grace spoke, Ellie hung on every word until everything about her own situation seemed unimportant.

"To help you understand, I'll have to begin even before my and Alfred's story began," Grace whispered, firelight bouncing off her face. Ellie nodded, waiting for more.

"You see, dear, our story reaches all the way back to the jealousy that my grandmother, my father's mother, held toward my mother. She didn't approve of my mother and she didn't want her only son marrying a woman like her. But my father was stubborn and he wasn't about to listen. He was going to marry my mother despite what anyone said." Grace smiled. "But, my grandmother was not going down without a fight. So, she took that ring that you're wearing now to a friend—a friend that had special *abilities*—and she asked her cast a spell on it."

Ellie stared at the old woman, listening closely, but Grace paused as if she were thinking of how to explain the rest.

"My aunt Calista, my father's sister, whom I adored, told me a story once about the night my grandmother went to visit that friend, whom many called a witch." Grace stopped and smiled again, momentarily. "It seems like just yesterday that I sat like you are now and listened to her tell me all of this."

Ellie stared ahead, anxiously waiting for her to continue.

"It was the night before my parents' wedding when Calista said she was lying awake staring at the ceiling of her bedroom," Grace said. "She was excited to see her only brother, my father, get married—but she was a bit jealous, too. You see, her mother had made a promise to both she and my father that whoever married first would keep the ring that her mother had given to her. Though she had hoped to marry before my father, deep down Calista had always known that her older brother would be the first.

"Calista was fond of my mother, but she wished that my father had chosen another ring for his bride. My grandmother had told them that the ring was very old, but even she didn't know how old it was. It intrigued Calista. She wanted to hold on to that piece of family history, but it was not meant to be."

Grace's voice trailed off as she paused for a moment to clear her throat and take a quick sip of tea from the cracked cup beside her. "Though Calista knew her mother disapproved of my mother, Isabelle, she also knew that my grandmother would stand by her promise and give my father the ring the following morning."

Grace shifted in her chair. "So as she lay there thinking about this ring, Calista said she heard the slow creak of the front gate opening. She peered out the window from behind a blowing curtain to see her mother, dressed all in black, standing at the end of the walk and staring back at the house as if she were making sure there was no movement inside. Calista said she slid back and pressed herself against the wall so her mother wouldn't see. Seeming satisfied then, her mother turned on her heels and headed down the dirt road toward town."

Ellie stared at the old woman as she continued her story with the reflection of the firelight dancing in her eyes.

"Filled with curiosity, Calista decided to follow her mother," Grace continued. "Ducking behind the large oak trees that lined the road, she trailed her mother as she passed through the town's main intersection. Once past this intersection, Calista knew there was only one person on the other side of town that her mother would go see. It was her old friend, Francesca Morano, whom many called a witch. Though she knew her mother was this woman's friend, Calista wondered why she would go see her at this late hour."

Ellie leaned forward in her chair.

"As her mother rounded the block where Francesca lived, Calista said she could see the moonlit silhouette of the towering walnut tree that stood in front of Francesca's home. There were so many rumors about that tree," Grace said, shaking her head. "Though it was overgrown with roots buckling through the dirt road, no one ever dared cut it down."

Ellie nodded as she imagined the tree, its roots emerging from the ground like skeletal fingers poking up from a grave.

Grace continued. "As her mother approached the house, Calista said the front door opened, allowing a dim light to escape onto the porch, but she never saw Francesca, and then both women disappeared inside. Standing on the other side of the street, behind the safety of another oak, my aunt mustered enough courage to cross the street. As she crouched in the bushes by the porch, she heard the women's muffled voices. She thought her mother was crying, but she couldn't tell for sure. With her curiosity growing stronger than her fear, Calista crawled up onto the porch and knelt beneath the open window."

The story unfolded, and Grace spoke slower and quieter as she talked about the encounter Calista had witnessed between her mother and the woman people called a witch. Ellie became immersed.

"The conversation Calista overheard that night has haunted my thoughts for years," Grace whispered. "My grandmother was so distraught at the thought of losing her only son to a woman she didn't approve of. She told Francesca that she knew in her heart my mother would betray my father. And so she begged her friend to cast a spell that would change his mind from marrying her. But Francesca was a careful witch and she refused."

Grace pointed her index finger toward the ceiling. "She didn't dabble on the dark side of magic. She knew that if she cast a negative spell, she would open herself up to danger. She warned my grandmother that a negative spell could sometimes reverse and cause threefold harm to the person casting it."

Ellie listened carefully.

"But, she also told my grandmother of another spell…one that *would* bind itself to that ring. But still, Francesca would not cast it. She told my grandmother that *she* would need to cast it. With this spell, the witch said, whoever wore the ring would be protected as long as they remained faithful. Good health, prosperity, and happiness could be theirs as long as love and truth ran plentifully within the marriage. But, if it didn't, there would be consequences. The degree of the consequences would depend on the degree of the betrayal. If the one wearing the ring betrayed the sacredness of the marriage the ring represented, then the spell would reverse. If *that* happened, whoever wore the ring would suffer, and consequently, whoever wore it next would pay for the sins of the one who came before. It would become a cycle that would unleash itself and continue on and on and on. It was a spell that would hold onto the ring so that no matter who wore it, the pain of betrayal would take hold somehow and someway. It wasn't the spell my grandmother mother was looking for," Grace said quietly, "but it was effective just the same. Sometimes desperate women do desperate things."

Ellie stared ahead, speechless. She couldn't believe what she was hearing.

Grace chuckled. "And *now* I can tell you how I met Alfred."

Chapter 6

Early June 1933

The cool breeze off the lake woke Grace from her slumber. She quickly sat up and wondered how long she had been lying there. Her skin felt as if it were on fire in the places where it wasn't covered by her bathing suit. Though her father disapproved of this suit because it was cut higher on her thighs than he preferred, she liked its black-and-white polka-dot pattern and the white belt that fit snugly around her waist. Though most of her friends still preferred a more modest swimsuit, Grace had found this one in the Sears catalog. Upon seeing the photo, her Aunt Calista had raved about how nice it would look on Grace; together, they ordered it without her father knowing. It was a reminder of the many reasons she was thankful to have her aunt in her life.

As she ran her fingers across her burnt skin, Grace reminded herself that she should have left the lake hours ago with Margaret and Beverly. But she had decided to stay and bask the afternoon sun, a decision she regretted now.

As the sun sank lower in the western sky, a cool breeze came up off the lake, making her shudder ever so slightly. She stood and began to feel dizzy as she gathered her things.

"Too much sun," she said to herself. She walked to the edge of the lake and peered at her reflection before dipping her hands into the cool water, bringing it to her face and letting in run down her neck and chest.

As she looked back again, she studied her reflection in the liquid. She could just make out her long, dark curls in the watery mirror, and her dark eyes gazed back at her as she breathed in slowly, taking in the warm summer air. She was glad she had decided not cut her hair short and style it with finger waves, which many of her girlfriends were now sporting. She liked the more natural look. Staring at herself, she noticed the sparkle of the ring on her right hand. The gold band glistened in the sunlight and she pinched it between her index finger and thumb, twisting it around her finger in a circular motion. It was something she often did. It was an odd but comforting habit that reminded her of the ring's presence—and of her mother.

Grace recalled the day her mother had given her the ring. She had already been weak and close to losing her battle with cancer, but as Grace sat with her that day, her mother had taken her wedding ring from her left hand and slid it onto Grace's right hand. With tears streaking her face, Grace had tried to stop her, but her mother insisted. "I want it to stay with you," she whispered as she held her daughter's hand.

Since that day, nearly two years ago, Grace had rarely taken the ring off. When she became caught up in her own little world, she often forgot it was there, as if it had almost become part of her hand. Then, when she suddenly remembered, she would squeeze it and anxiously twist it to keep the memory close.

Every time she did this, she saw her mother's face and could almost feel her essence draw near. As Grace looked down at her reflection and twisted the ring, a watery image emerged behind her. As the image became more vivid, she made out her mother's long, dark, flowing hair. Knowing that the image would disappear if she turned around, she reached toward the water. But, just like all the times before, the image rippled, distorted, and disappeared as soon as her fingertips skimmed the surface. Feeling empty, she sighed and turned away.

Realizing how late the day had become, and noticing the glow of the horizon as the sun began to set, she let go of the ring, slipped her old housedress over her bathing suit, and turned toward the pathway home. She knew she would have to hurry or she would soon be walking through the woods in darkness.

As she walked, Grace thought of Alfred, her father's new farmhand. He had kind green eyes and thick, black, curly hair that stuck out from beneath an old driving cap. She wondered where her father had found him and how long he would stay on the farm to help. She wondered if he had family or if he was from around here. She guessed not since she hadn't seen him before.

Her thoughts of Alfred kept her content as the sun dropped and she found herself alone, walking in the dark. She knew she wasn't far from home, but the darkness made her uneasy and she quickened her pace. She knew her father would wonder where she was and why she had missed supper. She hated how much he worried about her, and it had gotten worse since her mother died.

Most of the time he was a kind, gentle man, but his protective ways often sparked an argument. Just two weeks ago she had gone into town with her girlfriends for ice cream and to buy a new pair of shoes without telling her father. Since he had been in the hay field all day, Grace was certain she would make it to town and back before her father even came home. But she was wrong. Her father had come home while her aunt was gone to the market. With no dinner and no one waiting for him, he had grown angry. Evening was setting in by the time Grace left town and made her way down the dirt road toward home. Suddenly, a cloud of dust rumbled toward her as her father sped down the road in his old Ford. Grace could see the anger in his eyes before he even stopped the truck.

He shouted through the open window. "Where've you been?"

"I just went to town to see Margaret and to buy some shoes," she replied, holding up the sack from Bergstorff's Shoe Store. It contained the Mary Janes she'd been eyeing for weeks. She was stunned by her father's harsh reaction.

"Get in the truck! No one knew where you were," he snapped. "You've got to tell someone when you decide to disappear, Grace."

"I'm sorry," she mumbled as she stepped onto the rusty runner and slid onto the rough leather seat, slamming the heavy door beside her.

He continued his rant. "And you shouldn't be spending money on shoes, either. Money is tight. You know that."

As they drove home, Grace wished her mother were still alive. Her father had become a different person in the past few years. He was overbearing and almost possessive at times.

So now, as she walked on the path home from the lake, Grace quickened her pace and hoped her father wouldn't be angry again. The barn lights were on up ahead, and as she came closer, she made out a figure standing in the shadows and leaning against the barn door. Startled by her sudden appearance, the figure stepped into the light. It was Alfred.

"I'm sorry," Grace said. "I didn't mean to scare you." She walked up to the barn sweating and nearly out of breath.

"That's alright," Alfred answered, somewhat embarrassed. "I just wasn't expecting anyone to come down from the woods."

"Have you seen my father?" she asked, her eyes meeting his.

"He went up to the house about an hour ago. He said he was going to have dinner and come back down to the barn. The mare is about ready to go."

"She's ready now? I thought it'd be another week before Belle was ready to have the foal!"

Moving past Alfred, Grace made her way into the stable to where the horse was about to birth her first foal. Alfred followed quietly, like a shadow.

Feeling his presence behind her, Grace grew self-conscious. *I must look a fright from lounging in the sun all afternoon,* she thought. The dress she had pulled over her swimsuit was baggy and wrinkled and made her feel even more unattractive.

When she reached Belle's stall, she opened the door slowly so as to not frighten the horse. She lay on the straw and lifted her head slightly as Grace crept to her side. Belle was a beautiful horse; her coat was a smooth, dark-chocolate brown and she had the quintessential white spot on her long, slender nose. Her chestnut-colored eyes were full of fear. Grace lowered her head and rested it against the horse's face.

"It's alright, Belle," she whispered as she knelt to stroke the horse's dark, soft mane.

"It probably won't be long now," Alfred said as he grabbed the cap off his head, revealing curls that were matted from sweat. His overalls seemed to be a size too big and were torn in one knee, but Grace didn't care. She couldn't help but feel drawn to him. His disheveled appearance reminded her of her father, and they had the same soft eyes.

"Belle was my mother's horse," Grace said quietly, not turning toward Alfred.

"She's a good, strong mare," he answered, looking at the floor and kicking the dirt with his scuffed, worn work boots. "She should do just fine."

Just then, the barn door swung open as Grace's father walked in with Dr. Murphy, the veterinarian who frequently visited their farm.

"There you are, Grace. I was beginning to get worried when you didn't come up for supper. Calista said she hadn't heard from you all day." Her father's voice was stern.

"I'm sorry," she answered as she quickly rose to her feet. "I fell asleep at the lake. Aunt Calista knew I was going there with Beverly and Margaret."

"She didn't think you'd be there after dark," he snapped. "You know how I feel about you being in before dinner."

Embarrassed that she was being reprimanded in front of Alfred, Grace didn't respond. Her father's younger sister, Calista, had come to live with Grace and her father shortly after her mother's death. She and Grace had formed a special bond as time went by, and Grace often confided in her aunt when she needed someone to talk to.

"Oh, c'mon, Henry, Grace is almost all grown up now," Dr. Murphy said as he peered over his wire-rimmed glasses at Grace. Giving her a quick wink, he peered back toward her father. "You've gotta let her have some fun once in a while."

"She's not grown up yet," her father mumbled as he knelt down beside the horse. "Alfred, give us a hand here."

As the men huddled around the horse, Grace backed into the shadows to watch and wait. She was embarrassed by her father's actions in front of Alfred, but she was more concerned with the foaling of her mare.

Chapter 7

February 2, 2006, 6:26 p.m.

"Was the foal alright?" Ellie asked when Grace hesitated in her story and began to stroke Mayda, who still sat beside her on the arm of the flower-patterned wingback chair. Ellie thought the cat must sit there often because one arm was more worn-down than the other in a spot that almost perfectly matched the size of the cat's body.

"Oh, yes. He was fine. Belle gave birth to a fine little foal. We named him Rocco."

"What happened with Alfred? Did you fall in love right away?"

Grace chuckled and leaned forward in her chair to pat Ellie's knee. "No, child. Sometimes things take just a little longer. Alfred was a shy young man, but oh, how handsome he was. After that night, I was thinking of him for all but a minute or two each day. He was constantly on my mind."

Ellie smiled and settled back into her rocker.

"You're still wondering why you're here," Grace said, changing the subject.

"Yes. I don't understand any of this," Ellie replied.

"I can see why you would feel that way, Ellie," Grace said as she rose to put another log on the fire, which was growing weaker before them.

"Tell me about your Joe," she said.

"You know about Joe?" Ellie was startled. She hadn't mentioned his name since she had arrived.

"Of course, dear. I told you, I've been here a long time."

There was still much Ellie didn't understand about the situation, but at the mere mention of his name, she took comfort in telling this woman about her husband.

"Joe is a very hard-working man," Ellie said quietly.

Grace laughed sarcastically. "That's all you have to say about him?"

"No. He's a good man, but there are times when he seems so distant, like he's thinking of something else."

"Or someone?" Grace interrupted.

"Yes, or someone." Ellie looked away from Grace and into the fire.

"Does Joe make you happy?" Grace asked.

Ellie didn't answer right away, trying to choose her words carefully. "I love him very much."

Grace asked again. "But, does he make *you* happy?" Ellie felt the old woman's eyes upon her, waiting for an answer.

"I…yes. He makes me happy…most of the time."

Grace sighed and thought for a moment before she spoke again. "We often let love define us, Ellie. We think we can control it if we find it, and even if one person loves more than the other, we somehow justify it as being content—as being happy."

Ellie was silent, trying to take in what Grace had said. "But, Joe *does* love me, Grace," she said. "I know he loves me."

"I'm sure he does, Ellie, but you've kept a secret from him, haven't you? You're afraid to tell him because you know it's not what he wants, but it *is* what you want. Isn't that right?"

Ellie was bewildered at how this woman could pinpoint her feelings so eloquently. She didn't understand how Grace knew so much, but for the first time, she began to wonder if maybe she Grace was real.

"What do you want from him, Ellie?" she asked.

"I want him to feel comfortable with me."

Grace shook her head in disapproval. "No, Ellie. What do *you* want from him that he won't give you?"

Ellie looked at the floor and felt the emotion rise in her chest. "I want a baby," she whispered. It was the first time she had said it out loud to anyone. The topic had become so heated between Ellie and Joe that she didn't talk about it to anyone. Talking about it made the issue seem more real, and if she could pretend it didn't bother her outside the four walls of their home, then no one would ask her questions or make her think about it.

"And why don't you tell him this?" she asked.

"Because I know he doesn't."

"But it's too late now to turn back, yes?"

"Yes."

Grace sighed again. "You're afraid he won't want you or the child?"

"I don't want him to think I did it on purpose because he's made it so clear that he doesn't want a child."

"And something else scares you about having this child?"

"Yes. Joe's drinking scares me." Ellie lowered her head. "I'm afraid our child would have the same childhood I had."

Grace's questions were painful, but Ellie couldn't stop herself from spilling the truth. She had told no one about her real doubts in Joe. She only gave bits and pieces of the story when she couldn't hide it anymore. On the outside, everyone thought they were fine. They had a beautiful home on the lake that they had planned and built together. They had a comfortable bank account, and they seemed to live the perfect life most of the time. But since their marriage a few years before, distance had formed between them. She knew why and he knew why, but they rarely talked about it. Whenever the subject came up, Joe shut down and Ellie felt guilty all over again.

"He drinks all the time," Ellie whispered, still looking at the floor.

"And this scares you?"

"Yes."

"Why does it scare you?"

"Because of my dad." Ellie half whispered it. She had never admitted that out loud, either.

Grace settled back in her chair and continued to stroke Mayda, who purred softly.

Grace broke the silence that had begun to fill the room. "I think I know why we all have such trouble with marriage," she said softly.

Ellie wiped her eyes and was confused by the sudden change in conversation. She hadn't thought much of it until Grace pointed it out, but she suddenly realized that both her grandmother and mother had marriages that ended badly. Ellie's grandfather, Sam, had left her grandmother for another woman when her mother was ten years old, leaving her grandmother with little to live on and a daughter to raise. Ellie's mother, on the other hand, had left her husband when Ellie was a teenager; he later died of liver disease brought on by years of alcohol abuse. Ellie had few memories of her father that didn't involve drinking, and she often found herself angry with him even though he was no longer there to be angry with.

Though he had never been abusive to Ellie or her mother, alcohol had become an enemy to him and destroyed everything—his family, his work, his life. She had never understood the power of his addiction, and she hadn't been there when he passed. When Ellie thought about it long enough—when she let it in—she felt horribly guilty for not stepping in or trying to understand his dependence. But most of the time, she was simply too jaded and chose not to visit that place in her head.

Inside, Ellie knew her father and Joe were not the same person, but there were so many things about Joe that reminded her of him, perhaps too many things. As he started to drink more over the last few years, Ellie's fears that he was turning into her father shifted toward bitterness. Joe didn't understand why she felt this way, often shrugging it off, and it was one of the reasons they began to pull away from each other.

The other reason was much more obvious, at least to Joe. For Ellie, not having a child had become much more of an issue when she realized how determined he was not to have one. She wondered why he was adamant, and the more she wondered, the more she imagined the possibility of having a baby.

Chapter 8

February 3, 2006, 12:11 a.m.

The entire ride home from work was a fog, and Joe felt exhausted and groggy as he trudged into the house. His body tingled and he was chilled from the cold outside air. He convinced himself that all he needed was lie down next to Ellie. But, instead, he found the house eerily quiet. Ellie hadn't been back. He wondered if she had finally given up and left for good. After all, he had given her more than enough reasons to go.

He walked around the house looking for clues as to where she might be. There was no note, no missing clothes, and no wedding ring left behind as a small token of her disappointment. Knowing her as well as he did, Joe realized there was something strange about this scenario. If she had left him, there would have been a clue, some obvious gesture to tell him she had really gone.

He slumped into his recliner and rubbed his aching temple. Ellie hated this chair and often complained about how it didn't match a thing in their living room. When they bought their new leather couch with the chaise lounge on one end, she had tried to convince him that they didn't need that worn, torn, and faded recliner anymore. But like he always did, Joe argued and refused to let it go. Why hadn't he just talked to her? Things could have been easier, he thought. They could have been so much different if he had just tried to help her understand why he was so guarded, insistent and tightly wound. She deserved that much from him. But just as he started to let his defenses falter, he began to rationalize with himself again. “I never lied,” he said aloud. “I never told her we would have a family.”

And he hadn’t. But he also hadn’t fully shared his reasons with her. “It’s my life,” he said as he sat with his head in his hands, not speaking to anyone in particular. He wanted a drink, but he hesitated in standing and crossing the room to pour that soothing liquid into a glass. He so wanted to feel the brandy burn as it slipped down his throat, but he knew that drinking would restart what had transpired the night before.

Just as he was about to lean back in the chair, fighting off his urges, Joe noticed the answering machine’s light blinking from across the room. He stood and dragged his feet across the floor until he reached it, his finger shaking before hitting the button. Would it be her? If it were, what would she say? He knew he wasn’t prepared to hear her voice saying it was over.

His finger came down heavily on the button as he closed his eyes and held his breath. The voice on the machine was unfamiliar, and he had to play the message twice to understand it completely.

“Mr. McHugh, this is the emergency department at Oconomowoc Memorial Hospital. Your wife has been involved in a car accident. Please call us at this number immediately…”

His hands shook as he wrote down the number, and he could barely contain himself while he dialed the phone. When the voice on the other end spoke, he could hardly understand the words as his heart sank and he fell to his knees. The phone hit the floor.

Chapter 9

June 1933

Grace was exhausted when she finally came up from the barn after sitting with Belle until the early morning hours. The night's coolness still lingered in the air, and she glanced out her bedroom window as she took off her clothes to crawl into bed for a few hours' rest. She slipped off her old green, floral-patterned housedress and threw it into a heap on the floor. Calista had sewn its hem so many times. She wouldn't be caught dead wearing it to school, but it was just fine for here on the farm. The gathered waist was comfortable and it wasn't too short for her father to disapprove of.

From behind the safety of her curtain, Grace watched as Alfred came out of the barn, closing the door behind him. He took a long breath of the cool, fresh air as he turned and gently tipped his head back, peering up at the clear sky. His eyes closed and he stood there for a few minutes before walking toward the bunkhouse. Many laborers had used that bunkhouse as they came and went over the years, but never had Grace seen one quite like Alfred. She wondered what he was thinking as he looked up into the darkness.

When he was gone, she moved the curtain back, slipped into one of her mother's old silk chemise dresses, and crawled into her bed. Her mother had slept in these thin, slip-like dresses, and Grace had confiscated them from the closet before Calista had a chance to claim them for herself.

As Grace lay in the darkness, she spun the ring on her finger. Then she abruptly stopped and inspected it in the moonlight. She loved the look of this ring, its thick, gold band and the leaves etched into the metal. It was unique. As she turned over, she placed the ring on the bedside table and stared at it. She tried to remember what her mother's hand had looked like when she wore it.

Closing her eyes, Grace pictured her mother sitting in the chair near the window, her hands folded on her lap so the ring was on top. Her mother was so beautiful. Her long, dark hair had just the right amount of wave, unlike Grace's, which was wild with curls. And her mother was slender and shaped like a perfect hourglass. Grace wished she looked more like her instead of having a thin, boy-like figure.

As she tried to fall asleep, her thoughts shifted back to Alfred. She imagined him coming through her bedroom door, slowly removing his tattered overalls, never taking his eyes off her and then lying beside her. She would turn to face him as he lay next to her, but they wouldn't speak. He would kiss her, gingerly at first, but then passionately as their bodies intertwined. Just the thought of it made Grace shiver with excitement. Though she had never been with a man that way, she imagined how blissful it would be to taste Alfred's kisses. The thought carried her to sleep.

What seemed like just minutes later, Grace was slowly pulled from her slumber by a soft whistling in the air.

“Good morning, sunshine,” Calista said as she removed some of Grace’s neatly folded blouses from a basket on the floor and placed them in her bureau drawer.

Groaning, Grace turned to face the wall, covering her head with the blankets.

“I know you were up late, Grace, but I need your help today to get ready for the picnic,” Calista said as she continued to whistle, her small frame spinning on her heels as she turned back toward the bureau.

“The picnic isn’t until tomorrow,” Grace muttered from under the blankets.

“Yes, but I need you to go to the market with me and help me bake the pies,” Calista answered.

Every summer her father hosted a picnic on the farm to welcome the growing season. Everyone in town was invited, and it had become the event of the summer in their tiny, rural area. Since her mother died, her father had taken less interest in the occasion, so Calista happily took on the responsibilities instead.

Grace’s aunt was an attractive woman, but in a different way than her mother. While her mother had been naturally beautiful, Calista was more plain. Her mousy-brown hair was curly, like Grace’s, and it was cut to her shoulders. She always wore it pinned up on the sides, which accentuated her high cheekbones and blue eyes. Other than the color of their eyes, Grace thought there was little resemblance between her father and his only sister. While her father towered over six feet tall, Calista was small, barely reaching five-foot-three, and she weighed slightly over 100 pounds.

Though her aunt liked to wear many of Grace's mother's dresses, she could never quite fill them out the same way. Still, Grace had spent many a night watching her try on the fitted dresses that her mother had worn so eloquently. But neither Grace nor Calista could come close to looking as stunning in them as Isabelle had.

There was one dress in particular that both of them loved. It was a Greta Garbo-style low-back, raven-colored evening gown that her mother had purchased in Milwaukee when she and Grace's father had gone to the city for a weekend getaway years before. Her mother had no occasion to wear such a dress, but she bought it anyway. It was covered in ribbon embroidery with feather-shaped swirls and light blue crystals sprinkled throughout the dress. It had a full, unlined chiffon skirt and a metal zipper that made the top a snug fit. Even though she had been barely ten years old when her mother brought that dress home, Grace was enamored by it. Now she and Calista would take turns trying it on during quiet, playful nights, spinning in front of the mirror and giggling like children.

"Why is this here?" Calista said as she lifted the ring off the bedside table, where Grace had forgotten it.

"Oh, I took it off before I fell asleep," she replied, quickly snatching it from her aunt's hand and sliding it back onto her own.

Puzzled, Calista watched as Grace began to spin the ring. "You know, your mother used to do that," she said. Grace's eyes shot up to meet hers. "It was a habit she had," Calista continued. "Seems like you have the same one."

"Really? I didn't know that," Grace replied. She stopped spinning the ring and felt the metal's warmth on her skin. "Whenever I touch it, I just feel closer to her somehow."

Calista sat down and touched the ring again. "I think that's what she meant when she gave it to you." She sighed as she picked up Grace's right hand. "You know, that ring used to belong to your grandmother."

"Really?" Grace said with surprise. "Why haven't you ever told me that before?"

"Because it should always remind you of your mother," Calista said quietly. "When your parents were married, my mother gave it to your father, being that he was the oldest and the first of us to get married. I was always a little jealous that Isabelle had it, but I knew how much your father loved her. She was meant to have it."

Calista stopped talking and ran her fingers across the gold leafing. "You know, when I was little, my mother used to say that whoever wore this ring would be blessed with love, and it should always be worn by someone in love."

Grace stared at her aunt. "But I'm not in love, Calista."

"Not yet," she said, winking as she stood up. She had momentarily lost track of all that needed to be done to prepare for the following day.

As her aunt busied herself, Grace remained seated on the bed and began to twist the ring again. She looked out the window at Alfred standing in the yard and talking with her father. Suddenly in a hurry, she stood and began to dress. Instead of grabbing the old housedress, she chose tighter-fitting short slacks and a white, sleeveless blouse. Calista looked at

Grace with surprise and glanced in the same direction that her niece was looking. She shook her head, smiled, and turned back toward the bureau while mumbling under her breath. “Hmmm. Maybe a certain love interest isn’t so far away?”

Grace smiled coyly. “I’m just going to check on Belle.”

“Yes, and that boy.” Calista winked again as she finished putting away the clothes and made her way toward the door. “That ring might be on your left hand someday soon, but not *too* soon, I hope.”

Grace checked her reflection in the mirror and ran out to the barn. Her heart thumped with excitement as she opened the door and saw Alfred in the entrance to Belle’s stall. Today he wore a clean white T-shirt and loose-fitting denim dungarees. An old, dirty newspaper-boy hat was on his head. Grace liked it—it made him seem more boyish. Their eyes met as she came in, and they both smiled.

“Quick, come here,” Alfred said in a half-whisper as she rushed closer to the stall.

“Look, he’s standing.” Alfred pointed. The small, disheveled-looking foal clumsily shuffled his hooves in the straw as he hovered under Belle.

“He’s so beautiful.” Grace gasped, her eyes growing glassy. Noticing that Alfred was watching, she quickly looked away. “I’m sorry. I know it’s silly to be so emotional, but I’ve just been so worried about Belle.”

“It’s alright. There’s no shame in loving something.” A wide smile stretched across his face. Butterflies rose in Grace’s stomach as Alfred stared at her. He reached out to stroke Belle’s mane; as he ran his hands down her neck, Grace noticed the definition and strength in his arms.

Her nervous, self-conscious feelings were taking over, so she asked a question to shake them. "Are you going to the picnic tomorrow?"

"I guess so," he said, turning back to Belle. "I'm not much for social things, but I guess it'd be kind of hard to hide from it since it's right here on the farm."

Grace laughed. "Yeah, considering the whole town will be here, it would be *very* hard to hide. Aunt Calista makes an excellent apple pie, though, and we always make a huge fire and roast one the biggest pigs from the Trapp's farm up the road, so it'll be worth it for you."

"Ah, I guess I wouldn't want to miss that," he said shyly.

Grace moved closer to Belle and stroked her mane as the horse turned her head and nudged gently. Alfred watched, never taking his eyes off Grace as she moved. When she noticed his stare, he looked away quickly and nervously. The butterflies fluttered in her stomach again.

"I'm sorry about your mother," he said after a few minutes of awkward silence. Grace was surprised by this unexpected remark but continued running her hands over Belle's smooth, soft coat.

"Thanks," she half whispered. "She was sick for a long time."

"My mother knew her, I guess" Alfred said, looking nervously at his feet.

"Really? Is that how you got this job for my father? Because he knows your mother, too?" Grace asked.

"Yep, I guess. I just finished my first year at Marquette University and I needed to take a job before I enter St. Francis Seminary in the fall. "

"The seminary?" Grace's heart plummeted.

"Yeah, I'm studying to become a priest." He talked faster now. "My mother is very sick right now, too, and she really wants me to become a priest. It's her dream, I guess."

Grace stared at Alfred, unsure of what to say. It was the last thing she had expected to hear. "But, do *you* want to be a priest?"

Alfred laughed. "Of course I do. I believe in God's work, Grace. Don't you?"

"I guess, but we're not really church people," she replied, wondering if he could sense the disappointment in her voice.

Alfred looked down at his old, worn boots. "The life of a priest isn't all that bad, Grace. There are good things about it."

She walked out of Belle's stall, pushing past Alfred as she moved toward the barn door. "I never said it was bad. I've just never known anyone who wanted to become one."

Alfred called out to her as she walked away. "Will I see you at the picnic?"

"Yes, I'll be there," she said. She stopped and turned, realizing how rude she must seem. Though the butterflies were still there, she couldn't stop herself from being disheartened. Her family had never made church a priority. Sure, she believed in God and prayed sometimes, but her mother had always had different beliefs. She had believed in worshipping nature more than she'd believed in worshipping one unseen entity.

As she sauntered into the house, Grace shrugged and slumped into a chair at the kitchen table across from her father, who sat quietly reading the paper.

"What's with the long face?" Calista asked as she moved busily around the kitchen.

"Nothing," Grace quickly answered.

Calista smiled and looked at her brother, who was studying the newspaper. He mumbled something under his breath about what a tyrant Adolf Hitler was.

"You found out that boy is going to be a priest, didn't you?" Calista asked.

Graced looked up as her father, suddenly interested, peeked out from behind the paper.

"Who told you that?" she asked.

"Ask him," Calista answered, motioning toward her brother.

"I know his mother. The boy needed some money, so I hired him," he replied. "He's a good kid. He'll make a good priest."

"Too bad, hey Grace?" Calista said, touching Grace's shoulder as she passed.

"Yeah, too bad," Grace said as she rose from the table and made her way upstairs. As she flopped onto her bed, she let out a long, slow sigh. Even though Alfred was going to be a priest, she couldn't stop thinking about him. As she replayed their conversation in her mind, she couldn't help but recall how closely his eyes had followed her. She was convinced he was interested in her as well, but things were different now. If he were studying to be a priest, he would never fall for her.

Chapter 10

February 3, 2006, 12:45 a.m.

As he pushed through the hospital doorway, Joe's mind raced with fear. He had to get to Ellie, to be by her side. He rushed to the desk and could barely say her name when he asked the stout, emotionless woman behind it where his wife was.

When he finally did say her name, he could tell by the look in the woman's eyes that something wasn't right. She appeared stone-faced, like she was hiding something. She didn't look Joe in the eyes as she picked up the phone, whispered softly, and then replaced the receiver.

"Someone will be right out, Mr. McHugh."

He breathed heavily as sweat poured from his forehead and he looked wildly around the room. It was quiet here, and the glare of the clean floor almost blinded him. Soon the doors opened at the end of the hall and a tall, thin man in a white coat approached him. He looked serious and his forehead was wrinkled all the way up to his receding hairline.

"Mr. McHugh, please come with me." The man's voice was delicate and he took Joe by the arm.

Joe pleaded, pulling away. "Please, just tell me where my wife is. Is she okay?"

The man extended his arm, leading Joe into a small room with nothing but a couch and a few chairs. "Please sit down," he said as he motioned toward an uncomfortable-looking striped sofa.

Joe wasn't ready to sit. "Where is she?" he said, his voice rising.

"Mr. McHugh, my name is Dr. James. Your wife has been in a serious car accident." He hesitated. "As a result, she's suffered head trauma. We're doing all we can, but there have been a few complications."

Joe felt weak as he sank to the hard couch, which felt like concrete beneath him. "Is she going to be alright?"

The doctor moved slowly across the room and sat in a chair directly across from Joe. "We're trying to reduce the swelling of her brain, but there may be some other complications." His voice drifted off.

"What is it?" Joe asked poignantly.

The doctor sighed. "Your wife is pregnant, Mr. McHugh. We spoke with her obstetrician, and she told us your wife hadn't told you yet."

Joe's head spun and he suddenly felt nauseated. The doctor's voice became an echo inside his head.

"I know this is hard for you to grasp right now, but this is a very critical time for both your wife and your child, Mr. McHugh. If the swelling doesn't go down, we may lose them. If your wife pulls through, there may have been too much damage to sustain the child. It's just too early to tell."

The room wouldn't stop spinning as Joe struggled to his feet. "Can I see her?" he asked, trying to steady himself while wiping tears off his cheeks.

"Of course."

As the doctor led him into Ellie's room, Joe trembled with fear. How could she not tell him about a baby? How could he live without her if she didn't make it? Why hadn't he talked to her before all of this came about? He'd been so distant from her lately.

He hated himself as he looked at her lying in a bed surrounded by beeping and hissing machines. He didn't understand how this woman, this wonderful, beautiful woman, could be reduced to this. He had wasted so much of the time he had been given with her. At that instant, he wondered if this was how it would all end. He slumped into the chair beside the bed and covered his face with his hands.

Dr. James and the nurse locked eyes for a moment. "Is there anyone I can call for you?" the nurse asked.

"No, I'll do it." His voice trembled. He wondered how many other people knew they were expecting a child.

"We'll give you a few moments, then," she said as she and the doctor slipped out of the room.

Joe turned toward his wife and could barely recognize her swollen face. He took her hand and rested his head gently on top of it. "I'm sorry, Ellie," he whispered. "I'm here now. It's going to be alright. Everything is going to be alright."

He barely believed his own words. All he knew at that moment was how much he wanted her to be okay, baby or no baby.

As he sat motionless, clutching Ellie's hand, slow, hot tears streamed down his face. For the first time in a long time, he was afraid—afraid of losing Ellie, afraid of having this child, afraid to come to terms with his past.

The nurse slipped back into the room. “Are you sure there’s no one we can call?”

Joe didn’t even look up as she rounded the bed to monitor the machines connected to his wife. “No, I’ll call her mom,” he whispered.

The nurse nodded and left without another word.

Joe looked back at his wife, who lay still and looked so fragile. As he let go of her hand, he leaned back in the chair and wiped the tears from his face. He wished he had told her about his son, Andrew—a boy that was now being raised in another state, by another man, with a new name. Though it had all happened years before he met Ellie, he had sworn that he would never have another child. The guilt of letting his son go was always there, and he would never allow himself to enjoy another child’s love. It wasn’t fair to Ellie, but he had never made her false promises.

Joe and his son’s mother, Lisa, were very young when they learned they were expecting. Joe immediately knew he wanted to end the pregnancy, but Lisa didn’t. As time went by and his son was born, Joe felt himself changing in ways he’d never expected. He loved that dark-haired, strong-willed boy, but his relationship with Lisa had become a nightmare. She made constant threats about child support and visitation rights. Since he barely made enough money to support himself, he couldn’t imagine having to pay her on top of it. Lisa had wealthy parents who would always support her, but she would take anything of Joe’s just to prove she could. He could never quite understand why she was so bitter about him but also refused to let him go. They were polar opposites who brought out the worst in each other.

He was miserable, but he stayed in the relationship only because he loved his son. He hated Lisa more and more each day. Her threats, her nagging, her constant complaining—she was spoiled and couldn't stand not being in control. As time went by, he spent more and more time at work and the tavern. He failed to see the signs that Lisa put before him, or maybe he purposely ignored them. But one day, when he came home from work excited to see his boy but dreading to see Lisa, he walked into their apartment to find it empty. Lisa and Andrew were gone.

She left a note saying she couldn't live like this anymore and had taken their son to Florida with a man she had been seeing for some time behind Joe's back. Though he was devastated at the thought of not seeing Andrew, Joe suddenly felt free and more alive than he'd been in years. A few months later, papers came in the mail asking Joe to relinquish his parental rights. He ignored the papers, hoping that if he did so the case would go away and Andrew would someday come back into his life. He didn't have the strength to sign his son away. But when he failed to show up for a court hearing regarding Andrew, the judgment was granted anyway and Joe was no longer the eleven-month-old boy's legal father. Though he was hurt and confused, he knew it was for the best. Andrew deserved more than two parents who hated each other with a vengeance. Not long after, Joe decided he also needed a change and moved back to Wisconsin to be near his brothers and forget the past.

Two years later, he met Ellie. She had mesmerized Joe from the moment she walked into the party they were both attending. He didn't know a thing about her, but he knew she was the woman he would marry.

Chapter 11

June 1933

While helping Calista peel apples, Grace watched through the window as Alfred and her father set up the tables outside. It was a blistering hot day, and it was the kind of humid that made it hard to breathe. Alfred was shirtless beneath his dirty overalls, and his sweaty skin glistened in the sun.

"Would you stop staring at that boy and watch what you're doing?" Calista laughed as she handed Grace a towel to clean up the apple peels that had fallen and gathered around her feet.

Embarrassed, Grace smiled. She quickly wiped the floor and began peeling another apple. The room was filled with the aroma of baked apples and cinnamon, a scent so sweet she could almost taste it. Calista's pies were one of the things she loved most about this annual ritual, but making them took time and was hard work. As she placed the paring knife's blade against the green skin, Grace felt sweat pooling on her forehead. She looked out the window one more time, an action that didn't go unnoticed by Calista.

"You know that boy is off limits, Grace. You've got to let go of this crush." Her aunt shook her head and wiped her face on her apron.

Grace slid the knife into the apple and twisted it until a perfect spiral of green, moist skin touched her hand. “I know,” she said with a sigh. “He’s just different than the other boys. He seems so much more mature, and I…”

“You’ve never felt this way before. I know how you feel,” Calista said as she sprinkled flour on the wooden table and placed another mound of round, sticky dough in the center. Her red face was splotched with white.

“You do?”

“Of course I do,” she replied, reaching for the rolling pin. “When your Uncle Charlie and I first met back in school, I thought he was the most handsome thing I’d ever seen.”

Grace smiled. Calista rarely talked about her husband, who had died in an accident at the canning factory several years before. Her uncle had been sweet and funny. When she was little, he always played tricks. Grace loved it most when he would pretend to pull a quarter from behind her ear. He was handsome—always well-dressed—and he wore the biggest smile of anyone she knew. He was smaller in stature than her father, with a much more slender build, but his strawberry blond hair made his blue eyes sparkle like gems hiding behind long, ginger-colored eyelashes.

“You’re young, Grace. Just don’t go growing up too fast, now. You hear?”

Grace smirked as Calista turned away and pressed her weight down on the rolling pin.

Later that night, as the guests reveled in homemade wine and cider from Miller’s Orchard, Grace found herself alone and watching her father chat with the other men. The scent of the barbequed pork and roasted apples still lingered in the air even as the fire burned down in the pit. As he stood with the other men and nibbled on some of Calista's apple pie, Grace noticed that a line had formed near the center of her father's forehead. It made his skin look leathery and old. She knew it was from his constant stress and endless hours of hard work on the farm. Her mother had always been able to release that tension in his face—he lit up whenever she entered a room. But he had begun to change even before her mother had passed. Grace was never sure if it was from worrying about her mother's illness or if something else had changed him, but every year he looked older. Even his jet-black hair was turning more salt-and-pepper-colored.

Glancing through the crowd, Grace noticed Alfred talking to some of the other young men. She also noticed how much he stood out from the others. He was stronger, taller, and quieter. He wasn't wearing his normal newspaper-boy hat and overalls; instead, he wore a clean navy-blue button-down shirt and khaki slacks. His normally mussed hair was smoothed back and combed, making his tan, clean-shaven face more chiseled and his eyes even brighter than usual. Noticing her stare, he smiled coyly and then looked away. She shifted her gaze back toward her father but saw Alfred excuse himself from the group and begin walking toward her out of the corner of her eye. Her heart began to beat faster, and she wished she could slow it down. She didn't want to feel this anxious, excited feeling for Alfred now that he was going off to a seminary. But she couldn't stop. Whenever she looked into his deep green eyes, she didn't seem to care about his plans.

“There you are,” he said with a new glint in his eyes. “I was looking for you earlier.”

“I’ve been right sitting right here,” she replied, almost rudely.

“How come you’re not over there gossiping with the other girls?” He motioned toward a group of young girls that giggled as they watched the young men across the clearing. Grace looked at them in their skirts that widened softly at the hips, accentuating their trim waistlines. Unlike Grace, most of them had pale skin and thought it passé to tan in the sun. They wore too much rouge and tried too hard to look older than they really were. They huddled together and whispered about things that she wasn’t interested in. She seemed above them now; she didn’t want to be a part of their childish conversations.

Grace shrugged and looked back toward her father. “I just wanted some time alone.”

“Alone? Well, that’s no way to be.” Alfred nudged her arm and sat down beside her. Being this close to him made Grace feel uneasy. She stood just as the band began to play from atop a stage made of hay bales. Between the banjo, the accordion, and the crowd, the farm almost seemed transformed by the music and laughter. The night was warm and the stars were so bright that Grace could almost feel the electricity in the air.

“Do you wanna dance?” Alfred asked, motioning toward the others, who had started to circle around the clearing in a clumsy, unorganized square dance.

"No, not really. I was thinking of going to check on Belle," she said, barely meeting his glance. She was growing annoyed with Alfred's innocent flirtations.

"I'll come with you," he said, following close behind her.

Grace was nervous as they walked toward the barn in the darkness. She hadn't expected Alfred to follow, and even though she so wanted to reach out and take his hand, she knew there was no chance of things going any further between them. She wondered why he was tagging along.

As they walked through the barn door, he said, "Why are you so quiet?"

The air was less thick in the stable, and the cool air helped lift the heaviness that had settled on Grace's chest. "I'm sorry," she said, looking away. "I just don't know what to say."

"Is it because I told you about my plans? I really do want to be a priest, Grace. Honestly."

"That's good, Alfred. I'm glad for you." She tried to sound sincere.

"But do you want to know something else?" he said softly.

"What?" She turned toward him.

"I really want to kiss you."

They stared at each other in silence, both too afraid to move. Grace was unsure what to make of this sudden turn of events. And then Alfred stepped forward. His soft lips touched hers so tenderly that Grace wanted to melt into his arms. The kiss became deeper as he pulled her closer. She had never been kissed this way, and her body tingled with excitement. She smelled the musky scent of his skin and felt his heart beating beneath his clean cotton shirt.

But then, almost as quickly as the moment began, Alfred pushed her away. "I'm sorry. I shouldn't have done that," he said as he turned away. Grace was stunned as she watched him turn on his heels and push out the door with no further explanation.

Confused, she stared at the door. She hadn't asked for Alfred to come here, and she hadn't asked for him to kiss her, but still he had. None of it made sense, and the fury inside of her grew. Too angry to go back to the picnic, she walked in the woods instead. With her heart pounding, she had no fear of the dark trees that soon surrounded her. All she wanted was to get to the lake and peer into the water. Being there made her feel closer to her mother. She hoped her mother would appear when she arrived at the lake, even if it was only in her mind. She wanted her to manifest long enough to tell her what to do.

Even through the thick expanse of trees, Grace heard jovial voices and music from the picnic. She pictured Margaret and Beverly dancing and making eyes at young men. The thought filled her with more disdain. What she felt for Alfred wasn't infatuation or a childish game. Alfred was different. His smile, his demeanor, his determination—it was all so much larger than the aspirations of the other girls she knew. She had only known Alfred for a short time, but she knew he felt something, too. If he hadn't planned to enter the seminary, he would be walking with her right now.

How could he chose a life without the love of another human being and trust all of his love to a God he couldn't see?

How could he choose a life without tender touches between a husband and wife and without lust for a woman he truly loved? Would he ever know the feeling of lying next to a woman in the early morning hours, pushing aside with his finger the hair that fell across her face while she slept? *He must want that*, she thought. She walked faster once she could see the lake up ahead, its shimmering water looking like a silver blanket in the moonlight. Though she wanted to take off her clothes and sink beneath the cool, dark surface, she stopped at the edge, stared into the black water, and waited.

Chapter 12

February 2, 2006, 8:00 p.m.

"What happened when you got to the lake?" Ellie asked impatiently.

Grace sighed and turned her wrinkled face toward the fire. The shadows and the brightness from the flames licked at the old woman's serious face. "I stood there for a long time peering into the water. It looked like a shiny, black mirror in the darkness," she said quietly. "The moon wasn't quite full that night, but it was bright and I could see its reflection on the water.

"I waited for a long time and twisted that ring on my finger hoping my mother would appear. I could feel her, almost smell her, but she never appeared. After a while, I lay down in the cool grass near the shore and began to cry. I missed her so much, and I wanted to tell her so much, but the only thing that made me feel close to her was that ring."

Ellie's heart ached as Grace spoke. As much as her own mother annoyed her at times, she was glad to have her in her life. Still, she wished they could share more. Too often, Ellie was afraid to tell her what was really going on in her life. And Ellie had worn the ring all this time without her mother telling her the real story behind it. In that moment, she wanted to slip the ring off her finger and put it back on Grace's hand.

"It should stay on your hand," Grace said, looking point blank at Ellie, who had been so lost in thought that she hadn't noticed the old woman's stare. "If you love Joe, it should stay on your hand."

Ellie peered back at the woman with bewilderment. Had Grace read her mind?

Grace continued. "Remember, dear, my aunt Calista said that ring protects the marriage it binds." Ellie looked down, realizing she wore the ring on her right hand, not her left. "It doesn't matter which hand it's on," she said, watching Ellie's eyes.

"Did you fall out of love with Alfred? Is that why things ended the way they did?" Ellie wanted to know what had driven him to murder, and she was growing impatient.

Grace went quiet as she looked down at the floor. She turned back toward the fire as she began to speak. "It's not that simple, child," she said, her voice soft. "I killed him long before he killed me." She pulled at the red crocheted shawl that hung loosely across her shoulders. "Before he came to my father's farm, Alfred had a plan for his life, a destiny that was in his hands and no one else's. He wanted to serve God and be a good man. I didn't see it then, but I took all of that away."

"But you didn't do it alone. He chose you, didn't he?"

"He chose to deviate from his path for just a moment, just a small, un-thought-out detour that led him to a different place. If he'd known he would go there, he never would have strayed, but I called and he followed. Only figuratively, of course, but after that, his life wasn't the same. Nor was mine."

Ellie listened quietly and tried to imagine what could be so awful that it had led her great-grandparents to such a dark place.

Chapter 13

June 1933

When the morning sun hit her face, Grace blinked and struggled to focus. She watched the trees sway around her as she looked toward the sky. Confused and disorientated, she quickly realized she wasn't in bed. She sat up and looked around. *How did I fall asleep at the lake*?

Her stomach churned with acid and her head was pounding. The sun was warm, but the dew on the dead leaves told her it was still early, and she knew her father had to be wondering where she was. She was surprised to find her mother's ring in the palm of her hand instead of on her finger. She struggled to remember what had transpired the night before. She recalled Alfred's kiss and her anger as she stomped away from the farm, and she remembered lying down on the cool grass and looking up at the sky. She remembered wanting to see her mother, but her mother had never come—or had she?

Slowly, Grace brought the ring to her eye and peered through it. Even as she strained and squinted, all she could see on the other side was leaves and trees that danced in the early morning's light breeze. There was no noise around her other than a choir of crickets and the gentle wind blowing through the trees. Part of her wanted to stay and blend into the natural world around her. This world she could understand; everything had its place and purpose. In her world, nothing seemed to fit.

But then, remembering the flack she would face when she returned home, she decided it was better to slip back into the house and her bed in hopes that no one had noticed she was gone. She mustered the strength to stand and brushed dead grass and leaves from her long skirt. She jogged quickly when she reached the dirt pathway back to the farm, hoping with every step that her father had, for once, drank too much wine and worried about no one but himself. But she knew the idea was far-fetched. He was most likely worried sick that she had disappeared. He would no doubt turn his worry into anger when he realized she was fine.

As she jogged over the hill, breathing heavily and beginning to sweat, she saw the farm in the distance. As she drew closer, she was surprised by how calm it seemed. Perhaps they hadn't noticed she was gone.

Feeling a bit more relieved, she found herself staring at the window of the room where Alfred slept. She hesitated, wanting so much to go in and lie down beside him, but she continued walking.

"Good morning." A voice came from behind her. She jumped and whirled around, surprised to see Alfred behind her. "I'm sorry about last night, Grace. I didn't sleep a wink thinking about how you must've felt," he said as he moved toward her. Again she said nothing. She was tired and unable to muster the strength to tell him her feelings. She suddenly felt dizzy.

"Are you alright?" He rushed toward her as she faltered. His strong arms clutched her as he helped her to his room and guided her to the edge of his bed. His hand was shaky as he poured some water from a jug on the table, and it spilled a little as he handed it to her. "Here," he said. "This might help."

She drank the water slowly and looked around the room. It was drab and bleak, with nothing but a small, dirty window, wood floors, a rickety, uncomfortable-looking chair, a table with a book and the water jug resting on top, and the lumpy, neatly-made cot where she now sat.

"Feeling better?" he asked as he sat down beside her. The cot creaked under his weight.

"Alfred." When she began to speak, he brought his hand to her face and gently wiped away the perspiration that had begun to slide down her cheeks like tears. She stared into his eyes and he moved closer, but she hesitated and turned away. Embarrassed, he clutched his hands and looked at the floor.

"Grace, I'm so confused by what I feel for you. I barely know you, but every time I'm near you, I just want to be closer to you."

"I know. I feel it too, Alfred, but…"

Before she could finish, his lips softly touched hers. She closed her eyes. He pulled her closer and leaned her back on the neatly made bed. His hand clutched hers and his kisses grew deeper.

Suddenly there was a knock and the door flew open with bang.

"Alfred, get up! I can't find Grace!" Her father entered so quickly that he didn't realize Alfred wasn't alone. When Alfred and Grace quickly darted up, her father stood silhouetted in the doorway. He stared in bewilderment, looking from one face to the other. Nervously, Alfred stood up and stepped away from Grace.

"What are you doing?" her father asked as she sat motionless on the edge of the bed. She felt like a mouse about to be trapped beneath a bucket.

"It's not what you think," she pleaded as she waved her hands and stood up.

"Is this where you've been all night?" His voice was low, almost like a growl. He glared at Alfred, who stood cowering in the corner.

"No, I haven't," Grace said. "I was in the woods. I fell asleep and…"

Her father didn't buy her explanation. "Get up to the house now. Calista is worried sick."

As she pushed past her father, Grace stole a quick look at Alfred, who met her glance. He looked horrified. She knew her father would never believe that Alfred had just offered her a place to sit and catch her breath.

"You have work to do, Alfred," her father grumbled and stomped away without another word.

As she walked toward the house, she saw Calista standing on the porch with her hands clutched over her mouth. She had seen Henry enter Alfred's room and watched Grace exit. Grace knew how bad things looked. As close as she was to her aunt, she knew Calista wouldn't believe her story either.

Chapter 14

February 3, 2006, 8:00 a.m.

Something touched Joe's shoulder as he rested his head on Ellie's chest. Her heart beat against his head—or maybe he felt his own heartbeat. He wasn't sure, but it calmed him either way. Startled, he sat up to see his brother Peter standing behind him. Across the bed, Ellie's mother held her hand. Anna's face was blank, but it was obvious that she had been crying. Joe struggled to speak but couldn't find the words. He wondered how long Anna had been sitting there.

Peter spoke. "Why don't you come outside for a minute, Joe?"

He met his mother-in-law's eyes as he stood up, but she said nothing. "Anna, I…"

"It's alright, Joe. I'll stay," she said as she looked down at her daughter.

"It'll only be for a minute, Joe," Peter assured him as he led his brother out of the room.

Joe walked slowly and felt weak as he ran his fingers through his dark hair. He didn't smoke, but he knew Peter was leading him outside so he could light up. As they made their way through the automatic doors, Joe was taken aback by the crispness of the winter wind, and he was blinded by the sunlight. The cold air felt good on his face.

He watched as Peter pulled a cigarette from the pack in his shirt pocket and lit it, then inhaled deep and slow. He handed the cigarette to Joe, who also took a deep breath and exhaled quickly, before he could cough. He would have normally found it nauseating, but in that moment it was oddly comforting.

"So Ellie's expecting," Peter said, more as a statement than a question.

Joe coughed and handed the smoke back to his brother. "That's what they tell me."

"She didn't tell you?"

"No, I had no idea."

Joe sat on a bench that had dried in the bright sunlight. All around them, snow melted and water dripped off tree branches, creating slushy puddles that splashed a brown mush whenever cars passed by.

"For the life of me, Pete, I don't know why she didn't tell me," Joe said as he stared at the slush.

His brother laughed and sat down heavily. He exhaled another puff of smoke, which circled around him. The smell made Joe want to vomit, reminding him why he didn't smoke.

"Why didn't she tell you? C'mon, Joe. You can't really believe you made it easy for her."

Joe shot a dirty look at his brother. "I never told her about Lisa and..."

"She knows about Andrew," Peter said as he crushed the cigarette on the sidewalk beneath his black, shiny boot. Peter's boots were always shiny, probably from years of working as a city cop. He was a rigid and disciplined man, unlike his younger brothers.

Joe's head snapped around to look at Peter. "How?"

"I told her."

Joe stood up quickly. "You did *what*?"

Peter stayed seated and slowly looked his brother up and down, as if he were surveying a crime suspect. He wasn't rattled by Joe's anger.

"I thought she had a right to know what she was getting into when she married you. I didn't want you hiding it from her so that one day it would wake up and bite you in the ass like it would be doing right now if I hadn't."

"You had no right to do that!" Joe shouted as he sank back down on the bench. He was angry and exhausted at the same time. "Why didn't she ever tell me she knew?"

"Why didn't you tell her?" Peter responded as he stood and zipped his leather jacket. "You wanna know what she said when I told her you had a son that you gave up, Joe? She said it didn't matter, that she knew you would tell her when you were ready and there had to have been a good reason you would let him go. I see you decided that not telling her would be better, and now look where that got you."

"I'm not in the mood for this right now, Peter." Joe stood again and moved past his brother toward the hospital doors.

"She loves you, Joe, but I'm guessing she was as afraid to tell you about the baby as you were to tell her about Andrew." Joe stopped in his tracks and turned back.

"She told you about the baby? She told *you*?"

"No, she didn't tell me," Peter quickly responded. "But I'm not surprised that she didn't tell you."

Angry again, Joe turned and stomped back through the automatic doors. The sounds of the hospital were deafening—people talking, babies crying, doctors murmuring, and telephones ringing. It all started to sound like static in his head. A slow ache rose in his chest and he wanted to get away as fast as he could. He rushed into the men's restroom, raced into a stall, and slammed the metal door behind him. Here, in this place where people normally came to relieve themselves, he purged his soul and tried to gather his thoughts. He couldn't hear anyone else in the room so he let his emotions spill out. He wanted to scream, but all he could do was cry. Silent tears flowed through his fingers as he covered his face. His knees weakened and he sank down to sit on the toilet.

The conversation from a few nights before replayed in his head. Why hadn't he seen what she had been trying to say, and why hadn't she just come out and said it? He wished he could go back to that very moment. Maybe she would have told him about the baby if he hadn't spoken so sharply. Maybe she wouldn't have been so angry and tired if he hadn't spent the day drinking after that conversation. Maybe the accident never would have happened. Maybe she wouldn't be struggling to survive if he had just told her the truth.

He fought off the urge to think about his son. Andrew probably didn't even know he had a father other than the one who was raising him now. Joe wondered if his son looked like him, but then he winced away the thought and tried to free himself of the image. Since the day he let Andrew go, Joe had struggled not to think of Lisa or Andrew or the man who was raising his son. But now, here was another situation that brought him face to face with everything that happened. Ellie was pregnant, and as she struggled for her own life, she also struggled for the life of their unborn child. Joe wasn't sure he wanted a baby, but he knew he couldn't turn away from it; turning away would mean turning away from his wife, and he would never do that again.

As he sat in the stall and calmed himself, Joe remembered the first time he saw Ellie. It had been at a party for his friend John, and she was there with another friend. He had looked up at the door just as she came through it. He could still remember how she looked in that black sweater and blue jeans. She didn't make herself stand out in any way, yet she was stunning at the same time. Her dark hair was long and her eyes were deep brown—almost black—and they sparkled with obscurity. He didn't approach her right away but watched her from across the room for a long time. She didn't notice him until she stood at the keg pouring a beer, leaning the cup to one side to avoid getting too much foam in the glass. It was then that he finally mustered up enough courage to engage her in conversation.

"You know how to pour a beer," he said, not knowing what else to say.

She laughed, and he felt like taking his foot from the floor and jamming it directly into his mouth.

"I'm a Wisconsin girl, and Wisconsin girls drink beer," she said with a smile as she pushed the lever back on the keg, tipped the glass in his direction, and then brought it to her lips. After taking a long, slow sip, she pulled the glass away and ran her tongue across her top lip to taste the froth. "See? I'm not that good."

"I'm Joe," he said, extending his hand.

"Eliot," she reciprocated.

"Eliot? That's an interesting name for a woman." He laughed, again wishing he could smash his size tens into his teeth. Why was he talking this way?

She smiled and gave a nod. "My mother is a fan of George Eliot."

Joe looked confused. "Was he a baseball player or something?"

Ellie laughed again. "*She* was a writer. Do you know the classics, *The Mill on the Floss* or *Middlemarch*? That's her. George Eliot was her pen name. Her real name was Mary Ann Evans."

Joe shook his head. "I don't read much other than an instruction manual or an occasional magazine."

"My friends call me Ellie." Her smile radiated through him and Joe knew right then that he had come face-to-face with his future.

Joe began to feel nauseated as he sat in the bathroom stall. He stood facing the toilet and rested his back against the door. He bent over slowly, placing his hands on his knees. He waited for something else to surface, but all that came up was more memories of Ellie.

He remembered the first time they made love. Afterwards, he lay next to her on his living room floor watching as she stared at the ceiling. She was so different from any woman he had ever known; he was almost afraid of her. He had wondered what she was thinking and if she felt even close to the same way he did. She never said much about her feelings, and that made him want her even more. She was captivating as she lay there with her hair a mess and her black eyeliner running just a little. She rarely wore much make up, and this was another thing he loved about her. She was beautiful just the way she was.

"What are you looking at?" she had asked sheepishly, realizing he was watching her.

"You," he said. As he reached out and touched her face, she sat up and pulled the blankets around her. He said, "Are you staying?"

When things got heavy between them, Ellie normally gathered her things and left, usually coming up with some excuse about her dog being alone in her apartment for too long. He always wondered what made her so afraid to stay with him.

"Do you want me to stay?"

He pulled her back to him on the floor, cuddled up behind her, and pulled a blanket over them. "You know I do," he whispered.

She relaxed in his arms. Joe watched as their breathing became synchronized so the blanket rose and fell all at once, like it covered one person instead of two. He wanted things to stay this way. He didn't want either of them to ever leave the room, but he knew the sun would rise the following day and Ellie would walk away. He would count the minutes until he saw her again, and he'd hope she would let her guard down enough to let him in again. He didn't sleep that night.

Joe staggered out of the bathroom stall and walked to the automatic sink. He stuck his fingers beneath the spout, waiting for the water to turn on. When it didn't, he simply grabbed a rough paper towel and rubbed it across his face. He didn't even check his reflection as he tossed the towel in the trash and pushed open the door.

The hospital was still bustling and noisy as he made his way toward the elevator. Once inside, he watched the numbers slowly slip by until he reached the fifth floor. It seemed like an eternity before the doors slid open. As he walked into Ellie's room, a doctor was already there talking to her mother.

"Mr. McHugh, I'm Dr. Chase, Ellie's obstetrician," the woman said as she extended her hand. He took it with trepidation, but he had trouble meeting her eyes.

He had never met this doctor before, but he'd heard his wife talk about her. She was a tall, pretty woman with short, dark hair and glasses that made her look older than she probably was. She had a serious look, and he was immediately intimidated.

"Since Ellie hadn't told you about the baby, I was wondering if you had any questions or if there was anything Dr. James discussed that you'd like me to elaborate on."

His mind raced. He wasn't sure if he wanted to know more details. He looked at Ellie, still unconscious, still hooked to hissing and beeping machines, still unchanged. Noticing the look of concern on his face as he surveyed his wife, Dr. Chase motioned for Joe to follow her out of the room. He made eye contact with Anna, who remained silent but nodded to let him know it was okay to go.

In the hallway, he noticed it was oddly quiet. Night had fallen and he hadn't even realized it. The hospital clamor had settled down for now, and the doctors and nurses hunkered down for another ominous night.

"I can tell you she's about nine weeks along," the doctor said.

Nine weeks…nine weeks. He tried to remember the exact night it could have happened.

"She expressed a concern about telling you because this wasn't a planned pregnancy?" Her dark eyes scanned his face for a reaction. The tone of her voice was more an accusation than a question.

"No, it wasn't planned, and no, she hadn't told me."

"Well, despite Ellie's condition, I can tell you the baby's heartbeat is strong, so I'm hopeful things will go well." She watched as Joe's eyes darted back and forth on the floor. "If you'd like to hear the heartbeat…we can arrange that."

"I'd rather do that when I know my wife is okay," he said quietly, not wanting to offend her or act like he didn't care.

"I understand, but Joe, I think you should know that Ellie was both excited and nervous about this baby. I hope you know how much it means to her and how much she wants to share it with you."

Joe said nothing but nodded his head. He was beginning to understand.

As she said goodnight and walked down the hall, Joe couldn't help but feel jealous that a doctor he had never previously met knew more about his wife than he did, or so it seemed. When he came back into Ellie's room, he sat next to her. He wondered where her thoughts were. Did she know he was there? Did she know that he knew her secret, just like she knew his? He sighed and took her hand. Then Anna reached across Ellie's motionless body and placed her hand on top of Joe's. They exchanged a thoughtful glance but spoke no words. There was nothing to say.

Chapter 15

February 2, 2006, 8:45 p.m.

Grace stared silently into the fire for some time before she spoke. "Why did you marry Joe?"

"Because I love him," Ellie replied, wondering where this new turn of the conversation was headed.

"Could you see yourself with him forever?"

Ellie thought for a moment. "Yes," she said. "I mean, I know we aren't perfect. He hid some things from me…"

"Hid from you? What did he hide?" Grace asked as she took a quick sip from the cracked cup sitting beside her.

Ellie hesitated to tell Grace the secret Joe had kept from her and everyone else. He rarely spoke of it, yet she knew it was always there in the back of his mind. Sometimes, when she caught him staring off somewhere, she wondered if he was thinking of Andrew—maybe Lisa, too. In those moments, Ellie wondered if Joe regretted his decision. When he caught Ellie watching him, Joe would smile and turn back to whatever he had been doing. She would want to ask him about his past, but she never did. Something always stopped her.

"He has a son that he never told me about," Ellie said. She leaned her head back and began to slowly rock in the chair. It softly creaked as she moved forward and back.

"Hmmm, that's interesting." Grace sighed. "Do you think this is why he felt so strongly against having children?"

"I don't know any other reason why," Ellie answered. As she continued to rock, the chair continued to creak. "I tried to find him once…Joe's son."

"And did you?"

"No. The mother remarried and I couldn't find them without knowing her new name."

"Probably just as well, don't you think? What would you have done if you'd found them?"

Ellie stopped rocking and met Grace's glance. "I don't really know. I guess I just wanted to see his son…Andrew. I thought that maybe if I saw him, I'd know for sure he was real and not just a story his brother told me."

"Why would his brother tell you if it wasn't true?"

"I thought he was jealous of Joe at the time, maybe. I don't know. I just wasn't sure why he told me. I sometimes wish he hadn't."

"Or maybe he just wanted you to know so you couldn't find out later and be shocked?"

"Maybe, but Joe still hasn't told me."

"And you haven't told him about this baby," she said, pointing to Ellie's abdomen.

"I was going to, but he got so angry when I asked him about children. I just didn't know how. I'm afraid he'll resent me."

"And when were you planning to tell him?" Grace's stare was deep, and Ellie began to feel uneasy.

"I don't know," Ellie nervously replied.

She had thought of telling Joe from the first day she learned she was pregnant, but she could never find the right words or the right time. She wanted him to be as happy as she was, but she knew he wouldn't be. She wasn't ready to let go of being happy for herself so she chose to wait. She didn't want Joe to take the joy away from her, not yet.

Grace broke the silence. "Did you think he'd leave you if you told him?"

"I didn't know what he would do," Ellie answered. She looked down and rested her hand on her belly. She remembered the pains she'd had before her accident and realized she hadn't felt them since.

"If you knew it wasn't what he wanted, why did you do it, Ellie?"

"Do what? Get pregnant?"

"Yes."

"I didn't do it on my own. We'd never even had a scare before," she replied defensively. She hadn't done anything out of the ordinary that she could remember, other than missing one birth control pill, but she had doubled up the next day—just like she had every time before when she'd forgotten. She never thought twice about getting pregnant. But when it happened, she was both stunned and elated. She wanted it more than she let herself realize. But in another way, she knew it could be a mistake that would seal the fate of a marriage that was already on shaky ground.

"Funny, isn't it, how easily it can happen when there's such a small window of opportunity?" Grace stood and walked back toward the kitchen. "More tea?"

"Is that what happened to you?" Ellie asked candidly. Grace didn't speak at first. She poured herself another glass of steaming tea and brought the pot to the cup beside her visitor. Ellie touched the older woman's arm as Grace stood before her, almost shaking. "Is it?"

Grace turned away and took the pot back to the stove. "If I told you it was a mistake, I would be saying your grandmother, your mother, and you were a mistake, so I can't say that. I never thought of it as a mistake, but it meant everything in Alfred's world changed, and it was my fault."

She returned to the chair, where Mayda had taken a warm reprieve, and scooped the cat into her arms. Grace's voice was different—softer—as she dove back into her story.

Chapter 16

June 1933

As she lay on her bed, Grace heard Calista setting the dinner table downstairs. She hadn't left her bedroom, and neither her aunt nor her father had spoken to her all day. She was angry and they were angry, so it seemed best to hide away. Laying atop her soft quilt and staring at the white plaster ceiling, she thought about how ironic it was that her father had walked into Alfred's room right at that moment. Grace knew how awful it must have looked to him, and she wished there was a way she could make him understand that nothing had happened. She wondered how Alfred would be able to work side-by-side with her father now and not feel ashamed. Alfred had been planning to enter the seminary, but as far as her father and aunt knew, his plans had somehow changed in the few short days since he arrived on the farm. Grace wondered what her mother would have made of all this.

Some things happen for a reason, she thought as she remembered the two short kisses she and Alfred had shared. If he was still determined to become a priest, why had he done that? She knew the last one would have gone much further had her father not come in. She didn't know if she was thankful or upset that they had been interrupted.

She pulled herself off the bed and walked to the window, brushing aside the sheer curtain. Looking out across the farmyard, she could see her father in the closest cornfield walking among the rows. She wondered if he was looking for insect damage or if he was simply trying to keep busy. The corn was barely up to his knees since the growing season had just started. She wondered what he thought of her now. She hadn't given her innocence away, but she still felt ashamed. She turned from the window and lay back on the bed, not wanting to think anymore. She just wanted to lie still and clear her head. But then light footsteps approached.

"Grace, it's time for dinner." Calista's voice was quiet on the other side of the door. Grace lay still, staring at the ceiling and the tiny cracks in the plaster. She wondered how to make her father and aunt understand how trapped she felt. If Alfred had been any other boy, maybe they would have understood her feelings. But, maybe it wasn't her they were mad at. Maybe they were angry at him for making them believe he was something he wasn't. Or had he? She was confused about what he had said and done. It was all spinning too fast for her to hold onto.

"Grace?"

"I'm coming, Calista," Grace said as she wiped her face and swung her legs off the side of the bed.

The dinner table was silent as the three of them picked at their fried chicken and ignored the distance that stood between them like a deep ravine. No one wanted to call out to the other side, only to hear an echo travel back, bounce off again, and dissipate into the air.

Grace kept her eyes on her food, barely eating even though she loved Calista's chicken. She didn't want to see the look of disappointment on her father's face. She occasionally glanced up and met Calista's eyes. She wanted her aunt of all people to understand that nothing had happened with Alfred. She didn't want Calista to think less of her in any way.

"I wasn't there all night," she finally said as she set her fork on her plate, unable to eat and unable to take the silence any longer. No one said a word, though her father hesitated and then chewed slowly. He ground his teeth and the muscles in his jaw tensed. Grace knew he was angry.

"It wasn't Alfred's fault, Dad. He just offered me some water and a place to sit because I ran all the way back from the woods after I realized I'd fallen asleep at the lake."

Her father shot back. "How could you fall asleep at the lake? It was cold last night, Grace. Do you really expect me to believe you walked out there and fell asleep?"

"Did you have any of the wine?" Calista asked. If Grace said she had, the argument would be about something other than Alfred.

"No, I didn't. I—"

"You were thinking of no one but yourself. You're just like your mother that way, Grace."

"Henry!" Calista snapped. "This isn't about Isabelle."

Grace paused in surprise and looked back and forth from her father to her aunt, trying to figure out what he had meant. He had never spoken that way about her mother before. "Why do you think I'm like her *that* way?" Her voice quivered.

"You're old enough to know." His voice faltered and his hands shook. "Your mother was often fond of the farmhands as well."

"That's enough, Henry," Calista hissed as she watched Grace's face. "Isabelle being unfaithful has nothing to do with Grace and Alfred."

"What are you saying?" Grace's stomach began to churn. This was not the conversation she had expected—it was much worse. She had always believed her parents were perfect. She had never seen them show anything but love and affection for each other, and now her father was alluding that her mother had indulged in the dirty sanctuary of the farmhand bunkhouse. Grace's mind raced, trying to remember the men that had worked on the farm. There were only three she could recall: Tony Black, a student from Mississippi who was working to pay for his schooling in Whitewater; Jerod Alvarez from Iowa City, who worked only a few months before moving up north to be a logger; and Frank Larsen, who was younger than her father but older than the others. He had stayed on the farm until shortly before Grace's mother died. His family was near Chicago, and he moved back to be with them. Since Frank, there had been no one—until Alfred.

"Frank?" Grace whispered as she looked at her father.

Her father growled his response in a tone she had never heard before. "It wasn't just Frank. It was all of them." "You don't know that," Calista retorted. Then she turned and reached out to her niece. "He doesn't know that, Grace. Your mother was a free spirit and didn't have anyone else to talk to most of the time. Sometimes she enjoyed talking to the farmhands, and your father read into it too much. That's all."

"I saw them, Calista! I saw them with my own eyes!" Grace covered her ears as her father shouted.

"No," she said, turning away. "I don't want to hear any more."

"I don't want you seeing that boy anymore. Do you understand me?" Her father's voice was low and stern. "He's done. I want him off this farm tomorrow."

"No!" Grace shouted. "It's not his fault! He didn't do anything, and neither did I!"

Her shouting caught her father by such surprise that he leaned back in his chair, his mouth slightly open as if he were searching for something to say. Calista sat silent.

"He's gone," Henry repeated, his eyes hardening as he glared at Grace. "Tomorrow."

Grace rushed out of the house, horrified by what she had heard. She was angry that her father would blame Alfred for something that had happened in the past. Her father wasn't angry at her, and he wasn't even really angry at Alfred. He was angry at his wife for an infidelity that had occurred years ago. Grace had never seen this side of her father. As she ran, she could almost feel her mother there with her, willing her on and telling her to keep running, to get away and not be trapped on the farm anymore.

Running through the darkness with tears streaming down her face, Grace wasn't sure what she was running toward. She just knew that she wanted to get away. She was tired and afraid, but it felt good to run. When she finally reached the lake, she stopped, her breath labored. It was a warm night and the moon reflected off the cool, calm lake. She no longer felt her mother around her, only the anger that had followed her from the house.

Just then, someone came up behind her. Grace's heart leapt as Alfred rushed toward her, sweat pouring down his face. His green eyes weren't as bright as they had been that morning. Instead, they looked hollow and concerned.

"Are you alright, Grace?" he asked breathlessly. "I heard your father shouting."

She turned away from him. How could she tell him about what had happened and why her father was so angry? Alfred wouldn't understand. Maybe it was better if he left the farm before things got worse.

"I'm so sorry about this morning, Grace. I shouldn't have kissed you like that. It's my fault he's angry. I don't know what's wrong with me."

Grace began to sob. As Alfred walked around to face her, he pulled her chin up with his hand. She wanted to push him away, but she couldn't help the way she felt any more than he could.

"I think you're so beautiful, Grace, but I feel like I've been a burden to you since I got here. I think I should go, but first I want to make sure you'll be okay."

She laughed at first and then threw her head back to look at the stars. She was tired of playing games. "What good is God, Alfred? I don't know God, but you do, so tell me—if God is so good, why did He take my mother so that my father will hold onto me as long as he can and then bring you here to tell me you can't be with me?"

Alfred put his hands on her face and pulled her close when her voice trailed off. They kissed in the moonlight, and this time, he didn't stop. He gripped her tightly and she began to relax under his touch. His breath grew heavy as he kissed her neck and brought his hand to her breast. Grace quivered with excitement as she pulled at Alfred's damp T-shirt. She kissed his tan skin as they lowered themselves onto the cool grass.

Grace wondered for a moment if Alfred would stop again, but when he slipped his hand under her wrinkled skirt, she knew he was beyond turning back. She pulled at his belt. As he lowered his trousers, he looked into Grace's eyes with a look she hadn't seen in him before. As they lay there, exposed, he hesitated for a moment, then kissed her as he thrust himself forward. It was much more painful than Grace had imagined, but her body tingled with excitement as he continued. His breathing grew heavier and stronger. He moaned softly, then stopped moving. Alfred softly kissed Grace's neck as they lay there, coupled, under the moonlight.

Chapter 17

February 2, 2006, 9:26 p.m.

Ellie listened as Grace explained that she and Alfred had let go of their inhibitions and come together by the lake.

"Was Alfred sorry he chose you over entering the seminary?" Both women rocked slowly back and forth, their chairs creaking.

"He didn't choose me," she whispered, her face almost gray and stone-like. "He chose to give in to his weaknesses, and by doing so, his life changed course."

"You got pregnant that night, didn't you?" Now Ellie knew where the story was headed.

"I did. It just took that one time," Grace said, staring into the fire. "I didn't know it then, and neither did Alfred, but it's just one of those things that happens."

Ellie put her hand on her belly. She knew exactly what the old woman meant. But Ellie wasn't a seventeen-year-old girl on a farm in the country. She was a 32-year-old woman with a husband who claimed to love her. How could this child be wrong? She had imagined her son a thousand times—his first smile, first laugh, first steps, how magical it would all be. Joe would be there to guide him, and they would be a family—finally.

"Don't fool yourself with the illusion of bliss," Grace snapped as Ellie turned from her daydream back to the reality of the woman's stern face. "Just because you want it so badly, that doesn't mean he does."

"But Joe isn't Alfred. He's not the same."

"What makes you so sure? What makes you believe that he'll change when you have that child?" Grace's eyes glared through Ellie and her voice grew lower. "Why do you think you're really here?"

"I…I don't know why. I don't even know where *here* is…"

"*Here* is my prison, Ellie, because what I did to Alfred was selfish."

"But he chose to be with you, Grace. How could that be your fault?"

"Did he? Did he choose, or did I choose for him?" She looked at Ellie's hand and the ring on her finger. Ellie wanted to run away or wake up from this realistic dream. She didn't understand why Grace was saying these things. She hadn't trapped Joe, and Grace hadn't trapped Alfred. Those were just the cards that life had dealt them. It wasn't anyone's fault.

"Grace, I don't understand what you're telling me. Maybe it's time I leave." Ellie stood and moved toward the door. Glaring, Grace stayed seated.

"There's nowhere to go, Ellie. You can try to walk, but you'll end up right back here, just like me."

"Then tell me why I'm here. Tell me the *real* reason." Ellie was tired of the games. She just wanted to go home.

"Sit, child, and I will try to help you understand." Grace's voice became soothing again, but Ellie was reluctant. "Sit," Grace said. "I will tell you what you need to know."

Chapter 18

June 1933

Alfred and Grace returned to the farm in silence, holding hands and walking into the cool night breeze. It blew against them as if trying to warn them not to return. Grace replayed the moment they had shared by the lake. It all seemed so surreal. She tried not to think about the argument with her father or her mother's supposed infidelity. She was content to simply walk with Alfred in the darkness, holding his hand, no matter how short-lived the moment would be. His face was unyielding in the half-light and she knew he didn't feel as strongly as she did.

When they crested the hill and saw the farm below, they stopped and inhaled their last bit of freedom from reality. Things would be different now. Grace knew her father and Calista had probably grown even more upset since she had run off. If they realized Alfred was gone too, it would be even worse.

"I'm going to leave tonight," Alfred said as they stood in the darkness.

Grace had known this was coming. "None of this is your fault, Alfred. If we just give him time to calm down, he'll understand."

"It's not that, Grace. I just need to go. I can't stay here."

"To the seminary? You're still going?" She'd hoped their moment by the lake had made him realize he wanted to be with her, but deep down, she knew it was childish to believe that one moment would change his path.

Alfred looked troubled and dropped her hand. "I know you don't understand why I have to—I mean, why I *want* to do this. Things have been hard for my mother and me. I didn't have a family like yours."

Grace reached for his hand again, but he turned away. "Please, Grace," he whispered. "Try to understand. I do want to be with you, but I made a promise to my mother that I would go to the seminary."

Grace pleaded. "But do *you* really want to go, Alfred?"

"I do. I truly do," he said quietly. "I believe that I could do good as a priest—that it's what I was meant to do."

Grace tried not to appear disappointed. "But how do you know?"

Alfred stepped closer to her and grasped her hands. "Ever since I was a little boy, my mother read me stories from the Bible. I especially liked the stories about the disciples. They believed so much in Jesus that they gave up everything for him. I want to know what that's like. I want to give my life to something that has meaning."

"But there are other ways, Alfred..."

"Not for me, Grace, not now. What we just did..." He paused and touched her face. "We shouldn't have done that. I don't want to hurt you, and I don't want to make any more mistakes. That's why I have to go." He kissed her on the forehead, dropped her hands, and turned away.

Grace stood quietly and watched him go. She wanted to follow, but she knew it was no use. Even if she did follow him beyond the borders of this farm, he would always be walking away from her.

When he reached the bunkhouse, Alfred stopped and waited. "Do you understand?" His eyes were sincere and she knew he wouldn't change his mind no matter what she said.

"Yes, I understand." She didn't, but there was no point in begging him to stay. Even if she did convince him, her father would make him go. Grace approached Alfred slowly, touched his face, and kissed his lips one last time. His eyes stayed open, fixed on her every move. She turned away.

"I'll write you, Grace."

She didn't turn back. She knew there was no point.

The house was silent as she opened the door and slipped off her Mary Janes. It was well after midnight. On any other night, she would have expected Calista to run down the stairs and find out where she'd been, but tonight the house stayed silent. Even her father hadn't been out looking for her.

When Grace reached the top of the stairs, she stopped first in front of Calista's bedroom door and then her father's, but there was no sound. Since her father wasn't snoring, she knew he wasn't asleep. Grace touched his door and wanted to go inside to calm his fears, but then thoughts of her mother crept into her head. For a moment, she imagined her mother standing beside her and telling her to turn the knob, to go in and tell him how much she cared about Alfred, but she froze. What if the things her father had said about her mother were true?

She tried to recall every moment she'd spent with her mother before she died. She couldn't remember a single incident, not even a look or an expression, that suggested her mother had been unfaithful.

"He's been worried sick." A soft voice came from the darkness, and Grace turned to see Calista standing in an open doorway. "When he saw Alfred was gone, he assumed the two of you had run off."

"Alfred is leaving," Grace whispered as she walked toward her own door.

Calista sighed and followed. "I'm sorry, Grace, but maybe it's for the best."

Grace laughed sarcastically as she entered her dark bedroom and clicked on the lamp that sat atop her bedside table. As light poured out in every direction, she slumped onto her bed, tired, emotionally spent, and physically weak.

Calista followed, closing the door behind them. As she sat on the bed next to Grace, she paused as if she were carefully choosing the right words. She wrung her small hands in front of her and then placed them on her lap.

"Why didn't I know all those things about my mother?" Grace asked, her eyes filling with tears. "Why didn't I ever know about the farmhands and how unhappy she and Dad were?"

"They weren't unhappy, and your mother didn't sleep with the farmhands…just *one* farmhand." She walked to the window and saw the bunkhouse light was still on.

"It was Frank, wasn't it?" Grace asked.

"Yes," Calista answered, turning from the window to sit on the bed. "Your mother loved your father, Grace. Don't ever think she didn't, not for a minute. But she was lonely on this farm and Frank still talked to her like a woman, rather than talking to her like a mother and a housewife."

"Did she love him?"

"I think she cared deeply for him, but she loved you and your father." Calista touched Grace's cheek, wiping away a tear. "It was after she became intimate with Frank that she started changing somehow. She seemed happier, almost, but at the same time always tired and afraid."

"Why?"

"Fear of getting caught, maybe. Fear of losing you and your father, perhaps? It wasn't long after your father learned of the affair that she got sick. If my mother had been alive, she would have told me that's what Isabelle deserved because she broke the bindings of her marriage. Maybe it was that hex she put on the ring. I don't know if I believe all that, but that's what my mother would have said."

"I don't believe it," Grace snapped as she stood and walked to the window. The bunkhouse light had gone out.

"I'm sorry about Alfred," Calista said as she rose and stood behind her niece. Grace knew Alfred was out there somewhere, beyond the glass that separated her from the night, alone in the darkness and walking toward the train station.

"So Dad knew about my mother and Frank?" she said. Her reflection stared back at her in the window.

"He did after he found them one night." Calista turned from the window and lowered her voice to nearly a whisper. She said, "It was late one evening when he had come back early from the horse auction in Chicago. You had gone with him, but your mother said she wasn't feeling well and decided to stay behind. When the two of you came back, you had gone off to bed. Henry was surprised that your mother wasn't in the house.

"As he stood on the porch, he saw a small flicker of light in the bunkhouse. He wasn't sure what it was. As he walked across the yard and stood outside the door, he heard a low murmur and then a quick laugh—he recognized that laugh. As he pushed the door open, there they were, your mother and Frank in bed under a pile of blankets."

"Why didn't I ever know about this?" Grace asked again.

"Because they loved you and they didn't want you to know. Your father was devastated, but he believed your mother when she told him she was sorry and it would never happen again. Soon after, Frank left and your mother became ill."

"She died without ever telling me the truth," Grace said as she turned and sat on the bed. "Why didn't she tell me the truth?"

"What truth?" Calista asked with surprise.

"That she hated it here so much. What else did she want to do?"

"She didn't hate it here, she just felt trapped here…like you feel now."

Calista walked toward the door, turning one last time and meeting Grace's eyes from across the room as she grabbed the knob. "Your mother was a good woman. She loved you and she loved your father, but she settled, and that's something you should never do."

"Settled? She settled for this life?" Grace was growing angry.

"She settled here because she loved you. That's a sacrifice any mother would make." She turned and kissed Grace on the forehead. "Now get some rest."

As Calista shut the door behind her, Grace sat on her bed, confused and alone. She was beginning to realize that everything she believed about her parents was false. It was a harsh truth that she hadn't been ready to hear, let alone understand. And then there was Alfred, who had just made love to her but was now gone to pursue a life of celibacy. Nothing made sense.

As she closed her eyes, Grace desperately tried to push everything out of her mind. Before she fell asleep, she removed the ring her mother had given her and studied it in the moonlight that came through the window. She wondered if her grandmother had really put some sort of hex on it. Did it protect those who were true to their bond and haunt those who weren't? Why had her mother given it to her if it were tainted? Perhaps she hoped Grace could overturn the wrong she had done. As Grace slipped the ring back onto her finger and closed her eyes, she knew she wasn't off to a very good start.

Chapter 19

February 3, 2006, 10:00 a.m.

As he straightened his tie, Joe stared at himself in the mirror and took a long, slow breath. He was nervous. As his stomach churned, he felt the burn of acid rising in his throat. He reached into his pocket and felt the ring with his fingertips. *Okay, it's still there*, he thought as he headed back to the table where Ellie waited. He saw her as he made his way across the room; her back was to him and her shawl clumsily fell from one shoulder, revealing her shimmering skin. She hated to wear dresses—they made her feel awkward and uncomfortable—but he'd asked her to wear one that night. He thought this might give his plan away, but she had agreed with no question. Maybe she knew, but if she did, she never let on.

His initial plan had been to ask her after they ordered, but he couldn't bring himself to do it. The words weren't coming as easily as he had planned. He didn't want to fumble and make a mistake. As he took his seat, he noticed the check that lay between them. Ellie held a glass containing only a swallow of wine. She met his eyes.

"Everything okay?" she asked as he nervously reached for his water glass and took a long, hard gulp. Knowing he couldn't wait any longer, he reached into his pocket.

Slowly, he removed the ring and looked her straight in the eye. "I…I love you, Ellie. Will you marry me?"

Her eyes softened, but she seemed surprised as she rose from the table and came to his side, cupping his face in her hands as he rose to meet her. "Of course I will, you idiot." She laughed as tears welled in her dark eyes.

He slipped the ring onto her finger, almost in slow motion, as whispers grew louder around them and women smiled. Some even clapped.

Then a voice pulled him from his sleep. "Joe."

He opened his eyes and saw Peter standing before him. Joe rubbed his eyes and sat up. Nurses surrounded Ellie like worker bees. They watched her, took notes, and checked machines. Sunlight was sneaking in from behind the drawn curtains and Anna was no longer in the room.

"She went home to get a few hours' rest," Peter said as Joe looked around. "Maybe you should run home and get some rest, too. I'll stay."

"No, I'm fine." Joe stood and watched the nurses.

"Some coffee then, maybe? When's the last time you ate?" Peter's voice was filled with concern.

"Pete, I'm fine," Joe snapped.

One of the nurses took notice of the conversation. "It's alright if you want to head down to the cafeteria for just a little while," she said. "Dr. James will be in shortly and then he can tell you if there's been any change."

The nurse's eyes were kind and sincere, but Joe didn't want to leave. He wanted to hold his wife's hand and try to figure out just how things had gone so wrong between them. He reluctantly agreed, allowing Peter to lead him out of the room.

"You still mad?" Peter asked after they had sat in the crowded cafeteria for some time without speaking. Steaming Styrofoam cups of coffee sat in front of them, but neither had taken a sip.

"No, I'm not mad," Joe quickly replied. Had the circumstances been different, he would be mad—very mad—but now he didn't have it in him to be angry.

"She's been worried about you, you know," Peter said as he took a quick sip of the hot, steaming liquid. "She told Abby you didn't come home a few weeks ago."

Joe was quiet. He grew tense at the thought of Ellie talking to his brother's wife about their marriage. He knew the night that Peter spoke of, and it hadn't been the first time he didn't come home. It was all a bit hazy in his mind because he had drunk much more than he should have; all he remembered was waking up in the passenger seat of his truck, which was parked in front of a house he didn't recognize. He couldn't recall how he had ended up there or who had driven him. He'd sat there confused for some time, wondering how he could have let that happen. He thought of Ellie, who was at home alone, knowing full well she would be angry, hurt, and confused. He didn't want to face her so he waited just a little longer, knowing she would leave for work before he came home. That would buy him more time to think of an excuse. He'd hoped she would calm down enough to listen. The scenario didn't go as he would have liked.

"She's been worried about your drinking," Peter said when Joe didn't answer.

"I know," Joe said quietly.

He remembered coming through the door that morning. Ellie had already left for work. But as he lay down on the couch, his head swirling, he was befuddled that he still couldn't remember what he had done or who had driven his truck. He hoped it hadn't been a woman, but at that moment, he couldn't say for sure.

He knew there would be a huge fight when Ellie came home. He had no defense to offer other than that he had just planned on stopping at the bar for a couple drinks. He hadn't planned on staying, but somehow things got beyond his control, as they always did lately. He didn't have a way to calm her anger or her fear because he knew he would be furious if the tables were turned. But she would never do that to him.

He was wrong that night. Ellie didn't come home. She hadn't gone to the bar or stayed with friends; she had gone to her mother's house instead.

"What's going on in your head, Joe? Why are you screwing this up with her?" Peter watched as Joe ran his fingers through his hair and shifted nervously. He hadn't touched the coffee. "Are you cheating on her?"

"No," Joe shot back defensively.

"Then what is it?" Peter asked quickly.

"I don't know. I just feel restless sometimes. I just need to get out."

Peter laughed sarcastically, leaned forward, and looked his brother in the eye. "You think you're the only man that's ever felt trapped in his own skin? You have to stop running from the past and look at what you have. That woman loves you—would do anything for you—and she sure as hell deserves better than what you've been dealing her lately."

Joe knew Peter was right. Ellie hadn't done anything to deserve the things he was doing. But still, he couldn't shake the feeling he sometimes had when he was with her, as if it was all too much for him to handle. He had messed things up once, and he was sure he could do it again.

"She thinks you're trying to drive her away. Is that what you're doing?" Peter asked as Joe stared at the floor.

"No. I love her," he whispered.

"You've got a funny way of showing it, brother," Peter said as he walked across the cafeteria to a window. The sun was shining, but the newly fallen snow kept a chill in the air.

Joe sat motionless and felt heavy in his chair.

"What are you gonna do if she pulls through this?" Peter asked, never turning from the window.

"What do you mean?"

"I mean, are you gonna run away or are you gonna stop drinking and take care of your wife and baby?"

"I didn't ask for this, Peter, and I didn't run away the last time." Joe picked up the Styrofoam cup, which no longer steamed. He respected his brother, but he was growing tired of the father-like role Peter tried to play. He was well aware of his mistakes without his brother pointing them out.

"This is different, Joe. Ellie loves you, and if she pulls through this, you're going to have a child, whether you like it or not."

"Do you think I don't get that, Peter?" Joe was growing annoyed. "Do you think I don't understand that I'm having *another* unplanned child?"

Peter laughed again. "You're really something, Joe, you know that? You think no one has it worse than you do, and you walk around every day with this big chip on your shoulder thinking someone owes you something. If she pulls through this, be happy for once in your God damn life. Tell her you're sorry for being a fuck-up and tell her about your son. Then, when you're done, tell her you love her and you want this baby. Just because you didn't plan it doesn't mean it's gonna ruin your life."

Joe didn't respond. He was growing angry with Peter, but he knew his brother was right. None of this was Ellie's fault, and even if this baby wasn't what he had planned, he couldn't walk away again—especially not from Ellie.

"I gotta get back to work," Peter said, grabbing his black hat and placing it on his head. He straightened it in true disciplined military style. Joe always wondered if Peter had become a cop because of their father.

"Do you need anything?" Peter asked.

Peter was tough on his younger brother, but Joe knew Peter genuinely cared. Shaking his head, Joe looked out the window. "Alright then," Peter said. "I'll come back later. Let me know if you hear anything."

Joe nodded, but he was already a million miles away. As he made his way back to Ellie's room, he recalled all the nights he had taken advantage of in the last few years. Nights when he found himself restless and unsatisfied even when everything he needed was lying right beside him.

His mind drifted back to one particular rainy night when he hadn't been able to sleep. He had lain in bed for hours watching as Ellie slept beside him. Her breath had been slow and soft, and he had wondered what dreams were unfolding behind her closed eyes. When he couldn't relax on nights like these, he often watched her, knowing she was a far away in her own world.

Joe had also thought of his son that night. He had wondered what sort of father he could have been to Andrew. Would Ellie have accepted that he had son? Could they have formed a functional relationship that resembled some semblance of a family? As his thoughts had drifted from his son back to his wife, Joe knew there was so much about himself that he hadn't told her—so many secrets that he wondered if he deserved her love at all.

Quietly, so as to not disturb Ellie, he had slowly slipped from their bed and crept out of the room. The rain had grown harder and he knew there was no chance of falling back asleep. He'd seen Ellie's notebook lying on the kitchen counter; she often wrote short, horrible poems for him in this book. It was one of the small gestures that he often teased her about, but he found it intoxicating at the same time. He had run his fingers across the scribbles on the cover and then opened it to read some of the words he'd already read a thousand times.

My husband is my life,
I'm so lucky to be his wife.
I love him in the day and I love him in the night,

And I love him when he's wrong, because he knows I'm always right.

He had smiled as he read the words. Even though her poetry was usually terrible, it was beautiful just the same. She knew she had no gift for verse but she wrote it anyway; it was so much a part of who she was.

When he'd come to a blank page at the end of the notebook, he thought about writing her a letter to tell her about Andrew and Lisa. Maybe he could explain it better in writing, and he wouldn't have to see the look in her eyes when she realized how much he hadn't said, even after all this time. Sitting at the kitchen table and staring at the white page before him, he hadn't been sure what to say.

"What are you doing, honey?" her voice had made him jump. She'd stood sleepily before him in her flannel pajamas, her hair a mess. She had looked so beautiful that he nearly lost his breath.

A voice tugged him out of his thoughts. "Joe, are you okay? Can you breathe?" He suddenly realized he was in Ellie's hospital room. He blinked and saw his wife's best friend standing before him.

"Yeah, I'm okay, Lauren. I was…I was just dreaming. I didn't hear you come in."

"What have the doctors said? Is she going to be alright?" There was deep concern in her eyes, and he wondered if she knew about the baby.

"They said they'll know more in twenty-four hours. She hit her head pretty hard and there's been some swelling. They just don't know yet."

Lauren stepped around the bed and touched Ellie's hand. Joe wondered why Ellie thought Lauren was prettier than she was. He disagreed. Though Lauren was indeed an attractive woman, she never had the stunning glow he had always seen in his wife—the same glow that had left him breathless that night in the kitchen. Lauren had perfect blonde hair that was always done, and she would never be caught dead wearing a ponytail in public. She also had smooth, flawless skin and always just the right touch of makeup. She was slender and fit-looking even though she rarely worked out. She was normally well dressed, with a different purse to match every outfit, but today she wore tight black sweatpants and a pink track jacket. Her Nike tennis shoes were so clean, as if they had never seen a sidewalk, let alone a track.

"Did she tell you she was pregnant?" Joe asked, knowing Ellie told Lauren everything.

"No," she said quietly, not looking in his direction. "I can't believe she didn't. I don't know how she could keep it from me. I saw Anna outside—she told me."

"She didn't tell me either. I don't know how I let it get so bad between us."

Lauren swallowed hard. Joe knew there was so much she wanted to say, but she was holding back. In a way, he wished she wouldn't. He wished she would turn and tear into him. He knew he deserved it. Lauren disliked him, and he didn't blame her.

"I know I haven't made it easy for her lately," he stuttered.

"I just don't know what you're thinking sometimes, Joe," she gasped. "She would do anything for you, but you're able to toss her aside whenever you feel like it. At first I wondered if it was another woman, but I've seen you at the bar all by yourself, so I there must be something else wrong with you."

Joe sighed and sat in the chair next to the bed. "There's nothing wrong with me. I just…I…"

"What is it, Joe? You don't love her anymore? If you don't, you should find the balls to tell her and stop leading her on the way you do. I can't stand hearing her so upset that you'd rather be at the bar than at home with her. And then when you don't come home? I'd like to kick your ass myself, but then she makes an excuse for you. She tries to justify it in her head as something she hasn't done for you. And then you come back, you calm her fears, and you do it all over again. Why?"

Lauren's anger was palpable, and he had no defense. Everything she said was true. He tortured Ellie for no reason, hoping maybe she would leave him if he pushed her away, just like Lisa had. Then he wouldn't have to face the truth and try to move past it. It wasn't justifiable, but in those moments when he ran from her, he believed it was easier to hide in a bottle than tell his wife the truth about his past—a truth she had known all along. He was a fool and he knew it. Lauren knew it, too.

"She knows I have a son?" he asked, watching for the look on Lauren's face. If Ellie had known all along, she would know, too.

"Of course she does, you asshole," Lauren hissed. "She's known for a while. Is that what this is about?"

"I never knew how to tell her. I was afraid she wouldn't understand…"

"Do you *know* her at all?" Lauren glared at him. "Do you know how much she tortures herself because of you? She doesn't care that you have a son. She just loves you. Not for what you are or what you've accomplished, but because of who *you* are. To me you don't seem like much, but to her…Jesus, man. Why can't you just wake up?"

There was nothing Joe could say. He had been a fool, and he had damaged his relationship with Lauren so much that he wasn't sure it could ever be repaired. She was protective of Ellie, much more so than he had been, and he was just now beginning to understand.

In the beginning, he'd thought Lauren was a snob. She was critical of him, and he often mistook it as jealousy over Ellie spending more time with him than with her. Lauren was disappointed that Ellie had seemed to settle, while Lauren preferred to date whomever she wanted, whenever she wanted. Ellie was different than Lauren. She was quieter and more reserved than her friend, and Joe knew there was more depth to Ellie than Lauren because she felt and understood things better. While Lauren would jump the gun and make judgments based on an immediate emotional reaction, Ellie would take a step back, think carefully and try to rationalize every situation from every side.

"What are you going to do about this baby?" Lauren asked as she sat in the chair on the other side of Ellie's bed.

Joe shook his head and leaned back, taking in a long, deep breath. "I don't know, Lauren. I haven't thought about it. I'm more concerned right now with whether or not my wife is going to wake up."

He was tired of people asking what he was going to do about the baby. Did they all expect him to run? Lauren wasn't satisfied with his response as she sighed and stood up.

"She'll wake up, Joe, and when she does, you need to have a better answer than that."

With those words, she gave Ellie a soft kiss on the forehead and walked out the door. Joe watched her go and then gripped his wife's hand, looking for any expression in her beautiful, bruised face. He knew he deserved every angry word directed at him by the people who loved his wife, though he was certain no one could love her more than he did, no matter how much his recent actions suggested otherwise. "I'm gonna show you, Ellie," he whispered. "I'm gonna show you and all of them how much I love you. Please come back, please."

Chapter 20

February 2, 2006, 10:05 p.m.

Ellie touched the ring on her finger as Grace's voice trailed off. The older woman dabbed at her eyes with a white handkerchief. In the center, Ellie could make out half of a letter "G" embroidered in gold thread. It made her sad to know that her great-grandparents had been forced apart when Alfred left that way. She looked down at the ring on her finger and she wondered if this tiny object really had all the power that Grace seemed to think it did.

"So, how does the ring play into all this?"

Grace folded the handkerchief so the G was face up and then she rested it neatly on her lap.

"I believe it all started with my mother's affair," she said quickly.

"So your mother broke the bonds, and the ring took revenge on all of us. Is that what you're telling me?"

"It's difficult for you to understand, but yes, in a sense that is what I'm telling you."

"This is all just a little far-fetched," Ellie said. She breathed through her mouth, which made her words sound almost sarcastic.

Sensing Ellie's irritation, Grace grew frustrated. "Do you think you're here by chance?"

Reminded of her current situation, Ellie said nothing. She was growing tired and wondered what time it was.

"There is no time here," Grace snapped as she looked down at her weathered, wrinkled hands.

"You can read my thoughts?"

"Only sometimes, when they're strong enough." Grace traced the "G" with her bony finger.

Ellie wanted to lay her head down, and she wondered for the first time since arriving if she would ever see home again. She wondered if Joe had realized she was missing or if anyone else had noticed she was gone. There was so much wrong with her marriage, yet all she wanted at that moment was to get back to her husband.

"Did your mother know there was a spell on the ring?" She asked.

"She didn't until Calista told her. That was after she'd grown ill. Calista had always wanted that ring. I think she was jealous in a way that her mother had given it to my father to use as his wife's wedding band. I think that's why my mother gave it to me—so Calista wouldn't take it. She must have thought Calista told her that story to keep her from passing the ring on to me. Maybe it should have gone to Calista. Maybe none of this would have happened."

The story was beginning to make sense to Ellie now. "So when your mother was unfaithful, the ring's spell went into effect. Is that why your mother became ill?"

"I don't know for sure, but it seemed that way, yes," Grace answered.

"And when she passed it on to you, it changed the course of your life, too?"

"Maybe, though I didn't understand it until much later," Grace whispered.

"Then how did my mother come to have it?"

Grace was quiet for a moment. The tension returned to her face as the painful memories flooded back.

"I told your grandmother that my mother had given me that ring and that it should stay in the family, but she didn't want it and rarely wore it." She stared into the distance. "After her funeral, your mother cleaned out your grandmother's house. She found the ring and placed it on her right hand. Later, she passed it on to you. She had no way of knowing what would happen."

"And her marriage crumbled because of it?"

"Yes."

"And now my marriage will crumble?"

"I don't know, Ellie. You being here has given us an opportunity to make things right."

Ellie shook her head in disbelief. It was such a crazy story, yet each marriage had a similar outcome, though none as mysterious as Grace's had been. If the story were true, Ellie wondered if her marriage was already beyond repair. If this tiny object carried some kind of spell, was it too late to simply take the ring off and throw it away?

"Each woman who has worn that ring has found some comfort in it, whether from its beauty or its sentimental value," Grace said, breaking the silence. "Because of that value, no one has ever considered taking it off and leaving it behind. I'm not even sure that would end the spell that's already rooted within it."

"Then what should I do, Grace?" Ellie asked, eyes transfixed on the ring.

"Try to understand it, maybe. Try to learn from it. Try to take what I'm telling you and regain the trust that was originally placed in that ring. If you can do that, maybe you can save yourself."

"So I can go back?" Ellie asked, eager to wake from this dream.

"It's not that simple, child," Grace answered. "I haven't finished telling you my story. When I'm through, you may not want to go back."

Ellie anxiously sighed as Grace resumed her story.

Chapter 21

Late July 1933

Life on the farm slipped back into a comatose routine after Alfred left, but Grace's relationship with her father was permanently changed. They didn't speak of Alfred or her mother; they simply existed in quiet resolution, finding comfort only in everyday tasks. When she walked to the lake, Grace would revisit that night with Alfred. She wondered where he was and if he still thought of her. Now, instead of trying to conjure her mother's image in the water, she longed to see Alfred come out of the darkness.

As the weeks passed, Grace began to feel ill and tired. She shrugged it off, thinking the constant sadness made her feel this way. Her mother had always told her that lies will keep you sick, but the truth will set you free. She hadn't told any lies, but she felt as if she were living one just the same.

And then, late one summer night, as she prepared dinner with Calista, she felt her world turn. Her head grew hazy, and as she reached out for Calista, darkness closed around her like a long, black tunnel. As the energy was sucked from her body, her knees buckled and fell from underneath her. The next thing she remembered was waking up on the floor. Calista stared down at her with a befuddled, terrified look.

"Are you alright?" She said, breathlessly reaching toward the sink to grab the damp washcloth.

Grace struggled to sit up as her aunt dabbed her face with the cloth. "I don't know what's wrong with me," Grace said. "I just haven't been feeling well."

Calista helped her stand and maneuver to the kitchen chair. "Let me ring the doctor. You've never blacked out like this before."

Grace nodded, feeling nauseated as her aunt made her way to the hallway and toward the big, black telephone. As Calista spun the dial, Ellie slowly stood, feeling woozy. She smoothed her wrinkled black skirt as sweat began to pool on her forehead. Calista's muffled voice drifted in from the other room, and there was a loud click when her aunt hung up.

Surprised to see Grace standing, Calista jumped as she rounded the corner to the kitchen. "Oh, dear, you should sit back down. You're white as a ghost." She led Grace to the table. "The doctor will see you tomorrow, but you should get some rest."

Later that night, she was still nauseated. Lying in bed but too tired to sleep, Grace wondered if maybe she was falling ill the same way her mother had. In a way, she hoped she was so she could get away from the farm and rejoin her mother in a nicer place. She didn't really want to do die, but it seemed better than being trapped here. As she rolled onto her side, she stared into the bedroom's darkness and imagined her mother. She could almost feel her sitting at the edge of the bed and running her small, soft fingers through Grace's hair the way she used to do when Grace was a little girl. The thought carried her to sleep.

The following morning, Grace had a nervous twitch in her stomach as she and Calista sat in the waiting room at the doctor's office following her exam. The doctor didn't find anything wrong, but she was sweating again. She didn't realize it until he asked, but she was unsure of when her last menstrual cycle had been. As a result, he had asked her to take a urine test, and she knew what that meant. She glanced at Calista, who sat quietly thumbing through a copy of *LIFE* magazine. Grace's legs nervously twitched and she twisted the ring on her finger.

"Stop fidgeting, Grace," Calista whispered as she untied her headscarf and carelessly stuffed it into her purse. Calista usually wore the scarf to keep her curls from getting frizzy in the humidity, but today she had simply given up.

Moments later, the doctor called both women into his office. Grace felt faint but Calista seemed calm, unaware of what Grace now feared. The doctor stared at Grace over the wire rim of his glasses, like a judge behind a bench. The look in his eyes already told her what he was about to say.

"Well, Grace, it appears as though you're healthy, but I suspect you may be pregnant." His voice was low. "We'll have to wait and see if the rabbit dies before we'll know for sure."

Calista gasped and Grace felt as though the floor had dropped out from beneath her. She couldn't move.

"What?...How?...When?" Words escaped her as Calista tried to form a coherent sentence.

Grace said nothing and stared at the floor. She couldn't believe that one night with Alfred had led to this.

"What you're experiencing now is normal for someone who's expecting," the doctor said. "You should get some rest and drink plenty of water. We'll ring you with the results in a few days."

Grace heard his voice, but she didn't comprehend anything he said. Calista regained her composure and began asking the doctor question after question, none of which Grace heard. Everything around her sounded like static. She felt as though she might evaporate into thin air right there in the office. Moments later, Calista thanked the doctor and led Grace out of the room by her arm.

As they drove back to the farm, neither woman spoke right away. Grace leaned her head against the passenger-side window. Its coolness felt good on her forehead.

"Do you know where Alfred is?" Calista asked.

"No. He's probably in the seminary by now," Grace said quietly, tears dripping down her face. "What are we going to tell my father?"

"I don't know, Grace, but I know he won't understand. I think we need to find Alfred first. Wasn't he going to the St. Francis Seminary?"

Grace shook her head. "I don't know if that's the right thing to do, Calista. He didn't want to stay here. This would only make him feel guilty enough to come back."

"Precisely, Grace. He's the father."

Hot tears poured down Grace's cheeks. She knew that if Alfred came back, it wouldn't be by his own choice.

As they approached the farm, Grace wished her aunt would turn the car around and drive as far away as possible. It would only be a matter of time before her father learned the truth and their already damaged relationship would be beyond repair.

And as much as she wanted Alfred to come back, this wasn't how she wanted things to be. He hadn't planned on fathering children, and for all she knew, he was in the seminary right now making sure that would never happen.

"You have to tell him, Grace. He would want to know." Calista took her hand off the steering wheel and lightly touched Grace's arm. Grace instantly pulled away.

As they came up the drive toward the farm, Grace's father wiped grease from his hands with the red handkerchief he always kept in his pocket. As the car approached and he saw the stern looks on his sister and daughter's faces, the line on his forehead became more prevalent and his face wrinkled. He suddenly looked even older than usual. When the car groaned to a stop before him, neither woman could find the strength to look him in the eye.

"We can't lie, Grace. He already knows something's wrong," Calista said before opening the door. "We'll have to tell him now."

Grace froze in her seat and stared at the floor.

"I'll do it. Maybe he'll take it better from me," Calista said as she tapped Grace's knee with a shaky hand.

As the car door closed, Grace began to feel dizzy. Afraid to look up, she heard their muffled voices but was unable to make out the exact words. It didn't matter; she already knew what they were saying. When she finally mustered the strength to look up, Calista's hand was on her father's arm and his face had turned from its usual leathered tan to almost completely white. He looked at his daughter, who sat defenseless in the car, then back to his sister. He cast one more look at Grace, then looked down, turned, and walked away.

Though Calista called after him, he didn't look back and marched faster with every step. Grace sat frozen, watching her father's back as he went. It was real now that he knew, so real that Grace was unsure of what to do next. Her mind raced and she cursed herself for being so careless. *It was just one time, my first time*, she thought as the tears flowed. She wondered what her mother would have said. Would she have tried to comfort Grace or would she have been distant and disappointed, as her father now appeared to be? Calista opened the car door and bent to look Grace in the eye.

"He's your father, Grace. He will never stop loving you. He's just afraid to lose you."

Grace was thankful for her aunt at that moment. Without Calista's understanding, Grace would be tumbling into this unknown darkness alone. She nodded and took her aunt's hand. Together they walked up the front porch stairs and sat on the top step. With Calista's arm around her shoulder, Grace sobbed.

Chapter 22

February 2, 2006, 10:57 p.m.

Grace and Ellie sat quietly as the winter wind howled outside the cabin. Ellie was growing more tired; all she wanted was to rest and stop thinking about everything that had happened.

"Can you hear the whispers?" Grace said in a low, murmuring voice.

"What whispers?" Ellie said. She looked around the room, startled.

"He's calling you back," Grace said, still rocking but never looking in the younger woman's direction. Chills went up Ellie's back, but she didn't hear any voices.

"I can't hear anything but the wind, Grace. Who's calling me?"

"Joe is calling you. I can feel his heartache all the way here," she said. Her forehead tensed and she leaned her head back. "I could feel Alfred's heartache, too. When I first came here, people thought he was crazy for what he'd done, and he was tormented with grief. But his mind was clear when he held that gun to my head."

Ellie didn't speak as Grace kept talking.

"A few days after I saw the doctor, he rang us with the positive results. The rabbit had, indeed, died." Grace lowered her voice and looked at the floor, slightly shaking her head from side to side. "I was devastated, and I didn't know what to do. I didn't know if telling Alfred was what I wanted, but Calista convinced me that it was the right thing to do. When I finally found the courage to write him, I wasn't even sure where to send the letter since I didn't know if he had gone back home to his mother or to the St. Francis Seminary like he'd planned. I waited a long time before I sent the letter. I was already showing and people were beginning to ask questions. My father, of course, stayed distant."

Grace sighed, then resumed her story. "It was another couple months before I heard from Alfred again. There was a knock one cold November night. When my father opened the door and found Alfred standing there on the porch, neither of them could speak at first. They were both afraid and ashamed, but neither was more afraid than I was when I saw them standing face to face."

Chapter 23

Early November 1933

"I got a letter from Grace," Alfred finally said, breaking the wall of silence that had formed between the porch and the house. Alfred was dressed all in black, as if he had just come from a funeral. He wore a clerical shirt buttoned all the way to his neck, but he did not wear a white collar. The long, messy curls he'd had that summer were gone now, and his black hair was shorter and combed back. Henry stood like a statue, glaring at him. Alfred was unsure if Grace's father would reach out and strangle him or invite him in. He stood frozen, waiting for the older man to react.

"Henry, invite him in," Calista whispered as she appeared behind her brother. Henry said nothing and stepped aside, motioning Alfred to come inside. Alfred awkwardly stepped into the room and cleared his throat.

"Mr. Harper, I know there's nothing I can say to make things right between us." Alfred's voice shook as he spoke, never bringing his eyes up from the floor. "I didn't mean for any of this to happen, and I would have come sooner had I known, but I intend to do what's right by Grace and this family."

Hearing Alfred's voice, Grace ran from her bed, where she had been reading, but stopped short on the stairs when she saw Alfred facing her father. When Alfred looked up and saw Grace standing there, he stopped speaking mid-sentence. He looked from her face to her stomach and then smiled. Grace ran her fingers over her flower-print dress and suddenly felt extremely self-conscious.

"I'm sorry I waited so long, Grace," he said as she continued to stare.

"Alfred, we're all very happy to see you," Calista said as she shut the door and motioned for Grace to come down. "Henry is having trouble getting his arms around what's happened, so you'll need to excuse his rudeness."

Alfred shook his head and looked at the floor. "I understand," he whispered.

"You and Grace have a lot to talk about, so Henry and I will be in the living room. We can all talk tomorrow. I believe Grace knows where to find some fresh linens for the bunkhouse if you intend to stay," Calista said, glaring at Henry and leading him away.

"Thank you, Calista," Alfred said as he shot a look back up the stairs.

Grace descended the stairs slowly, feeling nauseated; she hadn't prepared herself for this moment.

"Would you like to talk on the porch?" Alfred asked, holding his hand toward her. She didn't take it, but instead walked to the closet to grab a coat.

As they stepped out into the chilly air, Grace wrapped her wool scarf tightly around her neck. Alfred followed behind her. She sat on the porch swing, but he leaned against the rail rather than taking a seat next to her. The air smelled of musty leaves, and the dampness chilled her to the bone.

"Sure is chilly tonight," he said as he looked toward the barn. Grace didn't respond. She was ashamed and unsure of what to say. Alfred moved in closer and sat beside her. "It's not your fault, Grace."

"You're not angry?" she asked with a shaky voice.

Alfred sighed and looked out again. His face became serious and she realized how much older he appeared. Without his old newspaper-boy hat and mussed curls, he looked more distinguished and not like the shy young man she had met just months ago. Even his face had a hint of dark stubble forming beneath his skin. "I was upset when I got your letter, but what happened wasn't your fault. I was there, too. I didn't know what to do at first, so I went to the grotto at the seminary and I prayed. But then I realized how you must be feeling, so I had to come back and try to make things right."

"What are we going to do, Alfred?"

"I know this might sound sudden and fast." He paused and cleared his throat, pulling at his shirt's top button as if to let more air into his constricted lungs. "But I think we should get married."

"Married?" Grace quickly stood. "But Alfred, we barely know each other. I haven't finished high school yet, and you're studying to be a priest. There's just so much…"

"There is no other choice, Grace. We did what we did, and now this is what we have to face. I've come here to make things right."

Grace had often daydreamed about Alfred coming back and saying these words, but it was happening so fast and he was so adamant. She realized now how unprepared she was, but she bit her tongue because she didn't feel like arguing.

"Do you plan to stay here tonight?" she asked, shivering in the cold.

"If I'm welcome."

"I'll go get the linens," she replied as she turned away. "We don't have to figure all of this out tonight. Let's just try to take it one step at a time."

Feeling weak in the knees, Grace turned on her heels and walked to the house. She knew she wasn't ready for marriage, or for a baby. She was beginning to feel as if telling Alfred had been a huge mistake. She wasn't sure what she'd expected him to do, but it wasn't marriage, and definitely not this quickly. She wished she hadn't written him at all.

She knew it must have taken an enormous amount of courage for him to come back. It was here that he'd lost a part of himself and changed from who he had been into what he felt he must become.

Grace gathered the linens. As she walked back onto the porch, she caught Alfred looking at her enlarged stomach, which poked from beneath her unbuttoned coat. His eyes darted up to meet hers and she quickly looked away, feeling ashamed. He could hide what they had done from everyone, but for her, the evidence was painfully apparent.

As they walked toward the bunkhouse in silence, Grace couldn't help but recall the last time they had been here together. She never imagined things would turn out the way they had.

As she clicked on the light, she looked around the cold, dusty room and plopped the linens on the cot. Her thoughts quickly turned to her mother and how unromantic this place suddenly seemed.

"I'll light a fire in the stove," Alfred said as he grabbed some kindling that had been neatly stacked and nearly forgotten outside the door.

As he lit the fire, Grace made up his bed. When she finished, she sat and watched his face while he warmed his hands. He shut the stove door and turned to face her.

"This is all so awkward, Alfred," Grace said. "I don't know what to say."

He moved closer. "I know. I wasn't sure I'd ever see you again until I got that letter."

"Did you ever think about that night? Before the letter, I mean?" Her voice was almost a whisper.

He sat beside her, removed his jacket, and laid it neatly beside him. "I thought about it all the time, Grace. I thought about it more than you'll ever know."

She was glad to hear those words, but she knew it was different for Alfred. "Before I came here I was prepared to live a life without intimacy, and I was determined that I could do that," he admitted. "But, on the first day I saw you, I knew I would fail. It happened so easily, and I was so uninhibited in committing the sin."

He went on to describe the day he'd received Grace's letter. He had been in the seminary just a few months. Although he found himself thinking of Grace often, Alfred had managed to put the incident behind him and move forward. "When I pulled the letter out of my box that day, I noticed it had been forwarded from my mother's home, and I recognized the return address immediately. I sat on the steps outside my dorm and I was almost afraid to open it. I knew I hadn't kept my promise that I would write." He looked down at the cold, dusty floor. "But I could still see your face in the moonlight on that night we shared. You looked so enchanting, almost bewitching, and I knew I failed an important test that night."

Grace was ashamed. She turned her head toward the door, wondering if she should get up and leave, but Alfred continued.

"I wasn't sure if I should open the letter and let all those feelings creep back into my head after I'd tried for so long to block them out, so I shoved the letter inside my prayer book and headed to my room. I studied for hours, trying to pretend it never came. Then, I prayed, trying desperately to get the thought of you off my mind."

Feeling uncomfortable, Grace stood to leave.

"No, wait," he said, reaching out toward her. "After a while, I couldn't take it anymore so I went out to the Our Lady of Lourdes Grotto. I walked a road lined by forty-nine tall maple trees, and I counted every one as I went, trying anything to get you off my mind. And then I sat down just outside the grotto and tried to listen to the natural world around me. The seminary is such a beautiful place, Grace. I have to take you there sometime." For a moment, his bright, boyish smile returned to his face. "But then I couldn't resist it anymore and I ripped open your letter because I had to know what it said. I knew then that my feelings for you were stronger than I had realized."

Alfred swallowed hard as he held Grace's hand and guided her to sit beside him. "I can't lie. I cried as I read that letter. It was almost as if I already knew what it would say. I can't remember the last time I cried before that." He paused and clasped both of her hands. "I know you didn't expect me to come back, Grace," he said, looking into her eyes. "But what sort of man would I be if I didn't?"

Grace's throat tightened and tears welled in her eyes.

"That very night, I realized what had to be done," he continued. "I had to come back and make you my wife. It's the only way to make things right."

Chapter 24

February 2, 2006, 11:35 p.m.

"So it was Alfred's decision to leave the seminary," Ellie said when Grace paused. "You didn't force him to go."

"That's true, but he never would have come had I not written that letter," she replied.

"But he was the father. It was only right to let him know, Grace."

"Is that so? Then why haven't you told Joe that he's going to be a father?"

Grace's dark eyes were piercing, and Ellie quickly fell silent. She thought for a moment about the words she had just said aloud and realized she was in no position to offer advice. An overwhelming feeling of regret came over her for not sharing this secret with her husband. She was too afraid it would send him reeling away and back out to the bars that he had begun to frequent. Such a distance had already grown between them. Telling him about this baby would only make things worse.

Still, Ellie couldn't help but feel happy about the pregnancy. She knew that even if she lost Joe, she would still have this piece of light to hold onto. For her, that would be enough. But Ellie was afraid Joe would feel as if everything he had planned and hoped for would be over. To her, it meant forging the best pieces of each of them into this tiny thing that would be a testament to who they were. Ellie convinced herself that Joe would see it in time, yet she wasn't ready to face his disappointment.

"Were you happy when Alfred came back?" She asked as Grace sat silently gazed toward the frost-covered window.

"I was happy he came back, but I was surprised at his reaction. He seemed so eager to get married and asked me so little about the baby. I should have seen it then."

"Seen what, Grace?"

"Seen how afraid he was of being considered a sinner, just like the rest of us."

"But you did get married?"

Grace inhaled slowly and looked at the ring on Ellie's finger. "Yes, we did, a few short weeks after he came back. I was reluctant, but he convinced me it was the right thing to do. Calista was overjoyed, and even my father seemed to approve after a time. We didn't have much money, so we used my mother's ring as my wedding band, and Calista gave him my Uncle Charlie's ring.

"Were you happy?" Ellie studied the old woman's face.

"I was happy, dear, but I was also very afraid. I was a young girl about to get married to a man I barely knew. How would you feel?"

Ellie looked away as Grace laughed sarcastically.

Chapter 25

February 3, 2006, 12:25 p.m.

As morning gave way to afternoon, Joe stood up from the chair next to his wife's bed, walked to the window, and peered at the parking lot below. A light snow had begun to fall, and his head ached from stress and lack of sleep. He felt helpless and alone. Joe longed for a drink, yet he knew that giving in to that indulgence would reinforce every negative perception that people had of him. He normally wouldn't care what they thought, but things were different now. He pressed his head against the window and felt the cold on his forehead.

Closing his eyes, he thought about how he had started to pull away from Ellie. It had nothing to do with her, really; it was just a feeling he had deep inside—an impending doom that seemed to follow him no matter what he did. After they were married, he stopped at the bar now and then for a drink or two with his friends and then he would leave. But then it became more frequent, and a few drinks quickly turned into late nights.

He loved his wife, and he knew he could never dream of having anyone other than her, yet he found himself restless and unable to live the calm day-to-day lifestyle she was designing for him. When he wasn't working, she wanted him home like clockwork. Most of the time, he obliged. But there were other times when he felt a longing in the pit of his stomach, an aching drive to get away. He was never really sure when it would happen, and he could certainly never predict or plan it, but it would eventually come. And when it did, there would be no turning back. He would pull his truck into the bar parking lot and be greeted with laughter and smiles when he walked through the door. He would block out the fact that his wife was at home wondering where he was and taking it personally that he didn't call to let her know he wouldn't be home.

As the liquor slid faster and the hours passed more quickly, he would dread going home. The feeling would intensify when the bartender would announce last call. His mind would be foggy with a drunken haze, and he often needed to be reminded where the door was. Sometimes he would even refuse to go, and he'd argue with whatever friend tried to usher him home. Though he lived close by, he often refused to walk and would pounce like a lion on anyone who dared take the keys to his truck.

When all was said and done, he knew Ellie would be waiting, and she wouldn't be hurt anymore—she would be angry. He knew she had every right to be furious; if the tables were turned, he would never understand why she did it. Therefore, he never fought back when her angry words tore at him in the darkness. When she heard him come through the door and met him at the bottom of the stairs, he wouldn't dare make eye contact. Instead, he would stagger to the kitchen and look for something to eat. Many times, Joe had found the meal she'd prepared hours ago, left untouched because she knew he wouldn't be home until bar time and she no longer felt hungry herself.

When he would refuse argue with her in the kitchen, he'd stagger to the living room couch. She would follow and continue her rant. Frustrated with his lack of response, she'd resort to insults. Still, he wouldn't respond. After a while, he wouldn't hear her voice at all. She would finally give in, bursting into the tears she'd previously managed to ward off. Then she would slowly make her way back up the stairs to their bedroom. She never slept on nights like that.

With Ellie defeated and back upstairs, Joe would lie on the couch and watch the ceiling spin above him. All he had to do was to sit up and focus in order to stop the spinning, but he didn't dare. It just felt right. He knew his life was good, yet he couldn't shake the feeling that he didn't deserve it so it was spinning out of control.

What he hadn't realized until the accident was that by torturing himself, he tortured his wife so much more. As he stood at the window in her hospital room, he wished he could go back and erase the things he'd done during the last few years. He couldn't remember a time in his life when he felt worse than he did at that moment, not even when he let Andrew go.

As he stood listening to the machines beep and hiss behind him, he began to imagine what it might be like to have another child. He loved Ellie, so he knew it would be better than it had been with Lisa, yet the thought still scared him to death. He knew it was a warning that he and Ellie had been brought to this place, and he was solely to blame. He had so many apologies to make. The thought made him sick to his stomach.

Even as he sat with his head against the window, his breath fogging the glass and making it difficult to see anything below, he wanted to run. Running would be so much easier than facing his mistakes.

It should've been easy to tell Ellie about his past, but he had let so much time and guilt accumulate that telling her seemed so much harder than it needed to be. It should have been simple, but now it was all so torrid. Had he told her in the beginning, way back when they were first discovering each other, it would have been easier. Yet back then he'd been afraid that telling her would scare her away. Later, he was afraid she would be hurt that he hadn't told her, and now—now to discover she had already known, he couldn't imagine what she must be thinking.

These thoughts made Joe feel even worse as he turned from the window and slumped into a nearby chair. He stared at his wife lying motionless in the bed. It was his fault she was here; he knew this. As his headache pounded even harder, he laid his head on the chair's hard back. It was uncomfortable and almost made his headache worse, but he didn't care. It was painful, and he wanted pain. He deserved pain.

Chapter 26

December 1933

Grace stood near the back door and reached down to touch the ring on her right hand. When she didn't feel its hard shell, she remembered that it was in the safety of Alfred's pocket as he slowly paced beneath the large oak tree in the backyard.

It was an unusually warm December day, almost spring-like, and they had decided at the last minute to marry under the oak tree rather than in the main barn. Calista had lined the aisle leading to the tree with candles that she made herself.

Grace watched Alfred from the window as he moved nervously in his dark suit, and she wished she could read his thoughts. Today he didn't look priest-like; he was just a scared, nervous young man about to get married. The uneasy twinge in her stomach made her suddenly nauseated. Alfred wiped his forehead with a handkerchief as he looked toward the house. She quickly stepped back from the window, hoping he hadn't seen her, and then she peered down at her right hand. She could still see the white band on her finger where the ring had been. Since she rarely took it off, the skin had changed color around it, almost as if the ring were a permanent fixture on her body. But now, she would never again wear it on her right hand. Like it had on her mother, the ring would take its place on her left.

She remembered what Calista had told her about the ring. No matter who had blessed or cursed it, Grace was afraid to wear it on her left hand. She had fallen for Alfred so quickly, almost obsessively, but she had never bargained for a baby, a husband, and an uncertain life. They would most likely stay on the farm forever—Alfred couldn't go back to the seminary now, and the university seemed a distant dream for her. But, despite all the uncertainty, she knew Alfred was a good man and would make a good father. Maybe it wasn't the type of father he'd planned to be, but he would be a father nonetheless.

As Grace peeked out the window once more, she saw that Alfred was still pacing beneath the tree. Pastor Richards stood beside him, waiting quietly. Alfred's mother sat alone in a wheelchair near her son, a black scarf wrapped tightly around her neck. She looked stern and serious, and she seemed less than happy to be there. A few others sat in the chairs beneath the big oak's shade. Margaret and Beverly were there, both in wool hats and faux-fur coats, trying to appear older and richer than they really were. Grace couldn't help but stare at her friends. She longed to trade places with one of them, either of them. Though they thought getting married and having a baby was exciting, they had no idea what Grace was about to face.

"I think it's time." Her father's voice came from behind and startled her. She spun around to see him standing in his only suit, a dark-blue tweed. With it he wore a black tie and shiny black shoes. It was the same suit he had worn to her mother's funeral. Grace found that almost prophetic.

Though her father looked somber and serious, Grace couldn't help but notice that he was handsome. He was a simple, hard-working man who had lost his wife to infidelity and illness, and now he would give his only daughter away to a man who he felt had betrayed him. Yet through it all, he remained strong and reserved, no matter how broken and scarred.

“You look beautiful,” he said as he stepped forward and gingerly kissed Grace on the forehead. He helped her into a long, off-white wool coat that Calista had found at the second-hand store in town. Both women had been shocked to find it; neither could imagine why anyone would want such a coat, but it was perfect for this occasion. As she fastened the gold buttons, it almost hid her pregnant belly and the white lace that stretched across it. She reached up and straightened her white pillbox hat as her father helped her pull down the veil that covered only half of her face. She was about to slide on a pair of white silk gloves—also from the second-hand store—but she changed her mind when she remembered that Alfred would soon slip a ring onto her cold finger. She didn’t want to fumble while pulling off the gloves, so she set them on the old chair in the foyer. When she reached out and took her father’s arm, she squeezed it hard. He had to know how afraid she was and how much she needed his approval.

He ran a rough, calloused finger from her eye to the base of her chin, then took a step back and smiled. “You look so much like your mother right now.”

A tear slowly slipped down her cheek, and he caught it with his big finger. “Alfred is a good man. This is the right thing to do.”

Grace said nothing. Her father wrapped her hand around his forearm and they moved toward the front door. Chin raised, he pushed through the screen door and began moving down the back steps. As the chilled wind hit her face, the people seated before them faded away. Grace only felt her father's strong arm gripping her hand. She saw nothing but Alfred standing before her, silhouetted by the light from Calista's candles.

When she finally reached him, Grace felt kindness radiate through Alfred and envelop her body. He was a good man, like her father had said.

When Pastor Richards asked Alfred to slip the ring onto her left hand, Grace whispered "I do" without hesitation. There it was, the ring on her left hand. Whatever its past, the ring had a new future now.

As she slipped her Uncle Charlie's ring onto Alfred's hand, he looked into her eyes, smiled, and said a firm "I do."

When the pastor announced that they were married, Alfred stepped forward and kissed Grace's waiting lips. When they turned, Grace noticed his mother looking down, as though she was sobbing. But Alfred looked at his new bride, smiling brightly. From his seat on the other side of the aisle, Henry winked at his daughter and Grace winked in return. Though they were both heartbroken, it was time to start mending all that needed to be fixed.

Chapter 27

February 2, 2006, 11:55 p.m.

"It sounds like you had a beautiful wedding," Ellie said.

"It was beautiful…and cursed," the old woman replied, clasping her wrinkled hands. The smile disappeared from Grace's face.

"Why cursed?" Ellie asked.

Grace sat stoically, choosing her words carefully. "Because it *was* cursed. The whole thing was cursed. My mother dying, Alfred coming along, getting pregnant, getting married. It wasn't at all anything that happened by chance."

"How do you know that?"

Grace laughed, which made her appear almost menacing. Though Ellie was beginning to feel more comfortable here, she found herself afraid at times like this, when the old woman's demeanor changed.

"My dear, chance is something that happens naturally, like the seasons changing—that's natural. Growing old, that's natural. But my mother's infidelity was not natural. Therefore, it began a whirlwind of unnatural occurrences that continue to radiate through our family even today. You don't see it because you choose not to believe it—not yet. But you will."

"You're talking about the curse again?"

"Curse? There is no curse." She stared at Ellie, her black eyes cutting through the younger woman like a light in the darkness. "It was a spell, Ellie. That's much different. That spell sent ripple effects through the ages, through the years, and through our lives."

Ellie stuttered. "If your mother broke the bond, then why are you here to tell me about it and not her? Why has she been allowed to move on while you stay here alone?"

"Because she didn't know—she didn't know that my grandmother had bound a spell to that ring. So when she broke her bond, the spell took flight. My mother died, so the spell attached itself to the next person who wore the ring, which was me. Calista tried to tell me about it, but I shrugged it off. I didn't believe it until the day that ring found itself on my left hand. I knew then that I had to find out what the spell was all about and stop it if I could."

"And did you?" Ellie asked, waiting anxiously for her to answer.

Grace looked at the fire and whispered low. "You wouldn't be here if I had."

Ellie exhaled. Her head ached and she was becoming cold, thirsty, and hungry. She wanted to wake up. As she leaned her head back, she thought, *wake up, wake up, wake up!* But when she opened her eyes, she was still in Grace's home.

"Do you ever sleep, Grace?"

"Yes, most of the time that's all I do. But with you here now, I don't want to sleep. I don't want to waste any time."

"Time?"

"Time with you, dear. Time with another voice to break the silence—that crushing, deafening silence that so often fills this room."

"I'm sorry, Grace."

"Sorry for what, dear?" Her voice grew tender now.

"Sorry that you're here and that I can't help you."

"My pain is not of your making, child, but you can help me. You just have to believe in what I say."

Ellie was befuddled. She didn't know what Grace meant. Did she need to believe in this strange dream or believe that a spell was haunting her family? She said, "Did you find the woman who created the spell?"

"I did. Calista finally helped me, but she dared not interfere."

"Was she afraid it would affect her as well?"

"Calista had had her own run of bad luck; she didn't want to bring more upon herself. She gave me the information I needed and she let me go."

Ellie nodded and leaned back again as Grace continued her story.

Chapter 28

Early February 1934

As the sun began to rise, Grace rolled to her side, away from Alfred, and peered out the window at the frosty world below. It wasn't fully light and she could see the sleepy world coming to life. Her stomach had grown noticeably large, and she ran her fingers across the flannel nightgown that covered her naked skin. She could no longer fit into her mother's fitted silk gowns, and the house was always cold this time of year, even with the fireplace constantly burning in the living room below.

She closed her eyes and listened to Alfred's steady breathing. They had been married only a few short months, but it already seemed like an eternity. Each day passed exactly like the day before. They would wake and eat breakfast as a family. Then Alfred and her father would work on the farm while Grace and Calista tended to the house. It was a simple, quiet existence, but one that seemed melancholy at the same time. No one spoke of the lingering bleakness, but they all felt it, each in his or her own way.

As the sun rose, Grace was determined to break the house's deafening silence. She touched the ring on her left hand and brought it to her face so she could peer at it in the bedroom's half-light. She needed to find the woman that had supposedly cast a spell on it. She thought maybe this woman could help her understand why the sadness lingered in a time when she and Alfred should be happy. If this woman knew more about the ring's history, she might be able to put the spell tales behind them once and for all.

As they finished the large breakfast of eggs, bacon, and hash browns that Calista had prepared, Alfred and Grace's father sipped the last drops of coffee and prepared to head outside.

"We need to fix that hay baler, Alfred," Henry said, folding his paper and laying it on the table.

Alfred nodded in agreement as he stood and put his cup near the sink. Turning back, he quickly pecked Grace on the cheek and headed toward the door. His heavy boots were still full of yesterday's dry mud, and he left a trail from the table to the door. Noticing this, he turned toward Calista apologetically.

"It's alright, Alfred," she smiled. "I was going to wash the floor today anyway."

As he put his red flannel cap atop his head, he smiled nervously as Henry stood and grabbed his old, thick canvas jacket off the rack. He gave his sister a nod as they headed out. Calista sighed as she flopped into one of the kitchen chairs and began to pile dishes atop one another.

"The work is never done around here," she mumbled. "But at least it's getting warmer. It feels like today will be even warmer than yesterday."

Grace shook her head, not really listening to what her aunt had said. She was distracted by trying to find a way to change the subject to the ring.

"Calista, can you tell me again about this ring?" Grace hesitated before picking up the breakfast dishes.

Calista wavered as she readied the water in the sink. "What do you want to know?"

"You told me it belonged to your mother and there was a spell bound to it. Tell me again about the spell."

"I thought you didn't believe in spells," Calista said as she wiped her hands with a towel and then turned to face her niece.

"I'm not sure I do, but I can feel something in the air. It feels almost…heavy. Can't you feel it?"

Calista smirked and placed the towel neatly on the rack. "I've felt if for a long time. It's been here much longer than you think."

"Can you tell me about the woman your mother took the ring to?"

"Why do you want to know about her?"

"Maybe she can tell me what to do," Grace said, reaching out to touch Calista's hands. Calista softened for a moment, but quickly pulled away.

"I'm not sure that's the right thing to do, Grace. That woman could do more damage than good. You should put it out of your mind and focus on the baby. A spell is only real if you believe it."

"Do you believe it, Calista?"

Suddenly there was a sharp cry from outside and Alfred's heavy footsteps ran across the porch. "Calista, Calista! Come quick!" He was breathless. "It's Henry…he…please come quick!" He shot a look at his wife, who quickly stood up from the table.

"What is it, Alfred?" She knew by the look on his face that something must be terribly wrong.

"Ring the doctor, Grace. Tell him to come quickly."

"But…"

"Grace, just do it," he said, trying to keep her calm. Sweat poured from his brow and there was blood on his pants. "Grab that towel, Calista."

Calista exchanged a worried look with Grace as she grabbed the towel and pulled on her galoshes. "Do as he says, Grace."

With that, they were out the door. As she stood in shock, Grace's heart began to pound and a swirl of nausea bubbled in her stomach. Before the panic took hold, she dialed the operator and asked to be connected to Dr. McMullen. Though she couldn't tell him what was wrong, the doctor knew by the sound of Grace's voice that whatever happened must be serious.

She paced in the hallway after hanging up the phone. Grace wanted to run outside to see what was happening. Peering out the window, she could see no one. She opened the door slowly and called out to Alfred and Calista, but neither answered. Biting her thumbnail, Grace stepped onto the porch and waited. She paced nervously and watched the barn, waiting for someone to come back. As each long minute passed, she contemplated ignoring Alfred's request to stay behind. Though she shivered against the frigid air, she didn't want to go back inside for her coat.

Soon the doctor's car came up the drive, kicking up muddy snow and sliding from side to side. Grace ran from the house and almost fell into the doctor's arms as he stepped out. At the same time, Calista appeared from behind the barn, her apron and hands covered in blood. Grace shrieked and ran toward her, but Calista was focused on the doctor.

"He's behind the barn," she said. She hesitated, looking at Grace. "He's was working on the hay baler. His jacket…his arm was caught."

The doctor didn't need to hear anything more. He grabbed his bag and ran around the barn. As Grace took off after him, Calista grabbed her by the arm.

"No Grace, you're in no condition to see it," she said, her grip tightening.

"I have to make sure he's alright, Calista. Please let me go. Please!"

Calista held her ground and grabbed Grace with both hands. "No, Grace," she said, staring at her point-blank. It was then that Grace knew the situation was far worse than she had imagined. "Go back to the house and wait for me, please. Just do as I say. You need to stay calm."

Grace stood in the yard shaking as Calista went back toward the barn. A strange calm had come over her aunt now. Calista moved slowly and didn't turn back. Watching her disappear, Grace felt helpless and burst into tears.

As she walked toward the house, there was a sudden rustle of feet in the sloppy mud behind her. Breathing heavily, Alfred and Dr. McMullen rounded the corner of the barn and stumbled forward. They carried an unconscious Henry, who was covered in blood and white as a ghost. His right arm was awkwardly wrapped with towels that were saturated in dark blood.

"Grace, open the car door," the doctor yelled. Grace spun into action as the two carried her father to the car. Alfred, carrying Henry's shoulders, climbed into the back and pulled his father-in-law into the car with him. The doctor placed Henry's legs inside.

He then turned, jumped in the front seat, and started the engine. It sputtered loudly. Calista, who had been running beside them, heaved herself into the passenger's seat as the tires kicked up more mud. The car rumbled away, leaving Grace standing in the driveway alone. Shell-shocked and afraid, she stood listening to the chilly wind whip past her.

Unsure what else to do, Grace stumbled up the stairs and sat on the porch swing. She stared ahead in a trance-like state and stayed there most of the day, thinking the worst as time passed painfully slowly. As evening crept in, she walked to the edge of the porch on shaky knees, wanting to see what had happened behind the barn. Before she could stop herself, she stepped off the porch in her rubber galoshes and headed across the drive.

As she walked, she saw the trail of dark blood that had spilled as her father was carried through the muddy snow. She instantly felt lightheaded and nauseated.

Turning the corner, she heard nothing but the cold wind whistling in from the fields of winter wheat that were still covered in snow. And then she saw the hay baler, the huge metal monster that her father had been working on. It looked like a giant bird with a beak pointing out to a chute below. It was still attached to the tractor, and beneath the rotating shaft she saw a tattered shred of her father's flannel shirt and a dark pool of blood.

Unable to hold back, a burning feeling rose in Grace's throat and her stomach contracted uncontrollably. She quickly turned away. Making her way back toward the house, she stopped and vomited violently. Her father was gravely injured. She staggered up the porch steps and lay on the porch swing, resting her head against its smooth wooden surface. Silent tears rolled down her face, and she was calmed by the swing's gentle swaying. She swore she felt a hand caress her face as the cold wind touched her skin, but when she opened her eyes, no one was there.

What seemed like minutes later, she was awakened by the touch of Alfred's hand gently pushing her tousled hair out of her face and tucking it behind her ear. Startled, she shot up as he sat down beside her. He put his strong arm around her back and pulled her closer to him. "You must be freezing," he said as he tightened the shawl around her shoulders and held her.

The blood on his clothing was still evident, and his eyes were tired and bloodshot. He said nothing at first. The sun had dropped and there was no sound other than the whistling of the wind pushing past the house.

"Alfred, tell me. Did he…?"

Alfred turned to face his wife, taking her face in both of his hands and bringing her head to rest against his. "He didn't make it, Grace. He lost too much blood." His voice was a whisper.

Grace was quiet. The tears that had come so easily before no longer flowed. She wasn't sure how to feel. It had been expected when her mother passed, but this was different. She was stunned and numb.

"Where is Calista?" she asked as Alfred wiped the tears from his own face.

"She stayed behind to talk to the pastor and make arrangements," he said, his voice shaking. "I wanted to come back and be with you. I'm so sorry, Grace."

Feeling weak, she walked to the edge of the porch. Grace was unsure of what to do as Alfred rose and stood behind her, cradling her in his arms and holding her close. "This farm. What will we do with this farm?" The question was more for herself than for her husband, but the reality of it all suddenly seemed like a heavy burden.

"Let's not worry about that now, Grace. Come inside. You should lie down."

As Alfred led her into the house, low thunder began to rumble overhead. She thought about how appropriate a late-winter thunderstorm would be right then. She felt like a storm was brewing inside of her, and she wanted nothing more than to burst into a fury of wind and rain. But for the moment, she couldn't muster a single tear. The powerful emotions she'd felt earlier were now dormant.

Noticing her blankness, Alfred took her by the hand and led her to their upstairs bedroom. As they passed her father's closed door, Grace stopped and touched the knob. Never again would he be there to touch it. Alfred watched his wife enter her father's room. He didn't try to stop her. Instead of following, he went to the bathroom to wash the blood and dirt from his face. Noticing his bloody clothing, he quickly stripped down to his shorts, gathered his clothes into a ball, and returned to the hallway. From there, he could see Grace sitting on her father's bed, emotionless. He watched her, unsure what to do. After a moment, he dropped his clothes on the floor and went to her. As she looked up at her husband, the heaviness of the moment returned.

She whispered. "He's really gone, Alfred?"

Alfred nodded and sat beside her, tightly wrapping his tired arms around her body. Together they cried until he scooped her up and carried her to their own bed, and then he closed Henry's door. He left their bedroom door open so he could hear when Calista returned home. They lay for hours in the darkness, listening to icy rain hitting the steel roof. Even in her husband's arms, Grace had never felt so alone.

Chapter 29

February 3, 2006, 10:00 p.m.

Joe slowly walked down the hospital hallway, almost dragging his feet beneath him. It was getting late, and the hospital was quiet other than the stir of nurses who routinely checked on patients. Though the nurses had tried to persuade him to leave and get some rest, he refused to go. He had convinced Ellie's mother to go home. With trepidation, Anna agreed on the condition that Joe would call if there was any changes.

So many memories flooded to him now, making him realize again the multitude of his mistakes. As he made his way down the hall for coffee, Joe couldn't shake the memory that was building in his mind. It was a night he and Ellie had never spoken of. He'd tried to block it out of his head, and he wondered if Ellie had done the same.

That night that had begun like many others; he had stopped at the bar on his way home from work and refused to call his wife to let her know he wouldn't be home. He'd turned his cell phone to vibrate mode so whomever he spoke to at the bar wouldn't hear its constant ring. He never turned it off, though many times he was tempted. He liked the comfort of knowing that Ellie was trying to reach him, but he would never give her the satisfaction of answering.

On that night, a lot like the others, Joe sat on a barstool and felt the burn of brandy and Coke sliding down his throat. He occasionally engaged in conversation with whomever sat next to him, but for the most part, he kept to himself—that is, until she sat beside him.

A woman he had never met before but often saw at the bar sat next to him and watched him swallow the last drop of his drink. He felt her eyes studying him, but he ignored her.

"Want another?" she asked as he set his empty glass on the bar.

He stared at the woman through his blurred vision and said nothing. She laughed, motioned the bartender, and ordered two brandy and Cokes. The bartender, a small, stout woman who knew Joe well, gave him an awkward glance as she sat the drinks in front of them.

"Thanks," he said as he picked up the glass and stirred the mixture with the small red straw that poked from between the ice cubes. He took a slow sip.

"I see you in here a lot," the woman said, looking at the wedding ring on Joe's finger. "But I never see you with your wife."

Joe laughed sarcastically but said nothing. As he set his glass back on the bar, she said, "Problems with the Mrs.?"

"No, just problems with me," he answered.

"I hear that," she replied, lifting her own drink.

The woman was mildly attractive, though she didn't hold a candle to his wife. Her hair was dirty blonde and bigger than Ellie liked to wear hers. This woman also wore too much makeup, thick eyeliner and a lot of light blue eye shadow. She had dim blue eyes and a nice smile with bright-white, perfect teeth. For some reason, this woman intrigued him. When the awkward silence grew between them, he said, "You married?"

"Not anymore," she said with a smile, turning to face him. The woman was less attractive to Joe from the full-frontal view, yet he still couldn't stop himself from talking to her.

Minutes soon slipped into hours, and he told this woman everything, as if she were a therapist pulling out all his secrets in one, long expensive session. He told her about Ellie, about Lisa and Andrew, and about his strange fear of being tied down. He told her how much he loved his wife and how much he feared the future they faced together. He didn't know why he told the woman all of these things, but the floodgates had opened. His cell phone vibrated in his inside jacket pocket. Ellie called every fifteen to thirty minutes. But still, he didn't answer.

When the bartender announced last call, Joe was still talking to the stranger, who seemed to hang on his every word.

As the few people left in the bar made their way toward the door, the woman spoke. "Are you going home tonight?"

"Where else would I go?" he asked.

She moved closer, put her hand on his knee, and leaned forward to whisper in his ear. "There's no one at my place."

The bartender once again shot a disapproving look at Joe, but he ignored it. He laughed, stood up, thanked the woman for her offer, and began making his way out of the bar. Not willing to give up that easily, the woman followed him out, taking him by the arm as she went.

In the darkness of the parking lot, she softly bit his ear as they walked. A tinge of excitement rose in Joe's stomach. He wanted to go home with this woman, but he felt a burning in the pit of his stomach that told him, *no, walk away*. As they rounded the corner of the building, Joe tried to ignore her and continue to his truck, but she was persistent. As he stuck his key in the driver's side door, she spun him around and began kissing his lips.

Joe was stunned at first, but the kiss felt good. For a moment, he didn't kiss back. She ran her hands through his hair and began to kiss his neck. His hands clenched the woman's arms and he began pushing her away, but she didn't stop.

"Just relax," she whispered. "No one is around. No one will know."

As she brought her lips back to his, Joe stopped resisting. His head began to spin as the woman kissed him deeply. She moved her hands down the front of his pants and began to unzip them. His head felt heavy from the alcohol and Joe grabbed her hand, but the woman lowered herself. He felt the warmth of her hands upon him now.

"No, stop," he said. But she continued, and though he knew it was wrong to let the woman go any further, he couldn't bring himself to stop her. It felt wrong, but it felt good at the same time.

When it was over, she stood and looked Joe in the eyes, but he quickly looked away, ashamed and distraught.

"Do you want to come home with me now?" She laughed.

Joe's eyes filled with tears as he realized what had just transpired. "I'm sorry," he gasped as he pushed the woman away and stepped into his truck. As she stood there with a bewildered look on her face, Joe fired the engine and sped away. He caught a glimpse of her in his rearview mirror, standing there stunned and angry.

Tears rolled from his eyes as Joe pulled into the driveway of his darkened home. Ellie had not called for at least an hour. He wiped his face and began to remove the key from the ignition when he realized his pants were still unzipped and unbuttoned. He quickly fastened them and began to sob, knowing he had made a horrible mistake. He had possibly traded his entire future with Ellie for a few minutes of pleasure.

Stepping out of the truck, he stumbled to the house and tried to compose himself. He opened the door with a dull creak. The house was dark and he couldn't hear anything other than the refrigerator's low hum. He closed the door softly behind him and slowly slid off his boots. As he made his way to the bottom of the stairs, he saw Ellie's silhouette at the top. Her shape was almost ghostly and he blinked his eyes, trying to clear his vision. Even though he couldn't see her eyes, he felt them upon him, almost like she knew what had happened. She said nothing at first and he froze there, defenseless, unsure of what to do. Joe was terrified that she would turn on the light, see his eyes, and know he had done something horrible—something much more horrible than not coming home when he was supposed to.

"Where've you been?" she asked with an emotionless, empty tone.

On most nights, Joe would have ignored this question and walked to the couch to watch the ceiling spin, but on this night he wanted to fall at Ellie's feet and tell her how sorry he was. Too afraid to move, he said nothing. He waited for Ellie's anger to erupt, but it didn't. Instead, she turned away.

"I'm sorry." Joe's voice was hoarse, but it cut through the darkness and Ellie stopped in her tracks. "I…I messed up tonight, I really messed up." His voice became shaky. She turned back toward him and sat on the top step as Joe made his way to her.

"Did you wreck the truck?" Her voice shook.

Joe stopped one step below her. With his back to the wall, he slid down to sit in front of her and rested his head on her knees.

"Joe," she whispered. "What did you do?"

He knew there was no point in lying or keeping it from her. The words fell from his lips so fast as he told her about the woman in the bar, as if they would sting less if delivered quickly. He grabbed her knees, buried his head in her lap, and sobbed. She said nothing.

"I'm gonna stop, Ellie, I promise. I'm not gonna be like this anymore. I love you. I don't know how I got here…"

Ellie stayed silent. She stood up slowly and moved away from him. He knew he had really done it now. She walked back to their bed, lay down, and stared at the wall. Joe crawled in next to her and grasped her tightly, but she didn't move. This terrified him even more; no emotion meant she was too upset to react.

As the memory unfolded in his head, Joe felt the same disgusting, sinking feeling he'd had that night. He stood before the hospital coffee machine and watched as the black, steamy liquid seeped into a paper cup that had fallen from the dispenser. As he waited, he recalled the morning after he told Ellie what he had done. Though he had expected her to pack a bag and leave, she didn't. She was silent, and although Joe was unsure of what she was thinking, he knew she'd had enough. He hated her silence; he almost would have preferred for her to yell at him—he could deal with that. But her silence scared him to the core.

The silence lasted over a week as the two of them functioned around each other. Ellie didn't mention the incident to anyone, and neither did Joe. He tried to talk to her, to reach out and touch her, but whenever he tried, she would walk away as if he were a ghost the she couldn't see or hear. There was nothing he could say to take away the hurt he had caused, so he waited until she came to terms with it on her own. He hadn't been sure that she would, but he was determined to prove that he could change. He hoped she would stay long enough to see it.

Chapter 30

February 3, 2006, 12:30 a.m.

"Why didn't you leave after you realized Joe had been unfaithful to you?" Grace asked as Ellie finished telling her about that horrible night. She had never shared that story with anyone. Saying the words aloud after all this time made her feel small and wrecked.

Ellie brought her hand to her head and rubbed it in frustration, unsure of how to respond. That night had destroyed her trust in Joe, but she recognized that his honesty might mean there was still some life left in him. A light had gone on inside of him, and there was still a glimmer of hope that he loved her enough to stop the things he was doing. As disgusting as it was, the night's events might have brought him to a turning point.

Ellie didn't look Grace in the eyes. "I believed he was sorry," Ellie said. She had never told anyone about that night for fear of being judged for staying with Joe. No one would have blamed her if she left, but staying…that was harder.

"I also believe he was sorry," Grace said effusively.

This statement surprised Ellie, though she knew Grace was thinking something more.

"Things got better for a little while after that, didn't they?"

"Yes. He kept his word and didn't go back to the bar…for a while." Ellie remembered those few months when it had seemed like Joe was his old self again. He came home when he was supposed to, they spent time together, and—for a short while—she even convinced herself that they had moved past the worst days. But, like most things that happen in circular motion, it didn't last.

Chapter 31

February 4, 2006, 7:00 a.m.

Joe was startled from his sleep by the sound of low voices. He sat up quickly, rubbing his eyes. Before him stood a tall, thin doctor with graying hair. The doctor seemed not to notice Joe as he examined Ellie's chart through rimless bifocals, a perplexed look on his face. A petite, nervous-looking nurse stood beside him. She glanced quickly from the doctor to Ellie, and then she moved skittishly, like a cat, to check the levels of an IV bag hanging next to Ellie's bed. Standing, Joe realized how stiff and tight his back was. As he stumbled to his feet, the doctor turned and looked at him over the top of his glasses.

"Mr. McHugh," the doctor said, extending a hand in Joe's direction, "I'm Dr. Eisenberg, a neurologist here at the hospital. I'm here to evaluate your wife's neurological functions."

Before he could continue, the door opened and Anna walked in holding some magazines and two cups of coffee. She was surprised to see the doctor and the worried look on Joe's face. The doctor extended a hand toward Ellie's mother and again explained his credentials. Neither Anna nor Joe said a word as they waited for the tall, stoic-looking man to continue.

"Over the last twenty-four hours, we've seen no signs that Ellie has experienced any brain damage."

Both husband and mother let out a sigh of relief.

"The fact that she hasn't shown signs of a brain injury is extremely positive at this point," the doctor continued, "but we're not sure how long she'll stay in this coma-like state since she has experienced head trauma." He glared at them as if waiting for a response. "It could be days, even weeks before she regains consciousness. We just don't know."

"Will that hurt the baby?" Anna asked.

"Well," he said, clearing his throat. "I'm not an obstetrician, but as far as I can tell, the baby seems to be doing fine. I know Dr. Flannery is scheduled to look in on her today and do some more evaluations, but overall, I think Ellie and the baby are doing well. If we give her a little more time to heal, I'm confident that she'll come out of this. We just need to be patient."

With that, the doctor handed Ellie's chart to the nurse, stuck his pen in the front pocket of his white coat, and removed his glasses. As if he were in a hurry to get to someplace more important, the man shook both Joe and Anna's hands once again and briskly left the room. The nurse smiled sheepishly as she finished her duties and also left. Joe wondered why the woman seemed so nervous.

For a moment, Anna and Joe didn't speak. Neither was sure what to make of the news. No brain injury, but also no projection for when Ellie would awake. Joe ran his fingers through his hair and walked to the window again. Peering out on the cold February morning, he was relieved that Ellie's prognosis was positive, but not knowing when she might wake up gave him little comfort. He needed to see her eyes to know she was really okay, to know she was still inside that sleeping body.

"I brought you some coffee," Anna said. "When was the last time you ate something, Joe?" She set the coffee on the windowsill beside him.

Joe sighed. He couldn't remember when he'd last eaten, but he wasn't the least bit hungry. The last twenty-four hours had been a blur.

"Why don't you step out for a little while, get something to eat, get some rest. I'll stay with her." Anna watched his eyes for a response.

Joe didn't want to leave, but his back ached horribly from trying to sleep in the chair, and the thought of a hot shower sounded like heaven. He turned to his mother-in-law and nodded in agreement.

"I'll be right here. If there's any change, I'll call you right away," she said, reading his look. "Are you okay to drive or should I call Peter?"

"No, no. I'm alright. I'll just run home, take a shower, and come right back."

"You should take a nap, Joe. Get a little rest and try to relax for just a little while."

Joe knew Anna meant well, but he didn't feel he deserved rest, comfort, or compassion—especially not from Ellie's mother. There was so much Anna didn't know about how bad things had become between he and his wife. He knew Ellie hadn't told her everything.

"I'll have my phone with me. Call me with any change," he said as he grabbed the coffee and turned to face Anna.

"I will, Joe. I will," she said as she watched him kiss Ellie on the forehead and make his way out of the room.

As he stepped out into the cold, crisp air, energy surged through Joe's body like electricity. The frigid air felt good. Before turning the ignition on his truck, he sat for minute, thinking of when he and Ellie could have conceived this baby. It had to have been the night he finally broke through to her after the incident at the bar.

There had been so much silence, so much distance between them since he'd come clean to her about what he'd done. He didn't regret telling her what had happened, but he was still so ashamed. Weeks later, on a cold, rainy Saturday, neither of them wanted to leave the house. As Joe watched a fire crackling in the fireplace, Ellie came down the stairs from their bedroom, where she had been reading. He watched as she descended. Her hair was pulled back and she wore her glasses, which always made her look studious and serious. She was wearing sweatpants and one of his old sweatshirts, which was entirely too big for her, but she looked gorgeous anyway. He always thought she was more beautiful in casual clothes then she ever was made up. She was stunning both ways, but she was naturally beautiful. As she reached the bottom of the stairs, her eyes quickly darted away when she caught his gaze. Joe was so tired of fighting. He wanted nothing more than to sit close to her and talk like they used to.

"I have a bottle of wine in the fridge," he said as she walked from the stairs toward the kitchen. "Do you want a glass?"

"Sure," she said softly.

He followed her to the kitchen. As she straightened a stack of unpaid bills on the countertop, he opened the cabinet above where she stood to reach the wine glasses. His body pressed against her back and he felt her warmth against his chest. He wanted to wrap his arms around her and beg her for forgiveness, but instead he grabbed the glasses and turned to put them on the island in the middle of the room. She stood behind him as he poured the wine. When he turned to hand her a glass, their eyes met and he smiled at her for what seemed like the first time in months. Again, she looked away.

As they sipped wine on the couch, Ellie moved closer to him and pulled the throw blanket over her legs. Joe could smell the sweetness of her honey shampoo and couldn't resist touching her. Pulling her closer, he rested his chin on the top of her head. He knew she was still angry, but it was this warmth he longed for. He shuddered at the image of another woman touching him. He didn't want to let go of what he had with Ellie. He wanted them to come through this.

As Joe held her, he began kissing her cheek and ear. She didn't respond at first but simply closed her eyes. He wanted to erase the past and be the man she needed him to be. But there was still so much fear, so much rage that kept him distant. He didn't want to think about the past or the future; he just wanted to feel safe and close to her.

As the rain continued, they held each other in silence until Ellie finally turned and looked into his eyes. The look on her face was like a knife to his chest. She looked so wounded. He touched her face and moved closer to kiss her. He knew she was tired of fighting, too. As they made love for the first time in weeks, both were able to let go of their troubles for just a little while and revel in each other. Afterward, they lay on the couch all night, not wanting to let go.

As he drove away from the hospital, Joe knew the baby had been conceived that night. He didn't blame Ellie or believe that she was trying to trap him the way Lisa had. That night had been different. It was something they both needed. Things were better for a while after that, but then, like always, they started to spiral out of control. Joe knew it was his fault. From that night until the evening of Ellie's accident, Joe had pushed her further and further away again, and even he didn't understand why. As he turned the corner and pulled into their driveway, he sighed and tried to push the memories away. He thought, *Why did I have to be such an asshole?*

Chapter 32

February 3, 2006, 1:11 a.m.

Grace wiped a tear as she recalled her father's death. Ellie found herself wanting to reach out to Grace for the first time since her arrival, but she hesitated. The two were silent for some time, each thinking of something different and wishing they were someplace else. Ellie couldn't stop thinking about Joe. She thought of all that had gone wrong between them and how she hated what they had become. Still, she wanted nothing more than to get back to him.

When the silence hung too heavily in the air, Ellie spoke. "Did you stay on the farm after your father passed?" "Yes," Grace said, looking down at the damp handkerchief in her hand. "Alfred and I tried to look forward to the birth of our child—your grandmother—but Calista retreated more and more into depression. I knew I had to stop procrastinating and take a deeper look into my family's secrets and the true story behind that ring." Grace pointed to Ellie's right hand.

"I still wasn't sure it held the key to everything that had happened, but I needed to know. I needed to do something to lift the melancholy that surrounded us day and night. I didn't want your grandmother coming into the world surrounded by such dread."

Ellie didn't say a word; she simply listened as Grace spoke. She had so many questions, but she was afraid Grace would become distracted if she interrupted.

"Calista didn't come out of her room on the morning of my father's funeral, so I knocked on her door," Grace said. "I didn't wait for her to answer. I slowly opened the door and saw her lying still in her bed. For a moment, I was afraid she had passed away, too, but then she lifted her hand and motioned for me to sit beside her."

Ellie interjected. "Did she know that you had come to ask her about the ring?"

"I think she did, but we didn't speak of it—not that day. I just sat with her and tried to persuade her to get out of bed. But she just kept telling me how tired she was. I didn't know it then, but she was talking about tiredness not only of the physical being, but a tiredness of the soul. It's that same exhaustion I feel every moment I spend here. I sometimes wonder if Calista had been trapped in some sort of purgatory that she created for herself. Her life had been filled with so much loss, too. Her parents, her husband, her only brother…I was all she had left. I suddenly felt so selfish that I hadn't seen how much pain she had been in.

"Things were different for me and Calista after that. I realized how much we needed each other to get through everything that had happened. Though I wanted to ask her about my mother and the ring, I waited. She needed comfort as much as I needed answers."

Chapter 33

February 1934

Grace grew tired as guests continued to stop by the farm on the afternoon of her father's funeral. It seemed everyone in the county had turned out to offer condolences. Though she very much appreciated their kind words, Grace began feeling claustrophobic in the house and needed to distance herself from the commotion. She looked across the room at her aunt, who greeted the guests and made sure to thank everyone. Something had kicked in and Calista was a different woman than she had been earlier that morning when she was barely strong enough to get out of bed.

Wrapping herself in her long wool jacket, Grace slipped out of the house to find solitude in the barn with the horses. Looking out the window, Alfred watched her cross the yard but didn't follow.

As she opened the barn door and stepped inside, Grace felt comforted and warm. Things were in place here, with everything was where it was supposed to be, so much unlike the life she lived outside these walls. Belle heard her come in and poked her head out of the stall. Rocco, who had grown into a gorgeous, strong colt, also appeared from a nearby stall and watched her approach.

"Hey, you two," Grace said softly. She smiled for what felt like the first time in days. She reached for a bucket of oats and offered some to the horses, who accepted graciously. So much had happened recently that Grace almost forgot how the horses made her feel centered. They were simple creatures and they didn't expect anything from her other than food and water.

As Rocco munched his oats, Grace turned back to Belle and stroked her long, soft face. The horse and gently nudged her hand.

"What will we do now, Belle?" Once again, the horse softly nudged her. During times like this, Grace had always been able to feel or imagine her mother close to her. All she'd had to do was close her eyes and visualize her mother's face, hands, and long, raven-colored hair. But she couldn't now. Grace wondered why she couldn't feel or see her mother during a time when she needed her the most.

Lost in her thoughts as she stood with Belle and Rocco, Grace didn't hear the door open as the old woman entered. It wasn't until a voice cut through the silence that Grace spun around in surprise. She didn't know how long the woman had been standing there.

"I'm sorry," the woman said quietly. "I didn't mean to startle you. I was looking for Mr. Harper's daughter. Are you his daughter?"

"Yes, I'm Grace," she answered, moving closer to the woman and extending her hand. The woman accepted, and Grace was almost startled by how cold her fingers were to the touch. Although she was a small, fragile-looking, gray-haired woman, her dark eyes were sharp and bright, like she knew a secret that she wasn't about to share. She was dressed in black and was a little hunched over. She walked with a cane, though she didn't seem like she really needed it.

"I'm sorry, have we met before?" Grace said. The woman studied her face. Grace felt uncomfortable and took a step back toward the horses.

"No," the woman said. "We haven't. I knew your parents…and your father's mother. Your grandmother loved your father very much."

"Yes, I'm sure she did," Grace said politely. "I don't remember my grandmother very well. She died when I was very young."

"You were two years old," the woman said as Grace looked up in surprise. "I remember seeing you at her funeral."

"Ah," Grace replied with a shy smile.

"I'm very sorry about your father," the woman said. "I just wanted to tell you that. He was a good man who loved his family."

"Thank you. I appreciate that." Grace nodded as she looked toward the floor.

"Your baby is a girl," the woman said as she pointed her cane toward Grace's abdomen.

The comment caught Grace by surprise. "How do you know that?"

"Your father told me," the woman said as she winked her wrinkled eyelid and then turned away.

"But…" Before Grace could ask another question, the woman disappeared and Alfred appeared in the doorway. Noticing the surprised look on Grace's face, he became concerned.

"Is everything alright? Who was that woman?"

"I…I don't know. She said she knew my grandmother and my father, but she never gave me her name."

Alfred reached out and took Grace's hand. "Calista is looking for you."

"Alfred, that woman just said our baby is a girl," she said, looking into his soft eyes.

He smiled and led her from the barn. "She's an old woman, Grace. She was probably just guessing."

"But she said my father told her it was a girl."

"Grace, maybe he saw her somewhere before the accident and told her he *thought* the baby was a girl." Alfred tried to rationalize what the woman had said.

"I know everyone my father knows, Alfred. I've never seen that woman before."

"I don't know, Grace, but Calista needs you. We should go." He coaxed her forward.

As they emerged into the chilly sunlight, Grace scanned the yard for the old woman, but she was nowhere to be found. She had gone just as mysteriously as she had appeared.

Busy pouring beverages in the kitchen, Calista smiled when Grace walked through the door. "There you are, honey. Could you help me with the coffee?"

"Ah, yes, sure," Grace replied. "Calista, did you see that old woman dressed all in black that came to see me in the barn?"

Calista snickered. "Grace, there's a handful of old women out there dressed in black. You'd have to be more specific." She handed her niece a silver tray filled with five steaming cups of coffee.

"I don't see her now, but she said she knew Grandma Harper." Calista hesitated for a moment. "She said she met me once at grandma's funeral, and she said Dad told her my baby is a girl."

"I'm sure it was just some old, distant relative Grace. I wouldn't give it another thought. Now please, can you take that coffee to the pastor's table?"

Though she sensed her aunt knew more than she was saying, Grace did as she was told and turned away to deliver the coffee. She was unsure of why Calista was acting this way, but she knew she wasn't about to find out.

Chapter 34

February 3, 2006, 1:45 a.m.

"The woman was Francesca Morano, the witch, wasn't it?" Ellie asked.

"Yes, it was, though I didn't know it at the time."

"Did you find her again?"

"Yes, but it wasn't until much later, after your grandmother was born," Grace answered.

"Were you surprised when the baby turned out to be a girl?" Ellie studied the old woman's pale, grayish face.

"No, I wasn't surprised at all. I just knew for some reason that the woman had told the truth. I didn't know why, and I didn't know anything about her, but the way she said it made me believe her." Then Grace changed the subject. "Tell me more about Joe," she said.

Ellie didn't want to talk about Joe. She wanted to know more about the woman in black and the day her grandmother was born, but she knew Grace was shifting away from the story for a reason.

"I'm not sure what more there is to say," Ellie said, though she knew Grace wouldn't be satisfied with the answer.

"Yes, you do. You know there's much more to say. Tell me what happened after he told you about the encounter at the tavern."

Ellie exhaled slowly. She didn't want to think about all of that. Remembering it made knots in her stomach. "Things were distant for a while, then we…well, I thought we'd made a breakthrough one night, but then it all went back to the way it was."

"Was that the night you conceived the baby?" Grace turned to watch the expression on Ellie's face.

"I think so, though I didn't plan it that way."

"Of course you didn't, dear. None of us planned for our daughters to be conceived," she retorted.

"Are you saying this baby is a girl?"

"If the tradition continues, I'm almost positive it is."

"But you don't know that for sure?" Ellie's eyes burned for answers, but Grace just chuckled.

"I don't know anything for sure, Ellie, other than I'm here, and now you're here." She paused, then said, "Let me hear more about Joe."

As Ellie told Grace about the last few weeks, the acid rose in her throat again. It burned horribly, until she was almost unable to speak. Everything had turned into such a whirlwind that even she couldn't get her arms around it.

After that night with the woman at the bar, Joe had promised to change his ways, and Ellie so wanted to believe him. He almost convinced her, until things turned around again. They spent one beautiful night together, and just a few weeks later she learned she was pregnant. But Joe was back to spending evenings at the bar by then, and she was terrified that telling him about the baby would push him over the edge. She was frustrated, scared, and out of ideas about how to make things change.

On nights when he stayed out late, Ellie would lay in bed alone, staring at the ceiling and trying to understand how they had landed in this place. She shuddered as she imagined him with another woman, and part of her wanted to go down to the bar to see what was happening with her own eyes. But she chose to lay silent, wait, and hope he would eventually see the light. She blamed herself for being too complacent and accepting, for not being enough of a challenge—but even then, she knew that Joe's struggles weren't about her. Still, that didn't make it hurt any less.

"What do you think he was going through?" Grace asked.

"I think it was a combination of things that had taken the faith out of him. His family, his ex, his lost child. I think he felt he didn't deserve me or anything good, even though most of the things that had happened to him weren't his fault."

Grace nodded and pursed her lips as if she knew exactly what Ellie meant. "I believe I did the same thing to Alfred that Joe has done to you," she said. "He loved me, gave up everything for me, and I tortured him until there was nothing left but the shell of a man who once had infinite potential."

Ellie was surprised by this revelation. She began to wonder if that was why Alfred had taken Grace's life. She couldn't imagine coming to a point where she could murder Joe, but there were times when she wanted to make him hurt just as badly as she did.

"You have to know that what Joe feels really has nothing to do with you, Ellie," Grace said as she folded her wrinkled, weathered hands in her lap. "He's stuck in a past that he can't overcome. I know how he feels."

"But you loved Alfred, didn't you?" Ellie asked.

"In the beginning I did, yes, but deep down we both knew that we hadn't made the right choices. And because of one choice—one simple, spur of the moment choice—our lives were forever changed. Alfred was so full of promise, so full of hope, even after he was forced to change his plans. But I…I, was so afraid, so unable to see past the moment."

Ellie said nothing as she thought of Joe and how he would react to the news about the baby. He would be like Grace. He wouldn't be able to see past the shock of it to envision the wonder that having a baby would bring. Ellie wanted so much to see him smile and be happy at the thought of their baby, but she knew he would revert back to that place inside where she was never allowed to go.

"Tell me about the last night with Joe before you came here," Grace said after a long moment of silence.

Ellie shrugged her shoulders. "There's really not much to tell," she responded. "It was like a hundred nights I'd been through before. I came home from work and Joe wasn't home. I knew as soon as I pulled in the driveway and didn't see his truck that he was most likely at the bar. I wanted to call his cell phone, but something inside me said 'don't bother.' So, I didn't."

"What did you do instead?" Grace asked, intensely studying the younger woman's face. Ellie was afraid Grace could read her every emotion, as if the expressions on her face had been written just for the older woman to interpret.

"I did what I always do," Ellie said with a sigh. "I walked the dog and ate dinner while watching the news. When it came time for me to go to bed, I went to bed."

"Did you sleep?"

"No, I never sleep on nights like that, though sometimes I just lie there praying that I could—or praying that Joe will come home and I can stop myself from flying to the stairs as soon as I hear him come in."

"And did he come home?" Grace asked, leading Ellie into a story she already seemed to know.

Ellie sat for a moment, staring ahead, confused. "You know, I can't remember now. I think so. Maybe I fell asleep."

"Why do you think you slept that time and not the others?"

Ellie hadn't thought about it until then, but it was odd that she hadn't confronted Joe like she had every time before.

"Maybe it was because I knew no matter what I did or said at that moment, that it wouldn't do any good."

"Precisely," Grace replied. "Maybe because you knew no matter how angry you became at him, *he* wouldn't change. He wouldn't stop what he was doing to think of you and your feelings."

"Maybe," Ellie replied.

"But you felt different than the times before, didn't you?"

Ellie thought for a minute. She *had* felt different. She felt more numb. She was still upset, but she was beginning to let go of the anger. "I didn't cry," she said almost surprised. "I didn't cry that time, I just lay there until my alarm clock went off, and then I got ready for work and just left."

Grace nodded as if she understood the emotions Ellie had gone through that night.

"What do you remember about your drive home?"

Ellie tried to remember every detail. "It was getting dark and the snow had just started falling. It was cold in my car so I waited, shivering until the car warmed up some. Then I started to drive, but I didn't get far before I could feel my eyelids getting heavy. I was so tired."

Grace nodded again.

"After that, I can't remember anything except waking up in the field."

Chapter 35

February 4, 2006, 10:00 a.m.

The house was eerily silent as Joe entered through the unlocked garage door. Ellie always hated when the door was left unlocked. Once inside, he clicked the lever to the locked position and momentarily leaned his back against the door. The blinking answering machine light caught his eye from across the room, but he ignored it this time. Now, he didn't care who it was.

Ellie's favorite beige sweater hung on the back of a kitchen chair and he touched it as he stood in the center of the room contemplating what to do next. Though the sweater was old and worn, it was still soft and smelled of lavender soap and the faint perfume his wife always wore. Joe had never been particularly fond of the perfume, but at that moment it was intoxicating. As he picked up the sweater and held it to his face, he pulled out a chair and sat at the table. He had a burning desire to drink, but again, he resisted the urge. *Now isn't the time,* he told himself.

Though he was physically exhausted and emotionally spent, he didn't allow himself to cry. He just sat at the table holding Ellie's sweater and wishing she was there to come up behind him, put her hands on his shoulders, and then slide them around his neck to kiss him on the cheek as she had done so many times before.

With this image vivid in his mind and her scent so strong in the sweater he held, Joe remembered their wedding day and how breathtaking Ellie had looked. Though he always thought she was beautiful, that day she had been the most perfect image of a woman that he had ever seen. Her long, fitted silk dress had clung to her body like a glove, and it had just the right touch of elegance. It was beaded on top and had an empire waist, but the dress was smooth and sleek all the way to her feet. She hadn't worn wear a veil, but her dark hair was pulled back and her brown eyes sparkled as they met his. As Ellie had walked toward him with her stepfather's arm wrapped around hers, he couldn't believe she was about to marry *him*. Tears had slipped down his cheeks when she smiled and took his hand. He had known then that he didn't deserve her, and he loved her more than she would ever know. But now, as he sat at their kitchen table while she lay in the hospital, Joe couldn't believe how far they had come from that day.

With their wedding still vivid in his mind, Joe recalled another incident that kept driving them apart. Though they had talked about children prior to getting married, Joe began to sense that Ellie had disguised her feelings on the subject as time went by in order to be closer to him. Her face would light up every time she held a friend or relative's newborn baby. She would look up at him and smile in a way he couldn't comprehend. He knew the tender look in her eyes was about something he would never give her. In times like that, he looked away quickly and quietly. Though they never talked about these moments, he was certain that Ellie knew what he was thinking.

Then one afternoon, as they drove home from visiting friends who had just welcomed their new baby, Ellie reached over and touched Joe's hand as he drove.

"Maybe we should have a baby," she said, almost laughing. Though her statement was innocent enough, Joe felt a large crack erupting in their relationship. He sighed, dropped her hand, and clutched the steering wheel. The warm October day suddenly seemed overcast and the smile melted from Ellie's face.

"Wow, was it something I said?" Her tone was sarcastic.

Joe sighed again. Without looking at his wife or taking his hands off the wheel, he said, "Ellie, you know I don't want kids. Kids complicate things. They're expensive and they monopolize everything about your life."

"As if you know," Ellie mumbled under her breath. She knew about his past, and it was times like this when she became resentful of his silence.

"I know that I don't want kids, Ellie," he said, his voice rising. "I've made that pretty clear to you."

"Why do you always make the decisions in this relationship, Joe? That's what I'd like to know."

"How do you figure that?" A fire rose in his throat. "You were the one who wanted to get married. I was perfectly fine with how things were before that."

He knew as soon as the words left his mouth that he had made a terrible mistake. He had wanted to marry Ellie, but as with everything else in their relationship, he had been afraid to make the move until Ellie gave him the push he needed. He always needed her to push.

"Are you saying you didn't want to get married?" Ellie's voice cracked. "Because I distinctly remember you were the one who asked me."

"Because you wouldn't stop asking me when it was gonna happen." He said it under his breath, digging himself into an even deeper hole.

Ellie's glare burned into the side of his face, but he refused to turn toward her.

"I don't recall pressuring you, Joe," she said.

He quickly cut her off. "You pressure me about everything, Ellie, and you know you do. When are we gonna get married? When are we gonna get a new house? And now you're asking about kids knowing full well that I don't want any. Every time I give in about one thing, you want something more."

Ellie was shocked and silent for a minute, and then she sneered back. "I'm sorry, Joe. I guess I thought it was just natural for human beings to strive for more, to set goals and try to attain them."

"Goals? When are your goals ever going to end? That's what I'd like to know," he replied harshly.

With those words, Ellie fell silent. She was too angry and stunned to respond. As Joe sat at the kitchen table and recalled the argument, he wished he could tell her that his life would stand still if it weren't for her pushing. Though he wanted Ellie to understand that she pressured him, he had been so wrong in the way he explained it.

Exhaustion set in as he stood from the table and made his way up the stairs. When he reached their bedroom, he lay down on their bed and allowed himself to close his eyes. Here he could smell Ellie's perfume even more strongly, and without opening his eyes, he reached across the bed, clutched her pillow and pulled it close.

Chapter 36

Late February 1934

Grace couldn't muster a word as she held her newborn daughter. There were no words to describe how awestruck she was by the tiny, screeching being that she had brought into the world. Though the long labor and difficult birth had exhausted her, she couldn't take her eyes off the baby. Throughout her pregnancy, she had imagined what her daughter would look like. Now that she was finally here, Grace was astonished that she had created something so amazing. Her fear and anguish evaporated as she realized that bringing this little girl into the world was the most important thing she would do in her lifetime.

"She looks like you," Alfred said as he took Grace's hand and gently touched the baby's nose with his large, calloused finger.

"Do you think so?" Grace asked without looking away.

"Absolutely," Alfred replied. "Have you decided what we should call her?"

With all that had happened, Grace hadn't completely decided on what to name the baby. She knew the baby would have been named Henry, after her father, if it had been a boy. But she hadn't decided on a name for a girl. She looked at Alfred, who shrugged his shoulders and smiled.

"I thought I'd leave this part up to you," he said.

Grace studied the baby's face for a few moments. "Mary Isabella—after both of our mothers?"

Alfred looked tense, but then he knelt beside them and smiled. "How about we call her Isabella, Izzy for short?"

When Alfred lifted the baby from her arms, Grace was amazed at how natural he seemed. For a man who had nearly sworn himself to God—never to marry, never to have children—he seemed completely at peace holding his daughter.

For the first time in months, Grace felt happy. She only wished her parents could be there to share this joy. She imagined the pair of them standing there, her mother in tears and her father being quiet and stoic, as always, but beaming with pride inside. As she looked past Alfred and into the corner of the room, she pictured them there. For a brief moment, she thought she could actually see them. The thought made her feel protected and calm. She knew they weren't real, but she could imagine them so vividly that it made them seem closer.

"Thank you, Grace," Alfred said, breaking her stare.

"For?"

"For giving me this beautiful gift," he replied, gazing glassy-eyed at the baby. Grace was astounded, but she was also grateful that Alfred seemed so happy. He barely resembled the reserved, sad man he had been since returning to the farm.

In the months that followed her daughter's birth, Grace found herself busy in the daily routine of caring for a new baby. She was comforted by the structure provided by looking after something outside of herself. Even Calista seemed drawn to the light that Isabella brought to their world. For the first time in months, the fog and depression surrounding all of them had lifted. Grace began to wonder if their bad luck was finally behind them.

Then, one late afternoon as the baby slept, the women sat on the front porch enjoying the cool wind coming in from the fields. After a warm early spring day, the breeze that blew across their skin felt refreshing and made them relax. Grace chuckled as Calista leaned back on the swing and unbuttoned the top two buttons on her dress, allowing the air to rush down onto her bosom. Grace soon followed suit, but she kept a watchful eye for Alfred because he wouldn't approve.

"It's nice to have a baby in the house again," Calista said as she lifted her head and looked toward the fields. "It reminds me of when you were a baby. Your parents were so happy again when you were born. They had just moved past some difficult times, and you made them whole again. It almost seems as if things have come full circle."

Grace smiled but didn't speak. Though she had so many questions about her parents, she didn't want to break the new contentment that had settled around them.

"I know there are things you want to know about them, Grace," Calista continued. "I wish I had all the answers for you."

Grace nodded and leaned back on the porch swing, looking at porch ceiling's chipping paint. "There are so many things I don't understand. I just wish I could ask them," she replied. "I feel like there's something that's been left undone or unsaid between us."

"I know you still carry their burden," Calista said as she touched her niece's hand and ran her fingers over the ring she wore on her left hand. "I think it's time you pay a visit to Francesca Morano."

"It *was* her at the funeral, wasn't it?" Grace asked. "You knew it was her! Why didn't you just tell me?"

Calista stood and walked toward the edge of the porch. Her heels clicked against the wooden floor and her cotton dress fanned around her as she walked. Her aunt looked so pretty at that moment, and it made Grace sad to think how lonely Calista must feel at times.

"I've always feared that woman, Grace. I don't even know why. But it seems that when she got involved in our family…things started to change."

"What do you mean?" Grace asked as she stood and walked toward her aunt.

"I'm saying she's the one you need to ask in order to find out what you want to know." Calista wrinkled her forehead and turned toward Grace.

"I knew she was at your father's funeral, and I also knew she had spoken to you, but, to be honest, I was too afraid to say anything."

"Why?"

"I don't know, Grace. I only know that my mother asked that woman to cast a spell on that ring." Calista pointed to Grace's hand. "But a spell is only good if you believe it—at least, that's what I've always thought. But still, that woman scares me. She knows things. She can see things. She just scares me."

"Where can I find her?" Grace quickly asked. "If she can tell me what happened between them, and if there really is something attached to this ring, maybe it'll help me understand..."

Calista told Grace the story of how she followed her mother on the night before her brother's wedding. "If it will bring you peace, then I think you should go—but be wary of that woman, Grace," Calista said as she held her niece's hands. "Some things aren't always what they seem."

When Calista explained where the old woman lived, Grace was surprised that she knew the place well and had passed many times on her way home from school. Francesca Morano lived in a worn-down house on the edge of town. A huge walnut tree almost overtook the entire front yard. Its roots poked through the ground in places and broke up the red brick pathway that separated the house from the street. It was a strange tree; it was always green, even in the dead of winter.

Grace was excited to meet Francesca again, but she was cautious since Calista seemed so uneasy. Still, if the old woman put an end to the idea of a spell or curse being attached to their family, Grace was certain she could let go of the past and make a better life with Alfred.

Later, as she lay awake next to her husband, she contemplated what she would say to Francesca. The night was eerily quiet. She heard nothing but the wind against the house and her husband's slow, steady breathing. She touched the ring on her left hand, felt the gold-leaf pattern, and began to twist it anxiously.

She decided to see Francesca the next day. Alfred would be readying the far fields and Calista could watch the baby. Grace would say she was going to the market, but she had never been a good liar so she knew Calista would be suspicious. Grace didn't care if Calista knew her plans, but she also didn't want her aunt attempting to change her mind.

As she rolled over, lying with her back to Alfred, she faced the wall and stared through the darkness. Grace wondered if her father had known how much his mother disapproved of his marriage, or if he knew she had visited Francesca the night before his wedding.

She closed her eyes tightly and thought of her mother. Whenever she allowed herself to imagine what life would be like if her mother were still there, Grace always had the same cavernous ache. There was so much she wanted to say to her, and so much that was left unsaid. She wished she could reach out to her now more than ever. Afraid that the vision of her mother would vanish if she opened her eyes, tears slipped from behind Grace's closed lids. She longed for the times when she could go to the lake and feel her mother's presence there. It had been so long since she felt that closeness. Now she could only see her mother from behind closed eyes, and she feared the memory of her mother would weaken as time slipped past.

Grace was tired when the sun rose the following morning, but she was also excited and ready to seek the answers she was looking for. She decided that today would be the day things would begin to change—hopefully for the better. It was a warm but exceptionally windy day, and as the morning dragged on, she found herself growing more anxious. She tried to keep herself busy by washing laundry. Rolling the clothes through the wringer kept her focused on something other than what she was about to do. With the smell of fresh linen filling the air, she decided to go through with her plan of visiting Francesca after lunch. The morning seemed to last all day as she nervously went from task to task.

When afternoon finally came, Isabella was hardly hungry so Grace rocked her in the old rocking chair in the upstairs nursery. This was the same chair that her own mother had rocked her in.

Holding Isabella made her feel centered and calm, and for a moment she wanted to stay right there with her daughter all day. But she knew that she had to go through with her plan despite her nerves. As she lay the baby down for a nap, Grace softly kissed her forehead and took another deep breath of the sweet baby smell before turning away. Though Isabella made her feel more complete, Grace would never truly feel whole until she figured out her past.

When she found Calista busy in the kitchen, nervous butterflies fluttered in her stomach. She didn't have to lie to her aunt, but she wasn't ready to tell her the truth.

"I think I'm going to run to the market for some things. Is there anything you need?"

Calista eyed her niece suspiciously. "As a matter of fact, I think we're running low on salt, and we're almost out of soap for the laundry." Calista reached for a piece of paper to write a short list.

As Calista wrote, Grace grew more anxious and made a mental note to stop at the market.

"Do you mind caring for Isabella while I'm gone?"

Calista never looked up from her writing. "Of course not, dear."

As Calista handed her the list, Grace found it difficult to look her aunt in the eye. "I'm going to take the Ford, but the truck is in the barn if you need anything." She turned toward the door.

"Sounds good, dear. Take your time."

As the old Ford rumbled to life, Grace tried to calm the butterflies by taking a long, deep breath and exhaling slowly. When she pulled out of the carport and headed down the drive, the wind kicked up a swirl of dry dust behind her, making the farm almost invisible in the rearview mirror. Though she hadn't written down the directions to Francesca Morano's house, Grace knew exactly where she was going.

When she pulled onto the narrow dirt road that led toward town, Grace nervously sighed. For a moment, she glanced at the ring on her finger and wondered if Francesca knew she was coming. To calm her fears, she tried to imagine the small, fragile woman that she had seen in the barn. She hardly seemed a person that should be feared, yet Grace couldn't stop herself from feeling uneasy.

Seeing houses ahead, she kept driving, bouncing into potholes as the dirt road soon turned to pavement. As she passed the market, she again reminded herself to stop before heading home. Near the center of town, she noticed her school friends gathered outside the ice cream parlor adjacent to the town square. They were laughing, and Grace briefly remembered what it was like to sit with those girls and talk about simple things, teenage things. She lifted her hand to honk the horn and get their attention, but then she hesitated. She realized she was no longer anything like them. They would all be going off to college at the end of the summer, and she would still be here in this dusty, gossipy town.

When she reached the other side of town, where the trees were thicker, Grace knew she was approaching Francesca's home. She knew the area well since she had gone to high school just a couple blocks up the street. She had often walked past the house with her friends when they were on their way to the ice cream shop after classes. That seemed like decades ago now.

The house was hard to miss with its tattered shutters and chipping paint. People rarely saw the old woman who lived there, but Grace knew the rumors well. They had never held much meaning to her in the past, but they did now. The tree that stood in Francesca's front yard had always intrigued her. Unlike the rest of the trees nearby, it wasn't a live oak, and it was huge—its trunk had to be at least five feet wide. As she rounded the corner, Grace saw the tree up ahead, towering above the others. Though it stood inside the steel fence that surrounded the old woman's yard, its leaves were scattered in the street and its black roots pushed through the brick sidewalk and buckled part of the road. Though it was a peculiar tree, no one in town seemed to mind its massive girth, and no one ever discussed trimming it back.

What struck Grace most, however, was the oddity of the tree's leaves. No matter the time of year, the leaves were always a deep emerald green. The color never changed. No one could explain it. Most brushed it off as a fluke or freak of nature, and one gentleman from the university in Whitewater had even tried to test the leaves, but his research was inconclusive and the mystery remained.

As she pulled up to the house, her palms beginning to sweat, the wind finally settled. Though it was still early afternoon, the oak trees on the opposite side of the street cast an eerie shadow over the road. Grace pulled the lever and heaved her weight against the car door before she could change her mind. As it opened, she took another deep breath and stepped onto the street. She caught a chill from the cool wind that pushed past, and she shuddered before moving forward. Though the house looked unkempt on the outside, it did not seem overly ominous or unlived in. A pair of rocking chairs on the porch rocked in the wind and a small pot of petunias sat neatly on the stoop.

Grace paused before the iron gate at the end of the walkway. Unsure of what to do next, she stared at the house. She couldn't see movement inside, and for the first time, she wondered if she could go through with her plan. Suddenly, the wind moved behind her once again. It was cold and almost nudged her forward. The wind became stronger as she moved toward the house, and a nervous lump rose in her throat as she stepped onto the rickety the porch. By the time she reached the door to knock, her throat was so tight that she wasn't sure if she could even speak. And then, without warning, the door creaked open and there stood the tiny woman that Grace had come to see.

Chapter 37

February 3, 2006, 2:20 a.m.

Grace paused. Ellie watched the older woman's glassy eyes, waiting for her to speak again, but Grace sat motionless, staring at nothing.

"What did she say?" Ellie asked impatiently.

Grace snapped back into the moment. "Oh, well, she knew who I was the moment she opened the door, and she was very courteous and polite. She looked exactly as she had that day in the barn. She seemed tiny and frail, yet you could tell the years had only made her body weak. Her mind was sharp as a tack. When I looked into her eyes, I wasn't afraid of her like I expected to be. She just smiled politely and welcomed me in."

"Did she know why you came?"

"I think she did, though she didn't let on right away. She just welcomed me in as if I was some long lost friend, and I was dumbfounded that people were actually afraid of that woman. She seemed more like a friendly grandmother than a witch."

Grace talked faster as her excitement grew. "Her home wasn't as small and dilapidated as it seemed from the outside. It was actually very bright and tidy on the inside. It was warm and inviting, and I immediately wondered why she lived alone. Her only company seemed to be a dark gray cat that slept on a pillow near the fireplace. The only movement that cat made the entire time I was there was to open one green eye to look me over. Then she shut it again and continued her nap. Before I even thought about what I was saying, I asked her if she knew why I had come."

Chapter 38

May 1934

Francesca laughed aloud. "It's the ring on your finger. I recognize it," the old woman said as Grace looked up in surprise. She continued. "It was your mother's ring, yes?"

Grace nodded as Francesca took her hand and ran her fingers over the leafing. "You want to know if I cast a spell on this ring?"

Grace nodded again.

"Tell me, what do you think?"

"I think I have a lot of unanswered questions," Grace replied.

Francesca smiled and tapped the back of Grace's hands with her cold, bony fingers. "Your mother was a beautiful woman. From the moment your father brought her home, your grandmother knew she was trouble, but she also knew your father loved her."

"Why didn't she trust my mother?" Grace asked.

"Beauty like your mother's usually only means one thing, my dear, and that's trouble." She laughed and coughed a little at the same time. "Your father was a good man—hardworking, trustworthy. But he was not rich or overly handsome. He was taken by your mother, and your mother fell for him as well. All of this worried your grandmother."

Grace shook her head. "But if he wasn't rich or overly handsome, what would my grandmother have to fear? My mother wasn't going to steal his money or break his heart."

"Take his money, no, but break his heart, possibly." Francesca turned and shuffled toward the kitchen. "A mother's love is a protective love, my dear. Henry was your grandmother's only son, and she was very protective of him. You see, Grace, when children are small, they depend on you, and you do everything for them, so they love you unconditionally. But when children grow, their love becomes *conditional* and they no longer depend on you like they once had. Your grandmother was never able to let go."

"So you *did* cast a spell on the ring?"

Francesca threw her head back and laughed. "Don't you know, child? A spell only works if you believe it does." With a wink, she turned toward the kitchen. "Would you like some tea?"

"I don't understand," Grace replied. "Didn't my grandmother ask you to cast a spell?"

"If I'm to answer that question," she said, "we're going to have to start at the very beginning." The old woman snickered. "There are many things about me that your grandmother, your mother, and you don't know. We had many things in common, and many things not in common." She paused. "Come. Let's sit out on the porch. I will tell you what they never had the chance to."

Grace followed the frail woman to the front porch and helped her take a seat in the rocking chair. Though Francesca claimed she never had visitors, there were two chairs on the porch, which Grace found rather odd. As she looked across the yard, Grace's eyes immediately settled on the walnut tree. Francesca noticed her stare.

"My great-grandmother brought the seeds of that tree with her from Italy," she said. "She lived in a place called Benevento. Have you ever heard of this place?"

Grace shook her head.

"Well, then, that's as good a place as any to start."

As the old woman began to speak, Grace twisted the ring on her finger. She wondered what Alfred would think if he knew she was there.

Francesca said, "Though she wasn't born there, my great-grandmother used to tell me about Benevento, a small town in Italy where she lived when she was young." Francesca noticed Grace's stare. "There was a tree there where a coven of *strega*, or witches as we call them here, would go to gather."

Grace quickly turned toward the old woman and honed in with child-like interest.

"Strega are very misunderstood, dear," she said as she reached out and touched Grace's hand. "Witches like myself draw our strength from the earth, and trees are especially powerful. There *are* witches that delve into the dark side, but we are not that kind. We don't make deals with the devil or cause harm to others."

Francesca smiled as she continued. "When word got out that witches gathered at that tree in Benevento, it scared people. They didn't understand it, and they didn't want to understand why these people were different from them. They wanted to believe that these women were dark and creating evil things. And that magnificent tree, which my great-grandmother said was in full, green bloom all year round, no matter the season, was ordered to be cut down. People thought this would stop the gatherings, but it didn't. The witches planted seeds from the old walnut tree in the same place, and within one year, it was back to what it had been before…or so I was told. The tree you see here is part of that tree."

"The same tree?" Grace asked as she stared in amazement at the large trunk and branches with deep emerald leaves. Its undergrowth fanned out like feathers, and it looked so strong, as if no wind—not even a blade—could bring it down.

"This tree is probably the only non-native tree you see on this street," she said proudly, pointing to the nearby trees. "When my great-grandmother came to America and settled here, she planted the seeds on this ground and it has been here ever since."

"How does it stay so green?" Grace asked.

"Well, that's a mystery even I can't answer any more than that professor from Whitewater could," Francesca replied, winking one of her dark brown eyes.

As Grace stared across the yard, Francesca watched her spin the ring on her finger. "May I hold it?"

Grace stopped, looked at ring, and then smiled nervously as she slid it off and placed it in Francesca's palm.

Noticing her trepidation, the old woman laughed. "It's alright, child. I'm not going to harm it. I just know there is much history in this ring, and it's easier for me to read that history if I can hold it in my hand."

Francesca stared at it for a moment, creasing her forehead as if deep in thought. Then she ran her rigid fingers over the smooth gold. As she did so, she closed her eyes, took in a deep breath, and slowly exhaled. She repeated this several times before speaking again.

"Your father's mother was not fond of your mother," she said as she opened her eyes and placed the ring back in Grace's palm.

"I know," Grace said, sliding the ring onto her finger and staring at it as her hand rested in her lap.

"She felt threatened by your mother because your mother also knew how to use magic."

Grace's eyes quickly darted up as she looked at the old woman in surprise.

"You feel her around you sometimes, don't you?"

Grace's heart raced with excitement. "I haven't felt her in a long time. I used to feel her all the time, but I…I can't feel her anymore."

"Since Alfred?"

Grace hadn't put the two together, but it was true. "No, not since Alfred and I came together. Wait, how do you know my husband's na—"

The old woman cut Grace off. "She's still with you, child. You mustn't worry."

Grace stared ahead, unsure of what to say.

"Even *she* knows you must figure things out on your own, but she is watching and she knows what she has done to you." Francesca stood and moved toward the door. "Come inside. I have something to show you."

Grace followed the old woman, questions dripping from her tongue. When she stepped into the small house, she began to wonder what time it was. As she looked around the room, she realized there were no clocks anywhere.

"An old woman doesn't need a clock to know what time it is." Francesca laughed. "Don't worry, dear, you are not missed yet."

The woman's bizarre ability to read Grace's thoughts made her uneasy, but Francesca seemed harmless, and she was intrigued as to how the woman knew so much about her family. Motioning for Grace to sit at a worn-out wooden table that looked as if it were ready to collapse, Francesca placed a faded, tattered photograph in front of her. There were two young women in the photo; both wore full black skirts, white blouses buttoned to the chin, and bonnets that covered their hair. The attire indicated to Grace that the photo had been taken during the 1800s. Both girls smiled in a young, girlish way. They appeared to be standing in front of the walnut tree that stood in Francesca's yard.

"That's me on the left and your grandmother on the right." She smiled as Grace stared at the photo. "It was taken more than 60 years ago, when we were young. Your grandmother was my schoolmate and my friend. Because of my family history, I didn't have many friends, but your grandmother—she became my friend. She didn't care about what the others said."

"What did they say?" Grace asked, her eyes glued to the photo. She'd never known her grandmother and had seen few pictures of her.

"Why, dear, they called me a witch, of course." Francesca laughed. "It's true that I come from a long line of women who practiced The Craft, but I didn't have any more choice in being part of my family than you had in being part of yours."

Grace met the old woman's glance. "Did my grandmother do magic, too?"

"Your grandmother's family was Catholic, so no, she didn't. But she wanted so much to learn. She wanted me to teach her, but my mother was very careful in what she revealed to me about who we were. She knew all too well the ridicule and danger that came with being a witch, especially in America. I shared some secrets with your grandmother, but I made her promise she would never tell a soul, and she never did."

Grace felt oddly disassociated from the woman in the photo. Her grandmother had died when Grace was only two years old so she felt no connection to her whatsoever. In the other photos she had seen of her grandmother, the woman was never smiling as she was in this photo. To Grace, her grandmother had always appeared cold and distant.

"She was happy there," Francesca continued. "She had just met your grandfather and was planning to marry."

Grace sighed and wished she could have known her grandmother's softer side.

"Your grandparents had two children, as you well know. Your father came first, and then your aunt Calista soon after him. From the moment he was born though, your father was the apple of his mother's eye. She was a protective mother, over both of her children, but more so of your father. You see, dear, women who give birth to girls know they must teach their daughters to be strong in order for them to survive in a man's world. Maybe she was tougher on Calista because of this, but she was very tender with your father. This turned into a problem as he grew older."

"A problem?"

"Yes. Your grandmother became overly protective of whatever he did." Francesca gazed at the photo. "There was one boy who used to give your father a hard time just because he was older and tougher, even though Henry was always a strong, tall lad. This boy challenged your father to a fight and, being quiet as he was, Henry refused. Well, the older boy needed to prove that he was stronger, so he followed your father after school one day. With a crowd of children around him, he continuously pushed Henry in the back. But, Henry never turned around. Finally, the boy pushed him hard enough where he fell and ripped his trousers. The boy and the other children laughed. But your father simply pulled himself up, brushed off his britches, and continued on his way."

It made Grace sad to think of her father being treated in such a way.

"By the time Henry made it home, Calista had already rushed ahead and told your grandmother what had happened. She became furious that anyone would dare pick on her boy. So, instead of hugging your father and telling him it would be alright, she went after the boy on her own." Francesca laughed.

"What did she do?" Grace asked.

"She waited until dark and found the boy alone, doing chores in his family's barn. She came up behind him, quiet as a mouse so he wouldn't hear her. When he turned around and saw her standing there all dressed in black, he let out such a yelp." She rolled back in laughter.

Grace smiled as she imagined her grandmother sneaking up on a schoolboy. It was an odd thought to place with the cold-looking woman she had seen in the photos. "What did she say to him?"

"She told him she knew what he'd done to her boy and if he ever did it again he could expect a bit of bad luck to come his way. And to prove she wasn't playing, she reached out and tugged a strand of his moppy hair so fast that the boy didn't have time to react. She held it out and said, 'Now I have your hair and I can use it in my spell.'"

Francesca laughed loudly. "That boy was utterly terrified."

"Did she cast a spell?"

"No, dear. Like I said, your grandmother didn't cast, but she soon gained the same reputation as I had. People were as afraid of her as they were of me. It bonded us together even though she didn't have the same gifts as I had. Not everyone has the ability to use magic. It's something handed down for many generations. People may dabble, yes, but these things cannot be taught. They are a gift. A gift that you also have inside of you."

Grace looked up in surprise. "Me?"

"Yes, dear. Though your grandmother didn't have a gift, your mother did. It lies within you, whether you recognize it or not. My guess is that your mother kept it from you so you didn't use it foolishly. Too often do people mistake foolery for fate."

Chapter 39

February 3, 2006, 2:40 a.m.

Ellie watched Grace's weathered face as she explained what Francesca had revealed on that day so many years ago.

"Learning that I was from a long line of witches wasn't a gift at all," she whispered. "If I had known earlier on what my mother was and what my grandmother had done, I would have understood everything better. I don't know why she never told me."

"Were you able to use it…the gift?" Ellie stuttered.

"No. She never taught me how. I don't know why, but she kept that key part of her history a secret from me.

"She often spoke of mystical things—dwarfs that played tricks on her, fairies that dwelled in the woods, the 'dark side' of the year when the veil between the living and the dead grows thinner, but I never took any of those things seriously. My father used to say that my mother was just eccentric and spiritual, but the word *witch*, that was something he never uttered to me."

Beneath the drama, Ellie knew there had to be a point in what Grace was trying to tell her, but she wasn't about to give it up easily.

"Tell me why I'm here, Grace," Ellie said, hoping for some insight.

"You know how the story ends between your great-grandfather and I, yes?"

"Yes."

"Then you know what you cannot repeat," she said, glaring at Ellie with fierce, cold eyes.

"I don't understand." Ellie rubbed her forehead in frustration.

"Tell me, Ellie, how do you feel when another man notices you?"

Ellie stuttered again. "What? I…I feel flattered, I guess, but what does this—"

"And guilty. Do you feel guilty?"

"I don't have anything to feel guilty about if I don't act on another man's flirtations."

"But Joe acted upon his, didn't he?"

The statement burned, but Ellie understood now where this was going. "That was entirely different. Joe was drinking and…confused."

"Are you justifying his actions?"

"No. I…I don't understand…"

"Though you have this baby inside you, do you find yourself wishing it wasn't Joe's? Do you ever wish there was someone else? Someone without issues? Without a past? Someone who wants to share the joy that this child will bring to your life?"

Ellie stood then, her body straight and stern. "If you're asking if I would be unfaithful, no, I wouldn't be. I couldn't."

Grace laughed and leaned back in her chair.

"Yes, we all feel that way at some point. Your husband felt that way too, once."

Ellie stared at Grace across the room and pondered the statement she had just made. Ellie knew what the old woman was insinuating, and the accusation stabbed at her like a knife. She didn't want to believe that Joe had been deceitful.

"What do you mean, Joe felt that way once?" Ellie asked as she tried to keep her emotions from spilling over.

"Your husband has been unfaithful more times than he's told you," she replied quickly. "He doesn't mean to be. He loves you deeply, but he just doesn't know how to change."

Ellie cupped her hands over her ears in an attempt to stop the words from reaching the inside of her head, where they continued to echo. She knew her husband had found himself in a situation that had gone too far, but now Grace was saying there had been more. She wanted to scream. She thought of all the nights that she lay alone in their bed while Joe was out until the early morning. He always came home the same way: drunk and reeking of cigarettes. She never knew for sure where he had been or what he had been doing. She had assumed he was just trying to kill the demons in his head by drowning them with alcohol; she didn't want to believe that there were other women helping to create even more.

"Indeed there was more than one encounter with another woman," Grace said sarcastically. "Infidelity is a funny thing, Ellie. You do it without a plan. One day, it just hits you out of nowhere. You didn't ask for it and you didn't seek it, but suddenly it's there and it changes everything. My mother knew it, and then I knew it."

"That's not me," Ellie snapped. "I love my husband."

Grace glared across the room, her eyes welling up with tears. "I wasn't talking about you, but can *you* forgive Joe?"

Acid churned in Ellie's throat and her breathing quickened as if she were about to hyperventilate.

“Can you forgive him?” Grace asked as Ellie looked up. She stared at Grace like a wounded animal.

“I…I don’t know what’s happening here. This is a dream. This is a dream!”

Covering her face with her hands, she squeezed her eyelids shut and attempted to talk herself awake. She wanted to sit up in bed and realize it was still night. Joe would be sleeping soundly beside her; she would roll over and cuddle up next to him, relieved that this entire thing was just a figment of her imagination.

When Ellie opened her eyes, Grace was still staring at her. “My story isn’t finished, child. You can’t go yet.”

Chapter 40

February 4, 2006, 12:30 p.m.

Clutching his wife's pillow, Joe tried to drift to sleep. His breathing slowed and his body relaxed, but his mind wouldn't rest. Although his eyes were closed, he could see clearly. Maybe it was because he knew the room so well, but it seemed as if he weren't really asleep at all, just on a different plane of consciousness. Through his closed eyes, he could see the wedding picture across the room. That day had been so perfect. He remembered Ellie's face, her smile, how she had whispered in his ear. From that day forward, he'd thought his life would finally be different. There would be no more complications, no more regrets. But the same demons always came back for him, no matter how much he tried to stop them.

When things went badly, he found himself wishing he had never been married at all—wishing he had stayed away from Ellie. She deserved much better than what he gave her. Yet Joe knew he could never leave her. He wanted to understand why he couldn't love her the way she deserved to be loved. He also wanted to know why she hadn't left him already.

As he tried to sleep for just a few hours before going back to the hospital, Joe recalled how his mother and father had interacted with each other. Most of the time they were cold and their conversations seemed forced. No matter how he tried, he couldn't remember any signs of affection between them…unless they were drinking. One particular scene that Joe couldn't erase was another recollection that he'd hidden from Ellie. It was a memory of his mother's eyes staring at him from across the room, tears streaming down her face. Joe turned over in bed trying to stop the repertoire from playing in his head again, but it came anyway.

Staring at him as he entered the room, his mother had said, "Joey, find your brothers and leave." Her voice was calm. Joe froze in his tracks and stared at his mother. His father held the barrel of a small handgun to his mother's temple. Joe's father was expressionless, his eyes glazed over in rage.

"Go, Joey. Take your brothers and go." His mother pleaded as tears fell from her eyes.

Joe didn't turn. His eyes shifted from his mother to his father, who began to shake and quiver. "You lying bitch," he mumbled under his breath, as if he hadn't even noticed his son walk into the room. Though he didn't know what had happened to provoke this scene, Joe knew his father was very jealous even though his mother had never been unfaithful. From behind him, Joe's older brother Peter entered the room and stopped suddenly, just as Joe had. Their mother's eyes shifted to her older son. "Peter," she whispered, "Take Joey and David and go."

Peter pulled the back of Joe's shirt, but the younger boy refused to move or take his eyes off his mother. The harder Peter pulled, the more Joe resisted. Finally, his father looked up and met his stare. As they locked eyes for what seemed like minutes, his father began to cry and dropped the gun from his wife's head. "Why do you make me do these things?" He said as he fell to his knees. She looked at her sons, who stood still, trembling with fear, and then at her husband in a heap on the floor. She stood up slowly and escorted her shell-shocked boys out the door, then shut and locked it behind them.

Peter, now crying, turned to his brother and led him down the hall to the bedroom they shared. Peter buried his face in his pillow and Joe lay on his own bed, facing the wall. He didn't cry.

As the scene played out in his mind, like it had a million times before, Joe snapped his eyes open, relieved to be back in his and Ellie's bedroom. He wondered if he was more like his father than he wanted to admit. The family never spoke of that day. The next morning, his mother and father acted as they always had. Sometimes Joe wondered if it had ever really happened at all. Afraid to find out, he had never asked Peter about it.

As he lifted his head off the pillow, Joe stumbled to the bathroom and looked at himself in the mirror. His blue eyes seemed darker now, and he realized how much he resembled his father. Though he had never raised a hand to Ellie, he wondered if his past was finally coming full circle. Then he remembered the day his mother died. He' held her hand and she had whispered, "Don't live in the past, Joseph." Now, it seemed as if that was all he *had* done.

As he splashed his face with water and glanced into the mirror, he looked into his own sunken eyes and wondered if he would ever escape his memories. He wondered why the bad things were so easy to hold onto and the good things always seemed to disappear. "I don't want to be like my father," he said out loud.

Giving up on sleep, Joe decided to drive back to the hospital. The sky was still gray and a fog lingered over the ground like a soft blanket. The warmer air mixed with the cold snow put an odd energy into the air. As he drove, he thought about Andrew again and remembered the first time he'd laid eyes on his son. Though he had been scared to death and clueless about what to do with a baby, Joe felt the connection as soon as the boy opened his eyes. Though he knew whole-heartedly that he didn't love Lisa, Joe suddenly found himself drawn to this baby.

Slamming his hand against the steering wheel, Joe tried to push Andrew's image from his mind. Thinking of that moment would bring back the same wave of guilt he always felt when he thought about his son, and right now he couldn't take it. But the thought wouldn't leave.

Andrew would be nearly ten years old by now, and Joe wondered what he looked like. Was his hair dark? Were his eyes still so blue? He hoped Lisa's husband was a good replacement father. He couldn't bear to think of what kind of man she might be with or what horrible things his son may have had to endure because he chose to walk away. Joe had always tried to convince himself that Andrew's life was better because he'd let him go. He wanted Andrew to have a childhood where his parents didn't fight. But now, now with this new child coming, he knew he couldn't walk away again. This child was a chance to get it right. If Ellie recovered, it would be his chance to change things.

Change was something he had promised Ellie before, but he had failed each time. And yet she had always chosen to stay. Joe wasn't sure how he had been lucky enough to keep her. He remembered someone saying once that there was no such thing as luck if you work hard enough at something. If you do things half-assed, then you deserve to fail. Joe knew what he deserved. After the incident at the bar, he'd known he had to stop his behavior. He wanted to change, but it wasn't long before he had fallen back into his old ways. If Ellie knew how low he had sunk, she would surely leave him for good.

On another night not so long ago, as he was on his way home from working the day shift, Joe found himself again driving into the familiar bar's parking lot. As he parked his truck and took the keys out of the ignition, he hesitated and looked at the cell phone on the seat beside him. He knew he should go home, but for some reason, he didn't want to yet. He could already smell the stale alcohol resonating in the air around him. It reached into his senses and made him crave the burning taste of brandy. Before he could change his mind, he hopped out of the truck and walked toward the front door. He saw through the window that the same old crowd was there, and he didn't particularly want to sit down and talk to any of them, but he went in anyway. As soon as he walked through the door, he locked eyes with the woman he had met a few weeks before. He instantly knew he'd made a mistake by coming here, but he didn't turn back. With no expression on his face, he quickly looked away. Noticing his friend John, Joe cleared his throat and crossed the room. With a smirk and a sarcastic laugh, the woman smashed her cigarette into the ashtray and continued talking to the woman seated next to her. Her eyes burned into his back and he knew she was laughing at him.

Joe lost track of time as he drank, and he began to drift into the same old drunken haze. When John rose to go to the bathroom, he left Joe alone at the bar. Seizing her chance, the woman approached him.

"Haven't seen you here for a while. The wife have you chained at home?" She sat close to him, closer than he was comfortable with. He shuffled nervously as he felt her smoky breath on his face.

"No, just haven't felt like being here for a while." He scanned the room for John or anyone else he knew, but there was no one.

"Are you nervous about something?"

Joe fidgeted with the change that sat on the bar in front of him and anxiously stirred his brandy and Coke. "No, I'm just sitting here enjoying my drink."

"I was pretty disappointed when you left me standing in the parking lot," she said without taking her eyes off his face.

"Sorry. I didn't know what I was doing," he said quietly.

"Oh, I think you did. I think you knew exactly what you were doing. I think you were just scared."

Joe laughed and turned to face her. Again he was reminded of how much prettier Ellie was than this woman. His wife was intoxicating at first glance, but this woman—this woman looked worn and her stare was like poison. "I wasn't scared. I…it just didn't feel right."

Moving her hand across his leg, she leaned closer and whispered. "Does it feel right now?"

"Nothing feels right to me anymore," he retorted, but he didn't move her hand. Though he knew it was wrong, the woman's touch excited him.

"Wanna go for a ride?" Her head was tipped down, but her eyes pierced straight ahead. She was like quicksand, and Joe knew she was trying to bait him. Though he wanted to say no, he stood and quickly scanned the room. John hadn't returned from the bathroom, and he didn't see anyone else who would notice him leaving with this woman. Stumbling forward, she grabbed his hand and they slipped out the door.

Before he knew what was happening, Joe found himself in the woman's car. It was as if someone else were in control of his mind and his body. The woman kissed his neck and ears, and he didn't stop her. Though he was already disgusted with himself, he didn't want her to stop. As he closed his eyes, he imagined Ellie. That thought made him kiss the woman harder. His hands trailed down her back and he lifted her shirt, feeling her breasts underneath. The woman sighed in surprise and responded by unbuttoning and unzipping Joe's pants, then lowering her own. When she crawled onto his lap and lowered herself onto him, Joe knew there was no turning back. As she moved back and forth, breathing heavier, Joe kept his eyes closed, imagining his wife. She thrusted faster, and Joe lost himself in the moment. He allowed her to kiss his face and neck, but he kept his eyes closed. When they had both climaxed, he laid his head back on the seat and the tension poured from his body. As she crawled off and pulled up her pants in the seat next to him, the woman lit a cigarette and stared at Joe's emotionless face.

"Now see what you missed last time?"

Without a word, Joe pulled up his pants and exited the car.

Chapter 41

May 1934

Grace stared at Francesca from across the table. She was still shocked at the old woman's suggestion that she had a gift for practicing magic. Grace stuttered. "What does it mean to have this gift?" The butterflies in her stomach fluttered again.

"That all depends, dear," the old woman answered, tucking a clump of gray hair that had fallen loose back into her bun. "This type of gift travels in generations, and you *are* your mother's daughter."

"But she never told me about any of this. I don't know anything about how to use magic."

"She never taught you because she wanted you to be different, but that doesn't mean you don't have it. You should be grateful. So many times, people long for what they don't have—like your grandmother did."

Grace stared at Francesca like a frightened animal wanting to run, and the old woman put her hand on top of Grace's folded fingers.

"Do you know what your grandmother asked me to do with this ring?"

Grace looked into Francesca's dark, oil-colored eyes. "She asked you to cast a spell on it?"

"Yes, she did, but I refused." Francesca stood. "Calista didn't hear the entire story when she cowered under my window that night."

Grace watched the woman closely, surprised to hear her mention Calista.

"Yes, I knew she was there, but I didn't say anything to her mother," she continued. "I knew why she had come, and I knew Calista would believe there was something more sinister going on than what actually was. That girl never did like me."

"What did she ask you to do?" Grace said effusively, trying to draw out the answers that she had come to find.

"Well, it's true that your grandmother asked me to cast a spell on that ring. But I didn't agree with what she was trying to accomplish. I told her I wouldn't do it, but she could try it herself."

"If you didn't agree, why did you let her try?" Grace asked.

"A spell works when the person casting it is able to tap into the spiritual realm and influence matters of the physical realm," the old woman explained as she looked into a corner of the room and then back again. "To make a spell true, we *must* be able to connect with the spirit realm. Your grandmother couldn't do that. She didn't have that gift."

Grace listened closely as her heart beat faster. She knew now what Francesca meant by having the gift. So many times she recalled seeing and feeling her mother, but she had never known if those images were real—until now. "What was the spell she wanted you to cast?"

"She wanted me to cast a negative spell, something that would hurt your mother if she betrayed your father, but I couldn't do that. You see, dear, in the world of magic, we believe there is a force that dwells in all things, and attempting to discord nature can leave a terrible imbalance."

"What?" Grace said, shaking her head in confusion.

Francesca sighed and thought for a moment before she continued. "How can I explain this better? My ancestors believed that there is a spirit within all things. It's this spirit that gives power to all things of nature—even stones or charms. Trees, like that walnut tree that stands in my yard, contain very powerful spirits."

"But what does that mean?" Grace asked as she looked at the ring on her finger.

"The strength of an object, like that ring on your finger, depends on the strength of the spirit it possesses," she continued. "In nature, all things influence each other. If someone were to cast a spell on that ring, like your grandmother was trying to do, they would need to connect with the spirit within the object. I told your grandmother to perform a ritual, but it was a ritual that I never thought in a million years would work."

Grace stared blankly at Francesca. "Are you saying my ring is haunted?"

Francesca scoffed. "In a way, yes. Somehow, and I still don't know how, your grandmother tapped into the spiritual realm and succeeded in what she set out to do."

"What did she do?"

"In order to protect your father, she boiled that ring in a pot of water and she chanted the words of her spell over and over until they fused with the water. She said that if your mother was unfaithful to your father, the power in that ring would unleash itself and torture your mother from the inside out. For your mother, it meant that she would be consumed with guilt if she wronged your father. Even though he didn't find out about her affair right away, she felt the overwhelming power of guilt and it destroyed her…even though she had every reason to do what she did."

Grace stared at the ring on her hand. "So it wasn't a curse that killed her?"

Francesca smiled and touched the ring. "No dear, cancer killed your mother. Her conscience killed her spirit."

"Is that spirit still in this ring?" Grace asked as she looked into Francesca's eyes.

"Like I said, there is a spirit in everything." She winked. "But if you're asking me if a spell is still attached to that ring, that is something I don't know."

Grace's heart sank. "It's so strange, but sometimes I feel such a heavy cloud of guilt around me and I never understood why. Could that be what I'm feeling?"

"Hmmm," Francesca murmured through pursed lips. "It is possible, yes."

"And if I take it off?"

"Taking it off will not change the course of your marriage. Only you can steer that."

"And you can't reverse it? The spell?"

"I can't reverse a spell I didn't cast, dear. Sometimes nature makes its own destiny. Just be sure your destiny doesn't follow your mother's."

Grace suddenly felt trapped. She cared for Alfred, but she wasn't naïve, either. She knew that what had transpired between them was more the result of infatuation than love, and she wondered if Alfred felt the same.

Francesca faced Grace as she led her to the porch.

"Love your husband, Grace, and only your husband, and hopefully he will do the same. You come back and see me if you want to awaken your sleeping gifts."

With that, Francesca smiled and closed the door. Grace felt dazed as she walked down the steps. She wasn't sure she understood anything that Francesca had said.

* * *

Later that night as she lay in bed watching Alfred undress across the room, Grace could still hear the old woman's words resonating through her head: *Love your husband and only your husband.*

When Alfred realized his wife was watching him, he faced her and smiled. "What are you thinking about?"

As he stood, Grace was reminded of how handsome he was. His face was sun-kissed, his curly, black hair was mussed, and his strength was visible as he stood before her bare-chested in his dirty trousers.

"Are you happy, Alfred?" she asked as she stood and walked toward him.

"Of course I am. Why wouldn't I be?"

"This wasn't your plan. You were going to the seminary. Do you regret not going?"

"I have no regrets," he whispered as he placed his hands on his wife's shoulders and kissed her forehead.

She pulled him closer. "I'm so sorry, Alfred," she said.

"Sorry for what?" He moved to look into her eyes.

"For so many things," she said before kissing his lips. He pulled away at first, trying to understand what she meant, but he leaned closer when he saw the look in her eyes. It had been weeks since they were last intimate.

Running her hands across his chest, Grace recalled that first night when they were together beside the lake. It was so innocent then. There were no heavy feelings of responsibility pushing them down.

As they kissed in the moonlight, Alfred lifted his wife and placed her gently on the bed. When they made love, Grace could feel how much Alfred loved her and she wished she felt the same. She knew he was a good man and had given up everything for her, yet she still felt a distance between them.

The following morning, Grace felt lost as she tried to understand all that Francesca had said. So much had transpired. How could she sort it all out? Feeling overwhelmed, she left Isabella with Calista and walked to the lake to clear her head. She hadn't been to the water in some time, and everything Francesca had told her made her want to believe that the images she'd seen of her mother were real. If she truly had the gift that the old woman spoke of, she might be able to reach out to her mother somehow.

As she walked through the cool trees, she thought of all the times she had walked this way before, waiting for her mother to appear. It had always happened the same way, always as she looked into the water. The watery image would be distorted at first and slowly grow clearer, until she could make out even her mother's dark brown eyes and warm smile. The first few times her mother appeared, Grace had turned quickly to see if she was standing behind her, but she never was. Then, upon looking back to the water, the image would be gone. But as time passed, Grace resisted the urge to turn so she could stare into her mother's eyes for just a few seconds longer before the image warped and faded.

This time, as she approached the lake's edge and stared into the water, the wind picked up behind her. Though the day was peaceful and calm, Grace thought she heard faint whispering in the breeze that gently pushed past her. Though she couldn't make out the words, or even a specific voice, she knew her mother was there. She looked into the water, but there was nothing staring back at her other than her own reflection. Saddened, that slow, deep ache returned to her chest. So many times she had tried to block the hurt, but right now it was no use. She missed her parents immensely. With all she had learned about them since her mother's death, she suddenly felt as if she had barely known them at all. She wondered how they could have hidden so much for so long.

As the whispering continued, Grace closed her eyes and allowed the breeze to blow across her face. It felt like warm, soft silk as it touched her. The harder she tried to tune into the voices, the quieter they became, until they were completely replaced by the natural sound of wind pushing through the leaves. As she opened her eyes and looked into the water again, she still saw only her own rippled reflection. Disappointed, she turned away. But as she turned, she caught a glimpse of a figure standing behind her. Startled, she gasped and focused her eyes, only to realize there was no one there. She turned back toward the water, only to see her own reflection yet again.

She said aloud, "If you're there, why don't you show yourself? Help me understand everything that you never told me."

Again, the only sound was the leaves rustling as the wind passed through.

Grace grew impatient. “Why aren’t you here now?”

Slowly, she lowered herself to the grass, closed her eyes, and listened. The soft whispering returned, but she still couldn’t make out what it was saying. It sounded like several voices talking at once, but not in unison. The confused chatter circled around her and a cold vapor enveloped her. Again, the harder she focused on the sounds, the fainter they became. Then they disappeared altogether. Frustrated, Grace opened her eyes and leaned back on the grass, looking toward the sky. Lying this way made her thoughts shift to Alfred. She remembered the first time she saw him. She had sat in this place on that same day, daydreaming about him and wanting to know more about him. And then, just a short time later, she had made love to him here and her old life quickly disappeared. This place hadn’t been the same since then.

As she rolled to her feet and brushed strands of grass from her skirt, Grace gave up and began walking back toward the farm. She thought of Alfred the entire way. She knew how much he cared for her, but she wondered if, deep down inside, he had the same doubts about their relationship that she had. She knew she could never tell him all the things that Francesca had said. Alfred wouldn’t understand talk of witchcraft and spells. He was a faithful man. He prayed each morning, at every meal, and every night before bed. It was almost ironic how fate had led them together.

As she reached the house, tired and dismayed, Grace sat on the porch swing and slowly began to rock. The sun was slipping lower in the sky and Alfred would be back soon.

"You seem distant today," Calista said as she carried the baby onto the porch.

"I'm sorry. I'm just distracted," Grace said as she lifted Isabella into her arms. "I was thinking about my mother."

"No need for apologies. Miss Izzy and I had a lovely time together," she replied as she dabbed the baby's cheek.

"I went to see Francesca Morano yesterday," Grace said, not looking at her aunt.

"I wondered if you had," Calista said sucking in her breath.

"She's not what I expected. She said she and your mother were close friends."

Calista leaned back into the swing and looked out across the field. "Yes, they were. They were best friends."

"Why didn't you ever tell me that?"

"I didn't think it mattered, Grace," Calista whispered.

"You said you were afraid of Francesca, yet you forgot to mention that she was your mother's best friend? That doesn't make sense to me, Calista."

"All I can tell you is that woman is a witch and my mother wanted her to protect your father," Calista replied softly.

"She also said my mother practiced witchcraft. Did you know that?"

"Yes."

Grace stood up quickly. "Did my father know?"

"Of course he did."

"Why didn't anyone tell *me* this?" Grace said as she shifted the baby in her arms and stared down at her aunt, who was still seated in the swing.

“Because, Grace, your mother had been through enough. She didn’t want you to go down the same path she had.”

Grace laughed sarcastically and stared at her aunt. “You all wanted to protect me and wanted me to be different, so you hid everything from me? Now here I am, on this farm, married and with a daughter—and surrounded by lies. Seems to me I’m exactly the same as all of you.” Full of anger, Grace kept her back to her aunt as she stared into the fields beyond the yard. The sky grew darker as Alfred walked from the barn with that same tired shuffle that Henry exhibited for all those years.

Chapter 42

February 4, 2006, 5:00 p.m.

Joe stared ahead as he turned off the truck's ignition. The hospital loomed before him and he dreaded going inside. If Ellie knew what he had done that last night at the bar—he couldn't bear the thought of what she might do. His stomach turned and he felt an urge to vomit. Clutching the truck's door handle, he waited for his heart rate to slow and his stomach to calm. He wasn't sure if he would make it all the way to Ellie's room without being sick.

As he waited, he tried to think of something happy. He recalled the last vacation they had taken. They had gone to the Mayan Riviera. They sat on the soft, silky sand during the final night of the trip and watched the sun disappear into the ocean. Just before it vanished, the sky turned a beautiful coral-colored shade of pink. As she stared into the distance, Ellie let out a long, slow sigh. "And the sun sets on another vacation," she whispered.

Joe had laughed and poured more wine into the empty glass beside her. As he looked up, he caught her gazing across the water again, strands of dark hair falling across her face. As she tucked them behind her ears, he noticed how soft her eyes had become. A devious little smile stretched across her face and he wondered what she was thinking. But, fearing he would lose this beautiful, peaceful image of her, he decided not to ask. He already knew that she was most likely imagining a happy future that included children he didn't want to have. Instead of bringing her back to reality, he decided just to watch and to give her this contented moment. He hoped her thoughts could gratify her...at least for the moment.

When she finally caught his glance, she smiled sheepishly. "Why are you watching me?"

"Because you look so happy right now," he said as he lifted the glass and handed it to his wife. She laughed, looked up at the now-dark sky, and took a long, slow drink of wine.

"Of course I'm happy," she said as she gulped her wine. This made Joe laugh and reminded him how much he loved her sometimes unladylike ways.

"Are you really?" He almost meant it as a rhetorical question.

She reached across the space between them and clutched his hand. "I'm happy when I'm with you. I'm happy that we're thousands of miles from home, and I'm happy there are no distractions here."

With that, she smiled and waited for his response. He knew exactly what she meant. Here it felt like they were the only two people that mattered. There was no past and no future, just the present. If only things could stay that way. There would be no problems if only he could be this person all the time.

Joe said nothing and simply extended a hand to brush the strands of hair from her face.

"Let's never go home," she whispered.

"Home is anywhere you are," he said softly, pulling her closer. For hours, they watched the waves in silence before heading back to their room.

Still clutching the door handle, Joe wished they had stayed in Mexico. He was fine when he was away with Ellie—*they* were fine. But back home, he always fell into his old ways. The pressures of work and the foreboding guilt of a past life stayed with him. He hadn't realized how much it pressed down on him until now. He had everything a man could ask for, yet he still wasn't satisfied and he still couldn't shake off everything that had happened in the past.

"It's not like you killed someone," Peter always said whenever Lisa and Andrew came up in conversation. But it felt like he had; he felt like he was covering up a murder. Maybe it was a metaphor for trying to murder his former self, but he wasn't sure he was a better man now than he had been before. Perhaps this man was worse. This man had a loving, beautiful wife, yet he was a functioning drunk who had been unfaithful.

Joe forced himself out of the truck and began walking toward the hospital. With acid still burning his throat, he remembered what his mother had once said about karma: "Whenever you wrong someone in this life, Joey, expect that wrong to come back around." How prophetic those words seemed now.

Chapter 43

February 3, 2006, 3:00 a.m.

The frigid wind outside Grace's cabin picked up again and Ellie rocked nervously in the chair. She was fuming from what Grace had just told her about Joe being unfaithful again. She didn't want to believe it, but deep down, she wasn't surprised. She wasn't sure if her tears were more from anger or sadness. She was furious that he couldn't change and be the man she needed him to be.

"I'm sorry I upset you," Grace said as she reached across the small table between them and touched Ellie's hand. Her fingers were cold, but the gesture was kind. Ellie looked up and wiped her tears away.

"I'm telling you these things so you can set us all free. That is why you are here. It's time we all stop telling secrets."

"I love Joe," Ellie whispered. "I know he doesn't deserve it sometimes, and I know maybe I could've been happier with someone else. But I won't give up. Not now, not after all this time."

Her cold hand gripped Ellie's harder. "Then you mustn't give up. I was young when I met Alfred, and I didn't think of the consequences of our actions. I didn't realize what would happen. Alfred was a good man."

"You were unfaithful to Alfred?" Ellie asked, knowing that must be what Grace was trying to say.

The old woman took a deep breath, as if Ellie had just stabbed her in the chest. "Yes, I was unfaithful. I didn't expect it, and I knew it was wrong. I knew all that Francesca had warned me about, but I did it anyway."

"Did you still love Alfred?"

"I will always love Alfred because he gave me my daughter, but ours was a love that spurred from a childish infatuation. It happened too fast and too soon. I was a child. I didn't understand what loving a man meant until much later. I should have let Alfred go. If I had never told him about your grandmother, he would've had a different life, and perhaps I would have had a different life as well. We all must live with the choices we make in life, Ellie, but sometimes it's so easy to wish you could change things. Joe wishes he could change things, too."

"He probably wishes he could change the fact that he married me."

"No, dear, that's the one thing he wouldn't change," Grace snapped. "He wishes to be a better man, a better husband. He wishes for the return of lost time and to take back the things he can't undo."

"How do you know all this?"

"Because those are the same things I wish for when I think of Alfred…though I would have set Alfred free."

"Can you tell me about what happened with you? With the affair?" Ellie straightened and sat up in her chair. She wanted to hear about anything other than what Joe was doing when she couldn't see him.

"It happened not long after I met Francesca that first time," Grace began. "Even though she had warned me to stay faithful, I felt things that I never thought I would feel again when I met Jack Snow. He changed me—not in the same way that Alfred changed me, but he made me realize that I was a woman and not a little girl. I knew how dangerous it was to love him, but once again, I allowed my heart to lead the way."

Ellie listened closely and watched the color return to Grace's face as she spoke. "How did you meet him?"

"Jack was the new veterinarian after Dr. Murphy retired. My horse, Belle, was getting older and she fell ill that spring. Alfred called the doctor and Jack showed up the very next morning. From the first time he stepped out of that truck, I knew I was in trouble." She laughed.

Chapter 44

June 1941

Grace stood next to Belle, stroking her mane and whispering softly in her ear. "It's alright, old girl. The doctor is on his way."

The mare had grown so thin from lack of eating, and her eyes seemed sad and sunken. From the stall across the way, her foal, Rocco, now fully grown, bucked his head and whinnied in a way that worried Grace even more. For a moment, she left Belle's side and stood before Rocco. His large head shook up and down, not violently, but in a troubled way. "Shhhh, Rocco," she whispered. "Be calm. It's going to be okay." She held out her hand. Rocco shifted his head to the side and sniffed Grace's fingers, his large nostrils curling up into a snort. She ran her fingers across the broad white spot on his nose and looked into his deep brown eyes. He was such a gorgeous horse, and she couldn't help but recall the night of his birth. How focused Alfred had been. How taken she was by his way with the horses. Though it had only been five years, it all seemed so long ago now.

Outside, a truck rattled up the drive. She knew it had to be Doc Murphy, and she sighed with relief as she walked toward the bright sunlight streaming through the barn entrance. The truck kicked up a cloud of dust when it stopped before her, and she was surprised to see a younger man with disheveled blonde hair and dirty khaki pants instead of Doc Murphy. As he jumped out of the truck with a medical bag in hand, he must have noticed the surprised look on her face.

"Hello, there. I'm Dr. Jack Snow. I spoke with your husband last night about your mare."

She stumbled on her words when she responded. "Ah, yes. I'm Mrs.…um…Grace."

"Nice to me you, Mrs. Grace," he said with a bright smile, extending his hand. He exuded such confidence that Grace found herself nervous and caught off guard.

"I'm sorry, it's just Grace, not Mrs. Grace," she said with an awkward laugh. Butterflies fluttered in her stomach as she shook his hand and looked away. "Let's take a look at that mare, shall we?" Jack said as he waited for Grace to lead him into the barn.

"Forgive me for seeming surprised," she said, "but Doc Murphy has been our veterinarian for years."

"Ah, yes. I apologize for not letting you know sooner, but Dr. Murphy recently retired. I've been his apprentice for about a year now and he left the practice in my care. I explained it to your husband on the telephone."

"I see." Grace sighed. "He must've forgotten to mention it to me. He's been preparing the fields for planting and has been a little distracted."

"I understand," Jack said with a smile. Grace couldn't help but notice his sparkling blue eyes and handsome face. His skin wasn't weathered from the sun like Alfred's was. As he walked ahead of her to Belle's stall, she noticed that even with his shabby, dirty pants and disheveled hair, there was something intriguing about him.

“Is your family from this area?” she asked, surprising herself with her forwardness.

“No, I’m actually from the Chicago area,” he said without facing her. His attention was focused on Belle. He looked into the horse’s eyes and ran his finger over her slender back. “My father was an old acquaintance of Doc’s, and when I finished school, he suggested I come up and see if Doc needed a hand. I’ve been here ever since. Tell me, what’s been happening with Belle?”

As he ran his hands across Belle’s ribs, Grace noticed he wasn’t wearing a wedding ring.

“She hasn’t been eating as heartily as usual and she seems to be drinking a lot more.”

“About how long has this been going on?” He opened Belle’s mouth to look at her tongue and gums.

“Maybe three weeks now with the lack of eating, but sometimes she gets picky about her oats and hay, so I tried not to worry right away.”

“Well, she’s definitely thin and dehydrated. Have you changed her feed at all lately?”

“No, she’s getting the same as usual. Rocco has been eating the same and hasn’t fallen ill.” She motioned to Rocco in the opposite stall.

“Well, I’m going draw blood for some tests that could help give us some idea as to what might be going on.”

Grace nodded and watched as Jack disappeared to retrieve what he needed from the truck. Watching him go, she took a slow, deep breath, trying to shake off the butterflies in her stomach. When he returned, she excused herself and slowly walked back toward the house.

When he was finished, Jack approached the porch, where Grace sat reading a book with Isabella. In the early evening light, his hair was dishwater blonde but his eyes were still bright. He wore wire-rimmed glasses now, which made him appear a bit more distinguished than he had earlier.

"What a beautiful little girl," he said, flashing a bright smile as he came closer.

"My name is Isabella. I'm seven," she said, extending a hand to the stranger. "You must be the horse doctor."

Grace laughed as she stood and put her hands on her daughter's shoulders. "She's forward. I apologize."

"No apologies necessary," he said as his eyes shifted from Grace to Isabella. "Indeed I am the horse doctor, and dog and cat and rabbit doctor, too. You and Belle have similar names."

"I'm named after my grandma, and Belle was her horse," the little girl said with a wide grin.

"That's very interesting. I'm sure she was a nice lady."

"I never met her, but Momma said she could make spells."

"Ah, yeah, that's enough honey," Grace cut in. "Why don't you go see if Aunt Calista needs help setting the table."

Isabella skipped off toward the kitchen and Grace looked back toward Jack. "She has a vivid imagination," she said.

"Most kids do," he said with a laugh.

"Do you have children?" Grace asked quickly.

Jack snickered. He looked down at his feet and kicked at the dusty ground. "No, I don't have kids, but someday I'd like to have a bunch."

Just then, Grace heard the sputtering sound of the tractor coming up from the field. Alfred waved from the driver's seat as he turned to drive toward the barn.

"Well, I guess I should be going. I just wanted to tell you that I gave Belle a thorough look-over and took some samples. I should know more about her condition in a few days. In the meantime, feel free to call me if things get any worse."

"I'll do that, and thank you," Grace said as Jack turned to go.

As Jack's truck left the drive, Alfred walked up from the barn, wiping sweat from his brow. He looked toward the road as he lifted his hat and pushed back the mop of black hair beneath it. The butterflies in Grace's stomach faded now.

"Was that the new doctor?" He asked as he kissed his wife on the forehead.

"Yes, it was," Grace replied, watching the dust cloud from Jack's truck settle before her.

"What'd he have to say about Belle?"

"He's running some tests and he'll get back to us soon."

"Alright, then. I'm going to get cleaned up for supper," he said as he shuffled up the stairs. When the screen door slammed behind him, Grace once again stared toward the road. She laughed at herself for the giddy feelings that left her insides tingling. It had been so long since she'd had a conversation with another man. She wasn't sure if it was Jack that excited her or just the interaction with someone outside her family. It felt good to look into a stranger's eyes. She hoped the young doctor would return soon.

Chapter 45

February 4, 2006, 5:30 p.m.

As he came off the elevator, Joe glanced quickly down the hallway at the empty nurses' station. As he turned to walk toward Ellie's room, he was surprised at how quiet the entire floor seemed, as if he were the only one there. He hesitated for a second and looked back down the hall to where he had seen several busy nurses earlier in the day, but now there was no one. He looked in the other direction and saw nothing but shiny floors and rows of doors. No doctors, no nurses, no people visiting patients. He felt oddly alone. Above him, halogen lights buzzed. He stopped, closed his eyes, and honed in on the sound. For some reason, it calmed him and drowned out the static inside his head. Suddenly, a voice came out of nowhere and snapped him back to reality.

"Mr. McHugh, are you alright?"

He spun around to see Ellie's obstetrician behind him.

"I…I'm fine," he said catching his breath. "I didn't hear you come up behind me."

"I'm sorry," she replied with a slight laugh. "I just came from the door behind you."

Joe nodded and shook his head, trying to lose the eerie feeling that had suddenly come over him.

"I was in to see Ellie earlier. She seems to be stable. That's good news." Her tone was optimistic.

"Yeah, that's good," he replied without making eye contact. For some reason, this woman made him nervous. He shifted awkwardly on his feet.

"The baby's heart rate is still normal and strong."

Joe looked up from the shiny floor. "That's good. Thank you."

The doctor shifted the file she held in her hand and touched the base of her glasses. "You know, Ellie told me you weren't expecting this baby. Is there anything you'd like to talk about or any questions I can answer for you?"

Joe wasn't surprised by the doctor's words, but he felt a tinge of guilt in realizing his wife had told this woman about his fears.

"I really…I really don't know how to feel about all this right now," he said quietly as he looked past her. "I wasn't expecting any of this."

The doctor sighed and shifted the folder again. "Ellie wasn't expecting this, either. You should know that. She was very indifferent about what to do when she came to me. I suggested she tell you, but she wasn't ready."

"I haven't made things easy for her lately," he mumbled.

The doctor seemed to know more than she was telling, and Joe wasn't sure what he should or should not say.

"I'll be checking in on Ellie from time to time, but feel free to call me if you have any questions," she said, handing Joe a business card.

"Thank you," he softly replied.

As she turned to go, she hesitated and spun to look at him over the top of her dark-framed glasses. "You know, this is really none of my business, but Ellie mentioned that you have another child that you never told her about."

The shaken and surprised look on Joe's face made her soften her tone and she stepped closer to him. "She really didn't want you to think she did this on purpose. That's all I wanted to say." She turned and walked away, the click of her heels echoing in the empty hall. Joe stood still as he watched her go. He knew that even this woman must be judging him.

As he pushed through the door to Ellie's room, he realized little had changed in the short time he had been away. She was still motionless and attached to machines. Anna slept in a chair across from the bed. He decided not to wake her as he quietly slipped into the chair beside Ellie. As he looked at his wife, he ran his fingers over the ring on her right hand. She had always worn this ring, even on the day he first met her. It was a family heirloom that Anna had given her. It wasn't worth much, she had always told him, but it belonged to four generations of her family and she wasn't about to break that tradition.

"I'm surprised she still wears that," Anna said, her voice breaking the silence. Joe didn't look up; he simply kept running his fingers along the back of Ellie's hand and over the ring.

"She never takes it off," he said, still watching her hand, waiting for it to move under his touch.

"I never took it off either, not until the day I gave it to her. She was seventeen then," Anna said, moving closer. "It was my mother's."

Joe looked up and noticed how red Anna's eyes were. She looked as if she had been crying while he was gone. "Anna, why don't you get some rest? I'll stay."

"You know, Joe, this girl is the best thing I've ever done with my life. She has been my entire world since the very day she came into it."

"I know, Anna."

"She's the only thing in my life that I've ever truly been proud of. She's strong, she's beautiful, and I'm so grateful to be a part of that. Nothing else in my life ever seemed as important as she is. Not my job, not even my husband."

"I know," he said, looking down at his wife.

"But, she is her own person, and she's never been a great judge of character."

He knew what was coming now.

"When she met you, she was so happy. You were everything she was looking for."

Joe stayed quiet.

"But something's changed, Joe, hasn't it? She won't tell me. She knows I worry, but I know there's something happening between the two of you that isn't right."

He let out a heavy sigh. "I haven't been a good husband to her lately," he whispered, knowing Anna was the last person he should be confessing to.

"What did you do Joe?"

"There's so much I haven't done and too much I can't undo," he said as his eyes filled with tears. "All I know is that's all over now. I just want her back. The rest doesn't matter anymore, and I'll do whatever I can to make her understand how sorry I am."

Anna didn't need to hear more. She put her hands on Joe's shoulders and squeezed gently. "Then make her understand," she said.

Chapter 46

February 3, 2006, 3:10 a.m.

"Have you thought of a name for your baby?" Grace asked as she rose from her chair and walked toward the window. Outside, a light snow had begun to fall and the sky was pitch-black.

"No. I've been so preoccupied with how to tell Joe that I haven't given it much thought," Ellie replied as she squinted into the blackness beyond the window.

"A child's name is so important. I should've given it more thought when I named your grandmother, but naming her after my mother seemed to make sense."

"Did you and Alfred consider having more children?" Ellie asked after pondering Grace's comment.

Grace laughed slightly. "That's an interesting question."

Ellie was unsure how to take her response, but she decided not to prod.

Grace continued. "We did talk of having more children, but it never seemed to happen." She turned away from the window, then slowly moved across the room to sit back down in her rocking chair. Ellie wondered how many times Grace engaged in the same routine every day. Time never seemed to pass here—there were just empty, timeless hours.

"Have you ever noticed that you come from a line of only-child mothers and daughters?"

Until then, the thought hadn't occurred to Ellie.

"My mother was an only-child daughter, as was I, as was your grandmother, and your mother…and you. Why is that, do you suppose?" She asked almost as if she expected Ellie to answer the question.

Ellie shrugged and shook her head. "I don't know, Grace."

"My mother once told me that the connection between a mother and a daughter is the strongest bond on earth," Grace continued. "It goes deeper than love. Deeper than any connection between a man and a woman, or even a mother and a son."

Her words made Ellie think of her relationship with her own mother. She loved her mother, of course. But, there were also many things she kept from her mother. Sometimes she preferred not to share things with Anna because Ellie knew how much her mother would worry.

"You'll soon see, dear, that birthing a child is messy," Grace continued, as if talking to herself. "It's dreadfully painful and goes on for hours. But when that pain and struggle are over, well—then you experience one of the true miracles in this life. A tiny being that grew inside of *you* has now entered the world. If that child is a boy, he will know right away that this is his world. He can go anywhere, do anything, and become exactly what he was meant to be. But if that child is a girl, well…things are different. She must prove who she is and what she is meant to be. Her will is not paved quite so easily. She must find it, develop it, and achieve it. And when all that is done, after she has forged her own path and is ready to bring forth more life into the world, she, too, will continue the painful circle and know what it means to be a woman."

Ellie blinked and stared at Grace's face. Her words were stern, but Ellie understood.

"Women know the pain of other women," Grace said with a nod.

"So why have there only been one-daughter families for so many generations?" Ellie asked, not intending to change the subject but wanting to know more.

"Because that is what is meant to happen in this family," Grace answered quickly. "Because we are strong women. We were stronger than any son could have possibly been, and we knew there was work to be done. We knew that it was time to prove a woman's worth."

Ellie squinted.

"Strength comes from strength," Grace said. "It's like that story Francesca Moreno told about the walnut tree. Some things just know the power they possess, and they won't stop no matter how many times you cut them down."

Chapter 47

Late June 1941

As Jack Snow pulled up the drive, Isabella rushed into the house with an excited burst of energy. She shouted, "Mommy, the animal doctor is back!"

Calista was slowly moving about the kitchen and Grace was readying linens to be washed. As her daughter clamored into the room, Grace felt a tinge of exhilaration.

"Alright, Izzy, I'm coming," she said, exchanging a glance with Calista, who turned from her work curious about this new doctor.

"Who is this young man?" Calista followed her niece to the porch.

"He replaced Doc Murphy," Grace mumbled as she pushed open the screen door to see Jack moving up the walkway leading to the porch. He wasn't dirty like he had been on the previous visit. This time he wore a fresh button-down shirt and pressed dungarees. His blonde hair was combed back and he wore his rimless glasses. But something else was different about Jack. He wasn't smiling—his face appeared almost sullen.

"Is it bad news?" Grace asked as she studied the look on his face.

He slowly nodded his head as Isabella suddenly burst past her mother.

"Hi, doctor!" she said loudly, a giant smile on her face.

Jack looked away from Grace and down to the little girl standing before him. His eyes softened as he placed one of his smooth hands on top of her head.

"Why, hello there, Isabella," he said softly.

"Have you come to see Belle and make her better? She's sick, you know."

He sighed, bent down, and touched the little girl's nose. "Yes, I know she's sick. That's why I've come to talk to your mom."

"Sweetie, why don't you come in the house and help me peel some apples for the pie," Calista said as she ushered the little girl away.

"Okay. Bye, doctor." Isabella turned to follow Calista.

"What is it?" Grace asked, her heartbeat quickening.

"It's not good, I'm afraid," Jack said, his tone serious. "The blood tests are showing some abnormalities. I'm not sure about everything yet, but I've seen this type of thing before."

"What is it?" She asked impatiently.

Jack hesitated and kicked at the sidewalk with his new-looking boots. "The other horses I've seen with these same symptoms were in early stages of renal failure…but I could be wrong. I just don't know enough yet to say that's what it is," he said, suddenly changing his tone.

Grace covered her face. Belle had been such an intricate part of her life for so long, and the horse was the only living part of her mother she had left.

"Will she be alright?"

Jack met her eyes. "It may just be that her kidneys are slowing down and not working quite like they were before. If I can stabilize her with fluids, she might be able to hang on for a few more years…or longer, maybe."

He lifted his hands, trying to reassure her, but Grace felt what was coming. "What…what should we do? I don't want her to suffer."

"I don't think we need to do anything drastic here," he said, raising his hands again. "I think we should just keep her drinking and give her some fluids to keep her from getting dehydrated. I'm also going to call some friends out West and see if they have any ideas. A change in diet might help."

"Alright." Grace sighed.

"I'm going to give her a check, if you'd like to come with me?" Jack motioned toward the barn.

Grace nodded and quickly stepped forward, but that excited feeling was now replaced with worry. They were silent as they walked. Suddenly, a sharp wind rushed past, cutting through her so swiftly that it made her catch her breath.

"Boy, it's windy today," Jack said with a half-smile as he noticed her surprise.

"Yes," Grace whispered, but there was something odd in the breeze that gave her an eerie, anxious feeling.

As they entered the barn, Rocco poked his head out of the stall with eyes bright and ears pricked. Jack rubbed his head. "He's a great-looking horse."

"He's Belle's only foal," Grace answered as she touched Rocco's face. She looked deep into his eyes, and he stared back without flinching. "He knows about Belle, I think."

"Animals have a funny way of figuring things out long before we do," Jack said as he turned toward Belle's stall. He stuck his hands deep into his pockets like a nervous schoolboy.

Belle stood quietly in her stall, but she seemed completely uninterested in anything around her. Her eyes were open and her ears were up, but she wasn't alert. She was gaunt and looked up slightly as Jack approached.

"She doesn't look good, but she doesn't look any worse than she did the other day," Jack said as he opened the stall door. "Has she been eating?"

"Very little," Grace replied as she entered the stall and stood near Belle, stroking her mane. From this close, she could smell Jack's musky aftershave.

"Her ears aren't pinned. That's a good sign," he said as he rubbed her ears and looked deep into her eyes. "When they're pinned, we know she's in pain. Right now, maybe she's just feeling some discomfort."

Grace rested her head against Belle's neck and ran her fingers across the horse's silky body. "I don't want her to be in pain," she whispered.

Jack stood straight and watched Grace. Her eyes closed and she leaned into the horse.

"What is she telling you?" He said after a couple minutes.

Grace quickly opened her eyes and stepped back. "I…I don't know what you mean."

"Yes, you do. She talks to you, doesn't she? I don't mean in a literal sense, but you know what she's feeling?"

"I wouldn't say that. I just feel like I can read her," Grace said.

“You can tell a lot by looking into an animal’s eyes and watching their body language,” he said as he stepped back and lifted Belle’s snout. She lifted her head nervously, but then calmed and blinked at him while twitching her mane.

“What is she telling you?” Grace asked as she looked into Jack’s deep, green eyes.

“That she’s not ready to leave you yet. She wants to stay here a while longer.” A smile stretched across his face.

Surprised, Grace turned and watched as Belle lifted her head and pricked her ears. With a slight laugh, Grace looked back at Jack. “I think you’re right.”

“She’s definitely sick, but I think we have some time to work on this,” he replied.

With that, he turned and headed out of the stall. Grace followed and they made their way out of the barn.

Stepping into the bright sunlight, Jack looked back and noticed Grace glancing into the fields.

“Is your husband close with Belle, too?”

She quickly turned to face him. “He adores her…and Rocco.”

“I see. Well, I’ll try my best not to let the two—er, three—of you down.”

Grace smiled awkwardly. Their first meeting had seemed so much more natural than this. She and Jack both fumbled for words now, unsure what to say.

“Well, I’ll make some calls and I’ll come back to see Belle in a few days. Be sure to call me if anything changes, and again, keep her drinking.”

“I will,” Grace replied.

With that, Grace watched him hop into his pickup truck. It was odd to have another male presence on the farm after all this time, yet she couldn't deny her curiosity about this man. He was much different than Alfred—not better, just different. He wasn't as quiet or reserved as Alfred, and that intrigued her. Still, she could hear Francesca's voice ringing in her ears: "Love your husband…and *only* your husband."

Chapter 48

February 4, 2006, 9:00 p.m.

Joe had fallen asleep in the chair again. When he awoke, the room was dimly lit and quiet. His back was stiff and he looked around to see if Anna was still there, but she wasn't. He thought she must have taken his advice and gone home to get some rest. As he stood and stretched his back, he felt a slow, painful ache that resonated from his neck straight through to his head. The pain made him nauseous. He quickly sat back down. A cold sweat formed on his forehead and he knew he needed to get to the bathroom before he vomited on the clean, shiny floor. He struggled to get up, but his body felt numb and clumsy as he staggered toward the door. He cupped his hand over his mouth as his stomach convulsed, yet he still couldn't maneuver his uncoordinated body fast enough. He stumbled, finally reaching the door. He fell to his knees in front of the stool just in time. As he vomited, the pain in his stomach intensified and he gagged uncontrollably. When it was finally over, he stayed on his knees, gasping, tears streaming down his face. He didn't move as he waited for his breathing to return to normal.

When his strength returned, he stood, shakily at first, flushed the toilet, and turned toward the sink. He turned on the faucet and splashed cold, crisp water over his face. As it ran down and soaked his T-shirt, he began to feel a bit better. Catching his reflection in the mirror, he barely recognized the man staring back at him. He was pale, his hair was a mess, and he hadn't shaved in days so the stubble on his face made him look older. His tired eyes seemed sunken. He blinked, hoping his image would go back to normal, but it didn't. Since there was no towel that he could use to dry his face, he grabbed a piece of paper towel from the dispenser and wiped it over his skin. It was coarse, even against his unshaven face.

As he emerged from the bathroom, he looked across the room at Ellie, who lay unchanged in the bed before him. He returned to his uncomfortable chair and watched her sleep, wondering if she were aware of what had just happened. Whenever he had been ill in the middle of the night, she would sit up in bed and whisper, "What's the matter, baby?" He wished she would do that now.

As he stared at her, he recalled the morning after his encounter with the woman in the car. He had come in late and slept on the couch as usual. He heard Ellie come down the stairs and stand over him, but he didn't open his eyes. She said nothing and simply walked away. The smell of her coffee wafted from the kitchen, its strong aroma making his stomach turn. She readied herself for work and left without a word.

When he heard her car pull out of the driveway, he opened his eyes and stared at the ceiling. He mentally replayed the drunken scene and remembered walking to the woman's car. How could he have let it happen? He didn't even want sex with her, yet he didn't stop himself.

It seemed surreal now, but he knew what he had done. He had gotten drunk and slept with a stranger—the same stranger he had told Ellie about before. He had no interest in her, but he wasn't strong enough to resist her. The sex wasn't even good. It had satisfied him for a few moments, but it would never be worth what he stood to lose. His stomach turned again.

"Baby, can you hear me?" He watched Ellie's face for any sign of movement. There was none. "I fucked up, honey. I fucked up so bad." His voice cracked.

As he whispered the words, there was still no movement. "It was dumb and it meant nothing to me. I…I never wanted it to happen."

Part of him wished Ellie was awake and part of him was thankful that she wasn't. Still, it made him feel better to say the words out loud.

Chapter 49

February 3, 2006, 3:33 a.m.

Grace hadn't spoken in some time, but she suddenly sat straight in her rocking chair and looked around the room.

"Do you hear that whispering?"

Ellie didn't hear anything, but she leaned forward, straining to hear.

"Do you hear it?"

"No," Ellie said as she looked around the room. She felt an eerie chill.

"I think I hear your Joe again, but I can't make out what he's saying."

Ellie wasn't sure what to think anymore. She longed to hear Joe's voice, but she heard nothing. She wasn't sure if Grace was just trying to convince her that she heard voices or if she actually *did* hear voices.

Mayda appeared from a dark corner of the room and moved closer to the firelight. She arched her back and stretched her body, then lay down and began grooming the silky fur on her paws.

"I think Mayda heard it, too," Grace said, leaning back in her chair. "I'm surprised you can't. You must not be ready yet."

"Ready for what?"

"Ready to hear what he has to say," she said. "I wasn't ready to listen to Alfred either, but my situation was also much different. I should've been the one talking to him."

Ellie nodded.

"I should have told him how I felt about things before he ever put that ring on my finger, but times were different then. Women had fewer choices than they have today. A young single mother today is very much a normality, but back then…then it was like being branded with a scarlet letter, only the letter was a 'P' rather than an 'A.'"

"P?"

"Promiscuous, dear. The word had a much different connotation in those days. It wasn't something you wanted to be called. Plus, our choices were not the same as yours now. Abortion was something you did if you were desperate, and it was dangerous. And adoption, well, that wasn't fondly looked upon either if you were the one carrying the baby. Nothing but marriage could make you right again."

Ellie thought about what it must have been like to be pregnant in Grace's time. Just the thought of giving birth without modern medicine made her shudder.

"Did you ever consider leaving Alfred?" Ellie asked, unsure of whether Grace would take the question seriously.

Grace drew in a long, silent breath and exhaled slowly. "I cared for Alfred, dear, I truly did, but again, the situation we were thrown into was not natural. We thought it was natural the first night we made love next to that lake. But it was an impulsive, quick decision. We were both meant for other things, but we stayed together. We made it work as best we could."

Recalling how horribly their story ended, Ellie wondered how Grace could even say these things.

"Absolution is a funny thing, dear. You can wait for it and try to achieve it, but it can be elusive."

"Absolution? You mean forgiveness?" Ellie was surprised Grace would speak of something somewhat religious when their family seemed to have such a pagan history.

"Absolution can mean different things. It can mean forgiving yourself, or forgiving each other. To Alfred, it meant forgiveness from God, but to me, it meant forgiving myself for making such a mistake and turning Alfred's entire life around. I will never regret your grandmother, but she, too, knows the pain I've caused."

Ellie began to think of her grandmother. She was a small wisp of a woman—quick-witted, tough, but also funny and charming. Her mother had said she was something of a hippie. When Anna was young, her family had left Wisconsin for a while, going north to Toronto for a few years, then to Seattle, down to California, over to Chicago and eventually back home. Anna had hated the constant moving, starting new schools, and leaving just when she had made her first friends or kissed a boy. It was one of the reasons she refused to move when Ellie was a child. It wasn't until Ellie was in college that Anna sold the home they had lived in for years and bought a comfortable condo where she wouldn't need to worry about mowing a lawn or shoveling snow. Ellie had been glad when her mother moved.

"Did you ever visit Francesca again?" Ellie asked, curious about her family's history with witchcraft.

"I did, but it wasn't until later. There were many distractions that began to lay my path in a new, unexpected direction. But one day, when I was putting some of Isabella's baby clothes away in the attic, I came across an old chest that had been long forgotten in that dusty place. Inside, I found some of my mother's books and writings, and then I realized who she really was."

Chapter 50

July 1941

The door creaked as Grace pulled against it. As soon as it was open, an old, musty smell rushed down the dark, dusty stairs and filled the air around her. Beside her on the floor sat a basket of Isabella's baby clothes—things she didn't want to discard or give away but no longer had room for in her daughter's bureau.

Staring into the darkness, she hesitated before climbing the stairs. It had been years she last went into the attic, but she knew she had to put these things away. She had always been uncomfortable up there even though she had no reason to be. As a child, she would follow her mother up the stairs to put something away or retrieve something from an old box. As her mother busied herself, Grace would stand behind her, peering into the dark corners, waiting for something to lunge at her.

"It's just an attic darling," her mother would say with a broad smile. Then she would softly touch Grace's face and hug her close, so close Grace could smell her lavender perfume. It smelled so good that Grace never wanted to let go.

"It's just an attic," Grace said aloud, laughing at herself as she put one foot forward and made her way up the stairs. Beneath her feet, the hardwood loudly creaked. The stairs were so rarely used that the wood wasn't worn, but it was dry and groaned as she walked. When she reached the top and searched for the cord to turn on the light, she felt that old, familiar sense of panic. Beyond the lighted hallway at the bottom of the stairs, Grace heard Isabella playing with her dolls in her bedroom. Again, Grace reassured herself that there was no need to be afraid. Reaching through the musty air, she let out a sigh of relief as the cord brushed across her palm. She gripped it tightly, pulling fast and quick. There was a "click" and the room filled with light. Grace quickly peered around to be sure there were no unseen forces waiting to surprise her. She once again laughed aloud and looked for a place to store Isabella's things.

There wasn't much in the attic other than an old highchair she assumed her parents had used when she was a baby, a rocking horse, boxes filled to the brim with odds and ends, and several old, dusty chests. She walked across the room, swatting the occasional cobweb that brushed across her face as she went. When she reached the first chest, she placed the basket on the floor and attempted to brush some of the dust from the front of the old box. There was no name on it, but she assumed it had belonged to one of her parents.

As she lifted the top, that same strong smell of must and mothballs filled the air. Inside was what appeared to be her father's clothes—old trousers and a black, formal suit. She removed the jacket and imagined her father filling out its broad shoulders. It must have been his wedding suit, she guessed, and she pulled it close to her body, hugging it as if she were hugging him. After a few moments, she placed it back into the wooden box and continued rifling through the contents. She found nothing but an old hat and a few pairs of dusty dress shoes. Disappointed, she closed the lid and looked around.

Across the way was another dusty, beat-up chest. She was surprised to find it locked when she attempted to lift the top, so she moved to another that was nearby. As she pulled open the lid on the third chest, she peered down at a pile of clothes that appeared to be her mother's. There were some old dresses, a summer hat, a nightgown. There was also a long, lacy dress that had probably been white once but was now a yellowish-brown color, most likely from sitting inside the chest for so long. It was her mother's wedding gown.

Grace gasped as she pulled it out. She imagined how beautiful it must have been with its white lace and high neckline. The sleeves were sheer but long, and they puffed up slightly at the shoulder. She wondered why her father had never told her it was there. He must have known. As she unfolded the dress, she stood to compare it to her own body. Her mother had always been so slender and beautiful. When the bottom of the dress unfurled, there was a clink as something metal hit the hardwood. Looking down, she saw an old skeleton key lying on the floor. As she picked it up and held it in her hand, she wondered what it could be for. She didn't know of any locks in the house that required such a key. She also wondered why it would be wrapped inside her mother's wedding gown.

Slipping the key into her apron pocket, Grace's attention turned back to the dress in her hands. Like she had with her father's suit, she held the dress to her face. She inhaled slowly but smelled nothing but must while imagining what her mother must have looked like on her wedding day. Her parents must have been a stunning couple, her father with his strong, broad shoulders and her mother small and beautiful with her dark hair blowing in the breeze.

She could almost see them as they joined hands and stared into each other's eyes while speaking their vows. The thought made her miss them all over again. Snapping back to reality, Grace gently folded the dress and placed it inside the trunk. Though she wasn't sure what to do with all of these old things, she was certain she couldn't discard them.

Remembering the basket of Isabella's clothes, Grace brushed the dust off her apron. As she did so, she felt the outline of the key she had slipped into her pocket. Pulling it out to inspect it more closely, she looked around the room and wondered what it could be for. Then she remembered the locked chest.

Kneeling before it, Grace slid the key into the lock and attempted to turn it. Applying little force, she heard a distinct "click." Before she could change her mind, she opened the lid and, with a rush of excitement, looked down to see a stack of books and a stack of journals. Beside the books lay a silver necklace with a star pendant, an odd-looking stick with carvings marking the wood, and something wrapped in a black velvet cloth. Picking it up, Grace quickly unfurled the cloth and was surprised to find a small, dull knife with an ivory handle. Confused, she next selected one of the journals. After brushing the dust off the cover, she opened the book and immediately recognized her mother's handwriting. The first entry was dated August 12, 1921.

It's a quiet summer night and Henry and Grace have long gone to bed. I decided to take a walk to the lake since the moon was so bright, though not quite full. Standing before the water, I could see my reflection and I recited the words of the Water Spell. I waited but felt nothing. I am so lonely. I cried and then swam in the cool, dark water. It felt good. I love Henry so much, but he works so hard on this farm. I long for more time with him. I miss the walks and the talks we would have until late into the night. His mother stopped by the other day. After all this time, I know she still disapproves of me. I'm not sure why.

"Momma?" Isabella cried from the bottom of the stairs. Grace closed the book with a snap as her daughter's feet trod heavily on the stairs. She quickly gathered the things she had removed from the chest and placed them back inside, slamming the lid just as Isabella reached the top step.

"What are you doing, Mommy?" The little girl looked around the room.

"Nothing, sweetie. Just putting some old things away." She attempted to usher her daughter back toward the stairs.

"Wow, what is this place?" Isabella's voice was filled with such childlike amazement that Grace couldn't help but smile. Isabella was a much more adventurous child than she had ever been.

"It's just the attic, honey—just a room where we store old things. Come, now. Let's go back downstairs. It's dusty and dirty up here."

"But I want to look around, Mommy! Please?"

"Maybe another day, honey. We've got to get downstairs and start dinner before daddy gets home."

Disappointed, Isabella stomped her feet as she turned to go. As Grace ushered her daughter down the stairs, she took one look back at the chest she had just discovered. The skeleton key was still stuck in the lock. Confident no one would discover what she had found, she pulled the light cord and followed her daughter down the stairs, closing the door behind them.

Chapter 51

February 3, 2006, 3:57 a.m.

"Did you read more of your mother's journal?" Ellie asked. She peered across the room at Grace, who calmly rocked back and forth in her chair. Mayda was peacefully perched on her lap and purred contently under her touch.

"I did. I stole away to that attic every chance I had to continue reading my mother's writings," she said. "Most of the entries were filled with her everyday tasks of life on the farm, but others talked of magic and spells she'd attempted. All very innocent, really, but truly fascinating to me at the same time. I realized how similar our lives had turned out to be. Both of us had fallen in love quickly and lived on that farm, most of the time lonely and confused. I began to understand her better."

"What were the other things in the chest?" Ellie asked, wondering about the necklace, the stick, and the knife.

"Ah, yes. I wasn't sure what those things were at first. But the more I read her journals, the more I came to understand. The necklace with the star was a pentagram."

Ellie raised her eyebrows.

"Not to worry, dear. A pentagram is not an evil sign—it's quite the contrary. A five-pointed star with two points at the bottom is a sign of witchcraft. If it's flipped the other way, with two points on the top, well…that's when you're dealing with black magic."

Ellie nodded.

"The stick with the odd carvings was my mother's wand, and the knife was her athame."

"Athame?"

"Yes, dear. An athame is a knife witches use in rituals. It represents the fire element and has the function of power sent."

Ellie stared ahead, a confused look crossing her face.

"It's used to maintain and send power, dear," Grace said as if Ellie should innately understand the concepts she explained. "The wand is a reception of power for the witch, but the athame draws power on the basis of its strength. It protects the witch."

Ellie continued to stare blankly at Grace, who laughed slightly.

"These are all tools witches use, my dear. To understand them, you must understand the witch."

"Did you understand them?"

"Not at first, but I wanted to know more about my mother so I found myself seeking to understand her ways. I often wondered what my father thought of her practices, or if he even knew. My grandmother knew, so I'm sure he had to have known."

"What sort of spells did she cast?" Ellie asked.

"I don't think she truly *cast* spells. I think she used spells as a form of protection and to ward off negativity. Never once did she write about casting a negative spell. You see, dear, again, witches don't believe in casting negativity because whatever bad things you cause will come back to you. If we remembered that more in our everyday lives, things would be much simpler."

"Do you believe that?" Ellie asked.

“You wouldn’t be here if I didn’t believe, dear.” Grace smiled.

Chapter 52

February 4, 2006, 11:30 p.m.

Joe was tired of the hospital chair and anxious to leave Ellie's sterile, quiet room. His legs began to shake as the feeling of the walls closing in grew stronger. His heart began beating faster and he rubbed his rough, calloused hands over his face.

Suddenly the door opened and in walked a plain-looking but somewhat pretty nurse. She seemed surprised to see Joe sitting in the chair and she hesitated at first, but then she continued into the room

"I'm sorry to disturb you. I'm here to check her fluids," she said without making eye contact.

Joe nodded and stood up from the chair. He stretched his back and walked to the window to peer at the snowy pavement below. The nurse came around the bedside and busied herself with checking the machines and squeezing the bags of fluid that hung from the IV pole.

"Have you been talking to her?" she asked without looking up from her work.

Joe turned from the window. "A little."

"You should keep talking to her—it helps. I know people say that all the time on TV and in movies, but it's true." She scribbled on Ellie's chart. When the nurse was finished, she looked up and met his eyes. The woman looked oddly familiar, but Joe couldn't place her. She held his stare for a few seconds. Then she looked away nervously and tidied the sheets on Ellie's bed.

"See you later, Joe," she said, briskly exiting the room.

Joe was surprised the nurse knew his name. It left him momentarily puzzled. He glanced back down at the chair next to the bed but didn't want to sit there anymore. He wanted to walk, but he didn't want to leave Ellie alone. He heaved himself back into the chair with a sigh. His legs immediately began to shake. Staring at Ellie, he tried to think of something to say. He had already made his confession and he wondered if, by some chance, she'd heard and understood what he had said. Leaning forward, he rested his chin on the cool, silver bar on the side of the bed.

"Can you hear me?" he said aloud. "I don't know what to say to you right now other than please come back. They tell me I'm supposed to keep talking to you, but all I know how to say right now is how sorry I am. You shouldn't be here. You didn't do anything wrong. It was all me."

As he grabbed her hand, a helpless feeling sunk back into his chest. He didn't like not having control over the situation in front of him, and he had spent most of his life running. It wasn't long before thoughts of his mother seeped into his mind. Soon he was ten years old again and lying on his bed. He awoke to a loud crash from down the hall. From the bed beside him, Peter sprang up and rushed to the door.

"No, Peter, don't look," he pleaded as his brother shushed him and slowly opened the door. Through the lighted crack, Peter peered from their dark bedroom into the hallway. Their father's angry voice boomed. He was slurring, a sure sign he'd had too much to drink again.

"You fucking whore!" Their father screamed. Joe lay in his bed covering his face with a pillow. He counted like he did when waiting for thunder to crack after a lightning flash, hoping the distraction would keep him from hearing the argument down the hall. *"One…two…three…"*

"I didn't do anything, John," his mother cried. "He only said hello!"

"Who the fuck is he? How long have you been fucking him, you God damn whore?"

Joe pulled the pillow tighter. He had anticipated this scene as soon as his mother had told them that she and their father were going to the tavern down the street. He knew they would come back drunk and his father would be belligerent. He wondered why his mother never realized this or refused to go.

"John, I didn't do anything wrong. I don't even know the man. He *just* said hello."

Another crash came from the kitchen. Joe guessed his father had thrown another dish.

"Clean up this mess, you bitch. If you're gonna whore around, you can at least keep this God damn house clean."

Peter opened the door and rushed down the hall.

"No, Peter, don't," Joe whispered. But it was too late. Peter was already gone.

"Stop yelling at her!"

At the sound of Peter's voice, Joe jumped from the safety of his bed and rushed to the doorway.

"Peter, go back to your room," his mother said. Then there was the rush of footsteps and a heavy thud against the wall.

"Don't back-talk me, boy," his father said coldly.

Joe knew his father had Peter pinned. Their mother screamed, "Let him go, John. You're choking him!"

"Maybe he'll learn to respect his father."

Joe could almost feel his father's hands tightening on his own neck, just as they were tightening on Peter's.

Their mother continued screaming, yet Joe couldn't move. Suddenly, there was a loud crack followed by the thud of something heavy hitting the floor. Frozen with fear, Joe wasn't sure what to do.

Joe's mother said, "Are you alright, Peter?" as his brother sobbed.

"Is he dead?" Peter asked.

"I don't think so, sweetie. I think I just knocked him out. Come here."

Joe made his way down the hall. He was afraid of what he might see, but he knew he couldn't hide in the bedroom any longer. Across the hall, his younger brother David peeked out of his bedroom, his little eyes full of fear. Tears streamed down his face. Joe grabbed David's hand and led him down the hall.

As they came around the corner, Joe saw his mother and brother huddled together on the floor, shaking and sobbing as they clung to each other. Nearby, his father lay in a heap on the floor, a dark red puddle forming beneath his head. The sight made Joe freeze again. Something warm and wet ran down his legs. Looking down, he realized he had wet his pants.

Through her tears, his mother said, "Oh, Joey, it's okay, honey. Come here." She held Peter in one arm and reached for Joe and David with the other.

Joe folded into her and sobbed next to his brothers. Their mother stroked their hair and kissed the tops of their heads. “It’s okay, boys. It’s okay. We’re going to be alright.”

After a few minutes, she pulled away from them and looked into their eyes one by one.

“Listen to me, boys. Don’t you ever turn out like him.” She motioned toward their father, who lay still on the floor. “Don’t you drink and treat women the way he does. You treat women with respect. You show them what a real man is. Do you understand?”

The boys nodded and wiped the tears from their faces. Joe was suddenly embarrassed that he’d wet himself.

“It’s alright, Joey,” she said as she touched his face and wiped the tears from her own. When she gathered herself, she stood, stepped over their father, and moved toward the phone.

“Yes, I…I need an officer, please. I’ve just knocked out my husband.” Her face was expressionless. “Yes, please send someone right away. If he wakes up, he’ll kill me.”

Joe wiped the sweat that had begun to pool on his forehead. Trying to shake the memory, he looked at Ellie again.

“I’m not him, I’m not him,” he whispered, fighting off the nauseated feeling once again. “Just come back, Ellie. Please, just come back. I need you to keep me sane.”

Chapter 53

Late July 1941

Grace lay in bed listening to the sound of Alfred's breathing. The house was still, quiet, and dark. For a moment, she tried to match her breathing to Alfred's in order to lull herself to sleep. She held her breath and slowly exhaled at the same time he did, then drew in her breath even slower, but even that didn't work.

Giving up on sleep, she stepped out of bed and tiptoed to the door so she wouldn't wake her husband. The hardwood floor was cold beneath her feet and she was careful where she stepped to avoid the creaky planks. She had walked this floor so many times and memorized every board that made a sound. Closing the door softly, she stood in the dark hall for a moment, straining to listen for sounds of stirring within the house. Satisfied, she felt her way through the darkness until she found the attic doorknob under her fingers. She wanted to read more of her mother's journals without Alfred and Calista knowing. The door creaked as she slowly pulled it open. Hoping no one had heard, she grimaced. The familiar musty smell hit her as she slipped through the half-open door, but the attic no longer made her feel uncomfortable. Since she had found her mother's things, the attic had almost begun to feel like a sanctuary.

As she felt through the darkness for the light cord, a hint of excitement rose in her throat. It was almost as if she was doing something she wasn't supposed to do, but the temptation of it was too much not to indulge.

She hesitated again as she knelt before the chest, making sure there were no sounds from downstairs. Hearing nothing, she opened the lid and looked down at her mother's belongings. She picked up one of the journals she hadn't yet read. It was nothing special, just regular paper with a plain black cover. The pages were slightly brittle and the ink a little faded. She opened the cover and dove into the words.

September 4, 1926

I'm so conflicted. I feel lost on this farm, but I don't want to leave my husband and child. I love them so much.

I made love to Frank while Henry was in town. I feel terrible even writing this down, for fear Henry might find this, but I have to tell someone—even if it is just this book. I didn't mean for this to happen. I love my family. But Frank is so tender, so sweet; he doesn't make life complicated or mundane. Yet still, I know I've broken my vows and I fear what this will mean. I shouldn't have done it, but it felt so right. It has been so long since a man's touch has made me feel so uninhibited. He touched me so passionately. What am I going to do?

Grace's throat tightened as she read the words. There it was: a written confession. Her father had told her this information, but she had refused to believe it. She closed the book, suddenly uninterested in reading on. Still, she couldn't help but feel drawn to her mother considering that, at times, she also felt trapped on this farm. She sighed and opened the journal again.

September 10, 1926

I've met Frank in the bunkhouse for the past three nights after Henry has gone to sleep. We make love and talk for hours. I feel myself being drawn closer to him, though I know I should end this now. Frank has a family of his own...children, a wife. We both know what we have is temporary, yet we can't find a way to make it stop. I haven't made love to Henry in months. He's sure to become suspicious.

I look at Grace, my sweet and innocent daughter, and I wonder what will become of her if I don't end this. Will she be poisoned because of my mistakes? She must never know of this. She needs to know that her father is a good, loving man. He's not a man that deserves a cheating wife. He's a wonderful man. What am I doing?

A tear slipped down Grace's cheek. Before she could catch it, it fell to the pages below and saturated the paper. She tried to wipe it, but it would leave a permanent, ring-shaped stain across her mother's words. Looking around the room, she was overwhelmed. Grace had no idea how unhappy her parents had been. How could two people so in love drift so helplessly apart? She hadn't wanted to believe what her father had said about her mother. She wished she could tell him how wrong she had been. He must have been so hurt when he realized the truth. And she wanted to tell her mother just how much she understood the conflict of loving the man but not the life.

Grace leaned against the chest as she sat on the floor and looked down at the ring on her finger—the wedding ring that had once been her mother's. She wondered what stories it would tell if it could. She also wished she could take it off.

Realizing she couldn't read more of the journal, Grace placed the book back in the box. Sifting through the remaining journals, she came across a brown, leather-covered book with a pentagram drawn on the front. She ran her fingers over the star, tracing it as she went. Outside, the wind picked up, making the house creak around her.

There was an inscription on the front page, written in her mother's handwriting:

Book of Shadows-Isabelle Harper

On the front inside cover was some sort of poem her mother had written. Grace whispered the words and a chill ran down her neck. "This must be her spell book," she said aloud. As she flipped through the pages, she saw more poetry along with rhymes about bindings and protecting loved-ones from harm. There were also diagrams explaining where to place candles or how to cast circles. She wasn't sure what to make of it all. Grace wondered again why her mother had never spoken to her about her true religion.

Closing the book, she traced her fingers over the pentagram and decided it was time to see Francesca again. Holding the book in her hand, she returned the journals to the chest and closed the lid. For the first time since she had found it, she locked the chest and removed the key.

Clutching the book tightly to her chest, Grace made her way back down the stairs. Once at the bottom, she closed the door slowly and turned toward her bedroom.

"What were you doing in the attic at this hour?"

Startled, Grace turned to see her aunt standing in the doorway. Her face wasn't visible through the darkness.

"My gosh, you scared me, Calista," Grace replied, grabbing her chest with her free hand. "I…I couldn't sleep. I was just cleaning up some things in the attic."

"What've you got there?" Her aunt's unusually eerie voice cut through the darkness. Realizing she still held the book, Grace flipped it over to hide the pentagram even though it was too dark for Calista to see it.

"This?" She said motioning toward the book. "Oh, nothing. I was just journaling some thoughts while I was up there. I didn't want to bother anyone so I took it up there."

"I see," Calista replied. "Well, I'm going back to bed. Good night, then."

Grace was dumbfounded by her aunt's odd behavior. "Good night."

Slipping quietly into their bedroom, Grace hesitated to make sure Alfred had not awoken. She could see his outline in the moonlight coming through the window. As he lay in bed, his breathing was soft and calm. She knew he was still lost in his own dreams.

Grace tiptoed to the bureau and gently opened the top drawer, where she kept her linens. She slipped the book and the key inside, knowing Alfred would never open that drawer.

Grace gently crawled back into bed beside him and tried to match her breathing to her husband's. It wasn't long before she began to think of her mother and Frank Larsen. She recalled Frank's strong arms and dark, wavy hair. He had a chiseled face and a perfect smile. He was always pleasant and courteous to the family and often shared a beer with her father after a long day's work on the farm. She guessed that was before Frank and her mother had become intimate.

Listening to Alfred's breathing, she imagined her mother and Frank in the bunkhouse, wrapped in blankets and making love. She thought of the time that she and Alfred had also been overtaken by a moment of passion in that room. Things were so different now.

Chapter 54

February 5, 2006, 12:30 a.m.

Feeling closed in again, Joe needed to get out of Ellie's room—at least for a little while. Anna had returned and was resting comfortably in the very chair that had begun to feel like his personal torture device. As he stepped into the hallway, Joe looked up and down the corridor. Again, it was oddly quiet. He wasn't sure where to go. At the end of the hall, past the rows of closed doors on either side, there was nothing but another elevator and a stairwell. Not wanting to feel the vertigo-like sensation that the elevator always gave him, he decided to take the stairs.

As he pushed through the door and started down, his footsteps echoed and bounced off the walls with heavy thuds. When he reached the next floor, he decided to continue down. Joe had the odd, eerie feeling that he wasn't alone. It was so intense that he stopped to listen, but once the echo of his own steps vanished, there was nothing—just the sound of his breathing and the humming of the fluorescent lights above him.

Though he couldn't shake the strange feeling, Joe started again, walking faster this time, as if he were trying to outrun something he couldn't see. On the next floor, he slipped through the door and looked behind him in case anyone followed. Again, he saw nothing. As he hurried down the corridor, he heard faint voices from behind closed doors and soon found himself in front of a long window. He stopped short and peered inside. On the other side of the glass, a half-dozen tiny pink and blue bundles were swaddled and encased in portable bassinets, each with a name card at the end. He had found the nursery.

He didn't know why, but he stared at the babies in amazement. He'd had the baby conversation with Ellie so many times; each time, he had refused to let the idea in. And yet here he was. His eyes filled with tears as he watched the babies sleep, or fuss, or coo. For the first time in his life, he realized what a miracle they were. Calmness came over him as he watched. Nurses occasionally tended to one of the children. They smiled as they looked up at Joe's emotional face; embarrassed, he looked away. They most likely mistook him for a relative. He didn't know why, but seeing those babies was exactly what he needed.

After a while, he decided to keep walking. When he came to an elevator at the end of the hall, he headed back to Ellie's room. Though he expected no change in his wife's condition, he would now feel less trapped when he sat beside her.

As the elevator doors swung open, he was surprised to see the familiar nurse that had been in Ellie's room earlier. The same stunned look crossed her face as he entered without a word. When the doors slid shut, they were awkwardly quiet as the lights on the numbers above the elevator illuminated to mark the passing floors.

"You don't recognize me, do you?" The woman asked, breaking the silence.

Joe turned to look at her face and his heart nearly stopped beating. With one glance into her eyes, he finally knew where he had seen her before. He hadn't recognized her dressed in blue scrubs and with her dishwater-blonde hair pulled back, but it was the woman from the bar. He couldn't even remember her name.

"Uh, yeah, I, uh…" He stumbled, not knowing how to react.

"It's alright. You don't have to say anything. I'm not the same person here as I am there." She leaned against the back of the elevator and watched Joe shift nervously in front of her. "I was a little surprised, though—after the last time I saw you—that you just walked away."

Joe stared down, embarrassed. After they'd had sex, he couldn't stand to look at her face. He was filled with regret, and the only thing he'd known how to do was leave.

"I'm sorry," he stuttered.

The woman sighed. "No, I'm sorry. I'm sorry I took advantage of you like that. I shouldn't have. You have a wife that you obviously care about or you wouldn't be here."

Joe couldn't find his voice so he simply stood still and stared at the floor. He wasn't sure if it was the elevator or his nerves, but as it moved, the vertigo set in. His knees weakened and he wanted to collapse.

"I'm sorry about your wife," the woman said as she watched Joe grow paler by the second. "I hope she and the baby are okay."

With a ding, the elevator reached the next floor and the doors slid open again.

"Well, this is me," she said as she stepped out. "I…I'm sorry, Joe," she said, hesitating outside the elevator door. He didn't look up until the doors were sliding shut. They made eye contact for a moment and then she was gone.

Joe let out a deep breath and steadied himself against the wall. He rested his head on the back of his hand and closed his eyes tightly, trying to ward off the wave of guilt that overcame him.

"This can't be happening, this can't be happening," he said aloud. When the doors finally slid open again, he found himself back on Ellie's quiet, still floor. His feet were heavy and he had broken out into a cold sweat, but all he could think about was getting back to his wife. He didn't want to think about the nurse coming back into Ellie's room when Anna was there. He knew she would be able to read the guilt on his face.

When he opened the door, Anna looked up to see him wiping sweat off his face. He walked past her and sat in the chair near the window, breathing heavily. Anna shot him a puzzled look but said nothing. She simply squeezed Ellie's hand tighter and returned her gaze to the book she held in her hand.

Chapter 55

February 3, 2006, 4:30 a.m.

The wind outside Grace's cabin seemed to get stronger as the women listened to the rattling windows and the whine of air whipping past the house. Ellie wasn't sure what to say anymore, and Grace slowly rocked in her chair, eyes locked on the fire. Ellie looked around the room and suddenly felt drawn to the framed photographs that lined the shelves near the fireplace.

"Do you mind if I look?"

Grace stopped rocking and smiled. "Of course not, dear."

Ellie felt as if she had been sitting for days in this quiet, lonely place. As she looked at the photos, she noticed one of a young, dark-haired woman standing next to a horse. Her hair was neatly done in tight, big curls and she appeared to be wearing red lipstick, though Ellie couldn't be sure. The woman wore a form-fitting white blouse and a straight, snug-fitting skirt topped with a wide black belt. She also wore black pumps. Ellie thought it was odd that she was dressed so well while standing next to a horse. The woman's smile looked familiar.

"Is this you?"

Grace looked up from stroking Mayda, who still purred contently on her lap. Her eyes strained a little as she looked to see what Ellie was holding. Then they softened and that familiar smile returned.

"Yes, that's me and Belle. Jack took that photo not long after Belle took sick."

Ellie stared at the image and smiled because Grace looked happy in the photo. Her eyes looked different—brighter—behind the frame's glass. The horse didn't appear ill at all.

"She looks okay in this photo," Ellie said, pointing to Belle.

"Yes, she had good days where she seemed like her old self and bad days when she refused to eat. It was some time before Jack was able to accurately determine that she had kidney failure."

As Ellie returned the photo to the shelf, she noticed another of Grace, a handsome dark-haired man, and a young girl.

"That's me, Alfred, and Isabella," Grace said with a smile. That was a few years before Calista died and Alfred was drafted."

"Alfred was drafted?" Ellie said, spinning to face the older woman.

"Yes, he served in the military during the Second World War. He had dutifully filled out his Selective Service card before he entered the seminary. It was funny, but until then the war seemed like it had forgotten all about us, and I was glad."

"How long was he gone?" Ellie asked, still looking at the photograph.

"Too long…and not long enough," Grace replied.

Ellie set the frame down and noticed another photo, this one of an older, more serious-looking couple. The woman was strikingly beautiful with thick, dark hair. She wore a shiny black, short-sleeved dress with buttons all the way down the front, and she also wore black pumps. Ellie wondered if they were the same pumps Grace wore in the other photo. The man was handsome and very tall, but he wasn't smiling. Instead, his absent eyes stared out from the frame as if he were looking straight at Ellie.

"That's my parents, Isabelle and Henry Harper."

"They don't look very happy in this photo," Ellie said without taking her eyes from the image.

"Yes." Grace sighed heavily. "I doubt they were."

As Ellie placed the photo back on the shelf, another caught her attention. A teenage girl with a large smile, dark hair, and dark eyes peered from behind the glass. That smile, too, looked familiar, but she knew it wasn't Grace. This girl had dark eyes and a mop of curly, dark hair. She wore a floral-printed dress and her bare feet were crossed in front of her. The photo comforted Ellie.

"That's Isabella," she smiled. "Your grandmother."

Ellie couldn't take her eyes off the photo. She remembered her grandmother fondly, and though she had seen countless photos of her, she had never seen one from when she was this young. Isabella had been striking in a natural way. She'd never needed makeup or fancy clothes to appear beautiful because she naturally was. Ellie liked to believe she was more like her grandmother than anyone else in her family.

"She was always smiling, that one," Grace said with a chuckle.

"Why isn't she here?" Ellie asked. Her grandmother had died when she was ten years old. Ellie remembered how sad her mother had been after her passing. She cried for days, and Ellie had never seen her so broken-hearted.

"Isabella died a natural death, dear," Grace said as she continued stroking Mayda. "My daughter was spared many truths that I should have told her, but she was a strong, happy child I didn't want to steal that from her."

"Did she know that her father murdered you?"

"Of course she did, and it wounded her deeply, but she loved her father and supported him. She tried to understand why he did what did. It's me she learned to despise."

Ellie placed the photo back on the shelf and returned to her chair. Though she didn't feel like sitting, she knew there wasn't much else to do.

"She despised you?"

Grace sighed.

"Not right away, but she learned to despise me when things began to change on the farm. The day Alfred received his draft letter, our whole universe turned upside down."

Chapter 56

August 1941

Sitting silently at the breakfast table, Grace anxiously nudged her eggs with a fork. She didn't feel much like eating. Thinking of her mother's book, which was hidden in the bureau drawer upstairs, made her both excited and nervous. She didn't understand what it was and hoped Francesca could explain it all. Alfred ate quietly, munching his toast and sipping black coffee. He occasionally glanced at Isabella, who wiggled in her chair and hummed contently as she picked at the eggs.

Grace noticed the way Alfred watched their daughter. His eyes were soft and he smiled sweetly when Isabella looked back at him. Grace knew Alfred loved that child, and she also knew Isabella was the bond that held them together. So much silence had grown between them. They were, after all, two people that had never really known each other before they were married and had a child. Still, Grace knew Alfred was a good man. He was hardworking and tender, and above all, he was loyal. She knew he would never leave them; she also knew she could have had a far worse life than the one she was leading now.

Alfred noticed Grace's stare. "What is it?" He asked as he set his cup back on the table and wiped his mouth with the linen napkin that had been draped over his left knee.

"Nothing, Alfred. I'm just noticing how much Isabella is like you," she replied as she reached out and touched Isabella's head.

"You think so? I'm not sure I've ever been that happy about anything," he said, smiling. Isabella giggled and shoved a forkful of scrambled eggs into her mouth. Then Alfred changed the subject. "I think Dr. Snow is coming by to see Belle again today."

"Is he?" Graced was suddenly interested.

"I thought he was. I called him a couple days ago to check Belle again. She hasn't been eating well the last few days. He said he would call and let us know when he was coming."

"I haven't heard from him," Grace said, remembering her plans to visit Francesca. "I was planning to go to the market today, but I can stop at his office and check if you'd like."

"If you think of it," Alfred responded. "Otherwise, I'm sure he'll come when he can."

Just then, Calista walked into the room looking haggard. She didn't say a word as she walked to the cupboard and took down a coffee mug. She placed it on the countertop, then stopped and stared at it. Grace and Alfred exchanged a puzzled glance.

"Calista, are you alright?" Grace asked.

"What? Oh, yes, dear. I'm sorry. I was just trying to remember if I bought coffee the last time I was at the market."

"Yes, you did. I made some this morning. It's right there in the pot," Grace said, motioning toward the coffee pot that still sat on the stove.

"Ah, there it is," Calista replied as she shuffled toward the stove.

Grace and Alfred again exchanged glances.

"Are you feeling alright, Calista?" Alfred asked as Calista poured her coffee with a shaky hand.

"Yes, Alfred, I'm fine. I'm just tired." She sat at the table across from Isabella, who looked up and smiled. Just then, a light knock sounded from the front door.

"I'll get it!" Isabella screamed as she clamored out of her chair with excitement and raced into the next room. She swung the door open before her parents had even stepped out of their chairs.

On the porch stood a sweaty, nervous young man in a dark green uniform. He removed his beret as Isabella stood in the doorway. His bright red face twitched as he reached into his jacket and pulled out a wrinkled envelope. He cleared his throat as he glanced down at the little girl.

"He…hello," he said in a shaky voice. "Is your father home?"

As Grace and Alfred walked to the door, she suddenly felt ill. There was only one reason a messenger would be at their door. She looked at Alfred as he moved closer, but his eyes were focused on the young man.

"I'm her father," Alfred said sternly as he stood behind Isabella.

"Alfred Johannis?"

Alfred nodded.

"Then this is for you," the young man said as he gave the envelope to Alfred, never looking into his eyes.

Alfred grabbed the letter without a word. The young man turned and nearly ran down the stairs to the bicycle waiting below. Grace watched as he pedaled furiously down the drive, as if someone were chasing him.

"What is it, Alfred?" Grace asked as she closed the door. She watched her husband rip open the envelope and read the letter.

"It's a telegram," he replied softly, his eyes darting back and forth across the page.

"What does it say?"

The color quickly drained from Alfred's face. When he finished, he lowered his hands and looked down at Isabella.

"What is it?" Grace asked again.

"I have hay to cut," he replied, handing the letter to his wife. He reached down, kissed Isabella on the top of her head, and walked out of the house without looking back.

"What is it, Momma?" Isabella asked.

Grace shuddered as she read the words.

You are hereby notified that pursuant to the act of Congress approved August 15, 1941, you are called to military service of the United States by this Local Board from among those persons whose registration cards are within the jurisdiction of this Local Board.

Alfred was to report for an Army physical examination in one week. The war had found them, and Grace was unsure what to do.

"What is it, Momma?" Isabella asked again.

Grace couldn't find the words to explain that her father was about to be sent away to a war they had never even discussed with her.

"Nothing, sweetie. Let's clean up the breakfast dishes." She tried to direct the little girl's attention to something else and wondered what was going through Alfred's mind. Had he expected this? What would they do with the farm? How would she, Isabella, and Calista get by without him?

Suddenly, she heard heavy footsteps on the porch. In all her distraction, Grace hadn't heard Jack's truck rumble up the drive.

"Hi, Dr. Snow!" Isabella said with a big, happy voice as she swung open the wooden door.

"Why, hello, Isabella," Jack said with a beaming smile. "Are your parents home?"

Grace shoved the letter into her apron pocket, wiped a tear from her face, and came through the main hallway to greet Jack.

"Ah, there she is," he said, his eyes sparkling.

"Please, come in," Grace said as she held the screen door open.

"Thanks," he replied, wiping his feet on the rug inside the door even though his rugged shoes weren't at all dirty. "I'm sorry I couldn't come right away. Mr. Collins' cattle came down with something and I've been out on his farm treating them."

"I'm sorry to hear that. I hope everything is okay." Grace tried to hide her emotions.

"I think they had some bad feed or ate a fungus off the grass in the field, perhaps, but they're alright now. Nothing like a bunch of cows with the flu to make your week."

Jack laughed and Grace smiled.

"So, your husband called me about Belle. Has her condition changed?"

Grace found herself lost in Jack's smile. He wore his glasses and a freshly pressed blue shirt, and a pencil stuck out of his left front pants pocket. His khakis were clean, but his shoes were scuffed and worn.

"Um, yes. Alfred said she's not eating well. I'm not sure why," Grace explained.

"Why don't we go take a look at her," Jack said, motioning toward the door.

"Calista, can you keep an eye on Isabella?" Grace said. She turned to see Calista sitting silently at the table, staring at nothing.

"Calista?"

"What? Um, yes, of course. Isabella and I will clean up the kitchen."

Grace hesitated for a moment, wondering what had provoked her aunt's strange behavior, but she turned to follow Jack out of the house.

"I'll be right back, honey," she said to Isabella as she lightly ran her finger across her daughter's cheek.

"Okay, Mommy," Isabella replied. Grace was glad she did not insist on following them to the barn.

As they walked, Grace noticed the sky darkening across the field. "Looks like rain," she commented.

"Yep, sounds like it's gonna rain all afternoon," Jack responded. "Are you okay? You seem a little distracted."

Grace was surprised at Jack's forwardness, but she didn't mind. "Oh, I'm fine. I'm just concerned about Belle."

Jack nodded as he opened the barn door. "After you."

He walked briskly toward Belle's stall, but the mare didn't stick her head out as she usually did when someone entered the barn. Instead, they found her lying on her side.

"That's not good," he said. "Let's get her on her feet so I can take a look."

“She never does that.” Grace breathed nervously as she cupped Belle’s head in her hands. “What’s wrong, old girl?”

Jack ran his hand along Belle’s side and moved around toward her backend. Then he knelt and placed his head on her stomach to listen. “Sounds like she may have colic. C’mon, girl, get up,” he said, pushing to help the horse to her feet.

Belle lifted her head but didn’t stand. Grace pulled on her bridle. “Please, Belle, get up. You can do it.”

As she ran her hand down the mare’s face and looked into her dark eyes, Belle suddenly struggled to her feet.

“There you go. Good girl!”

Jack ran his hands across the horse’s side. “Her stomach is rock hard. Let me see what we can do about this. I need to run back to my truck.”

Grace nodded. She walked to the main barn door and pulled it back with one forceful yank. The wind whipped inside. Belle and Rocco pricked their ears and stirred nervously. Grace watched as Jack left, then turned went to Belle. Saying nothing, she stroked the horse’s mane and rubbed her ears. Belle nudged back slightly.

In the distance, low thunder rolled across the sky. The sound always excited her a little; she loved a good summer storm. Being inside and watching dark clouds roll in usually made her feel protected, but not today. Today she was worried about Alfred, and now Belle.

“It’s alright, just a little wind,” she said as she approached Rocco in his stall. His chocolate brown eyes watched her and his large head lowered as she scratched between his ears.

Slow, low thunder rumbled again and she wondered what was keeping Jack so long. Suddenly, a quick flash of lightning lit up the sky and was followed by a loud thunderclap. Rocco bucked his head nervously and Belle backed up in her stall. Looking through the door, Grace saw Jack rushing toward the barn with his medical bag in hand. He made it into the barn just as the rain began to fall. Together they pulled the door closed.

"Whew, that was close," he said as he ran his hand through his mussed blonde hair. He walked back to Belle's stall, set his bag on the floor and opened it. "Has she eaten anything out of the ordinary lately?"

"I think Alfred may have switched their feed. He mentioned something about that last week."

"Ah," he said, reaching into his bag. "Different feed can certainly cause the bloat. I'm sure this issue is more to do with that than the other problems she's having. I'll give her some mineral oil to get her digestive system going again, and hopefully that'll do the trick."

Grace nodded and watched him intently. She was impressed by his quick action and gentle nature with the horses. Before he continued with Belle, he walked over to check Rocco.

"Has he been eating the same feed?"

"I think so, yes," Grace replied, standing next to Rocco and stroking his muscular neck.

Jack ran his hands along Rocco's side and stomach. "He looks good. Better keep an eye on him, though."

Grace nodded. The rain fell heavier and pounded on the roof like small hammers. Jack walked back to Belle and took a syringe and a bottle from his bag. Grace entered the stall, stroked the horse's side, and watched with interest.

"Did you always want to be a veterinarian?" She asked.

He continued working but smiled and let out a slight laugh. "Ever since I can remember. You might find this hard to believe, but when I was a kid, a dog saved my life."

"Really? How?" Grace asked with curiosity as she sat down on a hay bale inside the stall.

Jack stood, turned to Belle, and ran his hands down her face, trying to calm her so he could place the syringe in her mouth. He steadied her as he worked.

"Well, one winter afternoon when I was about ten years old, I decided to take a walk out on the river near my house. It was cold that day, but a warm spell had come through shortly before. Being ten years old, I didn't think much about thin spots in the ice, and when I got close to the center I heard the ice start to crack around me." Jack squeezed the mineral oil into Belle's mouth. She resisted some, but then relaxed again.

"You fell through the ice?" Grace asked, her eyes widening.

"When I heard that crack, I should've run—I might've made it to the other side. But I stood there frozen, scared half to death. On the bank behind me, the neighbor's dog started barking. He was a big black Labrador retriever, but he didn't like the water like most labs do. He wouldn't go near it. Even with the river frozen over, he was too scared to go out there. Then, all of a sudden, there was another big crack and the ice gave way. I plunged right down up to my neck."

Grace brought her hands to her mouth as she listened. Jack smiled and turned back to his medical bag.

"I was never so cold in my life, and the current was faster than I thought it would be under all that ice. It nearly pushed me under, but I managed to hold on so I wouldn't get swept away. But every time I tried to pull myself up out of the water, the ice would break and I'd fall back in. But then, wouldn't you know, that old Labrador who was so afraid of the water came trotting toward me like he didn't even know he was on the ice. He came right up to the hole, too, not afraid at all. I grabbed his collar and told him to pull—and he did. Somehow he didn't fall in with me. He just pulled backwards until I got up on the ice far enough that I could pull myself out. Then we high-tailed it for the shore. I think I was damn near frozen by the time we got back to my house."

Grace smiled.

"That's a true story, cliché as it sounds," he said, shaking his head. "I never forgot that dog, either. When he got older, I went to see him every day until he died. I fed him, I sat with him, did whatever he needed. He was almost like *my* dog."

"So you knew what you wanted to be because of that dog?" Grace asked.

"Yep. He made me understand a thing or two about animals."

"Which is?"

"That they're loyal," Jack said without looking in Grace's direction. "They're loyal and they don't judge. They just love."

Grace understood completely. She stood and walked toward Belle. She wondered what it was like to know exactly what your purpose was in the world.

"How about you? Did you always know this is what you wanted to do?"

"What, be a farmer's wife?" Grace said sarcastically as she sat down on a hay bale.

Jack looked at her with his head cocked to one side. "I was thinking more about being a mother *and* a wife."

Grace leaned forward, resting her elbows on her knees and looking down at the ring on her hand. "No, this isn't exactly how I thought my life would turn out."

Jack moved toward her, never taking his hand off Belle, sliding it along her silky coat until he sat down next to Grace. "I'm a firm believer that everything happens for a reason," he said.

Grace let out a quick laugh and began to spin the ring on her finger. Jack's leg touched hers and that familiar sense of excitement returned. It tickled her insides in a way she hadn't felt in years.

"You know, I don't know many people in this town yet," Jack said as she stood and walked toward Belle. "I like visiting here and seeing you…and your family."

Outside, the wind died down a bit, but suddenly the barn door slide open and Alfred appeared. He was rain-soaked and out of breath. Surprised, Grace quickly stood.

"Wow. That was a fast little storm," Alfred said as he shook the water from his hat. "How's our girl doing?"

"She's doing alright. I'm giving her some mineral oil." Jack jumped up, stealing a quick glance at Grace as she backed out of the stall.

"I'd better check on Isabella," she said, turning to go. Making her way toward the door, she turned back one last time. She was surprised at Alfred's reaction to the telegram, and she was confused about how Jack made her feel. She watched for a minute as the two of them talked, realizing how different they were from one another.

"Jack," she said. The men stopped talking in mid-sentence to stare at her. "Since you said you don't know many people in town, why don't you stop by for dinner on Sunday. We'd love to have you. Right, Alfred?"

"Um…sure," Alfred replied.

Jack smiled and nervously kicked the floor with his boot. "Well, I wouldn't want to put you two to any trouble."

"It's no trouble—we'd love to have you. We'll see you around 5:00."

Jack nodded and Grace turned to leave, her heart fluttering.

When she stepped onto the porch, she turned toward the barn again. Her heart slowed as she took in a long breath. Then she remembered that she had planned to pay another visit to Francesca and scurried into the house to find Calista.

Chapter 57

February 5, 2006, 9:00 a.m.

As Anna sat next to Ellie, clutching her daughter's hand and reading a book, Joe stared blankly out the window. The sun shone brightly on the fresh snow, and though it was still cold, the warmth was causing a slight thaw. He couldn't get the nurse's image out of his head, or the memory of the night he had stumbled into her car. He squeezed his eyes closed, wishing he could take it all back. Suddenly, a hand touched his shoulder.

"Are you alright, Joe?" Anna asked as she looked at his tortured face.

Sitting up in the chair, Joe looked at his wife and then back at Anna. There was genuine concern in her eyes, and he needed to confess what he had done. The heavy sickness churned in his stomach. Tears filled his eyes and he covered his face with his hands, no longer able to contain it all.

Anna moved her chair closer to her son-in-law and sat down to face him. She pulled his hands from his face and looked into his eyes.

"I know there's something wrong," she said quietly. "It's okay to tell me…whatever it is."

Joe wiped his eyes and cleared his throat. He knew it was time to let it out.

"I've done a lot of things I'm not proud of, Anna," he said with a quiet, cracking voice.

She nodded, waiting for him to continue.

"I have a son. Did you know that?" He waited for her to look surprised, but she wasn't.

"Yes, I knew that, Joe," she said softly. "What I don't know is why you never told Ellie."

"I was ashamed and I was afraid of losing her," he said, tears still flowing.

"She loves you, Joe. She would never be ashamed of you."

His tears grew heavier. "I…I haven't been faithful to her, Anna," he said. His voice was almost a whisper. The words were even harder to get out than he had imagined.

Anna sat quietly, staring at the floor. "I was afraid that's what you were holding in," she replied.

"I'm so sorry," he sobbed. "I never had an affair. It was just…it was just meaningless. I don't even know why it happened, or how I could let it happen. I love Ellie."

As he continued sobbing, Anna walked to the window and peered out at the white, sunlit ground below.

"I wish you could've met my mother," she said after a few minutes, not turning to look at him. "She was always so positive about life, so full of hope. Even after everything she had been through with her parents, she never seemed bitter."

Joe looked up, confused. He wondered if Anna had heard a word he'd said.

"I miss her every day," she said as she turned and sat down across from him. "Did Ellie ever tell you about my grandparents?"

Joe nodded. "She told me there was a murder."

“When they met, my grandmother fell fast and hard for my grandfather. He sacrificed everything for her and my mother. And in the end, they were all alone.”

Joe searched Anna’s face, trying to figure out why she was telling him this story.

“My mother had the amazing gift of rising above her circumstances, Joseph,” Anna said, reaching out and touching Joe’s hands. “I believe my daughter has the same gift, though she doesn’t always know it. Ellie loves you. Whatever you did, whatever you feel guilty for, it’s time to let it go. It’s time to tell her how you feel and let her decide if your worth will rise above your circumstance. Stop using the past as a crutch and live here and now, in this moment. Ellie is going to need you to do that, and so do I.”

Joe stared at Anna in disbelief. This was not how he had expected her to react. He had anticipated anger and hatred, but instead, he found understanding and forgiveness, things he was only used to receiving from his own mother. He rose to his feet and embraced Anna like a son.

“I’m so sorry, Anna,” he whispered.

As she pulled away, she looked deeply into his tortured eyes. “Don’t be sorry anymore, Joseph. Be the man my daughter needs…and deserves.”

Chapter 58

February 3, 2006, 5:10 a.m.

"Tell me more about Francesca," Ellie said when Grace finished telling her about the day Alfred received his telegram.

Grace was eager to oblige and thought for a moment before she spoke again.

"I went to see Francesca again a few days after Alfred received that letter and Jack came to see Belle. I opened my mother's book whenever I could find time to myself. I tried to understand what all of it meant. I knew there was only one person who could explain it."

Ellie nodded as Grace continued.

"When I went to see her that time, I followed the same route I always did when I went to town, but this time I wasn't scared or nervous. I just needed to know more about my mother's beliefs and why Francesca thought I possessed the same gifts. I was confused over what I felt for Jack and scared about what life would be like if Alfred went away to war. I didn't want him to go, yet part of me did. It all made me feel terribly guilty."

She stopped talking just long enough to stroke Mayda, who still lay purring in her lap.

"Well, lost in all my thoughts, I soon realized that I had missed the road to town and I didn't recognize where I was anymore. I went down one bumpy road after the next, trying to turn myself back in the right direction, but I only seemed to get more lost. I drove for what felt like hours, until the sun started sinking and I began to panic. Then, all of a sudden, I found myself back on the main road again. It was almost as if I'd made one giant circle and somehow ended up back in exactly the same place."

"Did you go back?" Ellie asked quickly, but Grace didn't seem to hear the question.

"Since it was so late in the day, I decided not to venture back toward town. As I turned into my own driveway, I glanced down for a brief moment at my mother's book sitting on the seat next to me. I wondered if she was trying to send me a sign that I shouldn't see the old woman. The thought perplexed me so." She paused. "And then, to my surprise, I looked up and there was Francesca Morano sitting on my porch swing."

Ellie gasped.

"Trust me, I was as surprised as you are right now. I couldn't imagine why that old woman would come to my home. Alfred wasn't aware of her and Calista seemed quite unnerved at even the mention of her name, so I felt rather nervous as I parked the car and made my way to meet her on the porch."

Chapter 59

August 1941

"Hello, dear," Francesca said as she rose from the porch swing. A cool, nervous sweat accumulated on Grace's palms as Francesca stepped forward with a surprised smile.

"I'm guessing you're wondering why I'm here," she said, her kind eyes flashing a hint of coyness.

"I am a bit surprised to see you, but please sit down," Grace said. "Of course you're welcome here."

As the words left her lips, Grace realized there was no car parked in front of the house. She wondered how Francesca had gotten there.

"Jack was nice enough to bring me by. He came to check on your horse and needed to run back to the office, but he'll be back to administer some medications."

Grace felt the color run from her face. "I…I didn't know you knew Jack."

"Oh, I don't, really, but my old cat became ill, so I asked my grocery delivery man to drive me to the veterinarian. And while I was there, Jack offered to drive me back home, but he mentioned that he had to make a house call first. And lo and behold, I ended up on your porch."

Still struck by the odd coincidences, Grace quickly stood up. “Can I get you anything to drink? Did Calista offer you any refreshments?”

Francesca laughed and pushed her cane against the floor, making the swing sway back and forth. The cane made a scraping sound as it dragged across the wooden floor. “Oh no, dear, I didn’t knock. I just told Jack I’d wait here until he returned.”

“Are you thirsty? Can I get you anything?” Grace asked nervously. It would have been easy for Jack to simply drop Francesca off at her house before coming out to the farm.

“Oh no, dear. Please, do sit down. I have a feeling there’s something you want to ask me.”

Grace tried to remember why she had initially wanted to see the old woman. Her motivation had disappeared in a cloud of shock.

“Where is your cat?” Grace asked without thinking.

“She’s back at the clinic. Jack needs her to stay for observation. I’m dreadfully worried about her, but she’s very old, and we all go when our time has come.”

Grace nodded and looked at the floor.

“Jack is a nice man,” Francesca said, watching Grace closely for a reaction.

She finally responded. “Yes, yes he is,” she said as the old woman studied her face.

“I have a feeling he visits this farm for more than simply caring for a horse,” she said.

“I…I don’t know what you mean.”

The old woman threw her head back slightly and laughed again. “Yes you do, my dear.”

Grace snapped out of her sudden coma and stared blankly at the old woman. "I was just coming back from trying to see you," she said, eyes fixed on Francesca.

"Really? That's very ironic." The old woman winked. "Why did you want to see me?"

Grace sat quietly, searching for the right words to explain the book her mother had kept hidden. She had forgotten it in the car because she was so surprised to see Francesca there on her porch.

"You told me my mother had a gift and practiced witchcraft, right?" Grace asked.

Francesca nodded in agreement.

"I found some things in our attic that belonged to my mother," Grace said. "One of them was a tablet—"

"Was it filled with spells and that sort of thing?" Francesca asked, cutting Grace short.

"Yes."

"Ah," the old woman said as she settled back against the swing. "It's very common for a witch to keep a book like this. It's a place where she can write the spells she's heard of or developed herself. Your mother, like me, was a solo witch without a coven, so she probably kept track of her work in that tablet, too. We sometimes call it a Book of Shadows"

"A Book of Shadows?" Grace asked curiously.

Francesca smiled. "It's not evil, dear. It's all very harmless."

"And what is a coven?"

"A coven is a group of witches that gathers and practices together. You're lucky to find a good coven to help you explore and worship with. I, unfortunately, have never found one in these parts," Francesca replied.

"If you knew my mother was a witch, why didn't you practice with her?"

The old woman let out another slight laugh and touched Grace's arm. "Remember, dear, I was friends with your grandmother, and your grandmother was not fond of your mother."

Grace nodded. She had a longing feeling in the pit of her stomach. "I want to understand what she was practicing. Can you help me?"

"Of course, my dear, but first there is something else we must talk about."

Grace stared at the old woman, waiting for an explanation.

"That ring you wear—do you remember what I told you about it?"

Grace nodded.

"I told you that your grandmother asked me to bless the ring, but I wasn't exactly truthful about that."

Grace's anxiety rose.

"You see, my dear, every good witch knows that you cannot…or should not cast a harmful spell on anyone or anything. If you do cast negativity, it will come back to you times three, as I explained before. This is a rule as old as The Craft itself."

Grace nodded again. "Okay, but what does this have to do with my mother and my grandmother?"

"I told you that I gave your grandmother a spell that I wouldn't do myself," the old woman said. She ran her small, bony finger over the ring on Grace's hand.

"Yes, I remember," Grace said nodding.

The old woman sighed again. "Your grandmother wanted a spell that would harm your mother if she betrayed your father."

Grace nodded, waiting for Francesca to continue.

"I shouldn't have let her do it, but since she didn't possess The Gift, I was convinced that the spell wouldn't work. But now I fear it has."

Grace felt nauseated. "What are you saying?"

"I'm saying the spell I gave her had negative intentions, and with what I have seen happen to your family, I believe it stayed with the ring and has continued to cause harm."

"Can it be undone?" Grace asked.

"I don't know, dear. It takes great will to undo a spell that another person cast, and I'm afraid I underestimated the amount of negativity your grandmother possessed when she cast the spell."

Grace stood and walked to the edge of the porch. She stared across the field.

"What does all of this mean for me?"

"I know you feel an attraction to Jack Snow, but you have made your life with Alfred. If you stay true to Alfred, the spell should lie dormant…that is, until I can figure out what to do."

Grace looked at the ground, almost ashamed. "I'm so confused," she whispered, almost to herself. "And Alfred received a draft notice."

Francesca gasped. "Oh, dear, I'm so sorry."

As the women talked, Jack's truck rumbled up the drive, kicking up its usual dust cloud. Grace looked up as he stopped in front of the house and hopped out of the driver's seat, that same bright smile lighting up his face. Her stomach twisted and she barely mustered enough strength to smile back.

"Why Jack, you've returned," the old woman said as she rose to her feet. "Grace and I were just talking about you."

Jack laughed shyly as he made his way up the stairs. "Is that a good thing or a bad thing?"

"Well, now, what bad could we ever say about you, young man?" Francesca rose from the swing.

Grace stood silent, unsure of what to do or say after what the old woman had just told her.

Jack read the concern on her face. "I drew more blood to run a few additional tests on Belle, but she seems good today. She even ate part of an apple I brought her."

"Thank you, Jack," Grace softly replied.

An awkward silence built between the three. Grace wanted to feel at ease around Jack, but Francesca's eyes were upon her, reading into every expression and reaction.

"Well, Jack, it's nearly dark. Could you please drive me home now?" Francesca broke the silence.

Grace stared at the floor and Jack shifted nervously on his feet.

"I'll be back on Friday to check on Belle and bring you the test results," he said.

Grace nodded.

"Come see me soon, Grace," Francesca said as she made her way off the porch and toward Jack's truck. "We have much to talk about."

"I will, Francesca. Thank you."

As he walked the old woman to his truck, Jack glanced toward Grace. She briefly locked eyes with him before turning toward the house. As he drove down the driveway, he took one last look in the rearview mirror.

Chapter 60

February 5, 2006, 8:00 p.m.

After her mother had left for the evening, Joe paced nervously in Ellie's room. Though he felt better for confessing to Anna, he was still restless from being trapped in this place for too long. He paced from the bed to the window and back again, over and over, always on the same path. He wished he could tell Ellie what he'd told her mother so they could put it all behind them.

With each passing hour, he wondered if Ellie would ever wake up. The doctors and nurses would come and go, make notes on her chart, tell him she was making progress, and leave again. Yet Ellie still didn't move. They reassured him that she had made it through the critical hours so she could regain consciousness at any time. It could be hours, days, even months—they just couldn't be sure.

He also thought about the baby Ellie carried and worried about what kind of father he would be.

Joe remembered what it had been like to hold Andrew in his arms and let him fall asleep on his chest as he rocked him. Despite all of his differences with Lisa, he knew how much he loved that child. After all these years of fighting that emotion and swearing he would never father another child, Joe thought about the possibility of having those sweet paternal feelings again.

As he sat next to his wife's bed, he remembered the first time she'd ever brought up the idea of having a child.

"You knew what I was when you married me," he'd said as he pounded the last swallow of brandy. Putting the glass back on the table, he gulped hard and stared at his wife, who stood across the room.

"I had no idea this topic couldn't even render a discussion," she said, holding her ground.

"There's nothing to discuss. I will never have a child with you or anyone else."

"Anyone else? Really?" Anger filled her voice and the air around them. She had turned and gone into their bedroom, closing the door behind her.

Joe knew she was going to cry and didn't want him to see. He hadn't known it at the time, but she knew about Andrew. Based on the comment she had made, he realized now that he'd stabbed her twice that night with his words.

As he stood over her bed now, watching her, he slowly ran his fingers through her hair and leaned down to kiss her lips. He placed his other hand on her stomach.

"I want you," he whispered.

Chapter 61

February 3, 2006, 5:40 a.m.

"How are you feeling about this baby you're carrying?" Grace glanced at Ellie's stomach.

"I…I'm scared, but happy, I guess," Ellie said as she placed a hand on top of her belly.

"Children are such a gift," Grace said with a smile.

"I just hope Joe sees it that way," Ellie replied softly.

"He does, dear. Sometimes we don't plan these things, but they happen anyway. Everything happens when it's supposed to happen; we just need to believe it."

"Do you believe that you and Alfred were meant to have a child the way you did?"

The old woman raised her eyebrows and paused.

"What happened between Alfred and me was supposed to happen, too. I just wish it would have happened differently. You see, dear, Alfred was a religious man, and that didn't change after he left the seminary. He still strongly believed in the teachings of the Bible and tried his best to live his life by them. I hid my family's secrets from him because I knew he wouldn't understand why my mother practiced witchcraft. He would believe that it came from a dark place, even though it didn't."

Ellie nodded and continued to listen.

"You see," Grace said, "that's why he became angry when he found my mother's Book of Shadows that I'd forgotten on the front seat of the car. It was the first time that I began to see the *other* side of Alfred. The side that believed no matter what we do in this life, our first obligation is to God."

Ellie stopped rocking in her chair. "What did he do when he found it?"

Grace clasped her hands on her lap. "He began to see me as a different person. I don't know if it was that book or the looming fact that he would most likely be going off to war, but something in Alfred changed that day."

Chapter 62

August 1941

A few hours after Francesca left the farm, Grace sat at the dinner table still befuddled and barely touching her dinner. Watching her quietly, Alfred stood and walked to the window.

"Looks like more rain is coming in."

"Yes, I think it's going to storm," Grace said, snapping back to reality. She quickly stood and began clearing dishes. She wanted to ask Alfred about the telegram, but she decided to wait until they were alone.

"I'd better park the car in the shed," he said as he opened the door and disappeared down the steps.

Grace continued cleaning up as Calista and Isabella went into the other room to play checkers.

A few moments later, Alfred came back in. Grace heard his heavy footsteps behind her but didn't turn as she washed and dried the dishes.

"What is this?" Alfred asked sternly as he dropped her mother's book on the kitchen table. It slapped against the tabletop with a heavy thud.

As Grace turned, panic shot from the pit of her stomach all the way to her head, leaving her shaken and a little woozy. With all that had transpired earlier, she forgot that her mother's Book of Shadows was in the car. She stood frozen, unable to move.

"What *is* this, Grace?" Alfred glared at her, his eyes full of anger. Grace backed away from him and felt for the edge of the kitchen counter to steady herself.

"I…it was my mother's, Alfred. I found it in the attic."

"What *is* it?" Judging by the tone of his voice, she knew that he had already opened it.

"It's just a book, Alfred. It's just some things she was writing."

"Just some things she was writing? Did you read this, Grace?" He shouted.

"Yes."

"This is witchcraft. These are spells! Your mother was a witch!"

"You don't know that, Alfred," Grace said, instinctively defending her mother. "I don't know what she was."

"Why didn't you tell me? I *am* your husband. I should be told things like this."

Grace was shocked by the sudden change in Alfred's demeanor. She said, "I didn't realize this would bother you so much, Alfred."

"I know who your mother was, Grace. She was unfaithful to your father, and now I find out that she was a witch on top of it? My mother was right about her." He sat at the table and ran his fingers through his hair. "We need to pray about this."

"What? Pray?" Grace felt herself becoming more defensive and angry. "I won't pray over something that we know nothing about. My mother was a good woman who allowed herself to be trapped on this farm. She wasn't what you think she was."

The anger in Alfred's eyes grew deeper. "Your mother was a sinning, adulterant witch."

Grace had never seen Alfred speak or act like this. The anger on his face frightened her and she stared at him stunned and speechless. He rose from the table and came toward her. Gripping her arms tightly, he put his face as close to hers as possible. She felt the heat of his breath as he hissed at her. "You *will* pray about this and you *will* destroy that book. I will *not* have the devil in *my* house."

Grace felt damaged and angry, yet she found the courage to speak before she could stop herself. "This is my father's house."

Without warning, Alfred's hand swung back and slapped her face. The shock of it sent her flailing backward, until she caught herself against the kitchen counter.

Calista appeared in the doorway. "What on earth? Alfred!"

Alfred suddenly snapped out of his daze as Calista stared at him from across the room. He composed himself and tried to reach for Grace to apologize, but then he stopped short. He spun around without another word, snatched the book from the table, and stomped out of the house.

"Are you alright dear? What happened?" Calista wiped the tears from Grace's face and lightly dabbed the thick red mark that had begun to appear on her cheek.

"I'm fine, Calista," Grace said through her tears. "Alfred just found out who my mother really was."

Calista sighed, looking her niece in the eyes. "You knew someday he would."

***

In the days following the argument, Alfred and Grace spoke very little to each other. Too afraid to speak to him and hurt by his reaction to her mother's writings, Grace had chosen to let him be. She knew he was angry over the book, but she also knew the telegram must have thrown him into a tailspin. Still, she couldn't help but wonder what Alfred had done with the tablet. Though there had been others, that book seemed to hold answers to most of her questions.

As she walked to the barn with Jack, who had stopped to check on Belle, Grace found herself oddly numb. She was tired of the wretchedness in the air and the doubts clouding her mind. Jack carried on with his usual small talk and Grace listened politely, but she didn't pay much attention to what he was saying.

"Is something wrong, Grace?" He asked as they walked into the barn's cool shade.

Grace shook her head as she walked toward Belle. "I'm sorry, Jack. I just have a lot on my mind."

"Anything I can help with?"

She turned and saw his handsome face staring back at her. The butterflies rose again. She wanted to stop thinking, walk across the barn, and kiss Jack, but the thought of her mother and Alfred stopped her.

"Alfred received a telegram from the Selective Service."

Jack closed his eyes and shook his head. "I'm sorry to hear that. When does he have to go?"

"He has his physical next week," Grace said as she rested her head against the wood of the stall and peered in at Belle. Jack came closer and stood beside her. She could smell his musky aftershave.

"Maybe they won't take him," he said in soft voice. "They didn't take me. At least, not for the war."

Grace turned quickly. "You were drafted?"

"Yes, but I didn't pass my physical." He turned away. "But since I had medical training, I served at Fort McCoy for six months administering shots before I came down here."

"Why didn't you pass your physical?" Grace asked.

"I have a slight heart defect that keeps me from doing a lot of running and that sort of thing. I've never been able to play football, either, which always bothered me. But, I have to tell you, not getting sent to war didn't bother me one bit." He shook his head.

Grace looked at the floor. "Alfred doesn't have any health conditions."

"You never know. They might find something. Do you want me to talk to him?"

Grace appreciated the concern in Jack's voice. But she knew the possibility of going to war wasn't the only thing plaguing her husband.

"No thank you, Jack. Alfred will come around in time."

Jack nodded and continued looking over Belle. "She seems better today."

"I think so, too," she replied as Jack moved around the horse and then stood directly beside her. Grace could smell his aftershave again, and she inhaled it with a long, slow breath.

"I think she's gonna be okay," he commented, oblivious to Grace.

"You're still welcome to come by for dinner on Sunday," Grace said, hoping Jack wouldn't move away from her too quickly.

He walked around the horse again. "You, know, I've been thinking about that, and I…well, I don't think it's a good idea."

"What? Why?" Grace asked.

Jack looked up shyly. "I just don't think it's a good time for you and Alfred. Maybe another time?"

Grace turned back to Belle. She knew Jack was right. "Alright, then. Another time."

As they walked out of the barn and toward Jack's waiting truck, they heard a tractor coming up from the field. Grace turned to see puffs of dark smoke coming from its exhaust stack.

Alfred looked past his wife but raised a hand to wave at Jack. Jack returned the gesture as the tractor bounced by, heading toward the far shed and sputtering as it went.

"Maybe I'll go see if he needs a hand," he said, turning toward Grace. "Sounds like he has a piston problem."

She nodded. As Grace turned away, Jack placed a hand on her shoulder. Surprised, she spun around to meet his eyes. "It's going to be alright," he said, his clear eyes seeing right through her. As much as she wanted to believe him, she knew there was so much more that Jack didn't understand.

"Thank you, Jack," she said, placing her hand on his. They stood that way for a brief moment, eyes locked, and then Grace turned away and walked toward the house. As she climbed the stairs, she turned back to see Jack disappear behind the shed where Alfred had gone.

Chapter 63

February 6, 2006, 2:00 a.m.

Joe stood and stretched his back. The night seemed endlessly long, and he wasn't sure how much longer he could stay confined to the hospital room. He didn't want to leave, but the walls felt more like a prison with every passing hour. He looked at the television remote control that sat on a table near Ellie's bed, but he decided not to pick it up. He didn't care what was happening in the outside world. The only things he cared about now were in this room. But feeling the itch to walk again, Joe decided to go to the cafeteria for more coffee. He was unable to eat, but coffee, he needed.

As he entered the quiet hallway, that familiar uneasiness began to return. He didn't know why this hallway gave him such a peculiar feeling. As he moved down the corridor, he recalled that his father had spent two nights in the hospital after his mother struck him with a cast iron frying pan. His skull had nearly been fractured, and Joe's father suffered a serious concussion from the blow. As Joe entered the common area where the coffee machines resided, he remembered sitting at a table in the hospital with his mother and brothers all those years ago. A gaunt, nervous-looking police officer interviewed them. The man's formalness had made Joe uneasy.

"Mrs. McHugh, can you tell me what happened?" The officer held a pen and a pad of paper.

Joe's mother said nothing at first but lifted a shaky hand and placed a cigarette in her mouth. She rarely smoked, and Joe didn't like the look of her when she did. It seemed unnatural. Under the circumstances, though, he didn't say anything.

After she inhaled an exaggerated drag off the cigarette, she exhaled in the direction of the young-looking officer and then flicked cigarette ashes onto the floor. "Are you married?"

"No ma'am," the officer responded.

"Then you're smarter than I am," she replied. She took a few more puffs off the cigarette and then dropped it on the floor, crushing it beneath her faux leather shoe. The officer looked down at the floor where the cigarette still smoldered and then gave her a disapproving look.

"What started the argument between you and your husband?"

Joe's mother snickered, pulled her shoulders back, and lifted her chin. "I used to be a fairly decent-looking woman," she replied dodging his question. "Not like I am now."

Even Joe couldn't deny that his mother had looked better. She was thin and pale now, and her dark, stick-straight hair was tangled and unkempt. Her eyes were red, and smeared mascara created dark circles beneath them. She wore a tight mini skirt and a purple wool sweater that was too big for her. The ensemble might have looked good on her at one time, but now it wore her more than she wore it. The sight of her made Joe sad.

The officer said nothing. He put down his pad of paper and replaced the pen cap. His eyes softened as he looked from Joe's mother to each of the boys sitting beside her.

"If you tell me what happened, I might be able to help you," he said.

Joe's mother laughed again.

"Help me? And how are *you* gonna help me?"

"I believe your husband is being abusive and that's why you struck him. If you just tell me what has been going on, I can help keep you out of jail and these three boys from going into a foster home."

Joe's mother became enraged. "My boys will never go into a foster home!"

"Mom, it's okay. Tell him what he did," Peter piped in.

His mother turned and looked at each of the boys. Joe wanted to cry, but not in front of the police officer.

As she reached out and touched Peter's face, Joe could see his mother beginning to soften. "My boys," she whispered.

"He hits my mom when he gets drunk," Joe said in a low voice. Afraid to look at his mother, he looked at the ground instead.

"He tried to choke me, too," Peter said more boldly. David said nothing. He clutched a teddy bear and sat hunched in a chair between the two older boys.

The officer picked up his pen and paper again. "Okay, now we're getting somewhere. Can you tell me what started the argument tonight, Mrs. McHugh?"

"Nothing ever starts it. He just gets drunk and loses his mind," she explained. "Tonight we went to a bar and a man walking past said hello to me. Just 'hello.' That was it." She shrugged.

"And then what happened?"

"We came home and he accused me of sleeping with the guy. I didn't even know him."

"I see," said the officer. "Did he strike you?"

"He was yelling at her and I wanted him to stop," Peter said, his eyes filling with tears.

"Peter came out of the bedroom. My husband backed our son up against a wall and choked him," Joe's mother said. "So I knocked the son-of-a-bitch out."

The officer nodded.

As Joe stood by the coffee machine recalling the scene, he wondered why no police officers had come to discuss Ellie's accident with him. It hadn't occurred to him until now, but he didn't even know what had caused it or if anyone else had been involved. He was so engrossed in his own misery that he hadn't even considered the event that brought Ellie to the hospital.

Without pouring any coffee, he walked back down the hallway, looking for the nurse's station so he could ask about the accident. He hoped the nurse he'd had sex with would not be there. The thought of seeing her again disgusted him. He had witnessed odd coincidences before, but having the woman he had been unfaithful with taking care of his wife while she was in a coma had to take the cake.

As he rounded the corner and approached the empty nurse's station, he heard footsteps behind him. Quickly spinning around, he saw no one. The uneasiness returned.

"Hello?" He looked back, toward where the noise had come from, but there was no response.

Shaking his head and convincing himself that he was suffering from sleep deprivation, Joe turned toward the desk. Finding no one there, he looked down each empty hallway and saw nothing. Light reflected on the shiny floor behind the large, oval-shaped counter of the nurse's station.

"Anyone back there?" He strained his neck to see inside the room. Still there was no response. Joe considered giving up and heading back to Ellie's room, but instead he decided to go behind the desk to see if anyone was actually there.

Finding the area empty, he noticed a stack of patient charts lying unattended on a table. He looked around to see if anyone was coming and then he began to flip through the pile. Not seeing his wife's name on any of the covers, Joe placed the stack back on the desk and looked around for more. Seeing none, he flipped open the chart at the top of the stack. As the cover flopped back, Joe was surprised to find the pages blank. He flipped from page to page, and each one was empty—there was no ink anywhere inside. The binder was filled with white paper. Finding it odd, he closed the chart and opened the next. It, too, was blank. Befuddled, Joe paged through the next chart. Also blank.

He thought, *Why would they do that?*

Placing the stack back on the desk, Joe looked around some more. It seemed strange that there were no nurses to be found. Then, just as the thought entered his mind, he heard footsteps coming down the hall. The soft, steady tapping of the shoes made Joe believe they belonged to a woman. Since the nurses usually wore rubber-soled shoes, he wondered if this could possibly be a doctor, or perhaps another visitor. He hesitated. He wasn't supposed to be back there, and he was unsure if he should stick his head out, greet the person, and make up an excuse or hide and hope he hadn't been seen.

The footsteps grew louder, and Joe stayed in the small room behind the desk. The person seemed to hesitate in front of the nurse's station but said nothing and then quickly headed off down an adjacent hallway. The clicking shoes grew quieter, then stopped. Joe heard the elevator ding. Whoever it was hadn't found what they were looking for. As the elevator's metal doors slid open, Joe decided it was safe to slowly stick his head out and catch a glimpse of the person who had walked by.

As she stepped onto the elevator, the woman turned in Joe's direction. A wisp of her long, straight hair moved through the air, revealing the woman's face. Her eyes followed him and she appeared to move in slow motion, but she never stopped. Joe froze, trying to comprehend what he was seeing.

"Mom?"

It was too late. The doors had closed.

Chapter 64

February 3, 2006, 6:15 a.m.

"Tell me, how is your mother?" Grace said as she lifted the cracked teacup from the table beside her.

"She's fine," Ellie responded. "She's had some rough years, but I think she's come out of everything okay."

"Good, that's very good," Grace said in a whisper-like voice. "I often worry about her."

"Did you know her?" Ellie asked.

"No, I was gone before she came. I wasn't there to experience being a grandmother when Isabella gave birth."

Grace's eyes misted over. "When you bring a child into the world, being a good mother becomes your most important job, but that doesn't always mean you do it well. Isabella was a good mother to Anna."

"I know my mother loved her very much," Ellie said as she glanced at the pictures on the mantel.

"Isabella was always a good girl," Grace said as she sipped her tea. "After Alfred came home from his physical for the Army, Isabella followed him around asking so many questions. She was proud that her father was going into the Army. But she didn't understand that it meant he would have to go away."

Ellie listened and continued staring at the photographs. She remembered her grandmother fondly.

"Did she ever speak of me? Your grandmother, I mean?" Grace asked.

Ellie thought for a minute. She couldn't remember a time when her grandmother spoke of her own mother. Ellie's mother had told her stories about Grace, but her Grandma Bell, as she called her, rarely discussed her own parents.

"No, I can't remember her ever bringing you up to me, Grace. I'm sorry."

Grace nodded. "I'm not surprised. She never dabbled in magic, either; she was more like her father that way."

"Did she know about all of that—the witchcraft?" Ellie asked.

"Oh, yes, she knew," Grace said as she clasped her hands on her lap and straightened her back. "As she grew older, I told her everything about my mother and Francesca and the world of witchcraft as I knew it. I didn't want her father filling her head with things that were untrue. But he did anyway, and Isabella believed him."

Ellie thought about her grandmother's warm eyes and sweet smile. Not believing in something mystical was a profile that didn't fit Grandma Bell. That carefree, exotic woman seemed exactly like the type of person who would believe in magic.

"That doesn't seem like the woman I remember," Ellie said.

"I believe she embraced it more when she was older, but she would never have told me. She was always very close to her father and she didn't want to disappoint him."

Ellie couldn't help but realize the contradiction between her great-grandparents' worldviews and how that must have affected their daughter.

"When you say she *embraced* doing magic, does that mean she also practiced it?" Ellie didn't recall Grandma Bell, or her own mother, for that matter, practicing magic or casting spells.

"That's the trouble with this family," Grace said as she pointed her bony finger at the photographs. "There are too many secrets. Isabella didn't always hate me. I did teach her a few things, which I hoped she would teach your mother, who I hoped would teach you."

Ellie shook her head. "She never taught me anything."

"I see. Well, I guess I'm not entirely surprised about that, either."

"What happened to your mother's book after Alfred took it away?" Ellie asked.

"Her Book of Shadows? Ah, yes. Before Alfred left for the war, I found out what he had done with it. That book drove a wedge between us deeper than I had imagined. It was then that the man I knew began to vanish before my very eyes. Maybe it was partly because of the war, but I think Alfred had also begun to realize his own mistakes. He didn't regret Isabella, but he resented me. That became apparent."

Chapter 65

Late August 1941

Grace paced in the kitchen as she thought of Alfred, who was receiving his Army physical at that very moment. She was anxious and unable to focus. Despite Alfred's dark new attitude, she didn't want him to go to war—but she didn't want him to stay, either.

"Are you alright, dear?" Calista asked as she entered the room and observed her niece scurrying about.

Feeling a surge of emotion rising inside her, Grace clutched her aunt's arms. "What are we going to do Calista? How will we get everything done on this farm? I don't even know how to drive the tractor."

For years Henry, and then Alfred, had tended to all the working details on the farm. When to plant, when to cultivate, when to sell, what to keep—Grace had stood by and watched it all, never learning or even taking notice of what needed to be done. She was overrun with panic.

Calista gripped her niece's hands and stepped back. "We will work it out. This was my father's farm before it belonged to my brother. I know a thing or two about making it work. We'll have to lease some of the fields to other farmers, and hopefully that will be enough to get us through. We can plant the winter wheat after this season, and then corn next summer, and then soybeans when that's done. It'll be a gamble, but it might yield some additional money."

Grace shook her head, astonished at her aunt's ability to take charge. She hadn't thought of renting out the land. "But how will we plant? Do you know how to plant?"

"We'll find someone to help us, Grace. You should be more concerned about what will happen to your husband."

Grace suddenly felt ashamed.

"I'm sorry…I just…I don't know what to feel," she stuttered.

"It's a lot to take in, I know," Calista said as she sat down at the table. "I know Alfred has been distant, but he has a lot on his mind."

Grace stopped pacing, sat down, and reached for her aunt's hand. She suddenly realized how hard it must have been for her aunt after losing her own husband. "I'm sorry about Charlie."

"Things would have been different for me had he not died. I often wonder what our life would have been like. He wasn't a farmer like your father or Alfred."

"Alfred wasn't a farmer, either—at least, that's not what he wanted to be," Grace whispered.

"He didn't want to be a soldier, either," her aunt responded.

Grace shook her head. She was suddenly consumed with guilt. Alfred had so few choices lately when it came to the course of his life. It was no wonder he seemed more and more resentful.

"I found some of my mother's things in the attic," she said as she rose from the table and turned toward the back door. The sky had begun to cloud up again.

"Oh?" Calista replied, not looking up at her niece.

"There's some sort of tools she must have been using to create spells, and there were some journals…"

"Ah, yes. I remember that she used to carry journals with her sometimes. She was always writing things down."

Grace shook her head and looked at the floor. "So many things I never noticed."

"You were young, dear. Children aren't supposed to notice what their parents do. Do you think Isabella notices what you do?"

Grace turned away from the door. "I just wish I would have opened my eyes while she was still here."

Calista nodded.

"I was going to take one of the books to Francesca so she could help me understand it, but Alfred found it."

"Oh dear," Calista gasped. "Is that what caused that awful fight?"

Grace nodded. "He doesn't understand."

"Where is the journal now?"

"He took it. I don't know what he did with it," Grace said quietly, staring off.

"I see. Well, we must find it before he leaves. That's not something that should fall into the wrong hands."

It was times like these that Grace wondered if her aunt knew more than she was telling. But, before she could say another word, the front screen door slammed and footsteps moved down the hall. Both women rose as Alfred walked into the room. He didn't look either of them in the eye as he snatched the hat off his head. His hair was freshly trimmed.

"I got a haircut on the way home," he said nervously. "I…passed the physical."

Grace felt her knees weaken. "Oh, Alfred," she whispered as she stepped forward, ready to comfort him, but he retreated.

"I have to get out to the fields. Please don't tell Isabella. I want to explain it to her myself."

"When do you to leave?" Calista asked.

"I have to report to Fort McCoy in two weeks," he said softly. "They might let me go in as a chaplain."

Grace reached out again and grabbed Alfred's hand. "I don't want you to go."

Alfred's eyes softened and he almost smiled. "I'll get to be a chaplain."

Grace said nothing as her eyes filled with tears. Though the thought of life without Alfred on the farm scared her, she was almost relieved that he was leaving. As he turned to walk out, Grace found herself at a loss for words. Even Calista remained silent. When the screen door slammed and Alfred hurried to the fields, Grace wondered if things would ever be the same between them again.

"It'll be alright, Grace. We'll get by," Calista said as she placed an arm around her niece.

"He doesn't even seem upset," Grace whispered.

"He's probably in shock," Calista replied. "He doesn't know what to expect."

"What will we tell Isabella?"

"You let Alfred talk to her first. That's what he asked for."

Grace nodded.

“Now,” Calista said as she walked to the window to make sure Alfred was out of sight. “We need to find that journal of your mother’s.”

Chapter 66

February 6, 2006, 3:33 a.m.

Joe stood still as he stared down the hallway toward the closed elevator doors. His heart pounded wildly in his chest. He rubbed his eyes and shook his head. Had he really just seen what he thought he had, or were his eyes playing tricks on him? His mother had passed away nearly seven years ago. He looked up and down the corridors again but saw no one. There was no movement on the entire floor. He looked down at his wristwatch, which read 3:33 a.m.

I'm not getting enough sleep, he thought. Looking back toward the elevator, his heart rate began to slow to a more regular pace. He wished his mother were here right now. She'd always had a way of making him feel safe and comforted. He hadn't realized until this moment how lost he felt without her. As he walked back toward Ellie's room, he took note of each door he passed. They were all closed, and the room numbers didn't appear to be in any particular order. The stillness on the floor made him uneasy. It seemed so odd that no one was in the corridor, even at this hour; it was a hospital, after all. Clutching the knob to his wife's room, he took one last look down the hallway. He almost wanted the vision of his mother to return. Rubbing his temple and making sure he was lucid, he glanced one last time at the dim emptiness in either direction.

Once inside Ellie's room, he was glad to find that everything was exactly as he had left it. The television remote control lay on the food tray next to Ellie's bed, and the blanket he had been using was strewn carelessly across that awful, uncomfortable chair he had been sitting in. An empty Styrofoam cup sat on the table near the window. Though he craved more coffee, he decided that trying to sleep might be better.

Before sitting back in the chair, he surveyed his wife. He watched for any movement in her fingers or a twitch of her face. There was none. But then her eyes suddenly began to dart around beneath their lids. She looked so peaceful, as if he could just nudge her and she would wake up. He hadn't seen her eyes move like this since the accident and he wondered if he should call someone, but the emptiness outside the room made him hesitate.

He whispered, "Ellie?" Then he grabbed her hand. "Can you hear me? Are you there?"

She didn't respond. Her eyes continued to move, and he wondered if she was in some sort of dream state. Or maybe he was—he couldn't tell anymore.

He held her hand and watched her fingertips, waiting for any sign of life, but nothing happened. Other than the movement of her eyes, her condition remained unchanged. Deciding not to leave the room, he pushed the nurse's call button from the remote hanging on the side of Ellie's bed. He waited nervously for a response.

"Yes?" A voice crackled over the intercom. "Can I help you?"

Glad to hear another person's voice, Joe quickly pressed the call button again. "It's my wife. Her eyes…I think she's dreaming."

There was a long pause before the voice returned. "Someone will be down shortly."

Surprised at the lack of urgency in the woman's voice, Joe leaned back, discouraged. Then, looking at his wife again, he noticed her eyes were still. He stood and placed his face closer to hers. "No, no, Ellie. Don't stop." Nothing. Now, the only movement came from her chest rising and falling with each breath. Though he was disappointed that there was no more movement in her eyes, the steady motion of her breathing comforted him. At least she was still breathing.

The door opened a moment later and a stout, disheveled-looking man entered. He wore a white doctor's coat, but Joe had not seen him before. He was chewing food. He wiped his stubby, greasy fingers on his pants and swallowed hard before extending his hand to Joe.

"I'm Dr. Lewis Montague. How are ya?"

As he shook the doctor's hand, Joe instantly knew that he didn't like him.

"What seems to be happening with Mrs.…?" He fumbled through Ellie's chart, looking for her name.

"McHugh. Her name is Eliot McHugh," Joe said as he gave the man an unfriendly glare.

"Ah, yes. Interesting name. What seems to be the problem?"

"Her eyes—they were moving. Like she was dreaming or something. That has to be a sign, doesn't it?" Joe's enthusiasm returned as he looked at Ellie.

"Hmm." Dr. Montague removed Ellie's sheets and ran a capped pen along the bottom of her foot. There was no movement. Joe felt the blood running out of his head. He knew she would move if she could feel the pen. She hated having her feet touched or tickled in any way.

The doctor covered her feet again and took out a small flashlight. He gently lifted each of her lids and shined the light into Ellie's eyes. "Her pupils are dilating. That's a good sign," he mumbled.

"And the movement—does that mean something?" Joe asked.

"It could mean she was in a deep REM sleep. I have heard of that happening in coma patients, but I've never actually seen it. It's rare."

"Is that good?" Joe asked.

"Well, yes…I would think so. See, people in a coma have a low-frequency component of EEG…er, electroencephalogram."

Joe stared at the man blank-faced.

"You see, coma patients don't show cycling through sleep-wake cycles, so normally they don't progress to REM sleep." The man began flipping through Ellie's chart. "Yes, it says here she has a mid-level brain trauma. You wouldn't normally see REM sleep with this sort of injury."

"I know what I saw," Joe stated. "Could she be trying to wake up?"

The man wiped the pooling sweat from his forehead with the back of his hand. He touched the base of his glasses as he squinted at the machines next to Ellie's bed. "I suppose it's possible, but it's hard to tell."

Joe was becoming more annoyed. "When will her normal doctor be in?"

The man flipped through the chart, again ignoring Joe's question. "Was your wife in a car accident?"

"Yes, she went off the road. Why?"

The doctor continued reading. The perplexed look on his face made Joe uneasy. "What does it say?"

"Her body temperature was unusually low when she was brought in," the doctor said as he flipped to the next page.

"What does that mean?" Joe asked.

"I'm not sure, but it has remained consistently low since she's been here. It doesn't seem to be rising."

Joe wondered why no one had mentioned this before.

"And she's pregnant?"

Joe nodded.

"It's odd because a pregnant woman's body temperature is usually slightly higher than normal, but your wife's isn't. Do you know what caused the accident?"

Joe shook his head. "No. No one has told me much about the accident."

"Does your wife have a history of blacking out for any reason?"

"Not that I know of. Why?"

"Well, I wonder if you wife blacked out and that's what caused the accident," the doctor said. "Her lower body temperature could have prevented her from sustaining a more significant head injury."

"What would cause her temperature to be so low?"

"Well, there can be many reasons," the doctor continued. "Has she been under any stress lately?"

Joe exhaled slowly. "Yes."

"That could do it, or the accident itself could do it. It's hard to tell. Normally body temperature recovers quickly after a trauma, but hers hasn't…and sometimes low body temperature can lead to drowsiness. I'm wondering if she lost consciousness while driving and it was low before the accident even occurred."

The weight of Joe's guilt returned and his chest constricted.

"Did she complain about being cold at all?"

"She always seems cold, especially this time of year," Joe replied. "She hates winter."

Dr. Montague nodded. "I'm going to look into this."

"And what about her eyes moving?" Joe asked before the doctor could slip out of the room.

"Call me if it happens again," he said as he produced a business card from his jacket's front pocket.

Joe held the white card and stared at it as the doctor disappeared into the dim hallway. Joe tried to comprehend all that the man had said. It was the most anyone had told him about Ellie's condition. He slipped the card into his pocket and sat down in the chair next to Ellie's bed. He stared at her face and picked up her hand, realizing now how cold and clammy it felt. He sighed and wondered if the warmth inside her was slipping away before his eyes.

Chapter 67

February 3, 2006, 7:25 a.m.

Grace stirred the fire with an iron poker and placed another log atop the hot coals that burned bright orange. The air inside the cabin had turned colder, and a chill ran down the back of Ellie's neck as she began to shiver.

"Would you like a blanket, dear?" Grace asked as she pulled her own shawl tighter around her shoulders.

"Yes, please, if it's not too much trouble," Ellie replied. Though she desperately wanted to get out of this place, she felt herself drawn more and more into Grace's story. She didn't want to leave until she had answers.

As Grace lifted a white crocheted blanket out of a chest that was across the room, Ellie said, "Was it hard when Alfred left for the war?"

"Yes, it was very hard," Grace replied as she unfurled the blanket and covered Ellie's legs. "I still cared about Alfred even though things had changed so much between us. Despite our differences, we shared a beautiful daughter that we both adored."

"Was he still angry with you when he left?"

The old woman sat back in her chair and slowly rocked. "I think his anger turned to disappointment. But I also think the thought of going off to war excited him in a way. It gave him a new sense of direction to know that he could possibly enter the Army as a chaplain. He wanted to help people and he wanted to spread the word of God—even if it meant he'd be surrounded by fighting."

Ellie shook her head. "It's so ironic that the two of you ended up together."

"Yes, it was," Grace said with a snicker. "But I believe that few things in life are purely chance. At least, not in our family."

"What do you mean?" Ellie asked. The cold chill that had begun on the back of her neck traveled further into the core of her body. She pulled the crocheted blanket up to her shoulders.

"Life is always a struggle between good and evil, Ellie. Though Alfred only chose to see the dark side of my mother's practices, I knew better. It was his form of worship that I had a much harder time understanding."

Ellie agreed. "Religion can definitely be dangerous."

"Indeed it can," Grace said, continuing to rock. "Alfred believed that there was only one way to view the world and God. He had a set form of rules that *he* felt he needed to live by, and if he didn't live by those rules, he was unhappy."

"Do you believe in God?" Ellie asked.

Grace stopped rocking and took a deep breath. "I believe in many things, and God has always been part of that, but after I learned more about my mother and my family history, my views began to change. It's not that I stopped believing in God. I just know now that whenever one believes in something so wholeheartedly, there is always a chance of missing the forest for the trees."

Ellie looked at the old woman puzzled.

"I believe sometimes, dear, that when we choose to put too much faith in one thing, we become more closed-minded about the possibility of other things. Alfred didn't want to believe that magic was real. He didn't want to believe that my mother created most of her spells for protection or for healing. He *wanted* to believe that she used it for dark reasons. He *wanted* to believe that she was trying to conjure evil."

"Did you reconcile before he left?" Ellie asked.

Grace looked toward the fire and began rocking again. "We did for the sake that he was leaving, but did we solve our differences? No, those we could never resolve."

"And the book. Did you get it back?"

"Yes. Our pastor paid me a visit after Alfred left for the war. I was surprised that Alfred hadn't destroyed it, but instead he had given the book to Pastor Richards. What Alfred didn't realize is that Pastor Richards had already known about my mother. And though I believe Alfred was hoping the pastor would try to counsel me back toward God, he didn't do that. He had his own story to tell about her."

Chapter 68

September 1941

Grace sat on the front porch steps with Isabella as Alfred packed his bag in the upstairs bedroom. Calista rocked quietly on the porch swing, watching as Grace stroked Isabella's hair and wiped the tears from her face.

"When will Daddy be back?" The little girl turned to face her mother. Grace cupped her daughter's face in her hands and swallowed hard before she spoke. "I don't know, baby."

"I don't want him to go," Isabella sobbed.

"I know, honey," Grace said as she pulled Isabella closer. Though she didn't want Alfred to go to war, she couldn't stop herself from feeling relieved that he was leaving. Still, she couldn't stand to see her daughter so distraught.

"Isabella, why don't you come sit by me here on the swing," Calista said. "I think your mother needs to talk with your father."

Knowing her aunt was right, Grace stood up, but Isabella clung to her skirt. "It's alright sweetie," she replied. "Go sit by your aunt. Daddy and I will be out in a minute."

Reluctantly, the little girl walked toward Calista, who reached out and swallowed Isabella in her arms. Grace watched and then turned away. Her heart beat faster as she stood at the bottom of the stairs listening to Alfred move about in their bedroom. As she took one shaky step forward on the stairs, her nerves begin to shred. She didn't know what to say to Alfred. The last seven years had gone by so quickly. They had shared so much, and yet they were so far apart. There was so much she wanted to say, but she couldn't find the words as she reached the top of the stairs. She stopped and took a breath before continuing down the hall. She hesitated in the bedroom doorway until Alfred looked up. His eyes were soft and kind, the way they used to be. Grace was reminded of why she had fallen for him in the first place.

He smiled slightly and went back to packing his things. She sat next to his bag, which lay open on the bed.

"I'm so sorry for everything, Alfred," she said quietly. It was the only thing she knew to say.

He stood across the room near the bureau. With his back to her, Alfred hesitated. He drew in a long, slow breath and then turned to face her. "You shouldn't blame yourself," he said, sitting beside her. "It wasn't all your fault. It was mine, too."

He took her hand and gazed into her eyes with a look she hadn't seen in what felt like years. "We don't want you to go," she whispered through a cracking voice.

"I know," he said. "I'll be back as soon as I can."

"I don't blame you for wanting to leave. I understand," Grace said as she released his hand. She stood and began tidying the things in his bag.

"So much has changed, Grace. I thought I knew you, but I realize now that I never really did."

"That's not true, Alfred," she said as she turned to face him. "I've never tried to hide anything from you. I know you don't approve of what my mother was, but that's not me."

Alfred stood and gently took her by the arm. “I’m sorry I struck you. I never wanted to hurt you.”

Grace wrapped her arms around him. “I’m sorry, too.”

As they pulled away from each other, Alfred took a step back. “I don’t want you to read any more of your mother’s writings, and I don’t want Isabella to know about any of it. Will you do that for me?”

Grace was shocked. “I...” She stumbled over her words as she searched for the right thing to say. She loved her mother and wanted to know more about her. She also wanted Isabella to know what a wonderful, eccentric woman she was named for. Alfred was asking the impossible.

Grace hesitated. She wanted to argue but then reconsidered. She knew she couldn’t keep that promise to Alfred, but he was about to leave for war so she reluctantly agreed. “I promise.”

Alfred smiled and hugged her again. She was surprised he hadn’t heard the insincerity in her voice. As he turned and closed the suitcase, she went numb. When he took her hand and left the room, Grace felt nauseated. She didn’t want to watch him say goodbye to Isabella.

When they reached the bottom of the stairs, Grace heard Calista humming softly to Isabella, who rested her head against her great-aunt’s chest. They seemed so calm that Grace didn’t want to disturb them. The screen door creaked when Alfred pushed it open. Isabella leapt to her feet, took a few steps toward Alfred, and jumped into his arms.

“Whoa, girl. You’re getting so big,” Alfred said as he hugged her tightly.

"Please don't go, Daddy, please!" Isabella begged.

Alfred lowered her back to the porch and crouched down to her level. He pushed the hair from her face and kissed the tip of her nose. "You're so pretty," he whispered. "You look just like your mommy."

"Can't you stay, Daddy? Please!" Isabella insisted.

Alfred looked down at the floor, Grace could tell he was fighting tears, but he wouldn't allow himself to cry.

"Isabella, I know this is hard for you to understand, but the Army needs me. I have to go and try to help where I can. I promise you, I'll be back as soon as I can. Things will be different when I come home," he said as he shot a quick look at Grace, who stood behind their daughter.

"No, Daddy!" Isabella sobbed as she wrapped her arms around his neck. He picked her up and clutched her tightly. This time, he didn't fight the tears. Grace turned away in time to see Pastor Richards' car pull up to the house.

Without a word, the pastor got out of his car, straightened his tie, and walked up the steps to retrieve Alfred's bag. He gently touched Grace's arm and gave her a slight smile. She reciprocated through tears.

"Alright, Isabella, Daddy has to go," Alfred whispered. He turned to Grace, who lifted the sobbing girl from his arms. He kissed both of them on the forehead and whispered, "I'll be back, I promise."

Grace held Isabella tightly and watched as Alfred embraced Calista, then turned and walked briskly toward the pastor's car. Isabella sobbed harder when they drove away, and Grace felt weak in the knees as she sat down on the front steps.

Calista sat beside her and wrapped an arm around her niece's back. The women rested their heads on one another and took turns stroking Isabella's hair. Grace didn't bother trying to stop her daughter from crying; there was no use. She simply waited as Isabella cried herself out. There was so much to fear, yet from somewhere deep inside, she felt released. Despite her weak promise to Alfred, she had every intention of learning more about her mother.

Chapter 69

February 6, 2006, 7:00 a.m.

Joe straightened in his chair when Anna came through the door. Bright sunlight lit the room, and he was thankful it was morning. The previous night's peculiar events had left him feeling dazed and confused. He hadn't even realized that he'd drifted off to sleep.

"You look awful," Anna said as she set a Starbucks cup on the table beside him. He was glad it wasn't another cup of the bitter, black tar that he had been drinking in the cafeteria.

"You need to go home and get some real sleep, Joe," Anna said sternly.

"She moved her eyes last night," Joe replied, ignoring Anna's comment.

"Is she waking up?" Anna said, spinning toward her daughter.

"I don't know. The doctor wasn't sure, but he said her body temperature is down and that it has been down since the accident."

"What does that mean?" Anna asked, her excitement draining.

"I don't know," Joe said as he stood and stretched his back. "He didn't offer a lot of explanation, but no one has ever said that before."

Anna cupped Ellie's hand between her own. "And her eyes—what about her eyes?"

"They were moving, almost as if she was dreaming or something."

"Did she open them?" Anna questioned as she moved closer to inspect her daughter's face.

"No, and the doctor said it's unlikely she was dreaming."

"What doctor?" Anna asked. "I just talked to Dr. James this morning and he didn't mention any of this."

"It was a different doctor, Dr. Monta-something. I hadn't seen him before last night. What did Dr. James say?"

"He said he really had nothing new to report. Why wouldn't he have told us about her body temperature being cold?"

Joe took a drink of his coffee and shook his head. "I don't know, but some strange things happened here last night, or maybe I was dreaming. I don't know anymore."

"What sort of strange things?" Anna said as she sat in the chair Joe had just vacated.

Joe was sorry he had even mentioned it, but he knew Anna would continue questioning him if he didn't explain. She was like Ellie that way. "I don't know," he said as he rubbed his stubbly face. "I tried to find some nurses at the end of the hall and it was like there was no one in this hospital, I mean no one. It was so quiet. It was weird."

Anna listened intently, pursing her forehead with that same look of concern that Ellie always had. He had never realized how similar the two women really were. Anna was smaller and plainer than her daughter, but he always thought she must have been attractive when she was younger. She and Ellie had the same hair color and the same deep brown eyes.

Joe continued. "Then I started to hear footsteps behind me, but when I turned around, there was no one there."

"Maybe it was someone going into another room?" Anna said trying to rationalize his story.

"I thought that at first, but when I couldn't find any nurses, I started looking behind the desk."

"You went behind the nurses' desk?" Anna asked, eyebrows raised.

"Yeah. There was no one there so I started looking for anything I could find about Ellie, but all I found were blank charts."

Anna nodded. "That doesn't seem strange. Maybe they were getting ready to use them."

"They weren't *just* blank charts," Joe continued. "They were full of white, blank paper. There wasn't a filled out chart, no doctor paperwork, nothing. There were just stacks of empty pages."

Anna watched as Joe crossed the room and stood in front of the window.

"And there's something else," he said as he turned around. "I started hearing footsteps again, but this time I hid in the back of the nurses' station."

Anna said nothing but watched Joe intently.

"I assumed it was a doctor or someone who wouldn't appreciate me snooping around, so I waited until the footsteps passed by before I came out."

Anna nodded.

"When I looked down the hall after whoever it was…" Joe stopped and shook his head again.

"Yes?" Anna prodded.

"I saw my mom," He replied sheepishly, afraid Anna would think he had completely lost his mind.

Anna raised her eyebrows again and then laughed. "Oh Joe, it was just a dream. You really need to get some rest. Please go home for a while."

"Was it a dream? It seemed so real, Anna. And right after that, I came back here. That's when I saw Ellie's eyes moving…and then that doctor came."

Anna looked at her daughter and then turned back toward Joe. "You're starting to worry me. Should I call Peter to drive you home?"

Joe sat down and ran his fingers through his hair. "No, I'm fine. I just…I just know what I saw."

"Joe, please," Anna begged.

"Alright, Anna, I'll go," he said as he stood up. "But please, if you see Dr. James again, ask him about her eyes moving and her body temperature. I want to know why they didn't tell us about that."

Anna nodded. Reluctantly, Joe grabbed his coat, kissed Ellie on the forehead, and prepared to leave the hospital for the second time.

Chapter 70

February 3, 2006, 6:55 a.m.

Ellie was growing tired. She felt the urge to close her eyes and sleep. At the same time, she felt herself growing colder and colder, as if her body could no longer hold in warmth. Even with the blanket that Grace had given her, she couldn't keep warm. The chill seemed to be rising from the core of her body.

"It's almost time, dear," Grace said, noticing Ellie leaning back and closing her eyes.

"Time for what?" Ellie asked as she cleared her throat and straightened up.

"Time for you to put the pieces together."

Ellie shook her head. "I've been trying to put the pieces together since the moment I woke up out there in the snow," she said, pointing out the frosted window. "I've been trying to understand where I am and what all of this means, but every time I think I'm beginning to understand something, I realize I don't. I want you to answer me…am I dead?"

"No, darling, you are not dead," Grace said, her voice weakening.

Ellie thought for sure the old woman would give her another elusive answer, so the directness took her by surprise. She said, "Are you dead?"

"Yes."

“Where am I?” Ellie asked. The chill made her shiver, and she stared at the old woman as she waited for a reply.

“When I first came here, I knew I was dead,” Grace said. She stood and walked toward the mantle, which contained the family photos. “I felt the heat off of Alfred’s gun and I knew why he did what he did. I’m not saying I deserved it, but I wasn’t surprised that the end came the way it had.”

Ellie stood and walked toward Grace. The blanket that had covered her legs fell to the floor. She shivered with every step.

“You can still feel the cold,” Grace said as she watched Ellie come toward her. “I can’t feel that. That should have been your first clue in knowing that you aren’t dead.”

“But why do you keep a fire, then?” Ellie asked as she crouched and warmed her hands in front of the flames. “And why do you cover yourself with that shawl?”

“These are the only comforts I have to remind me of what it feels like to be alive. But I’m dead, both inside and out,” Grace said as she touched Ellie’s hands.

Ellie felt the coldness in the woman’s hands and took a step back. “If I’m not dead, then what am I doing here?”

Grace turned away and went back to her chair. “Like I said, it’s time for you to put the pieces together. But first, I need you to tell me more about Joe.”

“Does he think I’m dead?” Ellie asked.

“He doesn’t know what to think right now. He’s in another place.”

“What do you mean? Is he here?” Ellie pleaded.

“No. He’s out there somewhere, looking for you.”

Ellie turned toward the door. “Out there? In the snow? Why didn’t you tell me he was out there? I have to find him!”

“You can’t, dear,” the old woman calmly said. “You can’t find him until he learns how to find you.”

Ellie was growing angry again. “Stop this! Stop this now! What are you talking about? You need to tell me what the hell is going on!”

Grace stood and gently took Ellie by the hand. “We’re almost there. Please, just let me finish.”

With the old woman’s cold fingers grasping her hand, Ellie weakened and her knees buckled. She collapsed into the chair and burst into tears. Grace picked up the blanket that had fallen to the floor and placed it around Ellie’s shoulders.

“There, there, darling. I promise you’ll see more clearly when I’m through.”

When she returned to her chair, she looked into the fire. “Now, where was I?”

Chapter 71

September 1941

Grace and Calista fixed dinner in silence as Isabella sat at the table and fidgeted with the edge of the tablecloth. She hadn't said a word since Alfred left a few hours before, but Grace was glad that she had finally stopped crying. No one was hungry, but Calista thought the three of them needed to do something to distract them from their somber mood.

"Isabella, darling, could you set the table?" Grace asked.

The little girl didn't move; she simply ignored her mother's request and continued pulling at a thread that had come loose from the edge of the tablecloth.

"Isabella, please?" Grace repeated.

"I'm not hungry," Isabella replied in a quiet, whisper-like voice.

Grace sat in the chair next to her daughter and took her by the hand. "I know you're upset, but everything is going to be alright. Daddy will be back as soon as he can."

"How do you know?" Isabella said without looking up.

"Because I have faith," Grace said as she lifted her daughter's chin with her index finger, forcing her to look directly into her mother's eyes.

"But Daddy says you don't believe in God," the little girl snapped.

Grace was taken aback and fumbled her words. "That's, um…well, that's not true Isabella."

"Daddy said Grandma was a witch. Why does he say that?"

"Your grandma liked to create spells sometimes, Isabella. That's all," Calista chimed in.

"What does that mean?" The little girl asked. "Don't witches make spells?"

"Yes, they do, but your grandma made spells to help people. She didn't do it to cause harm."

Isabella stared at her great-aunt with a confused look. "Was she a witch?"

Grace looked back at Calista, searching for the right thing to say.

"Your grandma practiced witchcraft, yes, Isabella, that's true. But she wasn't bad," Calista answered as she walked toward the table.

"Did she believe in God?" The little girl asked.

"Of course she did, darling. She wasn't a bad woman. She was very smart and funny…and beautiful, just like you." Grace touched the tip of Isabella's nose.

The little girl giggled for the first time all day. "Do you believe in God, Mommy?"

Grace swallowed hard. She wasn't sure what she believed in anymore. "Of course I do, Isabella. God gave me you."

"Daddy says God saves a place in Heaven for those who pray. How come you don't pray, mommy?"

Grace looked down. In the last few years, she hadn't spent much time praying. Since her path seemed to have been laid the minute Alfred walked onto the farm, she didn't see much use in praying for anything anymore. She had accepted the course of her fate and moved forward—that is until she realized she was living almost exactly the same life her mother had.

"I pray, Isabella," she lied. "I just pray by myself."

"Why?"

"Because some things I like to keep between just me and God," she answered. "Daddy believes in spreading God's word, but Mommy believes that quiet faith is just as good."

Isabella looked confused, but there was a heavy knock at the door before she could ask another question. Startled, Calista and Grace exchanged glances as Isabella leapt from the chair.

"Is it Daddy? Did he come back?" She raced down the hallway toward the door.

As Grace turned from the kitchen, she saw Pastor Richards on the other side of the screen door.

"Is my daddy back?" Isabella said as she opened the door. She pushed past the pastor and ran onto the porch.

"No, I'm afraid not, Isabella," he said as he turned to see the women coming out of the house. "I've actually come to have a word with your mother."

Calista and Grace exchanged glances again. "Is everything alright, Pastor?" Calista asked.

"Oh, yes. I saw Alfred off at the train station. Everything is just fine. But, he asked me to have a word with Grace. Would you mind taking a walk with me?"

"Of course," Grace said. "Calista, you and Isabella can go ahead and eat dinner. I'll fix myself a plate when I get back."

Calista nodded as she ushered Isabella back into the house.

As they stepped off the porch and began to make their way toward the path leading to the woods, Grace noticed that Pastor Richards kept his dark-blue suit jacket on even though beads of sweat had begun to form on his forehead. The late summer humidity was heavy in the air.

"Would you like to leave your coat before we walk?" Grace asked.

"Yes, I certainly would," the pastor said. He stopped and pulled a hanky out of his pocket, then dabbed at his forehead and wiped his bald head. He straightened his glasses and smiled. Pastor Richards had always been kind to her family, and Grace felt comfortable with him despite her questions of faith.

Taking off his jacket, the pastor removed a leather-bound journal that had been hidden beneath it. Grace gasped, recognizing it immediately.

"My mother's journal!"

"Yes," he said as he handed it to her, then rested his coat neatly over his arm as they began to walk.

"I thought Alfred had destroyed it. Thank you so much for returning it to me," Grace exclaimed as she held the book against her chest.

"He *wanted* me to destroy it—that's why he brought it to me," Pastor Richards said as he dabbed more sweat from his forehead. He shook his head slightly, as if he was afraid to make Grace angry. "He's convinced your mother was doing black magic and that these writings were part of that. He thinks if you continue to read them, you'll turn yourself into a witch."

Grace was silent. She wasn't surprised to hear what the pastor was saying.

"He wanted me to speak to you about faith and try to bring you back to the light. He said he has been praying hard, but he couldn't stop himself from believing it was your mother's fault that he became, well…"

"Trapped?" Grace said, finishing his sentence.

Pastor Richards pursed his lips and closed his eyes briefly. "Yes, trapped. He certainly doesn't regret having Isabella, but he believes your mother somehow bewitched him into seducing you."

"But she was dead before he even came to the farm," Grace responded. "She never even met Alfred."

"That's not entirely true, Grace. She knew Alfred's mother—*both* of your parents did."

Grace realized the pastor was right. Her father had told her that he'd known Alfred's mother. And though Grace had also met Alfred's mother at their wedding, the woman had kept her distance. Grace knew she did not approve of the marriage and she had hoped for her only son to become a priest. Alfred rarely spoke of her.

As they reached the edge of the woods, Grace wondered if they should turn back toward the house, but the pastor continued walking. The air became cooler as they entered the trees, and the shade felt good.

"My mother knew Alfred?" Grace asked.

"She saw him once," he replied, then stopped walking. "I want you to prepare yourself, Grace. What I am about to tell you may not be easy for you to hear."

Grace felt a nervous twitch in her stomach as she stood in front of him, preparing for whatever blow was about to come.

"What is it?"

"Alfred's mother was widowed shortly after Alfred was born. He never really knew his father," the pastor said as he began walking again. Grace followed closely beside him. "After her husband died, Mary briefly came down here from up north to live with her parents."

Grace listened intently; she knew little about Alfred's family.

"During that time, your father was sharecropping some of the fields that Alfred's grandfather owned and Mary worked in her family's vegetable stand at the edge of town, near those fields. Your father stopped by that stand regularly to buy vegetables for lunch or to take home."

"Okay," Grace replied. So far she hadn't heard anything horrifying.

"It wasn't long until they became friends."

"Okay," she repeated.

"And, well, then they became more than friends."

Grace stopped walking and felt the blood rush out of her head. "Are you saying my father had a relationship with Alfred's mother?"

"I'm afraid so. I'm sorry to have to tell you this, Grace."

Grace staggered. Her mother having an affair was one thing, but her father as well? She felt faint as she reached out and clutched the pastor's arm. "Are you sure? How do you know this is true?"

"Your mother was pregnant with you at the time and your father loved your mother very much. In time, he ended the relationship with Mary and told your mother everything."

Grace looked up toward the sky. "He was so angry with her about Frank and the affair, and it was him…he was the one who strayed first?"

"Yes. Your mother was understandably upset so she drove out to that vegetable stand the very next day after your father came clean and she confronted Mary. Alfred was there. He was three years old."

Grace spun around. "What did she do?"

"She threatened Mary. She told her to stay away from your father or…"

"Or what?"

"Or she would do something that would make her regret everything she had done."

"Do what? Cast a spell on her?"

Pastor Richards nodded.

Grace felt her legs go numb. "Of course she did," she said sarcastically. "And Alfred knew all of this?"

"Not until he was older, but yes."

"Then how did he end up here? Why would he come?"

"Mary's father died so she and Alfred came back for the funeral, and your father was there. He spoke to both of them. Your father felt horribly guilty for what had happened between them. He was impressed by the young gentleman that Alfred had become, and when he heard that Alfred was looking for work before entering the seminary, he offered him a job on the farm. Your mother was already gone by then."

Grace nodded. "And the spell—did my mother cast it?"

"I can't say for sure, but Mary and Alfred believe she did. That's why Alfred took that journal. He asked me to read it and help him pray over it to reverse any evil-doing your mother had done."

"But my mother wasn't evil!" Grace cried.

"I know that, Grace. That's why I'm telling you this now. Alfred should have told you himself, but Mary didn't tell Alfred the whole truth about what happened until after you were pregnant. At first, he didn't believe it. He stopped talking to his mother almost entirely, until…"

"Until he found this," Grace said looking at the journal in her hands.

"Yes," the pastor replied.

Grace sat down on a stump and covered her face with her hands. She thought she had been in the dark about her parents' relationship before, but now, now she felt complete anguish. Not only had they destroyed their own relationship, but her life was also in shambles because of their lies. For the first time since either of them had died, she was angry with them. She began to feel a deep burning resentment for all the silence about things she never knew.

Pastor Richards stepped closer and put a hand on her shoulder. "I'm so sorry. I thought it was time someone told you the truth."

Grace sat quietly, stewing in her fury and clasping her hands together. After a few minutes, she looked down, staring at her fingers and the ring on her left hand. "Pastor, do you know anything about the spell that my grandmother supposedly had placed on this ring?"

"Yes, I've heard some things about it." He watched her spin the ring in a circle between her thumb and index finger.

"Please tell me what you know."

Pastor Richards shook his head. "Your family has deep-rooted secrets, Grace. Dealings of witchcraft run on both sides. Your grandmother was very protective of her family, and she was friends with that woman who lives on the edge of town who folks say is a witch."

"Francesca Morano. Yes, I know all of this already."

The pastor nodded. "Well, from what I was told, Francesca knew your mother also practiced witchcraft, so when your grandmother asked Francesca to cast a spell on your father, she refused."

"Wait, my grandmother wanted Francesca to cast a spell *on my father*?" Grace asked as she stood up. "I thought she asked her do a spell for my mother."

"From what I was told, your grandmother did not want the wedding between your parents to ever take place, so she asked Francesca to cast a spell on your father to draw him away from your mother. I don't know what she did to that ring," he said.

"But they married anyway," she whispered.

"Yes, because you were on your way."

Grace stared at the pastor. "What? She was already…"

"Yes, your mother was already pregnant with you when your parents were married."

Grace quickly sank back to the stump. Her mind was racing from everything she had just heard. "It's all been a lie," she whispered. "All of it. Everything they told me was a lie."

"They loved you, Grace. They wanted to protect you."

"Protect me?" She shouted as she sprang up. "Protect me from what? Look at me now, Pastor. I *am* them! I'm living the exact same life, in the exact same place!"

"That's not true. You and Alfred are not them."

"We may as well be," she shouted. "I'm sorry, but I have to go. I need to get back to the house and I need to see Francesca Morano."

"I understand." Pastor Richards nodded. "Again, I'm so sorry to have been the one to tell you these things. Please ring me if you need anything. I won't be far away."

Grace didn't respond as she stomped back toward the house. She was driven by pure anger now and wondered if Calista had known these things all along.

Chapter 72

February 6, 2006, 9:00 a.m.

It was eerily quiet as Joe entered the house, which was just as he had left it. Ellie almost always had a television on when she was home, even though she wasn't watching it most of the time.

"I like the background noise," she would tell him. "It makes me feel less alone."

Right then, he couldn't have felt more alone. His head was pounding again. But instead of trying to sleep in their bed and being bombarded by all the same memories, he lay on the couch. He didn't even bother taking off his coat or his wet shoes. He knew Ellie hated it when he walked on the shiny hardwood floors without taking off his shoes, but right now he didn't care. All he wanted was to stop the pounding in his head.

When his head hit the pillow, Joe felt an immediate sense of comfort that he hadn't felt in days. Though he wanted desperately to sleep, he couldn't calm his mind. He had spent many nights on this couch trying to avoid an argument with Ellie after going out to the bars. It all seemed so useless now, and he wondered what on earth he had been so afraid of. Now there was so much more to fear.

As he tried to drift off to sleep, he couldn't help but think about whether he had seen his mother getting on the elevator at the hospital. It seemed like she had looked right at him. But why would she have walked away if it had really been her? Why wouldn't she let him know she was there and that everything was going to be fine? She had always been good at leveling his state of mind when everything else seemed so far off balance.

Before she died, they'd had many conversations that lasted late into the night about everything from her relationship with Joe's father to Andrew and, of course, Ellie. His mother was the only person he felt comfortable enough to talk to about Andrew. She had tried so many times to get Joe to find her grandson, but Joe refused. He was convinced his son was better off without him.

"Joey, you're a stronger man than you know," she would say.

"Mom, you don't know the half of it," he would reply, laughing sarcastically.

"Then tell me, Joey, why don't you believe in yourself?"

"Tell me why you stayed with dad for so long," he would respond.

"Touché, young man," she would reply. "Let's talk about something else. How about those Packers? Did you see Favre throw that interception?"

They would laugh and talk about something completely different. It had been seven years since his mother had passed away, and Joe wished he could have those conversations again.

When he tried to sleep, a faint hum started to ring in his ears. It was almost like the vibration of an idling engine, but it came from inside the house. At first, he passed it off as roadwork. Perhaps there was a crew down the street using heavy machinery that caused a ricochet effect, he thought. But then the hum grew louder and he felt the vibration throughout his body.

"What on earth?" He said aloud as he stood and walked to the front window. He looked out and tried to peer up the street, but he saw nothing out of the ordinary. Touching the window, he felt the vibration in the glass. He clamped his hands over his ears, but the noise was still there.

He sat back down on the couch and uncovered his ears. With his eyes closed, he tried to pinpoint the direction from which the sound originated, but it seemed to be coming from everywhere. It wasn't quite like a vibration anymore; it was more like electricity in the air. The hair on his arms rose and he stood again. The air seemed alive. Feeling unnerved, he walked up the stairs toward their bedroom, but the electricity followed. It was everywhere. With his heart racing, Joe broke into a sweat. He went into the bathroom, stripped off his clothes, and turned on the shower. As he stood under the warm water, hands still clasped over his ears, the humming grew quieter. The water helped clear his flooded mind. As it ran over his head, he began to feel calm again.

Suddenly, there was a loud crash and the sound of breaking glass from somewhere outside the shower. Startled, Joe shut off the water and stood still, listening. There was no sound, only his rapid breath and the blood pumping in his ears.

Snatching a towel off the rack and wrapping it around his waist, he slowly opened the bathroom door and looked around the bedroom. Sunlight poured in through the open curtains and he quickly blinked as he scanned the room. Nothing seemed out of place.

Dripping wet, he cautiously entered the hallway and made his way toward the stairs. There were shiny shards of glass all over the floor at the top of the stairs, and a picture frame was face-down on the carpet. He looked in the empty bedrooms and peered down the stairs before he bent to pick up the frame. It was a photograph of his parents that had been taken when Joe was a child. He had never liked it and was annoyed when Ellie hung it on the wall. But now here it was, face down on the floor. It looked like the glass had exploded out of the frame.

The vibration returned as he stared at the photograph. Confused, he dropped the picture and ran down the stairs, gripping the towel around his waist. Filling with anger, he checked every room in the house. The humming grew louder still. He ran down the basement stairs to see if the furnace had kicked on and was malfunctioning, but he found nothing there either. While standing at the bottom of the basement steps, he heard a door open and close on the first floor.

He froze, listening for footsteps, but he heard nothing but the humming. "Who's there?" He called out, but no one answered.

He ran up the basement stairs, taking two at a time, and stopped in the kitchen. Suddenly, the humming was gone. He stood there for a few seconds, trying to catch his breath.

"Is anyone here?"

The humming started again.

"Damn it!" He spun in a circle, trying to gauge where the noise came from. Feeling helpless, he ran over the broken glass, back up the stairs, and into their bedroom to get dressed. He decided that sleeping was no longer an option so he would go back to the hospital.

Before pulling his shirt over his head, he rushed into the bathroom and splashed water onto his face. When he looked into the mirror, he caught a glimpse of a woman with long, straight hair standing behind him. Startled, he spun around but saw nothing. His heart beat so fast now that he could barely catch his breath. He knew it had been his mother. He looked back to the mirror, but this time his own reflection was all he could see.

"What is happening?" He dressed quickly and ran down the stairs. He pulled on his shoes and grabbed his coat off the couch. Clamoring into his truck, he felt faint and tried to slow his breathing. "It's not real, it's not real," he whispered. His shaky hand stuck the key in the ignition. As he tore down the street, Joe looked into his rearview mirror and watched the house grow smaller behind him.

Chapter 73

February 3, 2006, 7:25 a.m.

"So your father cheated first?" Ellie said when Grace finished telling her about the conversation with Pastor Richards.

"Yes. It was the last thing I expected to hear," the old woman replied. "And to know that it was with Alfred's mother…well, I didn't exactly know what to do. Everything seemed so upside down at that moment. I couldn't believe the lengths that everyone had gone, including Alfred, to keep all of this information from me. If Alfred had known about his mother and my father *and* about the supposed spell my mother had cast, why did he even come to the farm?"

"Did you ever find the answers?" Ellie asked as she shivered beneath the blankets Grace had given her.

"No one ever finds the answers they seek until they really open their eyes," Grace said. "Like your Joe. He can never truly see what's in front of him until it's no longer there."

"You're right," Ellie whispered. "I wonder how he would feel if I never came back."

"Trust me, dear, he would be a ruined man," Grace said, lifting a corner of her mouth into a crooked smile. "Rather, he *is* a ruined man."

"Grace, when you said he was out there, what did you mean?"

Grace continued rocking and didn't answer at first as if she were choosing her words carefully. "Joe is in his own hell right now. It's different for everyone. I can't really explain it to you because you can't see it through your eyes."

"But do you mean he's literally out there in the snow?" she asked.

"Literally is never something we have here. This place doesn't truly exist," the old woman waved her hand in the air.

"It doesn't?"

"Of course not, dear," she continued. "I told you that *you* are not dead, but you know that I am. So tell me, *are we* really here?"

"So, I'm dreaming?"

"Something like that, but not entirely," Grace replied. "But, before we get ahead of ourselves again and your tears start flowing, let me finish my story.

Frustrated, Ellie slid back into her chair. "Okay, please go on," she said calmly.

"After my conversation with Pastor Richards, I went back to the house determined to confront Calista, and then I needed to see Francesca Morano. I was convinced those two women had not been entirely honest with me about everything they knew. In fact, they had been more elusive. Each had told me bits and pieces, but there were large pieces of the puzzle that didn't quite fit—at least not yet."

Chapter 74

September 1941

"Calista!" Grace yelled as she frantically entered the house. Her anger had grown with every step she had taken from the woods.

"What is it?" Calista said as she came out of the kitchen, wiping her hands. Isabella followed closely behind her.

"What's wrong, Mommy?" the little girl asked.

Grace only stared at Calista. "It was my father…my father cheated first. Why didn't you tell me?"

Calista took a step back. "I—oh, Grace, it wasn't like that. I don't…I…"

Grace shouted, "Pastor Richards told me everything," Grace said as she held the journal in front of her aunt. "Alfred gave this to him. He came by to return it, and he told me everything. My father cheated with Alfred's mother while my mother was pregnant with me. And the both of you…the both of you led me to believe that my mother was the one who ruined everything."

Calista dropped the dishtowel on the floor and moved closer to Grace, clasping her hands. "It wasn't like that, you must understand."

"Understand what?"

"Your father *did* love your mother very much, but you're right. There *is* more to the story."

Grace backed away and braced herself against the wall. Isabella stood in the kitchen doorway wide-eyed and silent.

"Tell me, Calista. Tell me all of it."

"My mother didn't just ask Francesca to bind a spell to that ring. She asked her for something else."

"Yes?"

"She wanted to drive your mother away. Isabelle had the gifts that my mother had always wanted but never had. She was beautiful, she was smart, and she also came from a family that possessed unique gifts."

"What kind of gifts?" Grace asked.

"You know what kind of gifts, Grace—the gifts that your mother wrote about in that book. She was a witch, but she had deep roots and possessed the ability to see things that others couldn't see."

"Grandma was a witch!" Isabella screamed as she covered her mouth with her hands.

"Oh, Isabella, honey, your grandma wasn't evil," Calista said, growing short of breath. "And Grace, your mother was special. Everyone knew it. Everyone was intoxicated by your mother, but my mother was afraid that she would destroy your father."

"So there were two spells?" Grace uttered.

"Yes, there were. The first was on that ring—and when it didn't have the effect she wanted it to have, my mother cast a second spell. She didn't know the harm she was doing, Grace. She didn't even know the spells worked. Francesca warned her of the consequences, but even she didn't know what my mother had done."

"What was the second spell?" Grace asked, her anger turning to anguish.

"It was a bewitching spell," Calista whispered. "She wanted your father to fall for someone else…and he did, for a little while. But, his love for your mother was strong, and she loved him too, so they were able to pull through it."

"Until my mother was unfaithful," Grace said as she looked at the ring on her hand.

"Yes, and then the second spell took hold."

"Do you have any idea how crazy this all sounds?" Grace said as she held her head in her hands. "How could any of this be true?"

"Maybe it isn't, Grace," Calista said as she moved closer to her niece. "Maybe none of it is true. Maybe sometimes things happen because they are *supposed* to happen. Like I've always told you, magic is only real if you believe it."

"What are you saying Calista? If all of this is true, why didn't my mother put it in her journals?" Grace asked. "Why didn't she ever write about my father having an affair?"

"Maybe you just haven't found that journal," Calista said as she sat down, wiped her brow, and tried to catch her breath.

Without another word, Grace turned and ran up the stairs toward the attic.

"Mommy, where are you going?" Isabella asked, following her mother.

As she opened the attic door, Grace turned and clutched Isabella's shoulders. "Please, Izzy, wait here. Mommy just wants to look for something."

"But what are you looking for?"

"Something that was Grandma's." Grace climbed the stairs more slowly now, hoping Isabella wouldn't question or try to follow. She wasn't ready to explain to her daughter all that had happened. But Isabella had already heard too much.

"Mommy, are you a witch, too?"

Grace stopped in her tracks. She turned and went back down the stairs. "Isabella, honey, there are people who believe different things about your grandma. That doesn't mean they're all true."

The little girl stared at her, confused.

"Honey, I don't know if all of these things about spells are true, but I know your grandmother—my mother—believed in magic. But she believed in *good* magic."

"So your grandma was bad because she made bad spells?" Isabella asked.

Grace stood up and looked back up the stairs. "I don't know, Isabella. She thought she knew, but that's why we should never do things like that unless we know what we're doing."

"I want to be a witch, too," Isabella said with excitement.

"Oh, honey—" Grace was interrupted by a thud and the sound of breaking glass below.

She ran down the stairs, nearly falling as she went, and when she rounded the hallway corner, she saw pieces of a broken water glass on the floor. Calista lay near it, breathing heavily and awkwardly clutching a dishtowel with one hand.

"Calista," Grace cried as she lifted her aunt's head and placed the towel beneath it. "What is it? What's wrong?"

Unable to speak, Calista stared at her niece and moved her face oddly, unable to speak.

“Isabella, sweetie, ring the operator. Tell her to send a doctor as fast as they can!”

The little girl stared for a moment and then did as her mother told her.

“Hold on, Calista. Please, hold on,” Grace cried. “Don’t leave me here like this.”

Chapter 75

February 6, 2006

Joe's mind began to feel foggy as he drove toward the hospital. He was so tired, more tired than he had ever been in his life. It was the kind of exhaustion that made him feel as if nothing were real anymore. The road ahead of him looked like a blur and the sky was black, though it had been daylight just minutes ago. He felt punchy and he knew he shouldn't be driving, but he couldn't go back to the house. He didn't know what was happening there, but he was afraid his mind was playing tricks on him and being there only made it worse.

Afraid that he was too jittery to drive on the highway, Joe decided to take a back road to the hospital. It was a narrow road he knew well, and it would get him to the hospital without the fear of hitting another car or injuring someone else. He rubbed his eyes as he weaved down the road. Looking into the rearview mirror, he saw nothing behind his truck but the soft swirling snow that had just begun to fall.

He thought of his mother and wondered why he had seen her image twice now. Was this his subconscious trying to tell him something? Was it his mind's way of preparing him to be a father again? Or was it possible that he was actually seeing a ghost? Nothing felt normal now.

He switched on the radio, hoping the sound would distract him, but all he heard was static. He pushed the button to change the station, but again, it was just static. He tried again. More static. Instead of switching it off, he let the static play. If nothing else, it would kill the silence in the cab.

As he drove on, the static began to seem more like voices—almost like a room full of people whispering all at once. He couldn't make out any words, but he focused in on the sound, trying to hear something that might not even be there.

"I'm here, Joey," a soft, murmuring voice proclaimed, suddenly becoming clear amongst the distortion.

He wasn't sure if he had heard it or if his mind was making it up, but he turned up the volume and listened more intently. The whispering voices filled the cab now.

"I'm here Joey," the voice said again. This time, he was sure he'd heard it. There was only one person that called him Joey. He pulled his truck to the side of the road.

"Mom, are you there?" he said, unafraid this time. "If it's you, tell me why you're here."

The whispers continued, but the voice didn't speak.

"Please, just tell me what's going on!" His voice was louder this time.

Still, there were only whispers. Frustrated, he shut off the radio and stared ahead at the snowy road. The sky had grown even darker now. A storm seemed to be moving in. The snowflakes, which had been so light and soft before, were turning into heavier, blowing snow.

Chapter 76

February 3, 2006, 7:49 a.m.

Grace dabbed her eye with the edge of her shawl as she told Ellie about finding Calista collapsed on the floor. "She died the next morning," she said quietly. "She had a very bad stroke."

"I'm sorry," Ellie said as she watched the look of pain cross Grace's face. Her life seemed to be filled with such loss, more loss than Ellie could comprehend. She had never lost anyone who was so close to her, but Grace had lost many.

"There were so many things I wanted to say to her before she died," Grace said as she looked out the frost-covered window. "There was so much I wanted to say to all of them. But the way I spoke to Calista that day, I couldn't help but feel responsible."

Ellie didn't know what to say, so she reached out and took the old woman's cold hand into her own.

Grace glanced up and looked deep into Ellie's eyes. "It's been so long since I've felt another person's touch."

"I'm sorry you had to live with such pain," Ellie whispered.

"Oh, I did have some good points as well," the old woman said as she pulled back her hand and straightened in her chair. "I had great love in my life as well. It just didn't happen the way I expected it would."

"You mean with Alfred?" Ellie asked.

The old woman snickered. "I did love Alfred, yes, but the greatest love of my life was with someone else."

Ellie stiffened her back and looked straight ahead. "With who?"

"With Jack. I followed in my parents' footsteps even more than I knew at the time. I had heard the warnings, felt the power of anger, guilt, and revenge, and yet I ignored it all. "

Ellie felt herself wanting to embrace the old woman, but she didn't. "If you loved Jack, why didn't you just leave Alfred?"

"If I thought that was ever an option, I would have. But, things were much more black and white in those days, dear. I was ashamed of what I had become, despite my feelings for Jack. I didn't want my daughter growing up thinking it was okay to do the things I was doing. And so I hid it. I hid it all from everyone, except myself. After a while, I realized why my mother had kept all those journals. I think it was less about the magic she wrote in them and more about trying to interpret what she felt inside."

"Will you tell me about Jack?" Ellie asked.

Grace's eyes lit up. "I'd love to, dear."

Chapter 77

September 1941

Grace stood in the hallway unsure of what to do or where to go. The doctor's words still rang in her ears. Calista was gone. Shell-shocked, Grace was immobile while Isabella clung to her skirt sobbing. Even her daughter's painful cries couldn't snap her out of the daze she now found herself in. She had lost her mother and father and had watched her husband go off to war without looking back, and now her aunt, whom she had relied on for all these years, was gone. Filled with so much loss, Grace didn't know where to put this latest pain. Like a balloon that will pop with just one more puff of air, Grace felt as if she could explode.

She looked down at Isabella, who had saturated her mother's skirt with tears. Mustering what strength she had left, Grace lifted the child into her arms and began walking toward the hospital entrance. She needed to get out of this cold, sterile place. Feeling surrounded by death, Grace had to escape the sinking feeling that there was a curse pressing down on her for things far beyond her control.

As she pushed through the doors with Isabella clinging to her like a cub, a rush of hot air hit her face. The late-summer heat made her stagger slightly, but she started down the concrete steps anyway. Halfway down, she was met by Pastor Richards and Jack.

"Grace, I am so sorry for your loss," Pastor Richards exclaimed as he reached out and stroked Isabella's back. The little girl's crying had not let up.

"Let me drive you home, please," Jack said, his eyes full of concern.

Grace stood stoic and emotionless. "I have my car over there," she mumbled, squinting in the sun.

"I will drive your car," the pastor said. "Please let Jack drive you home."

She nodded and Jack reached out to take Isabella.

"No!" Grace immediately realized the harshness of her tone. "I'm sorry," she said, "but no. I will carry my daughter."

"Alright," Jack replied. "Right this way."

Grace followed as Jack led her to his truck. Isabella held on tightly, burying her face in her mother's neck. The little girl's tears were wet against her skin, yet Grace couldn't find any of her own.

"How did you know I was here?" Grace murmured as the Chevrolet rumbled to life and jerked into gear.

"The doctor rang Pastor Richards," he said as he turned down the dusty road and headed away from the hospital. "The pastor rang me and thought you might need a ride…and maybe a friend."

Grace looked down and held Isabella tighter. The little girl had almost cried herself to sleep.

"I'm very sorry about Calista," Jack said. "I can help with anything you need—funeral arrangements, help on the farm…anything." Jack stole a glance in her direction.

"Thank you, Jack," she replied as she rolled down the dirty window and let the air hit her face. It was hot and not at all comforting, but it reminded her that she was still alive.

"Is there a way to contact Alfred?" Jack calmly asked as he stared down the road. "He just left. There may still be time to reach him before he's shipped to another base."

Grace hadn't thought about the possibility of Alfred coming back. Under the circumstances, and after all she had learned, she wasn't sure she wanted him to return. She needed to sort out the rest of her family secrets before she could start working on her relationship with Alfred.

"I won't be reaching Alfred," she murmured.

Jack looked at her again, but he said nothing.

As they turned down the dirt drive leading to the farm, the anxiety rose in Grace's chest. No matter where she went, she always felt the same anxious feeling when she returned here. It was as if gravity always pulled her back to the same place. She didn't want to be here anymore, especially now.

"Can you drive me back to town, Jack?" Grace asked. "I'd really like to speak with Francesca."

Jack glanced at her again, but she continued staring out the window, expressionless, her hair blowing back to reveal a redness in her cheeks. "Of course," he said.

As he circled the farmyard to leave again, Pastor Richards came up the drive in Grace's car. As Jack drove past him, he gave the pastor a wave and continued back to the road. There was a confused look on the pastor's face. He would be stranded there until they returned.

Grace remained silent as she held the now-sleeping Isabella in her arms. The little girl's weight made her conform to the uncomfortable seat. She wasn't sure what she would say to Francesca when they arrived, but she had to hear what was left of the story about her parents and the supposed spells. With Calista gone, there was no one left to explain it.

When Jack stopped the truck on the road in front of the old woman's house, Grace didn't move. She simply stared out at the walnut tree and its twisted roots coming through the ground. Though the trees around it had begun to lose some of their leaves, the walnut tree's leaves were still deep green. Large, browning walnuts were scattered about the ground beneath it, making it a virtual paradise to any neighboring squirrel, but the long, thin leaves clung to their host like they had no intention of ever falling away.

"That's one strange tree," Jack said as he followed Grace's stare.

"Her grandmother planted it," Grace uttered as she reached for the door handle and prepared to lift Isabella.

"Why don't you leave her on the seat," Jack said as he reached out. "Let her rest. She'll be fine here."

Grace hesitated at first, but then she nodded and lay Isabella down, her head resting on Jack's thigh.

"We'll wait here until you get back," he said with a nervous smile.

With a shaky step, Grace walked toward Francesca's front door. The old front porch stairs creaked with each movement, and the door opened just as she lifted a hand to knock.

"Hello Grace," Francesca said, her voice cheery. She was dressed in her usual black attire, but she wore a bright red apron over her skirt as if she had been cooking. "I saw you and Jack pull up. I'm happy to see you."

Grace smiled slightly as she met the old woman's glance, but Francesca's smile melted immediately. "Something is wrong. What is it dear? Please come in."

The house smelled of sweet rhubarb, and the scent made her feel more welcome as she stepped inside and cleared her throat.

"I'm sorry to bother you, but my Aunt Calista passed away this morning," she said, her voice quivering.

"Oh dear, I am so sorry. You must sit down," Francesca said as she reached for a handkerchief in the pocket of her dress. "Why is Jack waiting outside? He should come in."

As Francesca scurried around the sitting room, Grace sat in a large, floral-patterned high back chair. It was hard, as if no one had ever sat there before. "I came here to ask you about some things," Grace said as Francesca stopped moving and turned to listen.

"Yes?"

"I need to know about the spells that you gave to my grandmother, and I need to know if my mother cast a spell on Alfred's mother, Mary."

Francesca's face turned sour. She moved closer to Grace and sat opposite of her in a more worn-looking chair.

"I always knew this day would come," Francesca said as her eyes drifted to the floor and she nervously stroked her black linen skirt. "I should never have given those spells to your grandmother. I was young, but I should have known better. But as I told you before, your grandmother did not have the gift of connecting to the spirit world. I didn't think the spells would work."

"But they *did* work, didn't they?" Grace asked.

"Well my dear, *I* believe they did. But I'm a foolish old woman."

Grace sighed. "Please start telling me the truth."

Francesca shook her head. "Well, even though your grandmother didn't have the insight or a family history of practicing magic, she believed in those spells. She believed them so much..."

"That they came true?" Grace muttered.

"Yes," Francesca whispered.

"And that's why my father had an affair with Alfred's mother?"

"Yes."

"And that's why this ring is cursed?"

"Yes."

"Can I take it off and destroy it?"

Francesca stood up and walked to the window, looking out to where Jack sat in the truck with Isabella. "Destroying it won't undo the harm that's been done."

"What were the spells, Francesca? I want to know all of them." Grace was too weak to stand, but her voice was firm.

"The first was the love spell, which I should never have given her because she used it with the wrong intentions."

"And that's why my father was unfaithful...with Alfred's mother?" Saying the words out loud made a bubble of nausea rise in Grace's throat.

"Yes. She wanted your father to fall for someone else," Francesca said under her breath. "But she underestimated the depth of the love between your parents. It transcended even the spell."

"And the second spell?"

"The second spell was the binding spell. When your parents resigned to marry anyway, even after your father's infidelity, your grandmother became more desperate. That's when she came to me before the wedding. Initially, that spell should have been used to protect the marriage of whoever wore that ring. But instead of using the spell like I told her, she reversed it and turned it into a curse."

"What is the difference?" Grace asked.

"Curses use the destructive power of words, I'm afraid," Francesca muttered. "Your grandmother twisted them and uttered those words in the physical realm without connecting to the spirit realm."

Grace shook her head, confused.

"If the words are uttered the way your grandmother uttered them, they can sometimes influence the physical realm. Curses are channeled through people my dear. Spirits cannot curse; only people can do that. Like I told you before, your grandmother did not possess the gift of connecting to the spirit world, which, for most witches is what makes a spell take shape. Somehow, she did reach the other side, but it was a dark side—a cursed side. I should never have given her any spells. She didn't know the damage she could do."

"Then why did you give them to her?"

Francesca's eyes filled with tears and she looked down at the floor. "Because she was my friend…she was my only friend. I did it out of selfishness. I wanted to make her happy. Like I told you, I didn't think they would work. I'm not as talented of a witch as your mother was. I don't have the same gifts, and I knew your grandmother didn't have them. But she was so jealous of your mother that it made her stronger somehow."

Grace rose to her feet, angry. "You did this so you could keep a friend? A friend that was vindictive and thought she needed to use magic to stop her son from marrying the woman he loved? That's why you did it?"

Francesca stared at Grace, tears falling freely now. "Yes, and I'm so ashamed."

Grace glared back at the old woman in astonishment. "And my mother's spell on Mary, Alfred's mother—what was it?"

Francesca wiped her eyes. "That was a curse as well. A curse she made for Alfred."

Grace sank back into the chair as the old woman moved closer to her. "What?"

"Even with her keen insight, there was no way she could have known that out of all the places in the world Alfred could go, and all the women he could have met, he would find you. That was your mother's punishment for doing what no witch should ever do. Things have a funny way of always traveling in circles."

"What was the curse?" Grace asked.

"A curse is something different, like I said, and your mother knew it was different, but she did it anyway."

"I thought witches didn't cast negative spells or make curses. You told me that yourself," Grace replied.

"Ordinarily we don't, but your mother was scorned. She didn't know your grandmother's spell is what drove your father to stray. She believed Mary had lured him. But, instead of putting the curse on Mary, your mother decided it would hurt her more to put it on Alfred."

"And what was it?"

"I don't know exactly what it was, and if I did, I wouldn't repeat it. But what I do know is that it would cause Alfred to be forever restless. No matter what his good intentions are or where he goes, he will find no solace. By doing that, your mother took away Mary's hopes and aspirations for him. He would never attain the things that Mary wanted for him because he would destroy his own chances first. That is his curse. And as you know, dear, mothers place a lot of hope in their children. For Mary, her hope in Alfred was destroyed. And on the day he met you, she knew any chance she had of keeping Alfred on the right path, like sending him to the seminary, was shattered."

"Then why did she allow him to work on the farm?" Grace asked.

"She didn't. Alfred made that deal with your father, and it was done before she even had the chance to object. She tried to talk him out of it, but she never told him the whole truth either. All she could do was pray that Alfred would make the right choices."

"How do you know all of this?"

"I have my ways, child," Francesca replied without hesitation.

Grace thought of all they had been through and how ironic all of it seemed.

"My God," she whispered. "How can I undo all of it? I won't have my daughter dealing with this pain in *her* life."

"I'm afraid the only undoing is to stay away from it. Do the right things, make the right choices, and all will turn out in the end."

Grace laughed sarcastically. "That's your advice? To do nothing?"

"I can't undo what's done," Francesca said. She wiped her hands on the red apron as if she were trying to wipe away the proverbial dirt on her hands.

Grace wondered why anyone had ever feared this woman.

"I am sorry for what I did, Grace—for giving those spells to your grandmother." The old woman reached out and took Grace by the hand. She inspected the ring like it was the first time she had ever seen it. "But you must remember, there is still the possibility that the spells didn't work. There is a possibility that what happened between your father and Alfred's mother, and everything that came after, was by pure chance."

"Do you believe that?" Grace asked, remembering what Calista had said.

The old woman turned away and walked toward the door. She waved to Jack as she stepped onto the porch. He stared blank-faced toward the house. Then she turned back to Grace. "I don't know what I believe anymore," she said. "I am sorry for all that you've lost, but please be careful in what you do. That's all I can tell you."

As Grace stepped off the porch and walked toward the truck, she locked eyes with Jack. She was grateful he was here with her instead of Alfred. Alfred seemed like a different person after all that she had learned. As she passed beneath the walnut tree, a single, dry leaf gently floated down and landed on the ground in front of her. She looked up and was surprised to see that a number of leaves had turned from bright green to rusty brown and had begun to fall during the short time she had been in the house. As she walked to the truck, an uncomfortable feeling seeped inside her, like water filling a glass.

"Are you okay?" Jack asked as she climbed onto the seat next to him. She was careful not to disturb Isabella, who still slept between them.

"Yes, Jack. Please take me home now."

Chapter 78

February 2006

Joe broke out into a cold sweat as he pulled his truck back onto the road. He couldn't shake the eerie feeling that had settled inside of him. The road was less visible now, and he regretted taking this back way to the hospital. Though he wanted to turn back, a voice inside his head kept urging him on. *Get back to Ellie, just get back to her.*

The wind blew harder and Joe's tires slipped on the slick road, but he refused to let up on the gas. His windshield wipers slapped frantically, but they were no match for the sticking, blowing snow. His heavy breath caused the windows to fog. Though driving in heavy snow had never bothered him before, a panic rose in his chest. He used his sleeve to rub the condensation on the inside of the windshield.

Then, as quickly as the heavy snow had appeared, it began to slow. The road ahead became a little clearer. When he turned the defroster on high and slowed his breathing, even the condensation began to clear. *I must have driven out of it*, Joe thought. He punched his foot down harder on the gas.

Suddenly, from out of the darkness, a silhouette appeared. He made out the woman's long, dark hair as she walked in front of him and stopped directly in front of his truck. Joe instinctively hit the brakes with both feet and jerked the wheel. Though there was less snow here than what he had just passed through, his tires locked and the truck slid sideways. He turned the wheel and overcorrected, and he soon found himself spinning in a circle.

As everything moved in slow motion, the woman quickly flashed in his peripheral vision. Letting go of the steering wheel, he turned his head and clearly saw his mother standing in the middle of the road. She was expressionless, but her dark hair swirled around her head as if she were in motion and spinning with him.

Joe closed his eyes. The truck hit the curb with such a velocity that it rolled onto its side. As it continued to roll, he was tossed mercilessly around the cab. He heard breaking glass and twisting metal as he covered his face with one arm and put the other above his head to break his fall when the truck rolled upside down and forced him to the roof of the cab. After what seemed like minutes of spinning, the truck stopped right-side up with a vicious thud and slapped his body against the driver's side door.

Joe sat unable to move, but he felt no pain. He hadn't been wearing his seatbelt, so he instantly wondered if he was paralyzed. Afraid to open his eyes, he gasped for breath. Then he heard the crunch of footsteps coming through the snow and broken glass. He snapped his eyes open. As he shot a quick look down his body, he was surprised to see not even a drop of blood. He looked at the backs of his hands, wiped at his face, and felt down his legs. There were no injuries. As the footsteps neared, Joe rested his head on the back of the seat and started laughing. His strong, thick bellows came from a place deep inside, and even he didn't know why he was laughing. The laughter continued even when his mother's face appeared outside the window.

She smiled, reached in through the broken glass, and touched his cheek. Her hand was cold, but he remembered the softness of it. “I’m dead, aren’t I?” He said as he stared at his mother through watery eyes.

“You are,” she whispered. “But, it’s okay now.”

Chapter 79

September 1941

Pastor Richards was sitting on the front steps when Jack and Grace pulled up to the farmhouse. Grace could tell he was displeased with being abandoned on the farm. Though it wasn't quite dark, a heavy, warm haze still filled the air.

Grace was exhausted and she looked down at Isabella, who was still asleep on the truck's front seat. She decided it was best not to wake her.

"Let me carry her in for you," Jack said as he lifted the girl into his arms. He followed Grace into the house and up the stairs. As she watched him place her daughter in bed, she couldn't help but think of Alfred. She wondered where he was right then. A wave of guilt flowed over her at the thought of him keeping Calista's passing from him. He would surely want to know.

As Jack tucked the blankets around Isabella's chin, Grace wondered how her husband would feel if he knew that another man was in his house, putting his only child to bed. Though she knew the scenario was completely innocent, she couldn't shake the feeling that she was doing something wrong.

As they came out of Isabella's bedroom, Grace noticed the attic door was wide open and recalled how she had tried to go up there before Calista collapsed. She had wanted to look through more of her mother's journals, but it seemed less important now. She silently stared up the darkened stairs.

"Can I get you anything from up there?" Jack asked, following her gaze.

Grace closed the door and turned back toward him.

"No, but thank you, Jack," she said, taking him by the hand. "Thank you for everything."

Jack smiled as Grace led him down the stairs. It felt good to hold his hand, even though she had no idea why she was doing it. Alfred had only been gone a day. She wasn't sure if it was grief or exhaustion, but she didn't want Jack to leave. She released his hand when they reached the bottom of the stairs. Outside the door, Pastor Richards stood with his back to them and looked out at the cornfields. The door creaked as they opened it and joined him on the porch.

The pastor turned toward them. "Will you be okay alone out here, Grace?"

"I'll stay," Jack replied. "I don't think she should be alone tonight."

Both Pastor Richards and Grace looked at him with surprise.

"Jack, I'll be alright," she insisted.

"I'm staying, Grace. I think it's best." He met her eyes as he spoke.

The pastor cleared his throat and looked toward the vehicles in the drive. "Well, um…I don't have my car here, Jack."

"I'll drive you back to town," he said as he started down the porch stairs toward his truck.

Placing his hands on Grace's shoulders, the pastor spoke softly and slowly. "I'll be back tomorrow and we'll discuss the funeral. Please try to get some rest."

Grace nodded. As they drove away, she sat on the porch swing and listened to the sound of crickets and cicadas. The farm seemed so lonely now, so empty. She looked toward the cornfield and watched the tall stalks swaying in the breeze. She knew Alfred had made arrangements with local farmers to yield some of the crops, like the corn, but she began to wonder how long she could hold on here, alone. With Calista gone and knowing so little about farming herself, Grace was ashamed that she hadn't learned more about running the farm while her father was alive. He had never expected much from her in the way of doing farm chores or tending fields. She had happily cared for Belle and Rocco, but not once had she ever helped her father plant, sow, or harvest anything. She was suddenly aware that after all the time she had spent hating this place, the possibility of losing it was very real.

Overwhelmed, she stood and headed toward the barn. The breeze was cool on her face as she walked. Closing her eyes, she imagined her parents and her aunt together again. Calista would be reunited with her husband, Charlie, and she would be happy. Grace realized that, in a way, they were the lucky ones now—they weren't trapped; they were free.

As she slid the barn door open, both horses poked their long, narrow faces out of the stalls. Just seeing them calmed her. She walked straight to Belle and rested her head on the horse's face. Belle gently nudged her. It was then the floodgates finally opened and Grace let go of the tears that had eluded her all day. Belle stood stoic and patient as Grace held onto her.

As she cried, Grace thought of her parents, her grandmother, Calista, and Alfred. What a twisted circle all of them had created. She felt cheated to be the only one left, standing in the center of it. Even Francesca couldn't be certain of how to take away the pain they had caused. She no longer wanted to believe in the magic that her mother and the old woman practiced.

Lost in her grief, Grace didn't hear Jack return. When she felt his hand on her shoulder, she quickly turned and nearly collapsed into his arms. He said nothing but held her tightly. When she found the strength to pull away, she stared intensely into his kind eyes. She wanted to tell him to turn and walk away, to leave the farm and never come back before all of its darkness found a way to corrupt him, too. But she didn't.

Instead, she pulled him closer and kissed his lips. He reciprocated and held her tighter. His kiss was different than Alfred's. She felt his sincerity. His arms wove around her like branches, making her feel protected. As their kisses became more passionate, Grace allowed herself to let go. She wasn't a child anymore and she didn't have her father's foreboding eyes warning her not to make the same mistakes that her mother had.

She didn't allow herself to think of her husband, who was excited to rush off to war and leave her in the prison he had helped her create. She didn't think about Calista, either, or the warnings Francesca had given her. She didn't care about any of it anymore. She only thought of Jack and how good he made her feel. As he lay her down on a blanket of straw, Grace allowed herself to truly make love for the first time in her life. Though she had been infatuated with Alfred and became his wife, she had never given the woman inside of her a chance to reveal herself. She had been a child for too long. She felt more alive in Jack's arms than she had ever felt before, and she didn't care what the next day would bring.

Chapter 80

February 3, 2006, 8:30 a.m.

Ellie listened as Grace talked about Jack. Her love for him was apparent, and even the light in her eyes changed when she spoke of him. Ellie knew how the old woman felt—the feelings she described were the same feelings she had for Joe.

"What happened after that night?" Ellie asked when Grace grew quiet, a smile slowly curving across her face.

"I was a different woman after that day," she said, her eyes still sparkling. "I finally knew what it meant to be a woman and to know what honest love was all about. I can't blame Alfred for what happened, but Jack—Jack was so different. He had no direct ties to that place, or to me and my family. He saw me for who I really was."

"Why didn't you leave with him?" Ellie asked.

"We buried Calista a few days after, and Jack and I continued our relationship, but given the circumstances, we decided to hide it from everyone, including Isabella. Jack spent a lot of time on the farm, but he always made it look like he was working or tending to the horses so no one would question it. There were times he didn't come by during the daylight hours at all. But at night," Grace sighed and lifted a hand up to her heart, covering it as if it might beat out of her chest. "At night he would always come back after

Isabella was asleep. Most nights we made love, but others we just sat and talked. He made me feel so important, so relevant."

"And no one ever suspected you were having an affair?" Ellie wondered why the two of them just didn't expose the relationship.

"People talked, yes, but I was alone on the farm. They knew I needed help, and if I didn't get help from Jack, who else would have done it?"

"Why didn't the two of you just leave?"

"He wanted to," Grace said, looking down. "He asked me numerous times, but I couldn't go. I couldn't leave that farm even though I hated it there. It was the only home I had ever known, and it was the only place that made me feel connected to my parents."

"And the spells—did you disregard them?"

Grace briefly turned her eyes toward the ceiling. "I did. I became so lost in Jack that I forgot about everything. I didn't see Francesca anymore after that. I was afraid she would see right through me and know what I had done. But as the seasons changed, the consequences of losing touch with reality took their toll. I didn't lease the remaining fields like Calista had suggested, and I didn't plant new crops. The money began to run out."

Ellie nodded and looked down.

"It wasn't long before I began to sell my father's equipment, pieces of furniture, and anything I could just to get through the winter. It was harder for Jack to reach us as the snow piled up, and sometimes he didn't make it at all. On those cold, lonely nights, Isabella and I huddled near the fireplace in that big house all alone. After she fell asleep, I began writing. I wrote about everything. The questions I had about my parents, about witchcraft, and my questions of faith. I wrote about Alfred, and I wrote about my love for Jack."

"Did you ever hear from Alfred?"

"We received letters, yes," Grace continued. "He was stationed in Germany through most of his tour. He wrote how he loved us, and about his gratitude to God for keeping him alive through the horrors of war. Isabella hung on every word, but it was lost on me. I was no longer in love with Alfred. Some nights, I found myself hoping he would never return. He wrote how he couldn't wait to get back to us and get the farm running again. He also expressed his sadness in losing Calista.

"At times I felt guilty after reading Alfred's letters. He *was* my husband, after all, but as the months wore on, all that had happened seemed like a distant memory. Isabella was my only reminder of Alfred, and even she reminded me more of my mother every day."

"And what happened to the farm? Did you stay?" Ellie asked.

Grace shook her head and looked down at the floor. "In the spring of 1943, I ran out of money and had nothing left to sell. Jack begged me to leave with him and go out West. He had a friend that had started a successful horse breeding business and wanted Jack to tend to the horses' medical needs. It was the opportunity of a lifetime for him. But still, as much as I loved him, I didn't go. Isabella didn't know my true feelings for Jack, and she worshipped Alfred. I knew she would hate me if I left, and I couldn't bear the thought of that. Instead, I sold the farm to a young couple that had just moved to town. Pastor Richards had approached me and convinced me it was the best move—the only move—I could make. They agreed to board Belle and Rocco and allowed me to visit them as often as I liked. And so I bought a little house in town and tucked away what little money I had left. I was a saddened to lose the farm, but I felt a heavy burden lifted at the same time. The couple brought new life to the farm, and I was finally free of it. It was the right thing to do. I was optimistic that Jack would be happy and stay, too."

"Did he?" Ellie questioned.

Grace looked at the ceiling again before she spoke. "No, he didn't. He went to visit his friend with the job offer and he never returned. He wrote me furiously asking me and Isabella to join him, but I couldn't."

"It just ended?"

"Yes, dear, it just ended. Jack was the greatest love of my life, and I should have followed him, but I chose not to. I chose to stay and do what I thought was best for my daughter."

"And then?" Ellie asked.

"And then Alfred came home," Grace said. She picked up her cracked teacup and took a long sip.

Chapter 81

February 2006

Joe stared at his mother through the shattered window.

"It's alright, son. You can get out now," she said as she reached for him again.

When he pushed the door open and stepped out, Joe didn't know what to expect. He stared at his mother and then turned to survey the damage to his truck.

"What about Ellie? What about the baby?" He put his hands on top of his head.

"They'll be alright, Joey. There's much I need to explain to you. Come take a walk with me." His mother led him off the road and into the deeper snow.

"We're just going to leave the truck here? Just like that? Will anyone find it?"

His mother took his hand and continued walking. "You don't need to worry about your truck, son."

Joe stopped. "Wait. Where are we going?"

His mother continued without stopping. "I'm taking you to Ellie. If you want to see her, you have to come quickly, Joseph—before it's too late."

Joe picked up the pace and caught up to her, his feet trudging through the deepening snow. "Where is she, Mom?"

"I'm going to show you, Joey, but first you have to listen. We don't have much time."

"Is she dead, too? Did she die after I left the hospital? What about the baby?" The questions continued to flow until his mother stopped walking and turned to face him. "Did you see me in the hospital?"

"Yes, I saw you. Why didn't you stay?"

"Because you weren't ready yet to see what was really happening, Joseph. It wasn't the first time I'd tried to get you to see me," she said, touching his face again.

"What do you mean?"

"You've been lost, Joe. Lost to Ellie, lost to me, lost even to yourself, but you didn't see it."

Joe stared into her eyes. "What are you saying?"

"What do you remember about the last night you saw Ellie?" She took his hand and started walking again. The darkness was thick around them, and Joe had no idea how she knew where they were going.

"I was at the bar. She was mad at me again," he said, trying to recall what had happened.

"Do you remember the drive home?" She asked.

"Yeah…uh, well…no. I guess I don't."

"But you remember being home?"

He scratched his head. "Yeah, I remember Ellie coming out of the bedroom. She was mad, and then she left."

"And she never came back?"

"No. She was in an accident. She's been in the hospital ever since."

His mother nodded her head. As they started to crest a small hill, the sun began to rise in the distance.

"It's morning already?" Joe asked.

"It's anytime you want it to be. There isn't time anymore, not here."

"Where is *here*?" Joe asked. His mother smiled and cocked her head for a moment.

"'Here' is where you leave one road and learn to travel another. The journey can be smooth or it can be rough, depending on how you take that drive."

When they reached the top of the hill, they looked down into the snowy valley below. There, tucked near some trees, stood a small cabin with smoke billowing from the chimney.

"What is this place?" Joe asked as he began walking ahead.

"Wait, Joey," his mother said as she reached out and tugged his arm. "There's something I need to explain to you first."

"Okay?"

"The places where you've been during the last forty-eight hours never really existed, and it has actually been much longer than two days since you left the bar."

"What are you talking about?" Joe turned to face her.

"Ellie was not in the hospital, and neither were you."

"Was it a dream?"

"No, son," she continued. "It was a place you created for yourself with your guilt and your pain. It wasn't real. Seeing Ellie lying there was the scenario your mind created as your worst fear. Being bombarded with all those emotions, the fear and the memories, even the people—that was all your creation to help you deal with what you've done."

"None of it was real?" Tears welled in Joe's eyes as he thought about everyone he had been in contact with and recalled the conversations that had taken place. "So Ellie is okay? She isn't hurt?"

"No, son, she's not hurt."

"And there's no baby?"

His mother took his hand again and started walking slowly. "Yes, there is a baby, but she never had the chance to tell you before you passed. She was going to tell you the night you didn't come home—the night you actually died."

Joe wiped his eyes. "You said you were taking me to her. Does that mean she's dead now?"

"No, she's still alive," his mother explained. "She's been brought here for a short time because she's wavering between life and death. Something *has* happened to her, but she does not know why she's here. For her, time is not what it seems, either. She doesn't remember your death…not yet. You have to tell her."

Joe fell to his knees, breathing heavily. "What? Why? Can't she stay here?"

"No, son, she can't. Like you, she can't see what she needs to see just yet. She's been floundering since your death, trying to understand, and you owe her the truth now. Most people never get the opportunity that's being given to her…and to you. She's luckier than most. She comes from a very unique family that has been watching her. Now, they're able to make things right."

"What are you talking about?" Joe said breathlessly.

"Your wife comes from a long line of women who have a special insight, but that sight has been diminished with each new generation. Ellie doesn't know anything about it, and she doesn't know the secrets and lies of her family's past. But history repeats itself, Joseph, and now we have a chance to stop it. We can stop it for your daughter."

Though he still didn't understand what was happening, Joe followed his mother to the cabin. As they stepped onto the porch, he was surprised to feel his heart beating furiously. His mother placed a hand on his chest. "The heart isn't just a muscle, son. It still beats with love when you die."

The door swung open and Grace stepped onto the porch, locking eyes with Joe's mother. "Julia," she said with a nod.

"Grace," she reciprocated. "Is she ready?"

"I need a little more time. She's getting weaker," Grace said. "Hello, Joe. I'm Ellie's great-grandmother. Thank you for coming."

Joe shook her hand and stood in astonishment at the way the woman's eyes resembled his wife's.

"Please wait here for a few minutes," she said. She quickly opened the door and slipped back inside. Ellie had momentarily fallen asleep in her chair.

Hearing the door close, Ellie said, "Were you outside?" She was feeling even colder than she had before.

"I was just getting some fresh air, dear," the old woman responded. "Do you want to hear about Alfred's homecoming?"

"Yes," she said as she straightened up and adjusted the blanket. As she did so, she began to feel numbness in her hands and shook them slightly.

“I must hurry,” Grace said as she dove back into the story.

Chapter 82

April 1943

Grace sat on the front porch of the small, white house she had purchased months earlier and read a letter from Jack. He had been gone two months now, but it felt like he had been gone for years. Again, he had asked her to come to him, to tell Isabella the truth and leave all the bad memories and struggles behind. She could start over; they could get married, eventually, and start a new family. As she stuffed the letter back into the envelope, regret pushed down on her like a heavy weight. Still, she knew why she had to stay.

As she watched Isabella contently playing with her dolls in the front yard, she wondered if this was how her mother had felt all those years ago after Frank left the farm. Though Grace had combed her mother's journals after Calista passed away, she never found anything about her father's affair or the spell that her mother had supposedly cast on Alfred's mother. Grace began to wonder if any of it had ever been real.

She now kept the journals safely tucked away in her bedroom closet. They were full of spells to cure general ailments and described the spirits she had tried to conjure, but mostly they just detailed her mother's thoughts. Though Grace reveled in reading them, they also made her feel formidably sad because her mother had never spoken to anyone about her true feelings. As she thought of her mother, Grace took out her own journal, carefully tucked Jack's letter inside, and began writing. She was oblivious to everything around her when Isabella suddenly shrieked with excitement.

"Daddy!" the little girl screamed. She flew to her feet and out the front gate before Grace knew what was happening. And there on the sidewalk, wearing a dark-green uniform and shiny black shoes, stood a thinner, older-looking Alfred, a smile stretched across his face and his arms open wide. As Isabella jumped into them, Grace's heart dropped in her chest and she felt dizzy. She steadied herself as she rose to her feet and brought a hand to her mouth. Her eyes filled with tears. Though she masked them as happy tears when she met Alfred at the gate, Grace wanted to run back into the house and close the door. She hadn't prepared herself for his return.

As Isabella clung to his neck, Alfred's eyes locked on Grace and he smiled like he had when she first met him. "Hello, Grace," he said as he reached out and kissed her gently on the cheek.

"Oh, Alfred," she gasped. "Why didn't you tell us you were coming home?"

"I wanted it to be a surprise," he said as he looked back at Isabella. "My gosh, you're so big."

"I'm a whole year older and taller, too," Isabella giggled. "Come see the new house, Daddy! Come see my room!"

Alfred shot a look at Grace. "It looks just like your letters said it would, Isabella. It's wonderful."

"Come inside, Daddy! Come inside!" She tugged him along the sidewalk.

Shrugging his shoulders as he looked at Grace, Alfred followed Isabella into the house. Still standing on the sidewalk, Grace watched them go in. Then, with a loud gasp, she exhaled the breath she'd been tightly holding in her lungs. She turned around and looked out toward the street, but she saw no one. For a moment, she thought that no one would see her go if she ran. Still, she knew she couldn't leave Isabella, so she composed herself and walked inside.

As Isabella led Alfred from room to room, she said, "What do you think, Daddy?"

"It's not as big as the farmhouse, but it'll do," he said with a crooked smile.

When he let go of Isabella's hand, he walked over to Grace, who still stood in the doorway. He touched her face softly and then wrapped his arms around her. He was so much thinner than she remembered.

"I'm sorry I left everything on your shoulders," he whispered in her ear. "The house is perfect for our new start."

The trapped feeling seeped back into Grace's body and tears slipped down her face. She realized that by ridding herself of the farm but not leaving with Jack, she had traded one prison for another.

"Are you alright?" Alfred asked as he cupped her face in his hands.

"I'm just so happy you're back," she said, choking on the words and knowing they were lies.

Alfred smiled and kissed her lips. Though she knew he was sincere, Grace wanted to pull away. She didn't love Alfred anymore, and she wondered how long she could keep up the charade.

For the rest of the evening, Alfred sat on the sofa telling Isabella and Grace about his travels and the war. He almost seemed jovial, even as he talked about reading the last rites to dying soldiers on the battlefield. Grace thought it was strange, but she remembered that Francesca had told her about the curse her mother had supposedly placed on Alfred. Judging by the excitement in his voice as he talked about serving as a chaplain, she thought the curse couldn't possibly be real. Alfred seemed almost happy.

She interrupted as he told Isabella about walking through Germany in the snow looking for Hitler's army. "What will you do now that you're home, Alfred?"

"Well, now that we're free of the farm, I thought about maybe starting a church or a charity of some sort for soldiers returning from the war." There was enthusiasm in his voice. "I've been ordained by the Army."

"But what will we do for money?" She asked.

"Well, you sold the farm. Don't we have any money left from that? There should be enough to get the church rolling, and when I have a congregation…"

"Alfred, there isn't *that* much money, and we won't be starting a church with what is left," Grace said. The smile was erased from his face.

"Well," he said, looking at her with surprise and then clearing his throat, "we can talk more about that later. Right now, I think it's time for Isabella to get to bed. Grace, do we have any bourbon?"

"Bourbon?" Grace said with surprise. She had never seen Alfred drink before.

"Yes." He laughed. "I just returned from war, Grace."

"I'm sorry, Alfred, I only have homemade wine that was given as a gift when we moved into this house," she replied.

"That'll do," he said as he disappeared into the kitchen and started opening cupboards.

Grace was shocked at Alfred's transformation, and she was dazed as she readied Isabella for bed. When Alfred came into Isabella's bedroom to say goodnight, he handed Grace a glass of wine and clinked her glass. "Would you like Daddy to read you a story, Isabella?" he said cheerfully.

As Isabella picked out a book, Grace suddenly remembered the journal that she had left on the porch. Everything happened so fast that she had completely forgotten about it. As Alfred busied himself with Isabella, Grace slipped out of the room and breathlessly stepped onto the porch. She was relieved to see the leather-bound book still sitting in the place where she had left it.

"Oh, thank God," she said aloud.

Grace crept back into the house and slipped into her bedroom. She slid the book between her tidy bed's mattress and box spring and then looked around the room for anything else she may have left out that she didn't want Alfred to see. As she clicked on the closet light, she turned the key to lock her mother's trunk. She then removed the key and spread a blanket over the trunk to hide it.

Alfred surprised her as she came out of the closet. "What are you doing?" he asked.

"I was just looking for something special to wear for you," she said with a smile.

Alfred smiled and loosened his collar. “Let me make sure Isabella is asleep,” he said as he left the room.

Though her stomach turned, Grace knew Alfred would want to make love. For fear of making him suspicious, she knew she would have to oblige. She slid open her bureau drawer and dropped the key atop a pile of photographs. Before she closed the drawer, she touched her mother’s face in a photo that had been taken just months before she passed away.

When he returned with more wine, Alfred closed the bedroom door and removed his shirt. For the first time, Grace could see just how thin he had become. Though he was pale and skinnier than he used to be, Grace could still see the outline of muscle through his undershirt, and she briefly remembered how attracted to him she had once been. Nearly seven years had passed since then. Now, instead of making love to Alfred, she found herself wanting nothing more than to run away.

As he pulled her close and kissed her passionately, Grace’s tears returned. As he slipped off her dress and kissed her face, she wondered if he had any idea what a changed woman she truly was. But, as he looked her over and undressed himself, Alfred didn’t seem to care. Grace closed her eyes tightly and allowed Alfred to make love to her. Her tears flowed silently as she thought of nothing but Jack.

Chapter 83

February 3, 2006, 8:55 a.m.

Feeling lethargic and weak, Ellie listened as Grace spoke of Alfred's homecoming. She felt as if someone had sucked the life out of her.

"I know Alfred loved me, but it was too late for me to go back to the way things were," Grace said. "Even if I hadn't learned everything that I had been told, Jack had changed me."

Ellie stretched her fingers, attempting to shake off the numbness. "Did you ever hear from Jack again?"

"I received a few more letters after Alfred came home, but I could tell something had changed in him. He no longer asked me to come to him. He simply talked about his work and asked about Isabella. I knew he had found someone else. I missed my chance with him," Grace said as she looked down.

"What did you do?" Ellie asked, her eyes feeling heavy once again.

"I went on living."

"And what about Jack?"

Grace sighed. "Jack went on living, too."

"And Alfred never knew?"

The old woman laughed sarcastically. "No, not until much, much later, but by then things between us were very bad anyway. Are you alright, dear? You don't look well."

“I’m so tired and cold,” Ellie said. “My hands and feet are numb.”

Grace shook her head. “Yes, I know you’re weak, dear. Do you want to know why Alfred killed me?”

Ellie nodded.

Grace grabbed another blanket and tucked it around Ellie’s legs as she spoke.

“As the years went by, Alfred began drinking heavier. His idea of starting a church never came to fruition. Though I was thankful for that, he floundered from job to job without the steady work of the farm. He spoke less and less to me, and I supported us with crafty budgeting and odd jobs. I waited tables at a local diner and took work as a maid at a nearby hotel. The work was hard, but it kept my mind and my hands busy. All the while, Isabella grew faster. Since Alfred didn’t work regularly, the two of them spent a lot of time together. Alfred would walk her to and from school every day. He would usually sit at a local tavern in between.”

Ellie shivered as she listened.

“Most days passed by the same as the one before. We followed the same routines, day in and day out. We lived in a silent house. Though I had given up everything to stay for Isabella’s sake, I began to notice her pulling farther away from me and closer to Alfred. She seemed to be the only light left in his eyes.” Grace paused. “And then one day, when I was at work, Alfred found the key to my mother’s trunk. I have no idea why he was looking through my bureau, but he did. I don’t know how long it took him to find where the key belonged, but he did.”

“And he read the journals?” Ellie asked.

"Yes, he read them all. He found out about Jack and all the other things I wrote over the years that I never told him, or anyone."

"And then he killed you? Just like that?"

Grace laughed sarcastically. "Oh, no, dear. He let it fester for some time. And then he showed the journals to Isabella."

"Oh my God," Ellie gasped. "How did she take it?"

"Horribly," Grace said, her voice quivering.

As Ellie listened, she tried to imagine her grandmother, the happy woman she'd always known, as a bitter, hurt young girl.

"So, after all was said and done, I lost everything. I lost my parents, my home, my true love…and my daughter. So on the day that Alfred took my life, I wasn't afraid. You see, dear, when a woman has nothing left to lose, she has nothing left to fear, either."

"When did you know that he knew everything?" Ellie asked.

"When I came home from my cleaning job at the hotel on the day Alfred took my life, I walked in to find him sitting at the table drunk. I could tell he was angry, but when I asked him what was wrong, he said nothing. Since so much silence had already filled our house, I went into our bedroom to change my clothes, and there they were…my journals and Jack's letters spread neatly across the bed."

Ellie gasped.

"I should have left the house, but I was shell-shocked. I didn't know what to say to Alfred. There was no way to explain my way out of any of it. But what I didn't know at the time was that he had not only read my journals, but he had also read my mother's. He spent hours poring over her words and mine while I was at work. Though he never found the spell my mother supposedly cast on him, he became convinced that all of it was an abomination. And so, as I sat in a daze on the porch, trying to figure out what to do next, trying to understand all the things that Alfred and I would never be able to explain to each other about our feelings and a family history that couldn't be undone, he took my life."

Ellie stared at Grace with an open mouth.

"I knew when I heard that door open and his footsteps come across the porch that something bad was about to happen. But, I didn't run. I couldn't run. I had followed the same path as my mother."

Ellie began to cry. "So how did you end up here?"

Grace moved closer and took Ellie's hand. "When I came here, my mother was here. I was as confused as you are now. She created this place for herself after she passed away, and then when I came, she gave me all the answers that I had been looking for during my life.

"Which were?"

"That we cannot wait for the answers to life's questions."

"What?" Ellie said impatiently.

"You see, dear, my mother knew on her deathbed that she hadn't finished telling me all I needed to know about life. She left me with silence and speculation. So, I spent most of my life trying to find the truth—a truth that I never did find. My mother knew this would happen, and when she passed on, she became stuck between her former world and the next place where she was supposed to be. So, she created this place and she waited."

"Waited for what?"

"She waited for me," Grace said softly.

"And you waited for me?" Ellie asked.

"Yes, but it's not too late for you," Grace said as she stood and walked toward the door.

"What do you mean?" Ellie said, struggling to turn and follow Grace's movement.

"When I open this door everything will be clearer," she said. "Some years back I received a visitor. It was the one and only time anyone has ever knocked on this door. It was another woman looking for answers. Our stories intertwined, though we didn't know quite how much until we realized who our children were."

Ellie straightened in her chair as best she could and stared at Grace with a confused look on her face. "It was Jack's granddaughter. You see, I was wrong about that, too—I thought Jack had forgotten me. But he never forgot. He moved on, yes, but he didn't forget. He married a woman that he loved and was faithful to, but after she died, he told his granddaughter a story about another woman. A woman he loved…his first love."

Ellie pursed her eyebrows as she waited for Grace to continue. A nervous twinge rose in her stomach.

"Jack's granddaughter's name was Julia," Grace said as she put her hand on the doorknob. "You see, dear, that ring may not have been all bad luck. Though my marriage was a farce, true love always finds its way back."

As she opened the door, Grace nodded and motioned for Julia and Joe to enter. Upon seeing her husband, Ellie gasped and struggled to stand, but the numbness in her hands and feet caused her to stumble. Joe rushed forward and caught her in his arms.

"Ellie," he whispered, holding her tightly, as if his arms would never let go.

As she watched, Grace circled around them and then took her place next to Julia. "You see, Ellie, after I spoke to Joe's mother, I realized I wasn't saving this place for you—I was saving it for Joe. Joe is Jack's great-grandson, and *his* journey disrupted yours. You haven't done anything wrong, he did. But you have suffered because of it, the same way I suffered. But you can end it."

As the couple wiped tears from their faces, Julia smiled at her daughter-in-law and stepped forward. "I never knew how tightly our stories were wound until I left you," she said, touching Ellie's face and then her son's. She took Ellie's right hand and touched the ring on her finger.

"I don't believe this ring had anything to do with your bad luck, darling. But you've been given a great gift. You and my son have made many mistakes, just like the rest of us, but we can put an end to that now. Your child has the chance to know a different life, a life without the heavy silence that led the rest of us here."

"Does that mean we can go back?" Ellie muttered.

"*You* can go back," Julia responded. "But Joseph is one of us now."

Joe pressed his forehead against Ellie's. "I'm so sorry for everything I did to you," he whispered. "I should have talked to you—I should have told you the truth. But you have to know that it was never because I didn't love you."

Ellie felt weaker and the numbness in her legs crept higher. "I don't want to leave without Joe," she cried. Scenes began to flash through her mind uncontrollably. She saw flashing lights and the twisted metal of a truck. She saw herself on her knees wailing in pain. She felt close to fainting but saw one last vision of herself standing in front of a closed casket.

"What is happening to me?" She spoke as Joe lowered her to the floor.

"You're seeing the truth, my dear," Grace said. "It's what you've already been through but repressed when you came here. I needed you to hear what I had to say without the bitterness of what you had lost. Now you know the truth. It's what you do with it that matters."

"But what about the magic, the spells? Does any of that matter? Isn't that what brought me here? Why can't I stay here with Joe?" Ellie looked up at the women.

Julia and Grace exchanged glances.

"This is what happens on the other side of silence, Ellie. This *is* the other side of silence." Grace leaned down and touched Ellie's face. "When no one speaks about the past or the present…or even the truth…silence can become a room…a house, even a vast ravine. History tends to repeat itself, and history shapes who you are even though you don't recognize it. Actions are loud even when voices are not. Do I believe the magic and my family's spells brought you here? No, I don't believe in magic. Not anymore. I believe we make our own destiny. I believe all the energy that was put into believing in those spells is what *made* them true. We all shaped our lives around them. They were just words created by gifted and desperate women who were searching for something—be it revenge, or hope, or absolution, they were always searching."

Grace paused before continuing. "I have been wrong about many things. But what I do know is that we shouldn't be silent about who and what we are. We should scream it so loud that Heaven and all those we love can hear us. For it's when we hide who we are that the silence and the trenches grow deeper. Don't be quiet anymore, Ellie. Don't let your daughter be quiet, either. Wake up and live. Live enough for all of us that were silent and never found our way out of the world that we created for ourselves. That ring on your finger is a symbol of this family, but it does not shape your destiny. Wear it as a reminder of those who have gone before you, and pass it on when you're ready. Julia and I can go now, but Joe will be here waiting for you."

Ellie's eyes began to flutter and she struggled to hang onto Joe. She grabbed at his arms, but there was no strength left in her limbs. She could no longer feel. As everything grew dark, Joe whispered softly in her ear. "I love you, Ellie," he said. "I'll be right here."

Chapter 84

February 2, 2006, 5:15 p.m.

"We need the jaws!"

Ellie heard the shouting as she began to wake. Then a voice spoke to her. "Ma'am, can you hear me?" Ellie looked around and realized she was trapped inside of her car. She felt warm liquid running down her forehead, and she clutched her pregnant stomach, which pushed against the steering wheel.

"My baby!" She screamed, "Please, help my baby!"

"We're trying, ma'am. Just hold on."

Ellie slipped back into darkness. When she woke again, she saw her mother's face. It felt like only a minute or two had passed. As she blinked her eyes to ward off the bright sunlight that streamed through the open curtains, Anna's face became clearer. Before Ellie could speak, she coughed and gagged from the dryness in her throat.

"It's alright, honey. It's okay now," her mother said. She rubbed Ellie's back, which calmed down. Then her mother helped her to lean back.

"Where am I?"

Anna sat beside her daughter and gently rubbed her arm in the mothering, comforting way that she always did. "You're in the hospital, sweetie. You were in an accident on your way home from work."

Ellie looked down and clutched her stomach, which felt softer and smaller than before. “Oh my God, the baby.”

“It’s okay,” Anna said as she motioned toward a bassinet that was across the room, near the window. “They took her by C-section. She’s just fine. You’ve been through so much since Joe’s accident. They almost lost the both of you.”

“Please, can I see her?” Ellie pleaded.

“Of course,” Anna said with a smile, wiping tears from her face. She picked up the baby, who slept contently, and whispered, “Meet your mommy, sweetie.”

Ellie gasped as she took the baby and peered down at her face. She could immediately see Joe. “She’s so beautiful.”

Anna nodded in agreement as she sat beside Ellie and watched her granddaughter.

Touching her newborn daughter’s face, Ellie noticed that her hand was bruised and swollen and the ring on her right hand was missing.

“My ring?” she said as she turned toward her mother.

“They had to cut it off, honey. I’m sorry,” Anna said as she took her daughter’s hand. “I’m sure you can get it fixed.”

Ellie nodded and looked back down at her daughter. It didn’t matter now. She remembered the cabin, and Grace’s words still echoed inside her head. She wondered if any of it had been real or if it was just something her mind had created to deal with the sleep deprivation and grief over losing Joe.

She remembered his accident clearly now. Seven months ago, he had driven off the road on his way home from the bar and rolled his truck into a ditch. Never a believer in wearing his seatbelt, he had been killed instantly. He never knew she was pregnant.

"That ring was bad luck anyway," Anna said as she stood and crossed the room to get a bottle for the baby.

Ellie nodded as she stared into her daughter's eyes. "I had the strangest dream," she whispered.

"Oh?" Anna raised her eyebrows. "That's odd. So did I. I fell asleep in that chair and I thought I saw Joe here. It was the weirdest thing. We sat down and talked like we've never talked before."

Ellie smiled. "Mine was so real…"

Her mother interrupted Ellie's thought. "So, what did you decide to name this beautiful little girl?"

"I think I have the perfect name," she whispered as she once again ran her fingers across the baby's face. She cooed and crinkled her face. "Her name is Julia Grace."

Anna smiled. "My grandmother's name was Grace. Remember that story I used to tell you about her?"

Ellie smiled as she looked back down at her newborn daughter. Though nothing quite made sense, she didn't care in that moment. All that she needed was here in her arms.

"Yes," she whispered. "I remember."

www.ingramcontent.com/pod-product-compliance
Lightning Source LLC
Chambersburg PA
CBHW030807310726
48980CB00006B/415/J

* 9 7 8 0 6 1 5 7 2 5 7 7 2 *